A
BASKET
OF
REEDS

FREDERICK KEOGH

Dream World Books Publishing

Also by Frederick Keogh

Dream Weaver
Beneath the Turning Stars
Hurricane River

ISBN (Paperback): 979-8-9884740-2-9

ISBN (eBook): 979-8-9884740-3-6

In Gratitude:

to my sister Joan, for her wonderful cover art; to the works of Barbara Myerhoff, who showed that Cultural Anthropology is good for something; and as always, to Vicki, here from beginning to end.

CHAPTER 1

Lacey's Labyrinth

We all thought of him as an egotist, a deluded clod with a superiority complex or, in the vernacular of our progressive era, an asshole. After his death, these thoughts made me feel disrespectful, even guilty, if such bourgeoisie sentiments were still possible for me, until I reminded myself of who "we" were: academics. Academics, particularly those trapped in such insular and impractical fields as cultural anthropology, must believe that everyone's an asshole. They could not exist without such objective condescension, for their professions make them so ruthlessly introspective that they could not tolerate themselves otherwise. It is an unspoken fact that every soft-bellied, eye-strained, aloof intellectual so despises himself that without a countering expression of scorn, his ego would implode like an empty pop can under a garbage truck.

Still, we had a special hatred for Steven. Somehow we could tell, by the way he walked, by the small gestures of his hands, by his unwavering tone of argument, that his disdain for humanity was not rooted in an inherent struggle for self-preservation, but rather in the firm belief that he was the only truly sentient being in the universe. While it was abundantly clear that the hatred from us, his fellow graduate students, did not concern him one wit, the antagonism he generated among the faculty gave him no end of trouble. We were delighted that he had been denied scholarship money, forced to retake his doctoral exams, shuffled from the TA list, and had been rejected from one thing or another on minor technicalities and omissions. Steven's arrogance had broken the fundamental rule of the graduate student: that one must submit like a Chinese concubine to one's senior benefactors. Steven's inability to even conceive of quivering before a professor nearly disqualified him from academia. He could not grasp that professors had gone through the whole humiliating process themselves and now used their position to exact revenge on a world that had so debased them. To deny them the power to inflict on others the scars they bore sent them into a ruthless, although outwardly contained, fury.

Of course, Steven also had our grudging admiration, for our cowardice was our greatest wound and the engine for our fantasies of revenge, the same sentiments that had driven our professors to sadism years before. We were fortunate that the teaching assistants' offices were securely placed on the first floor of the Arts and Science building, where only a few other non-tenured professors shared our hall. There we could live our lives with some dignity.

But when we had to go to the second floor, the bottom would drop out. There, door after door concealed the lair of a tenured professor, each a tortured god in his own right, a crippled Loki seeking to ease his pain through the suffering of others. There we would walk stiff-legged to our destinies, eyes riveted ahead so as not to catch the glare of some vengeful deity who had opened his door to practice his perverse art. There, should one of Them so choose to engage us, the twists and turns and ambiguities in the conversation would force us to repeat the exchange in our minds again and again, combing our performance for errors that would lower our rating among the faculty.

The enterprise had driven more than one aspiring scholar to drink, but not Steven. He would, more often than not, curtly end any hallway discussion by letting the professor know that he was interfering with an important mission which, since it was Steven's, was always more important than the business of said professor. If any emotion would be evoked in Steven, it would be one of annoyance. The school, the teachers, the program only concerned him insofar as they brought him closer to his objectives. As much as I despised him, I could not help but envy his aloof conceit.

As I have said, none of Steven's qualities leant towards an oiled career path, but finally his perseverance, tempered by the firm belief that his outstanding genius could not be denied, bore fruit. At last the professors seemed to give up on stopping him at this phase of his career and allowed him to obtain a grant large enough to start on the fieldwork that would, in theory, lead to his Ph.D. While his first choice had been to live with the aborigines of the Borneo rain forest, which was still largely intact then in 1980, he was forced to follow his back-up plan. Far cheaper in every way, Steven would live with the peyote eaters of the high Sierra Madre mountains of central Mexico.

I can't remember the day, or even the week, that he left for the field. I do recall now in hindsight that this was about the time that Lacey moved from nervously plucking her eyebrows with her thin, white fingers, to plucking the top of her head. This led to one of the stranger results of obsessive-compulsive disorder that I have seen. Within a few weeks of Steven's absence, one could clearly see a bright pink circle of flesh shining through her straw-blond hair. Within a few months she simply gave up on any attempt to conceal the peak of her scalp that now was perfectly clean of hair in a pattern that was identical to the tonsure of a Catholic Monk.

If one knew Lacey, this held no small bit of irony. As with most of us in the social sciences, she could not believe in the possibility of a supreme being. She might give credence to the effectiveness of belief in a simple or traditional society, but she could not believe in the object of belief and would argue with righteous venom against the prospect that spiritual beliefs might have any beneficial effects in our own society. Hers and ours was a belief in the circle of logic, and that she would have a wreath or halo, a mark of a holy man, plucked into her head by her own hand seemed to point to the existence of a god with a sense of humor. Her conclusion that the universe was an intricate machine born from infinite time and random chance was so strong that when she finally had her nervous breakdown, I was puzzled by the details of her background.

I should have seen it coming, of course, etched as it was in her pulpy monk's cap, but my peers were all so neurologically challenged that it was impossible to cull the dead from the dying, so to speak. It would hurt to find afterwards that her girlfriends had seen it coming all along and had deigned me unworthy of their insights. This, too, should have been obvious, for they had clustered together like a tribe of nervous Amazons since the first year of graduate studies, but I had felt, as a fellow TA and inmate, that we shared a bond beyond gender. That a locus such as gender could exist after years of deconstructive philosophy was a surprise, but I digress. The point is that after her breakdown and subsequent departure, her girlfriends unleashed such a flood of startling information about the woman that it was difficult to believe she was the same Lacey who had graced the department for the last three years.

She had once mentioned that she had come from somewhere in New England, which, as a Midwesterner, I pictured in conflicting images of bright autumn leaves and grimy old factories, but it had never occurred to me that she was of the "Old Establishment." I had read of this long before in a poem about the Cabot's and Lodges of Boston and how one only spoke to the other, and the other only to God, but that whole system was so foreign that it seemed mythical. So it was surprising to find that Lacey had come from one of those families who spoke to both the Cabot's and Lodges, and even more surprising to see that her girlfriends were in awe of that fact. How could those who identified with the exotic and powerless become so breathless before archaic notions of pedigree and old money? And how could a woman who came from such impeccable Episcopalian roots be so aggressively atheistic?

The real shocker, however, was the news, well known to all the girls for over two years, that Lacey and Steven were, or had been, an item. This was almost impossible for me to envision, something on the order of picturing a male mastiff breeding with a toy poodle. Of course Lacey's attachment to Steven explained her decline and fall, but nothing could explain their attraction for one another. Steven was big, brisk, forceful, a loudspeaker in a hall of whispers. Lacey was self-contained, ordered and subtle, at home among the nuances and plotting of the department. Steven was broad and beefy, shaggy and ill-dressed and a devout conserver of water, while Lacey was neat and clean and properly and unostentatiously dressed for every occasion. To picture the two of them together in rut, the big, beefy, hairy, odorous man on the pale, hairless, antiseptic woman, was beyond the comical imaging of the dogs. It was almost sacrilegious.

Let me shake off that picture and get back to the point: Lacey's coming undone would allow me to inherit her desk, which would lead me back to Steven. Like everything else about Lacey's life, I would learn of her leaving the university only well after the fact. On a day just like any other, I would walk into the TA office and hear the girlfriends discuss her tragic departure. It was then that I heard of her involvement with Steven, and then that the reverence the girlfriends had for blue blood was revealed.

I would say nothing, but was left to wonder how anyone could envy another who was so panicked about her place in life that she pulled out her hair. It then dawned on me that to the girls, her breakdown enhanced her charm. When the "poor" collapse, they end up in a welfare motel or an alley behind a bar, but when the rich "come undone" they receive the intensive care of a wounded monarch. The care somehow accentuates their importance.

To the girlfriends, Lacey's tortured psyche elevated her recounts of sailing on the lake at Wellesley or summering on the Cape to romantic heights. In their talk they drew a picture of an elegant Lacey, of a woman in a loose cotton tunic that flowed with the breeze as she paused at the porch railing to glimpse with pathos the welling of the infinite sea. Never mind that this was the same woman who gossiped and flattered and trembled before her masters like the rest of us. Like a eulogy for Joe Everyman, her departure for Massachusetts had turned her into something of a saint, too high on a pedestal for reproach.

While the girls' talk made it impossible to avoid picturing Lacey in an ancestral mansion surrounded by fussing maids and frilly pillows and genteelly concerned suitors, it also led to the deduction that her desk would now be open for the first taker. It was one of three in the back-office, where one could talk without being overheard, work without being disturbed, or drink and smoke and curse if one so chose. The back office was not everyone's aspiration, but it was coveted enough so that its occupancy was decided by seniority privilege more than chance. With news of Lacey's tragic departure, I quickly volunteered my name for the vacant desk, and the girlfriends could not refuse: I had the seniority, and such a rush to take the pennies from Lacey's eyes would seem gauche to them. They gave me a few hard stares, but those were as wind on stone. As I have said, it hurt to discover that they had closed me out of the loop for so long. It seemed to me that the desk in the back room was my due.

Still, three long years in the department had cautioned me to never stick my neck out unless it could be done without detection. There would only be a few beginner courses to teach and a mid-afternoon seminar to attend the following day. I could afford to make a late night of it that very evening and move my files and notes and papers and knick-knacks and *Far Side* jokes and secret good luck charms to the back room without the baleful looks of the girlfriends.

I began the process around 10:00 PM, when a few lights were still on in the hall, and didn't look up for another hour, when every item from my former worksite, every little thing that might have given something away of myself, had been stacked on the gray steel desk of my good fortune. On the wall above it, pale squares were all that remained of Lacey's comic strips and calendar and bric-a-brac that had been removed quickly, perhaps a little too quickly, by the girlfriends. Their impatience triggered a cynical smile. But when I tried to open the doors to the desk and store my own articles, it shocked and angered me to find that they had apparently re-locked them for my inconvenience. I pondered their cupidity for a few seconds, then scanned the offices for a solution. To admit defeat was not an option. It would be too humiliating to be met, defeated, by their knowing and scornful glares the following morning.

Looking for nothing in particular, my eyes fell on the desk of a man who had just finished fieldwork in Haiti. On the wall in front of it, and above some kind of voodoo fetish, hung a good, useable machete, the kind meant for hard work in the cane fields. I briefly considered the damage it might suffer for my purpose, and the reaction of the owner, and then figured, what the hell. The machete was made for punishing labor, not a museum. Anyway, the owner was a fool. I took the tool from its nail hangers and shoved the blade forcibly into the top drawer. The lock bent and finally gave when the blade was wiggled up along the length of the edge. The same was done to the other drawers, after which the artifact was placed back on the wall, hardly worse for wear. If he should later detect the few dents and scratches, it would be suggested that it had fallen and needed to be hung more securely.

It then came time to examine the interior of the desk.

I opened the top drawer. Surprised, I opened a side door, then another, then another. Each was filled much as mine had been that morning, the only difference being the feminine handwriting that covered the familiar papers and forms. A sudden panic of trespass engulfed me, causing me to look around instinctively to see if anyone had been a witness. Then my eyes returned to the pile of papers, many of which undoubtedly held personal secrets and private thoughts, and I wondered what to do. In the same instant it came to me how fatuous a thought that was. The right thing to do was obvious. That it had been sidestepped signified just how far my moral compass had strayed. Clearly, all the material should be taken out and stacked neatly so that it might be boxed and sent to Lacey's home, without anyone ever having taken a peek.

Of course I couldn't do that, and my mind immediately assured me that a man of the social sciences, especially one with my particular gifts, should not pass up this wonderful opportunity to view the spontaneous records of a human profile. With the vestigial remnants of my conscience satisfied by that shallow sophistry, the real reasons for my need to pry then tumbled in. On one level, I felt a desperate need to find the limits of her professional adequacy. I wanted to know how smart she was, really, so that my abilities might be favorably compared with hers. Regardless of any show of affection or solidarity to the contrary, we were all in a desperate competition for a handful of jobs, even the girlfriends. The dog-eat-dog mentality was never far from the surface.

On another level, a much darker one, lurked the voyeur. It was not that I had any particular attraction for Lacey, even before her ordeal with the hair, or for the girlfriends either, for that matter. We played a constant game of intellectual chess with one another, a game equally suited for males and females, which lent a highly charged sense of androgyny to the air, like that between quarreling brothers and sisters. Still, I felt a glow of forbidden sexual pleasure when viewing her private papers, akin to that of an adolescent boy staring through a peephole into the girls' locker room. My rationalization had provided the hole in the wall for my lust, and once my target was in view, there was no stopping. Having resolved to go through with the crime, all my intellectual powers would then be turned to the cover-up.

While it was now apparent that the drawers had been locked all along, it was also probable that the girlfriends knew this and so had rightly assumed that there were still items within that should be protected. Still, we are creatures of habit and continue to take customary precautions when the dangers cannot possibly be present, just as we close the bathroom door when we have the house to ourselves. So, one might be convinced that the doors had been emptied of valuable content first, then locked from habit. Not much would have to be left to simulate this scenario. Some academic notebooks and references and outlines would be set aside to provide a sense of bulk along with a dozen or so innocuous greeting cards from relatives and some useless little keepsakes to give it the personal touch. These I would take from the desk and stack against the wall, where they would be casually brought to the girlfriends' attention the next day with a wave of the hand and a suggestion that they might want to send these things back to Lacey. Whatever else of use would stay with me.

To begin with, a box would have to be salvaged from the building dumpster to hold the selected items which would be spirited to my living quarters via the campus shuttle bus.

I went out the back door into the night to the docking area, and had to return again with a broom to poke out the raccoon that was pawing through the rotting food in the dumpster, fast food throwaways being man's greatest gift to nature. Rummaging through the debris, I discovered a strong box that had carried bulky introductory textbooks and brought it back to the office to tape the end flaps together again, looking about now and then with the alacrity of a cat burglar for any potential witnesses. I dropped it on the floor before the desk and dug into the drawers with my hands, noticing briefly that they were trembling. They touched on the birthday cards, the notebooks with labels like "Paleo Genetics" and "Post-Structuralist Thought" and a slew of notes for papers past and present, all of which were pushed against the wall for public viewing. Juicier items like a bulky first draft of a term paper and a mass of material for an NSF grant were tossed into my "take-out" box. I rummaged with greater speed and efficiency through one drawer, then another and then the next like a man going through the bases on a hot date, unlatching the bra, the belt, then….until my fingers came to rest on home plate in the bottom, right-hand compartment.

The mother lode was luridly conspicuous, not just a hot date but a baboon in estrus, a big bundle of envelopes and papers and letters tied together by a wide, purple ribbon bowed with the elegance of a Christmas gift. I tried to pull it out with one hand, but was forced to use two as envelopes slipped out. Before the bundle was even placed on the desk it was obvious that many, perhaps most of the correspondence had come from Mexico. There were big patriotic portraits of Hidalgo y Costilla and Zapata and Carranza on the postage, rubber-stamped with the deceptive designation, *aero postal.* My eye measured what must have been a dozen letters, and I could only imagine the wealth of information, of personal insights and field notes, that the bigger folders contained. Lacey's core, her emotional intersection of sex and bonding, dreams and desires, family and career, had been unearthed. So, too, most certainly, had been a dead man.

I prepared to take the bundle home, discarding much of the rest from the box as tangential bait, but within minutes of walking into the cold, black air of the Michigan winter night a sensation of disgust crept over me. While Lacey had never stirred me with desire, she was still a young woman and her personal life was tantalizing. But Steven. Had he been the stranger, the mystery man in a romantic novel, it would not have mattered, but I knew Steven. I detested Steven. I had no more interest in knowing Steven's private life than I had in seeing my parents entwined in passion. Even less. Theirs' was, at the core, a wholesome relationship. There could be little wholesome about Steven.

My conflicting thoughts continued on the bus home, the box bouncing on my lap all the while, shaking the sweater and backpack that were stuffed on top to conceal the treasure. As the rhythmic jostling measured time, the sense of the lurid wore off and more analytical thoughts coalesced in its place. As a new concept formed and assumed domination, it brought with it the certainty that this colder path would lead to more lasting satisfaction than the former jumble of urges. It told me that what was balanced on my knees, held in the fluorescent lights of an empty bus on its final run of the night, was power. As my professors liked to joke with an allusion to wisdom, Knowledge is Power. In my possession lay not just the lives of two people, but two people intimating their lives and experiences and contacts within my department. This was not just knowledge. This was knowledge that could lead to the greatest power of all: the ability to consummate revenge, to blackmail.

I left the bus at the top of North Campus with a new urgency and scuttled like a crab over the invisible ice that had refrozen since the salt pellets and sun had melted it several hours earlier. The box had to be dropped before the door of the Co-ops where I lived, then a glove pulled off with my teeth so that my fingers could search in pockets for the key needed after 11:00 at night. I tumbled through the outer doors into a hallway obscured in shadows and bumped an elbow on my neighbor's door handle, receiving all the customary pain of the "funny bone." Biting down on my urge to swear, the box had to be dropped again to open my own room door. I stumbled against my desk, nearly falling, then reached the table light. With the push of a button, the world again was under my command and the paper captives ripe for plunder.

Sitting down at my chair, it became apparent that the stress and late hours of the day had robbed much of my energy. The happy vision of myself delving into other's private lives for days on end would not be actualized this night, and with that realization came the thought that this is how it should be. As with all efforts that were worthwhile, this one should be afforded its due time, savored piece by piece at the appropriate moment. That would be easy. If I could wade through the muddy waters of Noam Chomsky and Jacques Derrida for three long, rough years, this little stream could be forded without effort. The temptation to have it all now was no temptation at all; in the great halls of the arcane, we had learned to delay gratification to the ends of time, if necessary.

It seemed right, though, that my evening struggle should be rewarded with one morsel, one little sweet fruit before sleep, one that most likely would be found in the stack of personal letters. Dumping the lot of them on the table, it occurred to me that they should be read chronologically, according to the dates on the postage, so that they would be experienced in the natural order, and it pleased me to note that they had already been sorted as such.

I looked to the first, sent from Laredo, Texas, May 5, 1980, took a deep breath and slipped a finger under the flap that had become resealed with dampness and age. Inside were several pages torn from a classroom notebook, scrawled by a sloppy but legible hand. I snickered. This was obviously the mark of a sloppy, shallow man. Steven. This was going to be fun.

CHAPTER 2

The Lonely Path

My Dearest Lacey,

It is so refreshing to be on the road again, to be free of the hot house that is our department. Even in bus stations slick with the blackness of diesel fumes, the air exudes the sweet scent of liberty!

Still, the real world is no paradise. On my ride to the land of big hats and snake skin boots, the heartland opened up like an oozing sore. While bus stops may not provide an accurate cross-section of America, enough of its diversity is present to afford a glimpse of the national ethos. Lacey, the nation is half asleep. I don't mean tired; I mean permanently dazed. This may well extend to humanity at large. In Saint Louis, a fat black woman reached into her pocketbook for one lifesaver after another, staring ahead at the walls with a blank look of defeat while her three kids kicked each other and rolled around in the wadded gum and tobacco spit on the floor. In Kansas City, a haggard white woman smacked her older boy for whining about pop money while she held the other so tightly by the wrist that he cried. Everyone has the look of gray. I doubt they are much happier back home in front of the TV, either. How can those women get beyond their indolent dullness with their attitude? Don't they realize the miracle of their own creations, their children? If they can't see that, how can they realize the wonder in anything?

Speaking of the blind, don't let your committee advisor get under your skin. He's undergoing tenure review this fall and he'd bury his own mother in an anthill for it, and kick some sand in her face just to show his enthusiasm. He's kissing up to Kronick to get him past Tourstein, who is Kronick's sworn enemy. Remember, he blocked Tourstein's favorite from getting the social science grant. That's because Tourstein failed Kronick's favorite on the exams. So, on and on and on. By no means should Kronick and Tourstein be put together on your committee. And don't get Greene on with Tourstein, either. Remember what happened between them. I still recall how she embarrassed the hell out of me by revealing every detail. We weren't even close. She just wanted to spread her version of the gossip to the first unaligned oddball available.

Which reminds me: why the heck did you decide to stay in that soap opera? Although you turned down my proposal, you could have come along regardless, on your own terms. Please let me know if you even wish to hear from me. Were concerns for your career involved? You know, you take this profession too seriously. If you are not having fun, leave it, really. The "immortals" in our department will most likely be forgotten before their emeritus chairs turn cold. These are marginal people in a small profession of little importance. In truth, it is probable that the daze of the common man contains more solemn wisdom than the works produced in our social science departments. It is understandable that you want to make it on your own, but fieldwork is vastly superior to the classroom. Again, is it me you are avoiding?

You have said that my critical stance on the department is only another form of egotism, and I have come to see, with no small shame, that you are right. It is my solemn promise, from this sentence forward, to find the humility to rectify this. Until now, the constant grating of competing personalities has led me to glorify myself in defense. Please forgive me. But is this the only problem? Is it this failing that caused you to reject me? Or do you really believe what you said, that marriage is simply a government intrusion on a personal relationship? Forgive me if I have overstepped my right to question your decision. It is really a last grasp at hope.

Anyway, by the time you get this letter, you will have already received my call from Monterey. What was said between us while these words slept in transit? Have we at least given each other our best, with honesty and trust?

I'm sitting on a bench with two heavy backpacks looking at the bridge that spans the Rio Grande to Mexico. It's hard to imagine that this dirty little city will look like a sterilized operating room when compared to the town across the border. There are about one hundred Mexicans at any one time on the bridge or in line at customs to get into the U.S. There are about a tenth as many going the other way. You would do well to practice your Spanish. In the end, the conquistadors are going to win one way or another.

Sorry to be such a grouch. The trip has left me tired and dirty and lonely and tense and hot, all at once. Perhaps I think of the troubling things left behind to feel lucky now. It is no comfort at all, however, to be here without you.

Hasta la Vista, until next time,

Steven

I stuffed the papers back into the envelope and closed my eyes. I had gotten, in one letter, the promise of everything hoped for, but still felt disturbed. The news of the professors' feuds and affairs was juicy and useful, but Steven's failed bid for marriage, which should have made me salivate, instead provoked nausea. He had a reputation as an arrogant bastard, and the letter didn't disprove that, but he had also revealed his vulnerability, which made me pity him. Pity for a man like Steven was the same thing as scorn. Whereas before he could at least be appreciated as an adversary, now he could be dismissed with disdain. The sour taste this left did not detract from my victory, however. I kicked off my shoes and reminisced over the pirated information until a deep, restful sleep took me away, clothes and all. What a good day it had been.

I awoke early the next morning with one thought in my mind: the notebooks. Coinciding with the letters would be dated notes that would add considerable text to his little missives. I rolled immediately from bed, changed my underwear, got first dibs on the hall bathroom, and returned brushed and shaved, eager to dig into the manila envelopes. It was Thursday, which meant no classes until 10 AM. That left an hour or so to root around in others' lives.

The cafeteria had opened for coffee, and after pouring a large cup, I returned to the pile of paper on my desk with a keen sense of anticipation. Pinching the cheap metal clasp on the largest envelope, I released the contents, three notebooks each of a different color and each smeared with soot and dirt and random grease. A quick look showed that my task had once again been made easy: the notebooks were actually numbered, presumably in chronological order, and each entry was dated. All that had to be done was to open book #1 and match the dates of the correspondence with the notebook entries. Thus a deeper meaning might be gleaned from the glib posturing and niceties of the letters.

The first few pages of the book were filled with Steven's itineraries, a long packing list, monetary budgets and the addresses of contacts in various parts of Mexico. After that, nearly half the book contained words and grammatical structures of Spanish paired with Nahuatl and a Uto-Aztecan corollary that presumably was the language of his subjects. As my specialty was the Algonquin speakers of the Great Lakes region, this left me at a complete loss. I flipped towards the back until prose writing appeared below the dates, then returned to the first of these entries, labeled May 4, 1980. Beautiful! This would coincide nicely with the letter to Lacey. The page was slightly smeared like the rest, and rumpled by water damage, but it was still easily read:

5/4/80

The monotony of the road is like a sedative that's been altered to produce not just a lack of energy, but malaise, Jimmy Carter's favorite word. God help him in the next election. Speaking of God, He knew that I would end up in buses, and so prepared me for the ordeal by an upbringing in Michigan City, where diesel fumes are mother's milk and axel grease is the paint of the warrior. Buses and diesel and grease bring up those thoughts of home as I sit numbed in my sweaty plastic seat, and it now occurs to me that an initiation of sorts into the fraternity of warriors was given to me in my youth. There were no feathers and ghosts and masks, to be sure, it being a stripped-down American initiation, but it had delivered the same message, with the same spirit, in the end. It came at a classic age, too, 14, just when I thought I could do a whole hell of a lot better in the world than the adults around me.

My dad was a mechanic and took on personal jobs at home in the garage for extra money, moonlighting. I'm not sure if that was ethical, but that's what paid for the extras like braces for my sister. Being the only boy in the family, it was my job to help my father, standing for hours by him when necessary. During adolescence, I started to resent this apparent waste of time, and I sighed and whispered obscenities under my breath while moving from side to side on the oily floor of our garage to show my displeasure. My dad never seemed to notice.

One nice summer day, a beautiful Saturday afternoon, I was once again stuck in the garage looking out at the trees and thinking about baseball, bicycling, ogling discarded old Playboys with the guys, anything, when my dad popped off a ratchet head. He had a car on a lift and was working underneath with the hanging drop light when it came off and he said, "Stevie, get that for me." While this was a typical request, this time it made me hit the wall. It had so angered me to be forced to stay inside and ordered around that I told him, "no."

"What?" he said as the legs that stuck out from under the car stopped moving. "What's that, Stevie?" The second question had a tone in it that froze me cold, but something made me stick to my guns.

"No."

My dad was on one of those mechanic's floor rollers and he pushed himself from underneath and tried to get up too soon and whacked his head on the drop light. It jerked around, the shadows dancing as it swung, making the garage and my dad's oil-streaked face look like a scene from a horror movie shot in an evening thunderstorm. I was scared and my legs trembled but I didn't move. I don't think I could have talked. My dad came up to me holding his head and swearing a blue streak and then said, "Listen, buddy, the day you hold down a job and support a wife and kids you can tell me where to go, but that ain't yet by a long ways. Now just cut the crap and start helping out like you ought."

Something stony and tough got a hold of my jaws and said, "The day I work under a car to support anything ain't ever comin'. I'd rather starve to death than be some grease monkey on his back like you."

It felt as if my awareness had come out of my body and was watching this whole terrible scene from some other place. It was out of my hands. My dad flared up like a match and smacked me on the cheek. He had the strong, stringy, vein-streaked arms that working guys have, and the power of that hit almost knocked me off my feet. It was only the second time in my life that my father had hit me, and the only time I saw stars. But I regained my footing and stared back at him, the one eye that got hit making tears. It was crazy. He stood dazed before me, as shocked as I was. After a few seconds he started to laugh. Then he told me in a calm, quiet way,

"All right. I can see you're starting to make up your mind about things. That's good. You've got to think for yourself in this world." He

24

looked at me sideways with a funny squint and laughed again.

"I tell you what. From now on I'll give you an apprentice wage. When you get old enough for an outside job, you never have to pick up a wrench again, OK? This isn't a punishment. You can see that we need every man to pull his weight around here, don't you?" He had stopped smiling and was looking at me somberly. "Now, why don't you go inside and wash your face. You look like a fucking Indian." He started laughing again and ducked back under the car. I went back to the house and looked in the bathroom mirror and saw the big patch of grease on my cheek, with the long lines of my father's fingers stretching out to my scalp. I touched the ends of the fingerprints with my own hand and thought, "he called me a man." My shock had turned into awe.

It's true. People have always needed rituals for accepting new stations of life and shedding the old. Looking around the bus stations I see misfits, beetles cast with thin, hard shells that inadequately cover the soft and formless guts beneath. Most people do not know who they are or what they are meant for. We social scientists have found that this has to do with modern forms of commerce and the technologies that coincide with them, but since we are aware of our deficiencies, why do we continue to be controlled by them? Instead of trying to restore those important bits of culture that make sense of life, we fight continually to tear down the old forms to make way for the fringe elements, for the exotic, for anything new we think might help. It has been a disaster. For the first time in all of human history, the mass of humanity is being sacrificed for the benefit of a small number of misfits and their ideas.

Oddly, the commercial changes that have made the modern world proceeded from Christian fanaticism. This same fanaticism also fathered the secular humanism that now strives to crush religious belief and the culture it was made from. I sense that, underneath the exoskeletons that hide the quivering jelly of the modern psyche, we understand that the elite are leading us into a bottomless pit. There is no bedrock beneath the secular humanism that now directs us. Whatever is proclaimed "right" is only right because "they" say it is. There is no God, no Bible, no stone tablets for its foundation. We know what we believe to be right will only shift with the winds of ideological fashion. We know that with it we will never find strength for our inner core.

It is my hope that sharing life with the Indians will yield knowledge for the restoration of this lost self. From my window I can see that we desperately need it, and it is clear that our institutions will not provide it. Who would think that an heir to Christian dominance would look for a spiritual source in the realm of the superstitious 'heathen'? How far from God have we gone that we must look over our shoulders to catch sight of Him again?

Off to sleep. Drowsy and delirious, talking to self. These last comments will never appear in my thesis.   S T

I could hardly believe what I had just read. Steven was a holy roller! It would never have occurred to me that his arrogance stemmed from this. Most religious nuts wear it on their sleeve. At universities you learn to recognize them and avoid them or snub them before they even reach you. What, then, did this make Lacey? Was she a closet Bible thumper? After thinking about it for a few seconds, it came to me that this was one of their problems. No: she was one of us, a bedrock materialist. That must have been the underlying reason for the dispute on the marriage proposal. It made me laugh again. Perhaps he had begged God forgiveness for fornicating and had sought to legitimize the object of his sin. Pathetic.

In any case, that he seemed to embrace discredited religion was an outrage. Every anthropologist knows that religions hold diametrically opposed positions on many different things, negating any sort of unified message from a single deity. Steven should have surmised that we are beyond believing in spirits and can never go back. To accept them is to accept a crutch when we have perfectly good legs. If you're looking for paradise, vacation in Aruba. It will do no good searching for it in the sky.

26

Steven's revelation about his religious nature took some of my enthusiasm for his correspondence and notes from me, and I dropped the notebook back in the box to proceed with more pressing work. Later, however, while preparing to leave for the university, my curiosity began to formulate titillating questions, so many that they rolled around in my mind like a mouthful of hard candy on the long walk to campus. What would Lacey's response be to Monterey? Obviously it had been somewhat positive because many letters were to follow. How would this god business work into the mix? Did Steven have time to write about his god at the time of his death?

Of course, the answer to the last might never be known, and even the cause of his death might remain a mystery. I presumed Lacey knew, but if she wouldn't talk about her relationship with Steven to me, it is doubtful that she would share the details of his demise, if indeed she ever returned to the university. But the 'girlfriends' might know this and more, and might be persuaded to part with this knowledge one way or another.

The questions had caused me to stow the notebook and a few letters in the backpack at the last minute, information to be gleaned after class if the back room happened to be unoccupied.

First, though, the day would begin with a run through the gauntlet within the social science building. I slipped into the department office for my mail, said hello meekly to a professor who replied with a short "hrumpff," grinned a little too much for the office secretary then hurried down the hall to the TA office. The window in the door showed that all four of the girlfriends were there, talking animatedly by the backroom. With Lacey's personal effects lying in the open by her former desk, this had not been unexpected. I took a deep breath, put on a business-like frown and opened the door. There, four pairs of eyes bore into me for a silent moment before the inquisition began.

"How did you open her locked drawers?" "Is that all her things?" "Did you actually read those personal greeting cards?" I had replies for those questions and then some.

"What do you mean, 'locked?' I never lock mine, do you? It was wide open. I came in late last night to change desks and saw that she had left some of her papers in the drawers. They were in a mess. She must have rifled through them before she left to get the more personal items out. All that was left is stacked in the pile. I didn't look to see if there were any birthday cards, or whatever. I assumed that you guys would know what to do with it all." I shrugged and slid past them into the backroom. After sitting down at my new desk, one of the girls swung into the room on the door. She looked at me with unwavering suspicion.

"All the drawers were locked when we checked them yesterday afternoon."

"Really? All the drawers were unlocked when I came in last night. Maybe you didn't try to open them right. Sometimes you have to jiggle them to get over the latch." I showed her how the top drawer stuck unless it was lifted up and shaken several times. The latches had been bent with the machete the night before, and now the damage was working to my advantage. She came over and tried another drawer, and found she had to do the same thing.

"Yes. I guess you're right. We'll just get a box and send her things back to her." Her look of suspicion and righteous anger had dissolved into a puzzled fret. She had been beaten. And now, if Lacey asked for the Steven papers, they all would know that the desk had been open to everyone all along. The claim could either be made that someone else had taken them, or that Lacey's recollection of them was merely the delirium of a mentally strained woman.

"Anytime you want." I shifted my chair firmly towards the desk, took a book from my backpack, removed my glasses and let the world know that it was shut out from my studies. From the corner of my eye I could see the girlfriend, Suzanne, linger about the door, wanting to say something that she apparently was incapable of putting into words. It was hard to keep from laughing. At last she left, closing the door quietly.

It was difficult restraining myself from reading the notebook and letter until the evening, and my agitation would have been apparent to anyone who was paying attention. Fortunately, in the seminar that afternoon the grad students were either too eager to show off their intelligence or too preoccupied with ingratiating themselves with the professor to notice anything else. As for my students in 101, they could not pay attention to anything at all except the boys to the girls and the girls to their fantasies of picket-fenced bliss.

Throughout the day I slid past these semi-conscious beings like a Greek hero through the shades of Hades until I finally arrived, late, to the land of the living in my backroom office. It was blissfully unoccupied, and my hand was in the backpack before reaching the desk.

Which to read first, I thought with greedy anticipation, the letter or the notebook? It was a hard thing to guess which medium Steven would first use to describe his discussion with Lacey in Monterey. Would he be 'Steven the lovesick mope,' and so write his lost love first, or 'Steven the Man of God,' and so consult his conscience through his notes? I gambled on 'lovesick mope,' and removed the letter from the pack delicately with two fingers. It would prove to be the correct choice:

Lacey, Love,

Just being able to reach you from Monterrey was a pleasant surprise. I was not sure you would be there to answer. It is true that graduate school messes with the normal rhythms of life. We are both in our mid and late 20's and old enough for commitment, yet still in the juvenile role of student. Please be assured that I will never let this issue come between us. Perhaps it was my pride that needed to know that your rejection of the proposal was not a rejection of me. Since there is so much uncertainty, we should agree to continue as friends and see what happens over the next few years. This has been painful for me, but your acceptance of my correspondence is deeply needed and appreciated. The bus is not long out of Monterey now and already it seems that I am on a lonely path.

Oh, I know; we are taught that "love" is only a manifestation of sexual chemistry. Marriage is essentially a framework for the sustenance of the young and the transmission of culture and values to these young. But still, it is so much more: it is a sacred trust that must be held deeply in our hearts.

Through the bus stations of the USA and through the filthy streets of Monterrey one can see the disastrous results of people who measure their fealty to others by the passion of the moment. The land is littered with poor children, the tossed-off spawn of men who are swayed by passion unfettered by responsibility. These kids are crippled from the start. We all agree that we must try to help them, but then why do we also wish to downplay or adulterate marriage and fidelity? Are we really thinking first of the poor, or of our own desire to do what we want without censure?

All right, then. Back to the land.

It feels exotic to be surrounded again by Spanish and all the things of Latin America that are oddly both transnational and completely out of place in America: children selling *chicle*, men with roosters tethered to their wrists traveling to the next cock fight, and the women with their *botánicas,* the herbs and curios for healing and magical spells that are spread out on blankets in the streets and bus stations. I don't know if there is any other border in the world that so neatly delineates two very different ways of life. It is like crossing from one state of consciousness to another.

It will still be a few days before we enter the real backwoods, although the Sonora Desert is not exactly Broadway. But the roads are good and straight and fast, and it's prickly pear season. If you have the patience to peel them, they're very tasty. If it is possible I will send you some.

Please don't worry so much about the department. You must keep in mind that you are doing this for enlightenment, not money. Hold on to that truth until you are delivered into the field. There you can separate the pearls from the swine. What little remains will still be enough.

Take Care,
Steven

Oh, so they remained just "friends." That at least put Lacey up a notch or two in my book. But then, she couldn't be condemned for slumming it once in her youth. It was also gratifying that Steven didn't sob all over the page. He apparently was smart enough to know that he was playing way out of his league. It still made me cringe to think of his little homily about his grease monkey father. Grass-roots philosophers should stick to writing folk tunes for starry-eyed girls. What seemed to be developing more fully, though, was Steven's conservative, perhaps even Christian critique of society. It made me wonder, only half in jest, if he hadn't gotten some kind of Vatican grant to come to grad school. Thank God, at least, that Lacey had not followed the Pope and forgone birth control. Then again, maybe Steven had insisted they wait until marriage to go 'all the way.' That would be the most humorous thing of all. It would be no small irony if the possibility of Steven's genetic continuance had been snuffed out by the rules of a religion that were directly responsible for much of the world's overpopulation.

As amusing as that thought might be, I found Steven's antiquarian stance on our evolving morality downright disturbing. A shrinking world has exposed the lies of religion by granting us a clear look at each other's beliefs. Every parochial element falls apart before this universal view, and it is not possible to sustain social rules with known lies. As Max Weber wrote, the only hope we have of caring for fatherless children and other victims of modernity's sharp edge is to expand the mechanism of the state bureaucracy. The science behind that is really the social scientists' "Raison d'etre." It is why I once thought that we are so essential for the future of the world.

I turned to the notebook and Steven's next entry. Of great interest would be the difference in information between the letters and the notes - what secrets would be kept, what would be revealed? This was a perfect opportunity to practice a little deconstructive interpretation. Of more practical concern would be information that afforded leverage with the girlfriends, the faculty, and perhaps even with the lady of pedigree, Lacey, if she ever returned. I found the appropriate date:

On the Road, May 7

Jesus, the mess of urban Mexico! It's as if someone took a reeking medieval city, stripped it of all its charm and order, and stirred in the sounds and smells of a million cars without mufflers. Just miles and miles of filth and noise and uniform concrete. At the stations, thousands of starving children crush in to sell a few pesos of candy, or steal or beg while withered old ladies sit by paltry piles of goods on ragged blankets staring blankly ahead as if any thought has long since been crushed from their minds. Young men strut in their cheap plastic-knit clothing while young women keep their eyes to the ground or to themselves. The old personality structures continue to play on a stage where a master of subjugation and corruption choreographs every move. The actors, the people, are too enthralled to see that their old standards of behavior have been perverted to create the horrific injustice that holds them in desperate poverty. They can't see the proof in the implausible fact that a nation awash in oil and tourist wealth keeps sending more and more of its people to live in orange crate houses by filthy streams of industrial waste, or out of the country altogether.

It would be astounding, for instance, if they could see the destructiveness of certain aspects of *machismo*, if they would replace the bloated sense of honor enshrined by this ethic of revenge and domination with the simple virtues of commitment and compassion. Corruption thrives on egotism, while it can find no purchase in actions based on a communal sense of right and wrong. Yet self-promotion is cool and hip, while responsible caring is dated and homely, a victim of a scientific positivism that denies spirit. Passion is no longer tempered by humbling values. Now everyone moves about the litter and stench of this broken system like a cartoon character, each a flat and thoughtless caricature drawn by a shallow and cynical hand. Liberation from moral bedrock has made us slaves to impulse.

Let it pass. Nature has led me beyond such dreary thoughts. We have survived the cesspools of Monterrey and Saltillo and are now sailing into the sharp beauty of an evening desert sky. The colors of sunset are stupendous, the closing darkness slashed by exuberant reds and purples that glow like the tails of comets. The cactus and creosote bushes rub against the remnants of light like pig bristles. Otherwise the land is a void. Unlike in the US, there is not an electric light to be seen anywhere in this great flatness. The bus could be a stagecoach in colonial times for all the signs of modernity.

Thoughts of Lacey still bring pain. There was a distance in her voice that made her sound farther away than mere geographical miles. It is clearly over. Although it seems cliché, perhaps our contrasting backgrounds made this rupture inevitable. Then again, the lives of those in my profession are marked by movement, and movement always brings change. I am fortunate that she still remains as a confidant, someone to receive my letters and assuage loneliness. Perhaps it is for the better that the anxieties of hope are now extinguished. Despite any plan, fieldwork will be started afresh, the way it's supposed to be.

Can't write anymore, no more light. Just as well. Many miles more to go, and I must sleep.

ST 5/80

I was both relieved and disappointed that Steven's romantic plans had been abandoned, but that had become of secondary importance; first and foremost, it was clear that the forces of reason were calling upon me to contest Steven's desire to return us to the theocratic state. Not that I could see that there was anything to fight, any external spiritual intelligence, behind his zealotry. Suffering and horror and senseless tragedy enveloped the noble and the wicked alike. Where were the signs of almighty justice in the world? Indeed, if there were a god, our miseries appeared to prove that 'It' was consumed with a perverse hatred for Its creations, giving us both our disruptive desires and the cruel and inevitable facts of nature. As such, it was laughable to believe that this god would give us immortal souls for an eternal paradise.

I flipped through the letters and noticed that the next was postmarked more than a week after the last. This pattern of diminishing returns continued, the letters to and from Lacey becoming more infrequent. This was consistent with the end of a romantic relationship, causing me to surmise that the notes, rather than the letters, would become of increasing importance in the future. Still, I had already gathered something from the disparity between Steven's writings. It was obvious that he patronized Lacey in the manner of a Victorian gentleman. He withheld his harder comments and observations to protect Lacey's feminine "weakness," and, along with a dollop of cheap tenderness, he probably thought of himself as quite the hero. This did not surprise me, and in fact I expected him to lay it on thicker and thicker as he plunged into his personal Heart of Darkness.

However, questions did arise from the diminished correspondence: why was Lacey sent the notebooks, and by whom? I could not imagine some illiterate Indian even thinking to do so, nor imagine some poor Mexican willing to spend his last peso on a pile of scribbled notes. Maybe a local missionary helped, but, still, why would there be this connection to Lacey? It was known that Steven's mother was alive, at least during his last year, and he had written of a sister. Why would his final personal effects go to an ex-girlfriend?

I shrugged it off. What did it matter? Perhaps Steven had only written letters to Lacey, leaving only that address for his "executor" to use. The important thing was that the notes were now in my hands, and that there was still time left in the night for a few more pages. The next date in the series was quickly located:

Valparaiso 5/9/80

Am beat and getting my first dose of *turista*. I've stopped for a day in the ideally named town of Valparaiso, which is anything but. Have taken a room at the only hotel in town, and it is like a prison for "disappeared" political prisoners. It is a cubicle of concrete with no more than a slit for a window in the bathroom. I expect uniformed men to break down the door at any minute and attach wires from a car battery to my genitals and shock me again and again until I confess to everything they want to hear. It wouldn't make a difference. The pain of intestinal cramps and a burning rectum make me long for a distraction, no matter how unpleasant. It couldn't get much worse.

I reached Fresnillo late last night and found that no busses would be running until about four in the morning. The bus stop was besides a broken fountain built around a statue of Benito Juarez, one of the most beloved of Mexican leaders. A fascinating fellow and so reflective of Mexico's needs and failures. He was of Indian descent, and ushered in a liberal government and constitution in the 1850's that promised to end the feudal oligarchy that had run Mexico since the time of Cortez. In time, it would only lead to the authoritarian rule of Porfirio Diaz. Such continued the sad story of Mexico.

However, the fountain provided a good place to lean my bags while I tried to pass the next five hours in a hoped-for half sleep, just deep enough to give rest but shallow enough to remain aware of the thieves who slipped through the shadows like hyenas circling a carcass. It couldn't have been more than fifteen minutes before the rats came.

I've seen rats around the dumpsters in our cities, but never like this. They flowed from a circle of darkness towards the fountain, covering the red bricks with dull gray fur. One got on my backpack just behind me and was shaken off, but the others were barely intimidated by my movements. For some reason this was their feeding station. Maybe there were crumbs left from daily lunches and handouts to pigeons, but, in any case, they quickly forced me to leave. I had to prop myself against the closed door of the ticket office and stay awake and aware for most of the night. My *turista* kicked in right about the time the bus came and it was just hell keeping a tight sphincter until we got to Valparaiso, 'Valley of Paradise.' Fate does have a sense of humor.

It is a seething pit. Its one main street is a strip of muck fouled by sewage that empties straight out of the crumbling old stucco villas as well as from the new, ugly cement-block houses. An exploding population has caused unplanned side streets to form that lead to hovels made of sticks and rocks and flotsam. One can only guess where the excretion goes from there. I have been careful not to drink the tap water, but that's a fool's game. The water that you buy is just as likely to be from the same tap that you strenuously avoided. I lie here, sick as a dog, as living proof. In a corrupt land, no amount of careful planning can keep you safe for long.

While we all must confront the inevitable hardships of life, in Mexico unpleasantness plagues one on an everyday basis. Original sin strikes us all in the end, but in America most of our suffering is caused by the perversions of our individual free will. Here, the whole world is perverse.

Jesus, keep thoughts like that away. Too sick. My stomach's wracked by barbed wire and my anus is forced to pass molten lava every few minutes. Puking is a nice, simple relief in comparison.

Back to the town: As tattered as it is, it is only a small blight on a large and changing landscape. It is apart from the northern desert, in a pocket of foothills near the Sierra. If I had a window, I could look out directly to a small valley coursed by a stream that runs from steep grass-covered hills - actual green grass. It's refreshing to notice green after so much desert, even in my miserable state. A few pine trees can be seen on the farthest rises. Some excitement stirs through my misery. In just a few days the road should end and the adventure begin.

Must go, quickly. Tomorrow will come, I trust.

ST

FREDERICK KEOGH

I finished the entry unimpressed. So our boy gets intestinal illness? One would think from his description that he is Superman touched by kryptonite, so alien is ill health to him. He seemed to babble something about original sin, too. It frustrated me to know that he was so well educated and yet so superstitious. His course work had certainly taught him that the concept of unavoidable sin was a product of a hierarchical patriarchy that created our world of struggle, where nature and the "other" are seen as enemies to be conquered. It was hard to grasp that Steven could believe that *any* of our suffering was the result of a creation myth.

I was about to dig into a few more entries to find something of genuine interest when the office phone shook me from solitude. After answering it with suspicion, the caller identified herself as Shari, a first year grad student who had on occasion stopped by the office. It was very odd that she would call so late, and even odder that she would call specifically for me. She said that her apartment was only a few blocks away, and that she had looked through the window and saw the light coming from my office and thought to give me a ring. Oddest of all was her invitation to join her, along with her offering of all manner of delights, starting with a bottle of wine and ending with a hint at the possibility of sex. As any man would, I shrugged off any doubts about her motives to dash over, where all that was promised was delivered and then some.

It was after, when she insisted we go out to a diner for a snack, that the piper claimed his due. By the time we reached the 'greasy spoon' it was quite clear that she was a clinical nut case, a psycho with deep schizophrenic tendencies kept loosely in check by powerful medication. Over a burger she growled, changed her voice and personality like a puppeteer, laughed hysterically and then sunk into anger, all without a word from me. I looked around nervously to see if the waitress was calling the police, then desperately sought an excuse to leave immediately without being scarred for life by her threatening fingernails. It took some

37

doing, but necessity brought forth an incantation of lies and promises that set me free. I dashed to the office to pick up the notebook that had been carelessly left on my desk, and then walked the long, dark route back to North Campus because the bus lines had stopped for the night.

A long walk in a winter night was never so welcome. The fresh air came into my lungs like the first breathes to a man freed from a trap of weeds beneath a scummy pond. It was obvious that Shari would have to be avoided at all costs in the future. Her psychosis would not harm her standing in the department, however. With her aberrations and sexual proclivities, it was almost certain that she would climb to the top of our profession in no time.

Midterms descended like firebombs, as usual, and what with the flatness of Steven's last entry and all the work to be done, the notes were forgotten until the following Sunday. It was then, after sleeping late and grabbing a last bitter cup of coffee from the cafeteria, that I settled in my room and read an article in the Detroit Free Press about the dangers of intestinal parasites in Nepal. This made me recall Steven's own intestinal distress and his final speculation that he would reach the end of the road in the next few days. It occurred to me that perhaps this turn of events might bring him to write something more compelling. Besides, there were more letters to read. The romance, if it could be so called, might be mercifully over, but the aftermath of a physical relationship often carries surprises.

With just enough allure and a moment of free time before me, I pulled out the papers and turned first to the notebook. The right page came up immediately:

Hueuquilla 5/13

Spent an extra few days in Valparaiso thanks to the hideous microbes that oddly exist only within the artificially drawn borders of Mexico.

Montezuma's revenge, for sure. It would be just like the Aztec priests to curse their enemies rather than attempt to reform them. It was no wonder that Christianity won out over the natives, even as poorly practiced as it was. Whatever god or curse was responsible, it seemed doubtful that my disease could ever be cured. While I could not eat and drink much during the painful recovery, this still had to be done, bringing the possibility of new infection with every swallow.

Miraculously, though, the disease finally broke, freeing me again for the journey towards the mountains. Once on the road, only a few miles passed before the landscape changed from grass-covered hills to rocky crags and cliffs. The passage was not what one normally expects. One usually progresses from flatlands to taller and taller hills until the hills become mountains. Here, there were no rising hills, just heaps of rock which seemed to have been tossed at random from an enormous volcano. The land became drier, too, rather than greener, no doubt an effect of the rain shadow cast on the eastern side of the Sierras.

Just at the point where the dwindling grasslands verged on full-blown desert the town of Hueuquilla appeared, rising before us from the boulders and scree like an Anasazi ruin in the rugged cliffs of Arizona. Unlike everyplace else in Mexico, there were no signs of population growth here, and few even of recent births. A small number of souls meandered along the narrow streets that were squeezed between ancient blocks of adobe houses, houses that were the color of the ambient pale gray rubble they were made from. They shimmered in the pervasive dust like a mirage. The illness had left me weak and groggy, and whenever people emerged from these buildings it seemed as miraculous as three-dimensional people walking from a television set. If I had had the energy, it might even have been alarming.

This passage is now being written from the same sparse little café that I first came to several years before. I have just finished having a beer with a fellow passenger who told me about sightings of Extra Terrestrials in the nearby mountains. These, he claimed, foretold the coming apocalypse and the New Order. As he talked, the beer went into my system so fast that it left me dizzy, then nauseous. My friend offered proof of UFO interventions in world history by citing Aztec codices that he believes depicted alien spacecraft. The clincher, he claims, is in the famous myth of Quetzalcoatl.

Aztec legend has it that the emissary of this winged serpent was to return as a white man from the east "on giant wings" at approximately the time of Cortez. The "wings," my friend claimed, clearly described sails. Scholars know that the Aztecs did expect an emissary, but they did not expect what followed from his coming. I asked him about this and he replied, "Can we ever predict the vision of the gods?" He reminded me that the Jews had expected an earthly king, not a world savior.

We both concurred that the Mayan calendar predicted a cataclysmic end of the current age and the beginning of a new one in the Christian year 2013. After much upheaval, the modern reading has it, we will be led into an era of peace and well-being. I would have drunk to that if my stomach could have tolerated another beer.

My friend has left and writing is tiring. Until tomorrow and Tutzingo. ST

Following was a letter to Lacey post-marked the next day.

Dear Lacey,

The good old Mexican bug had me for a few days, but has gratefully departed. I am in Hueuquilla and within a day of the last Mexican town before it all becomes Indian Territory. I may have told you about my adventure here several years ago with my friend Will. It seemed such an alien, exotic place then. Coming here again, it is clear that my recollections were not mere fantasies of youth. The sense of magic is just as it was before.

A wise man said that we only see the world once as a child, and then rely on that memory for the rest of our lives, but it is pleasing to find that

this is not always the case. The magic I'm talking about is the same as the spell cast by a book, or by a movie, or by love for that matter. No real dragons appear from a wand, no miscreants are turned into frogs. But real actions do come from such feelings. Couldn't we say then that magic, this ephemeral magic, is still a prime mover in this universe? Hasn't that been said about love?

Forgive my drift into sentimentality. It is the stuff of memory, and there are more than a few fond memories of Mexico thanks to goofy Will. He had a habit of getting us into the worst trouble, and then delivering us to safety. We were Bing Crosby and Bob Hope on the road. It's still hard to believe that he settled down with his high school sweetheart in Michigan City, but we had our days. When we arrived in Hueuquilla, the police chief approached us only seconds after we got off the bus. Neither of us understood Spanish that well but it became obvious as he talked that he wanted money from us - or else. We stood dumbfounded until he glowered at us and motioned several times at our packs, saying the word "drogas" many times. We then understood that he was threatening to plant contraband on us and have us locked in an electric shock torture cell until our worried parents were drained of their home equity and savings.

I was about to hand him everything we had when Will played the wide-eyed idiot. He repeated again and again, in a louder and louder voice, "No, policia, no quiero comprar drogas. No me gustan!," this said in Gringo high-school Spanish meaning, "No, officer, I don't want to buy drugs. I don't like them!" Of course the officer kept repeating that WE were the ones who had drugs, but his tone had been so low and conspiratorial that the crowd heard Will first and was convinced that their policeman was trying to enrich himself by selling marijuana. There were even words from the people that sounded like insults directed towards him. They forced him to leave us, his face full of frustration and fury. With Mexico the way it is, it is most probable that the people in the crowd were angry because the policeman had not bought his supply from THEM. The same officer's face hasn't appeared so far today, thank God. Will's wacky wisdom isn't here to help this time around.

Tomorrow I will try to get a bus to Tutzingo. Last time there, we only stayed for a few hours, finding the tiny village without any accommodations or much of anything else. We hadn't known then that any rural community in Mexico would have a family that was willing and able to rent a room or house to a relatively rich North American. The few extra dollars would be the equivalent to what might be saved in a week of hard work. The picture of Tutzingo that comes to mind is one of the most serene that my memory holds. It is truly at the end of the road, with nothing beyond it but the high mountains and the blue sky.

These memories have long seemed a dream, and now the dream is rising into reality like a childhood fantasy coming true. Still, it is hard to express how lonely I feel. We learn that this is part of the fieldwork experience, but still... I have set up a postal box in Hueuquilla and am sending you the address. The bus comes out to Tutzingo from here a few times a week, and the mail will come to me one way or another on a fairly regular basis. Any correspondence that you might send that is not stolen should get to me in less than a month, unless I am up in the mountains. It is a tenuous connection, but one that will keep us in touch. With the payment of a few dollars, many things suddenly function in Mexico.

Concerning our last conversation about Suzanne and "Low Brow" Bernini: your advice to her to graciously back out of the relationship is wise but too late. Once she has stroked the ego of a professor with a sexual relationship, she can only wait until he grows tired of her if she doesn't want to suffer consequences. It may seem unfair, but she made her bed, and besides, truth be told, it seems she has thoroughly enjoyed sleeping in it. And yes, Ben is probably the most obnoxious grad student in all the social sciences, but he is also inadvertently hilarious. He is the perfect caricature of the haughty professor he wishes to become, but without the layers of deceptive armor that only time can make. Don't trust him, but invite him to your dinner parties. He never fails to make all the other guests feel better about their own relatively small imperfections.

Hasta La Proxima,

Steven

This last bit angered me for a moment. Ah, my old friend, so you had fun at my expense, did you? No matter. He was gone from this world, and his notes had now given me an excellent handle on Suzanne. It was hard to believe: although Suzanne thought higher of herself than she should have, she could have gotten a respectable, if unimaginative, mate. But Low Brow? Not only was he married with kids and nearly fifty, but he was also the ugliest man I knew who was not a genetic mutant. That he was a paleoanthropologist was the best part of the joke, for he looked all the world like the old portraits of Neanderthals that still inhabit the popular imagination, from his thick coat of black "fur" to the large brow ridges that gave him his pet name. If I had imagined Steven and Lacey a bad match, this was positively decadent, like a girl and pony show in Tijuana. Oh my, Suzanne, it was written that we would have an interesting time together someday.

As for the notes overall, they were still pretty pedestrian. It had been my desire to read more about "Tutzingo" that morning, but it was past time to head to the office and get some of the students' tests out of the way. Choosing to walk to campus, I discovered too late that the powdery snow that had blown around for so many weeks had turned into eight inches of slush. By the time I got to the department, my feet were soaked and my pants drenched past the ankle. Avoiding the professors, I quickly snatched my mail and sloshed down the hall to the grad offices, hoping to slip past the other TAs into the back room. There I expected to kick off my shoes and relax behind a desk piled high with the lamest excuses for scholarship to be found in the western world, my student's exams. On opening the door, however, two situations more unpleasant than the mud dripping off my cuffs lauded my arrival. The first concerned the machete.

The door had not closed behind me before Andy came into view, sitting on his desk with the big blade in his hands. He had apparently just spoken and was eyeing the other TA's suspiciously as he slid a thumb along the dented edge. He looked over as I entered and immediately grilled me with the same pointed questions he must have given the others.

"Hey, Ben, what do you know about this, huh? This machete was blessed in a Santeria ceremony. It's special. You have any idea who would want to desecrate it?" He held the blade up higher so that the dings and scratches could be clearly seen. I had to stifle a laugh. Andy was usually a pretty good-natured klutz, clueless and harmless. He had never appeared so upset before. This would be like shooting fish in a barrel.

"Jeez, Andy, you'd think you got your Papal miter caught in an escalator. I've seen that knife nearly come loose every time the door slammed. The janitor probably knocked it off with his broom. Now maybe you'll tie it up a little better. Besides, I'm sure it remains as beautiful as ever to the spirit world."

"I don't think so. This looks like it was purposefully jammed into something and used as a tool. I think it was done on purpose and someone here knows about it."

"Yes, the janitor knows all about prying it off the floor from behind your desk. Ask him. Be careful, though. If that blade cut him, he might sue. Now if you don't mind, I've got work to do. I'll light a candle for your machete if you'd like, though."

His smoldering eyes burned into my back as I walked to my office and closed the door. With that over, I dropped into my chair with relief and began to lean over to peel off my clingy shoes, glimpsing a partly folded letter at the edge of the desk in the process. After taking off my shoes, the paper was smoothed out and opened. On it was a deeply pressed and erratic scrawl that raised the hair on my neck:

"You said you'd call. You promised. Nobody makes a fool of me like that."

Oh Shit. It wasn't signed but it didn't take a Sherlock Holmes to deduce that it was from Shari. Before I could begin to formulate a solution for this nutcase, Suzanne walked in to deliver the other part of the one-two punch. She closed the door quietly behind herself while my hand slid the note carefully into the top drawer. Her smile was not pleasing. It was the smile that has been worn throughout time by the victor when he puts his heel on the skull of his enemy.

"I think I know who used poor Andy's sacred mojo as a tool. Don't you?" She purred her words like a cat over a half-dead mouse.

"What are you talking about?"

"The desk, Benny. You pried it open with the machete. That explains the bent latches, doesn't it?" Her smile now hardened into the tight lips of a prosecuting attorney. I returned with a smile meant to frighten her. If it didn't, it should have.

"Not that I can recall, Suzanne. However, I'm sure a forensic expert could clear this up. How about we call in your friend Dr. Bernini? I've heard you're a very good friend of his. Very good. I'm sure you've even met his wife and family, haven't you?" It was now my turn to harden my gaze. It felt good.

"You bastard."

"Not me. My mother was married to her lover."

"Asshole."

"Well, now that you've demonstrated your command of the language, I think we can get back to work, can't we?" I could see the hate seethe as her hand twitched towards the door. She was mine.

"Oh, but wait, Suzanne. I might have something you can help me with."

"Go fuck yourself."

"Thanks for the pleasant thought, but you are more right than you know. It does have something to do with that. But we can talk about it later, can't we? When our emotions aren't so high and we can think clearly?" I held out my hand like the reasonable diplomat. She gave me another look of loathing and closed the door behind her, without saying a word. Wonderful! My personal research was already paying off!

This episode increased my desire to immediately read more from the purloined notes, but this impulse had to be carefully restrained. It was apparent that the papers should never be in the office at any time, let alone held there before a light to read. Between Shari and Suzanne, my little back room had become insecure. I would have to wait until that evening at North Campus to open Steven's dead little world, one that still held so many consequences for the living.

CHAPTER 3

Tutzingo

5/12/80

I arrived today in Tutzingo, and the ride in was so stereotypically Mexican that even many Mexicans would not believe it. The bus was at the end of its useful life, painted and repainted blue and red so many times that various shades poked out at once, displaying its history like a slice through a sandstone cliff. All windows had cracks and outright holes, if they had glass in them at all, and the seats had been reduced to the hard wood platforms that had once held cushions. A wooden rack had been bolted onto the roof for baggage, but when I arrived it was already full, so the aisles were being used to hold additional sacks of grain and cages of various poultry.

Climbing over them was the exercise for the day. Of course the bus's tires were smooth as marbles and the metal body as pocked as the moon. Perhaps because of this, the driver – or better put, the pilot – had an even greater altar than usual displayed on his dashboard, looking from the rear like an ornate Hindu temple. On closer inspection one could see statues of various saints and likenesses of both officially sanctioned and unsanctioned holy people who could help with specific troubles, all of them adorned with brightly colored tassels under a cross holding a graphically suffering Christ. I did not remember the route to be dangerous, so I wondered: what was the pilot so afraid of?

Not long out of Hueuquilla we entered a dead zone, an alien desert covered with flat, bleached rock slabs that were themselves piled with rubble and boulders that stood up like angry guardians with fists raised along the road, ready to crush all comers at the slightest offense to the gods of the land. We stopped in this wasteland to pick up a man standing by a small group of homes that looked like a Flintstone's cartoon drawn by Salvador Dali. Apparently, a cluster of slabs had been geologically arranged so that an excavation of the smaller boulders and rubble around and under them made for usable housing structures with thick rock walls and roofs, each deformed by one side or top that slanted at an unpredictable angle. Ancient dirty wool tapestries hung as doors across different sized openings while goats searched hopelessly for graze on the gravel between the rocks. Two women could be seen in the partial shade of a slab house as they carefully and expertly slit long reeds with their thumbnails and folded them into the basketry they were making. The man we picked up carried three of these baskets and a chicken, the former probably for trade. How else could they get enough to live on?

The going was slow and tough. The road had never seen a bulldozer, and the pits and chunks that had been taken out by flash floods had been carelessly replaced with piles of rock so that certain stretches were like slightly raked avalanches. The pilot has to be given credit, though – he was able to subdue the genetic code that makes all inheritors of Mediterranean blood drive recklessly fast, allowing the old rusted bolts that held on the tires and frame to remain intact. Barely. Still, he took what seemed to me unnecessary risks, but a passenger is always less certain of the road than a driver.

After several hours of teeth rattling and kidney jolting, I was able to take my mind off my carsickness and notice the new signs of life that came at the appearance of the real Sierra foothills. Shady sides of hills held some green and occasionally cupped a trickle of water that was bordered by clumps of living brush. At one turn in the road we came to a steep decline that held at its bottom a genuine, running river. It was fast but not deep and wouldn't have been that formidable except for the small canyon it had carved in its course.

Our bus would have to cross this on the most rudimentary and decrepit of bridges. I did not recall this danger from before, which meant that the bridge had either deteriorated with time or that age had made me more cautious. In either case, it did not seem like it would hold our weight as it once must have. In fact, I wouldn't have crossed it by foot on a bet. On closer inspection it became apparent that it was no longer a bridge at all, but simply two tracks of two-by- tens nailed together, one for the left and the other for the right set of wheels. There had to be some form of bracing underneath it all, but there was nothing that could be readily seen.

Here's where the navigator came in. Until now, he had only opened the door for passengers and helped stack luggage and goods, and it barely seemed he earned his keep. But here he was essential. After the pilot stopped perilously close to the "bridge," the navigator got out and crossed most the way to the other side on one track. The drop to the river wasn't huge, maybe 30 or so feet, but such a drop into shallow water and hard rock could have maimed or killed several of us. I started to get up to follow the navigator, figuring we would all walk across just in case, but the pilot waved me down. No need for the inconvenience, gringo, he conveyed silently, it was all under control. At that he followed the hand signals of the navigator, steering a little to the right and then to the left as was gestured. At the half-way point the engine had to be revved to climb up the large bow the weight of the bus had made in the boards.

Finally, the back wheels left the planks with a loud "sproing," and we were home free.

I asked the pilot if the bridge had become worse over the past several years, and he emphatically replied, "Si, carray!" He said that plans to improve the road and even bring electricity all the way to Tutzingo had been abandoned because of the poor economy. When I asked him where all the money had gone from the fat years of the OPEC oil embargo, he shrugged and smiled. The economy is always bad for *campesinos*. Maybe if more tourists like me came out, things would improve?

Tutzingo was just five or so more miles up the road after that. In fact, the very river we crossed passes right through the village on its way from the high Sierra. Where it comes from in the mountains is a mystery to me, just as the village is a revelation, a mystery solved, to the unsuspecting traveler. While the hills get bigger and greener as one moves in its direction, the changes on the ground are incremental and unremarkable. It's at the last turn where one is suddenly and stunningly presented with both the village and the mountains. This illusion is attained by the curves of the road and the hills that hide the mountains behind them. At the last turn, one suddenly finds oneself looking down into the valley of Tutzingo and up into the great black mountains behind it. Today, the sight was as stunning as it had been years before, if not better: now my good fortune was to actually get to live in the area.

The mountains aren't naturally black, but look so after early afternoon when the sun casts huge shadows eastward. It's then that I arrived, and the mountains made a penumbra of the valley, letting it shine in a half-light like that of a partial eclipse. It was like driving into a dreamscape, the long curved green oval of the valley running about two miles east-west from the pass to another curve that disappears in the mountains, and about one mile north-south before the grass gives way to cliffs. Off somewhat to the south side runs the river, disappearing at the other end in the western canyon that it had carved millions of years before. The water glistened, too, in that mixture of brightness and shade that gave everything a celestial glow. I could not have been happier when the dust of the road in the hinterland turned into the rutted muddy main street of the village, where fate hid unseen promise and adventure.

The bus was not driven back to Hueuquilla right away, but was turned slowly around, slipping here and there in the red greasy earth, and then parked before the government-built store. The pilot and his navigator yelled their hellos outside before entering, and I followed, first turning to get a good look at the place.

Overall, only a few things of significance have changed. One is the additional slab of cement that juts into the mud before a building that serves as a garage (the other slab of cement is before the government store, where it had been before. Everything else in town is adobe or mud). There is only one vehicle in town, owned by the local rich man, but plans have been made for a motorized future. For the time being, though, it looks like the garage exists for the rich fellow and the bus, which is probably what keeps it in business. Each and every drive on that wreck of a road probably calls for an overhaul.

The other difference, and this struck a discordant note, is the cluster of electrical wiring that stretches between two poles behind the government store. This must have been from the time the pilot had talked about, when plans had been made for road improvements and electrification. It is surprising that the wires have not been sold for scrap, at least by a local thief. Perhaps it's the town's totem of a brighter future and their removal would constitute an intolerable desecration: where once religion brought the people pie in the sky, now science has brought them dangling wires in the air.

The government store is a box structure of cement blocks with a zinc roof that was built about ten years ago, back when there had been a surge of interest among some politicians to introduce a socialist bureaucracy that would shape Mexico in the image of Western Europe. The urge, as well as any additional funding, was siphoned off quickly by the oligarchy, but the store remains. When I walked in, it was almost into blackness. The building had been built for electrical lights, with only two tiny windows chiseled out on either side that let in just enough natural light to see down to your feet. It must either close at night or the proprietor must burn some of his profits in kerosene.

After my eyes adjusted, I could see a well-used lantern on the counter, behind which stood a large, gloomy man (with a mustache, of course. All men grow mustaches here, and the bushier they are, the more European blood they claim, and the better off they usually are). It seemed his eyes were bloodshot, but it could have been the lack of light. Behind him and to the sides were shelves that were almost all depressingly empty. There were some flashlight batteries and tins of sardines, along with some subsidized corn meal in big burlap sacks on the floor (many were marked with UNICEF or USA), along with a stack of Coke and beer in bottles. All warm, of course. I asked the man for a Coke, and then about a place to stay for a few weeks. He started to tell me, and then sent a boy who had been sitting invisibly against the wall to get the man he thought could help. Within a few minutes, the voice of my future landlord called me outside.

I could barely see anything at first because of the glare of daylight. When it was possible to take my arm from my eyes, I shook hands with Rafael Calderón, who took mine in the gentle way that the rural mestizos and Indians do. He is of nearly pure Indian stock, as most are in this area, with a small, delicate stature and dark reddish-brown skin and the thinnest wisp of a mustache. He wore a white shirt and dark pants of artificial fabric and leather sandals and the "straw" hat of the area, made expertly of cactus fiber that peaked at the top like a roof and was circled below the crown with a bright band of red. He spoke to me in the meek formal language of the campesino before a moneyed "blanco:"

"How may I serve you, sir?"

Of course his meekness is only skin deep, as is typical of subservience to a boss. One does what one must to survive. Still, being treated this way has always made me feel uncomfortable. After a while, you start to see yourself as the White Man, and pretty soon you lay yourself open to the abuse of the "lesser minions," who feel they can steal from you with a clear conscience. I hope it will be different with the mountain Indians.

But it has worked out pleasantly enough, with each of us, it seems, believing we got a bargain. To stay in his newly constructed adobe will cost an equivalent of two dollars a day, including breakfast and lunch. He pardoned himself and said that meat dishes would require a little extra (!) He will make at least a dollar a day profit for doing little more than having his wife make a few extra tortillas (perhaps with subsidized corn), but where could I find anything like this in the US? There will be no modern luxuries, but just to be able to have enough to eat, food made by someone else, no less, and a serviceable place to stay for that amount is unbelievable.

So here I sit, or lie, as the case is, writing from my new home. To say that it has no luxuries is a risible understatement. To pretend to be the White Saheeb at this moment is beyond imagination. Although it is new, it was obviously built either for the eternally hoped-for tourist industry or a newlywed son's starter house. It is, simply, an adobe square of about 12 feet by 12 feet with a thatch roof and a hard dirt floor. There is no other furniture besides a bed and an old crate of some kind that I was able to wheedle for a table. The bed consists of a mattress on rough wood slats, and the mattress looks like a hand-me-down from the Spaniards who lived here in the colonial era. The lice and fleas that it will probably transmit will serve as merit badges of fieldwork. There are no facilities such as a sink or shower or toilet. My guess is that one defecates behind the stonewall in the nearby field. Anything to do with water must be provided by the river. There are two windows, squared-out holes in the wall with no glass or screen so that the flies come in at will, and there are millions of them, with the animals and people providing hearty manure for them everywhere. I am writing lying stomach-first on the bed, sweating under my sleeping bag in an attempt to keep the horde of flies from lifting me into the air.

Still, I consider myself lucky. I finished eating at the landlord's house an hour ago, a late meal set up especially for me, and was impressed with his family. There live Rafael, his wife and four children, his mother, his brother (whose wife and children had recently left him) and an older man and women referred to as *tíos* (uncles and aunts). The place has been expanded from a one room like mine to many, still with only the two windows in front, so entering it is like entering an extensive cave.

It was almost night when I arrived there, and one candle lit the entire scene as we sat cross-legged on the floor and dipped tortillas into beans and chili sauce that had been put in terra cotta bowls on a blanket. It was all very polite and essentialist, but there was some family tension in the air that will in all probability come to light shortly. If this or some other issue proves to be messy, my move to the Indians in the mountains will provide the necessary escape.

I love the way the women dress here, with the layered, ankle-long dresses and the shawls or blankets over the shoulders, and all with bare feet, unlike the men in their sandals. I love the way they look, too, so delicate and small-boned with the shiny straight black hair and big black eyes. Sitting down at the meal, the females were like tables unto themselves, flows of fabric that seemed to hold them from the waist-up like pedestals.

More later. The government store *is* open into the evening, which allowed me to purchase six celebratory beers. The proprietor promised that a new lot came in every month whether called for or not, and I promised him that my presence would certainly bite into the supply. It is now time to release the bubbly spirits so that a temporary peace might be made with my new vermin friends. Then a little reading and lantern out. Tomorrow begins the search for information on the Indians. ST

I continued to the next entry:

5/15

What a disappointment! What started out so well with Rafael has become a mess. He came by this morning and gave me a chicken for a gift. Of course I insisted on paying him a dollar for it and also insisted that we share it for the big meal, our lunch, which was probably expected. But his talk shifted to the facts of his poverty, how farming brought in almost nothing and how he wanted his oldest son to go to school in Guadalajara or Mexico City. I told him that, as a student myself, I understood poverty first hand, but this only made him more emphatic about his own troubles. He then asked if perhaps I knew some wealthy Americans in the US? If perhaps they would be interested in buying large quantities of marijuana? It was all very good, grown right here in the hills, and the price was certainly a bargain. What were my thoughts about setting up a little business?

Of course this appalled me because now I will be forced to dissimulate at every turn. Not even my disgust for his offer could be shown, for that could have aroused a fear of betrayal on his part to the law. Now every contact in town has to be treated with extraordinary care. It's not that growing pot brings moral outrage to Mexican law enforcers - they couldn't care less, as the drugs, so they say, only go to rich, decadent Americans - but that it can be used for blackmail and power. The officers of the law can demand and get any cut they wish with the whip the law gives them, for they can throw any one of these peasants into jail for years on a whim.

As a young, unkempt American, Rafael just assumed that I had come for business. Why else would one leave a land of wealth and gleaming machinery for a fly-infested hamlet at the end of the road? Rafael knows he is open to blackmail, and has no reason to believe that this leverage will not be used. A Three-D game of chess has now begun involving the whole village that was not asked for and cannot be stopped.

That this affair will not remain private is very clear. In this old and tiny and insular village, what happens to one person affects everyone. Which, to get back to my reason for being here, has opened up some interesting angles. Every person here has referred to Rafael as a relative-either as a cousin or an in-law, which shows that the bonds of blood and marriage are deep. Could they reflect elements of a clan-like system from the pre-Christian era?

In a place this size, however, everyone must be related to everyone else both as an affine *and* blood relative. The question is, how is it determined that one is classified as one and not the other? Do they follow patrilines, and marry only cousins from their mother's brother's line (with mother's sister's line going to one's father's brother's line)? If such a system is in place, does it mirror the system still held by the mountain Indians? And how mixed are the people here with the Indians? If to a high degree, what delineates one as Mexican and one as Indian? So many questions, but will they trust me enough to answer them? Maybe I should buy a pound or two of weed to fit in. Then again, maybe they would sell me to the *Federales*. Best to leave it alone.

The village itself is easy to describe. There is Main Street, which is a one hundred yard-long rut of mud that ends abruptly at the cattle path running west. This latter goes on (they tell me) into several higher valleys that are owned by a few large cattle ranches, each with its own set of hereditary ranch hands, or so it seems. More on that later. On the north side, away from where I am staying, are the two commercial buildings, four domiciles, and the school. On the south side are two large (or one large partitioned) houses, and three other standard ones. Out in the fields to the other side are my house, just built, Rafael's, and four others scattered about, apparently without a pattern. Ours is the side with the river, and nobody lives in the north fields. That makes up fourteen houses. Using the standard calculation of five people per house, that would amount to 70 residents, a number about twice the size of the average primitive band. While these people cannot be compared to hunters and gatherers, the number, 35, is the upper limit at which people may feel that all are part of a single family. Greater numbers than that and artificial abstractions or sanctions must be used to govern the social unit.

Concerning subsistence, it does not seem possible that the small arable acreage here could support them all. The primary food, corn, is obviously supplemented by aid agencies. There are also a fair number of grazing animals, notably cattle and sheep, but it is doubtful that these are sufficient for everyday nutrition, except for the milk from the cows. The sheep, too, are obviously kept for wool, as I have seen women spinning the yarn for the blankets and shawls used here by everyone. It seems that either the aid they receive has allowed them to expand their population, or that the marijuana industry here is more extensive than meets the eye.

I did manage to talk to my landlord about the Indians, and then to Manolo, a cousin of Rafael from the main street who joined us in conversation. There are two groups in the region, the Tarahumara, who are famous for the 120 mile run that the young men do every year, at night, nonstop, while kicking a small ball between them. It is claimed that this is possible because of the use of peyote. The other group, the more isolated of the two, are the Huichol, who are just now becoming known in Western art circles for their incredible, bright yarn paintings. These depict scenes from their mythology and are also influenced by the ritual use of peyote. It was, in fact, one of these yarn paintings that brought me to Tutzingo. I had bought one of these from a Huichol in Fresnillo on my first visit to the area, a beautiful depiction of a deer dying besides a cactus plant, its spirit leaving its nostrils in a white plume.

When questioned, the Indian gave me directions to his homeland, which I wrote on the back of the plywood plank that served as the canvas for the painting. That day, the Mexicans had crowded around us as we talked, then mocked the picture, as the spirit coming from the nose reminded them of snot or semen. You can see how this humiliation would make young people give up traditional ways.

Rafael and Manolo told me that some Huichols come into town about twice a week to trade herbs and wild game for flashlights and sardines and local brandy. There are two Huichol women in town married to Tutzingo men. It is possible, even probable, that everyone here is related directly to Huichols, although it is something people prefer not to speak about. They are, they claim, Mexican *racionales*, regular folks fully part of the mainstream. It's obvious that the sting of inferiority and servitude that being Indian has meant for so many centuries is still alive and well. The men also told me that the schoolteacher knew much more about the Indians, as some of the Indian children stay in town with relatives to learn how to read and write and to speak Spanish properly. I went to see her, but she had gone to Hueuquilla on the bus to obtain school supplies. They say she will be back in a few days.

Until then I will wait for the Indians and get to know the townsfolk and work out a better system for bathing and performing other essential functions, especially defecating. One of the town pigs has figured out my routine, and has to be shooed away while I am squatting. As soon as I stand, however, he cannot be kept from this treat. It will be hard to eat pork the next time it is offered.

Hasta Manana. ST

My gag reflex had to be checked as the rambling notes were digested. It seemed as if the trail had suddenly turned cold. The text not only did not contain any juicy tidbits of gossip, but was devoid of fresh ideas as well. Cross-cousin marriage? Social bonding? This guy was dealing in old British Structural-Functionalism, about as original as spats and muttonchops. His brief allusion to cultural ecology with the garden and livestock comments was equally as tiresome. It would be immediately clear to any buffoon that a town such as he described would not have the isolation necessary to justify the notion of a closed economic system. And better left unsaid was his attempt at camp humor, bringing to mind his great, hairy buttocks. It left me wishing that he had died a little sooner.

I put the notebook down and thought hopefully of the letters. They had turned up gems before. A quick look at the neatly wrapped bundle revealed that the exposed envelope on top had been postmarked from Hueuquilla only three days after the date of the notes just read. After removing it perfunctorily for opening, a glance at the letter beneath made me jump with delight. The postage on that was from Ann Arbor, sent three days before the one from Mexico. It was addressed to Steven in a feminine hand, with the return address, without name, of our own department. The rich bitch had written! For some reason I had never expected anything from her, even though the notes had obviously been sent to her from the field. Of course he would have saved her letters.

Thinking of it, it was obvious that she would have sent at least one, the one that undoubtedly formalized their break-up. Beyond that, part of me hoped that others would follow while another that they would not. It was a curious position of ambiguity, but not one that caused discomfort. Everything that would happen was all tied up here in the folders, and it was already known that the lovers' tale had, for me, a happy ending. The endeavor was like entertaining oneself with a formulaic movie, watched solely for the special effects sandwiched between a known beginning and end.

I slipped a thumb along the frail top of the air-mail envelope and pulled out a little piece of Lacey:

Dear Steven,

I am so sorry for having to disappoint you, if that may be said with humility. I thought it would be best for you to be unencumbered in your work, free to pursue any avenue you see fit. Also, we have to face it: neither one of us is in a position to take on the responsibilities of married life. You know that there is money in my family, and that this makes it so much harder. A husband in debt and without a job would instantly lose the respect of my parents, especially my father. He would guess you had married for money and it is possible, given our profession, that future events might seem to prove him right. We are a tight family that can count back a dozen generations, and we have been taught respect for the traditions of our ancestors. If you were to first find a position, you would be welcome with open arms, but this might take many years. It does not seem fair to hold you to only a possibility for so long.

I do worry about you, though, and am now feeling the emptiness that is left when one loses a good friend and confidant. I wake in the morning expecting to find you warming my bed, but have to wait for coffee to cast off the chill. It is still just so vicious here, and it would be so much nicer to be in the field with you, but I have to prove myself and win my credentials. Such is my family. I know it might all sound provincial to a man from the Heartland, but it is also a strength. When even God lost his thunder to modern reason a few generations ago, we still had our heritage to cling to. This has become our one and only staff and rod. It has occurred to me now and then to rebel, to become a free individual, but too many people, both living and dead, would suffer in the process.

In the department, the same old struggle of ambitions continues, complicated by an entanglement of gossip and payback. You may disapprove of Suzanne's affair, but at least it is human. Ben (Solomon) had a little tryst with Greene that was as sleazy as you would expect, catching her on the rebound as he did, but that is still within the bounds of average selfishness. More pernicious are the fights between professors that unfairly involve the students, as happened to you. Now it has become Andy's turn. Kronick insists that he return to his field site for some small, very specific data, which will certainly cost him months in time and thousands of dollars, if he can manage it at all. This is happening because Friedman, Andy's advisor, criticized Kronick for the lack of rigorous methodology in his latest book. Given that he has tenure and security, why should he care? Why must he destroy someone as inoffensive as Andy?

Anna has become engaged to her boyfriend Aden from Statistics, the one you call the Idiot Savant. She seems happy, as they have found that his part-time job will become full time after he completes his Masters this month. Anna is already talking about children, and Aden does not disagree.

I have found myself hoping for some kind of happiness these days. It is becoming clear that this will not come from our profession. The miserable state of the professors' lives should be proof enough of that. As my enthusiasm for my work recedes, there seems to be nothing to take its place. Maybe marriage would have solved this problem, but, then, one shouldn't marry to become happy. One should marry out of happiness. It's not that you failed to make me happy, but rather that my capacity for happiness has diminished along with everything else.

Even this letter is unsatisfactory. It reads so cold, so snobbish, especially where it concerns my family, but you deserve the truth in this matter. There is, in retrospect, a lot of selfishness in my life, a selfishness that now threatens to pull everything apart. I wish you were here with me now, but it would be just as selfish to use you as a crutch. I have to solve this thing in my heart, by myself.

Please take care and write. I would like to send you a new compilation of articles concerning the new Native American rights movement in Latin America, but you say that anything that is sent beyond a simple letter may be stolen. Is that really true? Is it really that corrupt down there? How can people live like that?

Again, take care,

Love, Lacey

I closed the letter with a flush of anger. I had believed that my little "conquest" of Professor Greene was our secret, although it is hard to depict a woman who practically dragged me to her couch as a conquest. It was in her office, no less. She was the first black woman to have shared her dusky flesh with me, although it happened that once the heat was on, the feast tasted the same. But she had talked, the slut! In retrospect, this should have been obvious, as she had started free-associating about her broken affair with Professor Tourstein before our sweat had dried. And what the hell was Lacey's comment about my sleaziness? Sleazy is screwing a greaser from a rust-belt shantytown. She should have remembered her benighted ancestors' Good Book and its admonition about the splinter and the beam in one's eye.

My anger subsided once the titillation of the other gossip sank in. More importantly, Lacey had exposed her soft spot. Most certainly, other useful facts would come to light if she continued to write. It was disappointing to read that she had not kissed Steven off completely, and the undeniable revelation that the two were indeed involved in a sexual affair was revolting, but her subtle put-down of Steven's lumpen-proletariat ways was a pure delight. It was doubtful he would even catch it. "Heartland" meant "fly-over country," and "free individual" meant "lawless mongrel." While I have had little contact with the rich, never mind old Boston money, I have met many of their intellectual counterparts in Chicago, and know their language and prejudices. Lacey had given Steven a good little spanking, padded nicely as a humble apology.

There was more: it would not take a Freud to figure out that Lacey was headed for a psychological meltdown. As certain as she wore her family pride, she had lost her personal reason for living. She envied dull little Anna her future as a wet nurse, and even briefly reconsidered her wise rejection of Steven. She had, as the old families of New England might say, lost her mooring. In the tempests of the department, she feared that she would crash on the rocks.

Perhaps my stance towards her should have been more sympathetic, but Lacey's heart was no less flinty than my own. Even had her condition been evident at the time, she would have resented my help once she regained her strength. Then her ego would have demanded that mine be reduced to hers at its former abject level.

I shrugged off my brief flirtation with kindness and reached for the next letter, Steven's, written after Lacey's but completed and sent well before hers could be received. The interplay of actual and postal times proved to make even Steven's dull script intellectually enjoyable:

Dear Lacey,

The weather is so perfect here, like Mexico City without the smog. The sun shines every day, the temperature wavers in the 70's, and the nights are crisp and perfect for huddling beneath blankets. And the stars! Tutzingo is about a mile high with a dry climate and no ambient light, which opens the sky to the universe. Here the Milky Way is no thin strand, but a vast veil of shimmering white painted in the style of a grandiose impressionist, the great starry fabric woven from a billion dots of light when observed closely. It pulls me out of my own mind to see it, sensing that we are like that galactic slash, a unity of light composed of billions of individuals. The satellites float by like small harbor boats, as if we humans were hugging the coast, waiting to cast off into the great glittering sea.

You can see that the quiet isolation here has brought on a great deal of introspection, if not an epiphany. Yesterday I walked upstream to the bend in the valley before the mountains and waded to a rock in the river where I sat in the afternoon sun and drank several beers chilled in the mountain water. Some cowboys rode past, reigning down horses excited about going home, and they waved to me with their great, wide *vaquero* hats. While the villagers often cower in false servitude to gain from my presence, the spirit of the cowboys is still present, epitomized by the buoyancy of their horses in the open valleys and tall mountains. This tells me that we are all yearning for the right time and place, the good fortune to be free, free of the chains of our work, our obligations, our disappointments. To be free, though, one is first obliged to make an honest self-assessment, one that for me is long overdue.

I have blamed the professors for the horror of our department, but they have only taken on the baggage of a soulless system made brutal by the competition of so many for so little. It is obvious that the bitterness has entered my soul as well, even more so for thinking that it hasn't. As Karl Marx observed, the work environment shapes the man, at least those of little faith. And who can keep the faith in a department of social science? Isn't violence done to our nature just in making the 'social' a science? Even so, this leaves no excuse for the honest man. It is, in the end, up to him and him alone to provide the attitude necessary for the enjoyment of life and the fulfillment of his goals. The stars soar without rancor or pity; we should do no less.

Not that this is accomplished perfectly anywhere. What is it about *campasino* life that makes people so envious? I disagree with Faulkner's depiction of our own peasants, the southern red necks – in reality, the depravity of a few was balanced by a far greater humanity than he allows - but the meanness he portrayed was no doubt real and is apparent here. The other day while at the store looking for kerosene, a boy politely commanded me to come visit his father, the rich man in town who owns the truck. I agreed, and found that the two houses he owns had been made into a single compound in an attempt to form a regal courtyard in the Spanish tradition. Made by simply connecting the houses by rounded adobe walls, the boy was careful to take me in one house and lead me through this courtyard to the other. There, a kitchen and two bedrooms were isolated one from the other by plaster walls, such separation of quarters probably unique to the village. In the larger of the two bedrooms we found the father lying glumly in bed. The covers had been pulled down below his chest, which was wrapped several layers deep in medical gauze. He was in his mid-forties, strongly built with light skin covered with black, curly hair. While it seemed certain he would recover, he did not look well: his eyes were bloodshot and tinged with yellow, and his expression was one of smoldering anger. He had me sit, and he answered my obvious question.

He had been drinking with his brother-in-law in the afternoon when the latter had demanded the use of the truck. When his request was refused because the vehicle was being repaired, his in-law accused him of being stingy. "Why, you have always thought that your family was better than ours. You are such a big man, squeezing money out of us farmers and giving us back nothing. The only things you give back are the bastard children you have disgraced us with."

The rich man, Senor Gonzalez, or Chico as the men call him, shot back a reminder that the other man had disgraced Chico's sister by having intercourse with here before they were married. Then he threw him out of the house.

Shortly afterward, Chico walked into the street to check on his car and was met by his in-law, who shot him three times with a pistol. It was lucky that Chico was strong and the in-law a poor shot or the latter would be rotting in the state penitentiary. I asked that if he was not to be incarcerated now, how would he be punished for the attempted murder?

"The *cabron* is still wasting his ancestor's land with his laziness. Why would I send him to jail? It would only make my sister and her children suffer. But you may be certain that I will find a suitable revenge for him."

He stared with blank hatred for a moment at the ceiling and then asked if I was a mechanic. He thought all American men were good at mechanics, but it so happens that I was able to tell him in truth that I actually knew a thing or two. My father's patience had paid off. He hoped for help in the garage, and claimed that people would pay me for it. Even though it was obvious that this was not true, I happily volunteered to lend a hand. With only one truck and one bus to watch over, the work won't be much, and the capital made in good will should more than compensate my time. Besides, a little tinkering now and then is good for the soul.

Yesterday was a busy day for meeting important people. At the afternoon meal I was introduced to a pretty young woman who was described with great pride as the schoolteacher. Then Rafael's wife, who had never talked to me directly before, let me know that she was her sister. The teacher is quiet like her sister, but fully self-possessed. It is clear that her softness of nature is born from serenity, not shyness. She had her toddler son with her, and after we ate, she asked if I would like to see the school building. With that, we walked over the field to the other side of the street, her son carried tenderly in her shawl.

The school is about twenty yards up from the street and fronted by small, dense trees and cacti, obscuring its view from the street. It is one of the three buildings in town made from concrete, but she pointed out how shabby the textbooks were and how inadequate the writing supplies that she had bought in Hueuquilla. She hoped to get some help from the American doctor who is supposed to come this afternoon. He works for a US relief agency and often flies in to bring supplies for the children.

She also told me, without my asking, that her son had no legitimate father. Her *novio* had gotten her pregnant when she was in school in Guadalajara, and then refused to have anything more to do with her. The town had managed to get her enough money to finish her degree, so that she would come home and teach. Her utility was obviously greater than her disgrace. It's funny – as much as I dislike the feminist intelligentsia, I find myself disliking more the machismo attitude that causes a man to reject a woman because she has giving in to his desires and lies. It's all about him! So a woman is good only if she keeps the man on a leash until his frustration forces him to marriage. No wonder the Latinos are so filled with frustrated passion. While this system once created a successful warrior culture, now it seems to exist only to create misery.

Alert! The plane is coming, remarkably on time! Must be a gringo flying it. I'm off to meet him to see what he has to say, and maybe get this letter to you a little earlier. Take heart Lacey,

Love, Steven

CHAPTER 4

A Mountain and a Mole Hill

I woke late the next morning, and numbly realized that I was still in my pants and lying on Steven's notebook. A quick look at the clock showed that there was just enough time to pull on my boots and make it to class. It wasn't until I crunched over the refrozen snow and sat down in the campus bus that thoughts returned of Steven's last letter. Of course, his cheap attempts at lyricism annoyed me - how often must we hear of someone's joyful leap into nature?- but it was his penchant for moral reflection that really struck a nerve. It was no wonder the faculty had slapped him down so often, pugnacious arrogance aside.

His "forgiving" of the department and his penitent shouldering of the perceived sin induced hyper-glycemic nausea. Not only were the declarations fatuous, but they also betrayed a prejudice of mind that disqualified him from progressive social circles. Where did he get off telling anyone what a proper social environment should be? How could he have the arrogance to conclude that what prevailed in the department was to blame for our blemishes? While it is true that we didn't exactly live in perfect harmony, who did? To what abstract ideal did he compare us?

Of course, I knew: his was the picture of the Christian brotherhood, a society of peaceful men bent on contemplation and trust and the cultivation of great, open hearts. This may sound good, but it is a fairytale, an ideal that is not reachable, and, given the real-world effects of Christianity, a striking contradiction. Who couldn't see that an insistence on an idealized belief would lead to intolerance and war? The traps hidden in the Western moral system had been proven, "outed." For instance, who could deny that chivalry reduced women to idealized images? And who could deny that honor held a man to his debts, that patriotism held him to defend the status quo, that a humbleness of spirit allowed for a usurious hierarchy?

But as a professional anthropologist, his letter revealed a more disturbing bent. If he believed that one form of behavior was better than another, this might lead to the condemnation of other cultures that did not share his values. Isn't that what the colonials did, giving themselves excuses for selfish atrocities along the way? This also would ally him with the discredited theory of social evolutionism, the belief that humankind was working towards a more perfect complexity. This had also been used by colonials to "teach the savages" as they enslaved them and pillaged their resources. No, he must accept that all things are morally relative, that no law comes from a Creator God, that one way of doing things is simply another way. His lack of self-perception accurately reflected his deprived pedigree.

The bus brought me in time for class, a long, three-hour seminar on exactly this subject, attended by graduate students and several undergrads who were obviously lesbians. With their piercings and butch haircuts and baggy, torn clothing, it was clear that the male gender was missing nothing by their alternative choice of sexual partners. They were sharp, though. The theory that morality was a class-based tool of oppression had been taken by the lot of them as Gospel, and the leader among them was revered as a prophet who could roll out this philosophy as adroitly as a rabbi could unroll the Torah.

It was amusing but also made the class dynamics problematic for me: as a graduate student, I would be expected to master the material at a higher level than the little zealot freaks, even though the material meant nothing to me nor helped my career. I had counted on Angela Greene, the professor of the course and my once-passionate lover, to get me over that hump, so to speak, but she had allowed our relationship to bleed into gossip (as revealed in the letters) for revenge against Tourstein. That left me with little leverage.

So it was that a somber mood predominated on the way back to the office. Schemes for cementing a new alliance with Greene filled my head until the door to the back room swung open at my touch. A single glance within gave the immediate impression that my desk had been violated. Perhaps slight changes in the position of the pens and papers had alerted my subconscious to the fact that something was terribly wrong and, by smell or some other trace sense, brought to mind the probable perpetrator. I quickly opened two of my drawers, and at first could not fathom what I saw. It took several seconds to grasp that the drawers had been stuffed full with toilet paper. A quick check showed that all had suffered the same fate. It then came to my attention that the papers had been discolored: used, in fact, for their intended purpose. Brown streaks and splotches smeared every strip. It was not long before I noticed the smell, and soon after that, the handy-work on my calendar.

It was one of those nature homilies that are sent out for advertising by heating oil companies and hardware stores. It was opened to March, of course, and the scene was of melting snowdrifts in the Rockies that fed a gushing creek. Against the whiteness of the picture had been scrawled the word "SHIT," formed in big capital letters with excrement. Below it on the actual calendar the word "HEAD" completed the phrase with the same substance and style. Fingerprints could clearly be detected in the smears.

Some kind of vengeance from Shari had been expected, but not so quickly or so graphically. I had envisioned something on the order of an angry rant in the department office, something that could be parried by well-planted gossip about her mental health, but now it was obvious that she was the physical sort, and as such, dangerous. Women of her kind had cooked their children in ovens because angels had told them to do so. Fortunately, an empty box left over from the dumpster still lay by the desk, and several sheets of writing paper served as gloves to empty my drawers of Shari's filth into it. The other grads could not find out about this. There was no telling how it could be used against me.

There was only one potential confidante to help me with my predicament, and when I opened my door slightly for a peek into the main office, it was heartening to see that she had arrived during the cleanup. I nudged the door again until the outer fluorescent lights illuminated the backroom.

"Suzanne, would you mind coming into my office for a moment? I have a few things to discuss about some students." She had picked her head up quickly with the sound of her name, then hardened her face when she saw me.

"I would think that a man of your great intelligence could handle a few undergraduates on his own."

"Oh, come on! I need to know something about these guys. I think they may have plagiarized their papers. It'll just take a minute." She looked at a couple of her friends and rolled her eyes, but came to the door. I waved my arm for her to enter and offered my chair.

"Oh, no, that's yours. My legs will hold for a minute. You did say it would only take a minute?" Her seething sarcasm was somehow very feminine and attractive. It brightened things up for the first time that day. I closed the door, sat down and pushed the chair against the wall to face her.

"Suit yourself. It's not really about papers, though."

"Surprise, surprise. I have work to do."

"No, wait. You might find this amusing. It's about me and that new girl, Shari."

"New woman, you mean. That's old news. And so is your taking advantage of every trusting woman in the university. Are we done?"

"I can promise you that it's more than that. For one thing, it was all her idea. I barely knew she existed."

"Yes, who could resist you?"

"For another, and here it gets interesting, she's fucking nuts. I mean certifiable. Hard core schizophrenic."

"Have you talked with her doctor? It might be that you drive everyone crazy."

"Listen, really, I'm serious. After our, uh, night, we went out, and the way she behaved, I thought they would tow her away on the spot. Really. She seemed to be possessed in the classic sense, with demons. Then I remembered a few of the medicine labels that were in her bathroom. I looked them up. She's one sick girl."

"So you hooked into a pathetic, emotionally ill woman and now want me to help you dump her, is that it?"

"Well, yes, but it's more than that. If you promise to keep it to yourself, I'll show you something."

"I won't promise anything. You know, it's not that I dislike you. I hate you. You blackmailed me. That can only go so far. He won't be the first professor to have been caught in an affair."

"And you won't be the first grad student to go down in flames because of it. You think your dignity trumps tenure? Forget it."

"I don't care. It won't fly anymore, Ben. One for one is enough."

"All right, all right. This is serious. Look. See this note? I got that the day after my little romp with 'Shari dearest.' Now, check out this calendar. And look in the box. That was all stuffed in my desk." Her curiosity had been captured, and she examined the evidence with a sardonic smirk until she realized what she was pawing through. She jumped in horror as if a ghost had just appeared.

"That's excrement! You bastard, and I touched it!" She turned to go out the door to wash, but I caught her by the elbow.

"See? This puppy's sick. And dangerous. I really need your help."

"Serves you right. Have fun."

"As I was saying, there is something more to trade with." At that, she turned and eyed me suspiciously, her hands held up as if she were wearing surgical gloves. I read her look and felt her buried guilt, her sense that she had a few more things in her life to hide, as did we all, and knew there was an opening.

"It's nothing about you. Well, maybe a little about you, but not blackmail. You see, I may have just fallen into a few letters between Lacey and Steven."

"Scumbag."

"I said, 'may have.' And maybe a few notebooks. Some contain some pretty surprising stuff about the department. I mean, 'may.' Some shocking stuff, really. About some of our great professors."

"How would she know any more than we do?"

"How would *they* know. The two of them, together. And we all know something that someone else doesn't. That's what drives our whole social system here, isn't it?"

"Some of us have friends." Her reply was disdainful, but I could see that she was hooked. Again. Last time with vinegar, this time with honey. Forbidden honey. I helped her make excuses for herself, but we both knew the deal was done.

"You should really send them back to Lacey. You know that."

"I don't know that. The sight of them could send her over the edge. Really over the edge. Who knows?"

"Then you should keep them tied up until she asks for them."

"For how long? Then what do I do, burn them? Look, both of them are out of the system now..."

"She might come back."

"OK, then, you would know what I know. You could tell if I were using this information for my own advantage. In a way, you would safeguard her from me."

"Are you really that afraid of Shari? She's only a 'girl.'"

"I never said women were harmless. Since the invention of weapons, no one is harmless. Yes, I'm afraid of her. Wouldn't you be?" I looked at her squarely in the eyes then, and saw an expression that, for the first time, was not filled with hate or contempt. As a matter of fact, there wasn't much in it at all except a glint of curiosity, especially for the forbidden. She couldn't resist a portal into the private lives of others any more than I could.

She began to sit against the edge of the desk, then noticed her hands again and jumped up. "I've got to go. We can talk later."

"Sure." I nodded with a tight smile as she swung out the door with her hands raised before her. I wanted to yell, "scrub up well, doctor!" but knew that a semblance of seriousness was warranted. She must believe that she was better, nobler than I. She was doing this for Lacey. Sure. Although it was funny: for the first time since the beginning of my career it struck me that Suzanne was actually a good-looking woman. A little too serious and scholarly, yes, but when she pursed her lips before leaning to sit on the desk, there was something. Maybe it was simply the dropping of our facades. Maybe it was more a sense of kinship than sex. Maybe the former would make the latter incestuous and I should forget the whole thing, as had been done since the beginning.

Having an ally to rid me of the psychopath eased my mind considerably, but still my eyes roved carefully around and behind me before I entered the bus back to North Campus. The same caution was repeated after flicking the lights on in my room. What Shari had done was so visceral, in every sense, that it was probable that she would do anything. Scenes from Clint Eastwood's movie, "Play Misty for Me" couldn't help but crop up.

Having secured the perimeter, which consisted of the closet and the space beneath the bed and desk in my cubical quarters, the package was brought out again. The notebooks that slid out elicited a sigh of boredom. While the letters gave me something now and then, the notes did little for me. Steven interested me no more now than when he was around in person. I was tempted to go straight for the letters again and skip the notes, but something made me resist this impulse. Perhaps it was the compulsion of the scholar who must delve into every dank archive, no matter how trivial or redundant. Perhaps it was the morbid curiosity of one who awaits a certain death and lingers on all the preceding details. But it was most probably the former, the curiosity of the social scientist with the need to explore every detail that went into Lacey's breakdown; the need to know how someone could fall apart so completely.

5/23 Tutzingo

I met the schoolteacher again yesterday, as beautiful and graceful a young woman as remembered. She mentioned the difficulty of getting supplies for the children, not because the funding wasn't legislated, but because it was stolen before it got to her district. She claimed that 90% of funding for all projects is stolen, and that is why so little progress is ever made in Mexico. While one can buy less pencils and books for a school, one cannot buy, say, half an airplane for an agricultural improvement project. She mentioned again the American doctor who flies in every two weeks to administer medical care and delivers any sort of material he can that might help the general population. She had asked him for the remainder of textbooks and supplies needed, and was waiting for his arrival with the kind of hope of a sailor stranded at sea.

Fortunately he had come, about 11:00 in the morning, and was able to fulfill her request. It was a pleasure to see her delight. She behaves like a woman who prays a lot and believes that the Lord will fulfill anything that is unselfishly desired and that is, in His infinite knowledge, good for the world.

Speaking of God: I met the doctor with Angelica after he landed and helped bring the supplies to the schoolhouse. He is a tall, lean, late-middle-aged man with intense blue eyes and thinning white hair, the classic gringo philanthropist. He also is intensely religious, and he talked in good Spanish with Angelica about things in boldly theistic ways. Even though I have not abandoned faith entirely, I find such openness about God embarrassing, as if it were a chat about masturbation fantasies. It all seems too personal and revealing, but as I write, those emotions have to be questioned. Why should this be so? A belief in science may be expressed in any crowd, containing talk about black holes and time travel and other such things that are absolutely beyond the human grasp, yet a mention of God deflates the whole party. Is it because talking about belief may cause conflict? But this has seldom stopped anyone with a few drinks in him from bringing up politics. No, it is because God is embarrassing, like an adult belief in Santa Claus, especially among the educated classes.

This has disturbed me before, not so much because our intelligentsia is so preposterously conceited that it believes it has the right to shove beliefs held dear by the majority of the world into the closet, but because we anthropologists study religion everywhere we go and yet are forbidden to express our own experiences with the sacred. The answer always given is this: ours is a science, and we study what science can study. We may detect the affects a *belief* in a god might have on the individual or social level, but it is not our province to determine whether or not that god exists. But would a scientist settle for determining the affects a *belief* in black holes has rather than the reality of them? We have, after all, an advantage over the astronomer: our sources of information, people, usually have long-practiced techniques to communicate with their gods. Shouldn't we explore these with open hearts and minds?

Still, theory could not overcome training. I felt relief and, of course, open interest when the conversation turned to the Indians. They were one of the reasons that the doctor was here. Although his organization claimed to be non-denominational, it was clear that they had at least general Christian conversion in mind. However, as happens with most of us in the field, and with medical doctors in particular, practical matters often swallow up the fancy abstract reasons we have for being there. His chief concern now is with a case of typhoid fever that had shown up a few months before at the nearest Huichol village.

He had had to ride up by mule and direct the extermination of head lice to make sure the disease didn't become epidemic. He was anxious to see that everything was now under control. He had told the regional director of Indian affairs that he would be arriving today if the weather permitted, and he hoped that the director had remembered to send someone with news of the sickness. Even so, some Indians would usually come down from the mountains when they heard his plane, for health reasons or for trinkets and treats they might get, but they sometimes would not arrive until late in the evening. Doctor Gary could stay no later than 5:00 PM before he was scheduled elsewhere.

That the Indians might be arriving soon was a good bit of news. The time seems right to get away from the flies and the tedious social undulations of the village.

It's lunch time and too hot now. More later.   ST

Tutzingo, 5/24

Good luck has come for my project! But first to other events. I have been skipping extensive notes recently either from lack of anything new, or from too much that is new. The last 24 hours have been a time of too much. First came something horrible. Shortly after noon I used the siesta break to visit the garage for a little tinkering. I started the truck - the keys were left in as there was no possibility that anyone could get away with car theft here - and noticed some off-firing probably caused by poor timing.

I had popped the hood and was looking around for anything like a timing light (always the optimist –where is the electricity?) when Chico, the owner, hobbled in with the aid of his son and a crutch. It seemed like a really bad idea, as the wounds had produced some fresh patches of blood on his bandages, but he insisted that sitting in his truck would do him a world of good. After his son helped him gain a piece of the seat, he told him to go get that "lazy good-for-nothing husband of my sister (Simon) up here to help the North American." No protestations on my part could change his mind, as Chico was determined to squeeze Simon *por cuanto que me debe,* "for everything that he owes me."

I was fiddling with the engine when Simon showed up, a thin, reddish-faced man whose gaunt appearance wasn't helped by his surliness. Chico immediately ordered him to stand in front of the car and hold a flashlight to dispel the shadows under the fan. I told Chico that all it needed was a few small adjustments that could be made by feel, but he insisted, forcing Simon to lean, smoldering with anger, against the radiator with the flashlight loosely pointed at the engine block. Then a sudden screech of tires made me jump and literally fall in a stack of WWII surplus jerry cans behind me. A second later came the sound of twisting metal and a shattering scream.

There is no use to waste paper on suspense. The short of it is that Chico got his revenge by crushing Simon's legs against the wall. One, the right, seemed simply swollen, but the left was shattered. Two bone splinters jutted out from his pants, one with a chunk of meat on it. It's always a shock when we realize that our substance is no different than livestock. Chico backed up immediately after the scream, apparently satisfied, and I yelled at his poor son to go find the doctor immediately. He arrived shortly after and was able to stop Simon from bleeding to death, and then flew him out so that he might save the leg.

Of course it was the news of the day, and after helping Simon get packed into the plane, Rafael and Mando and I spent the evening talking over several shots of mescal and a few beers. It has led to a slow morning, but it was just the thing for me. The incident has really shaken me up. Thank goodness that packing for a new adventure has given me something to do.

Anyway, with the drinking came quite a bit of gossip. Back in the 20's, Simon's grandfather had been a lay minister (deacon) of the Catholic Church when the area came under the control of the *Cristeros,* the force of counterrevolutionaries that tried to overturn the secularization of Mexico and the new "revolutionary" government of the PRI. His *abuelo* was given control of the communal lands because of his position in the Church until the *Federales* returned and killed everyone connected to the *Cristero* hierarchy.

It was payback time when the a*buelo* was forced to turn over the land to Chico's grandfather for his efforts to save him and his family. Chico eventually replaced his grandfather's son, his father, as leader through primogeniture, and so his relative wealth in the community was explained. The strange thing is, Tutzingo is officially an *ejido,* where land tenure can only be claimed through current use. There are no hereditary rights, yet Chico gets richer than the rest. Apparently there are systems of debt and honor at work here, as well as deep resentments that are continually bridged by the long-standing rule of intermarriage. Something to look into later, if I have time.

There's also an anomaly. Rafael's family is somewhat outside of the Chico-Simon system. His wife Teresa is from Simon's family, but their children will be of Rafael's line. He claims he has no allegiance to Chico and gets to farm with the Simon family because of his marriage and his right to the *montaña.* I suspect he has deep Indian roots.

After Rafael was good and drunk, he also let me know that he would not be unhappy if a North American who also happened to be a decent mechanic took an interest in his sister-in-law (the teacher). He said that the teacher's son was free (from another man's claim) to become my own. I told him that any such arrangement must depend on the interest of the lady. Since I will be off to the mountains in a few minutes, it seems fate has rescued me from another village subterfuge.

As it turned out, the Indians did come down, but after the doctor had left. They stayed the night in the school house- their place is a six hour fast walk away - and in the morning Angelica suggested they talk to me. Their Spanish was of trade caliber, surprisingly limited, but they seemed very agreeable to the idea that I come back with them once their request for money to buy "sardines" was honored. They gave me until high noon to prepare, which will come any minute now. They are used to picking up fast. Unlike the Mexican stereotype, life is for now, not *mañana*.

As quickly as possible, this is my present impression of them:

The first thing you notice is that they are beautiful. They wear baggy white peasant pants and loose pullover white shirts that are embroidered extensively with brilliantly colored geometric designs, especially around the cuffs, and brilliant sash-like belts that dangle to the knees. They have carrying bags held by straps that run across the body from the right shoulder to the hip, where they hang convenient to the left hand. These are also embroidered with bright patterns as well as vivid, stylized animals. Both the Indians are very young men, probably in their late teens or early twenties, with perfect complexions and perfect, very white teeth. They are trim and look agile and strong for their size, about 5 foot 4 inches and 130 pounds. They have nearly black eyes that shine with vigor and a little something else - some touch of the wild, as if thought and action were more united and less parsed with them than with us. Their hair is long, straight, shiny and jet-black, like a raven's, left to flow freely.

It was because of this blackness that the white, tiny grains of rice in the hair could be detected, rice that moved. They are infested with head lice. I hope the doctor snuffed out the typhus, for these things are mobile and spread their eggs everywhere. It will only be a matter of time before my own infestation.

Must leave, they're here.

ST

It gave me pleasure that my assessment of Steven's attachment to religion proved correct. He was certainly a believer, and had been taken in by quasi-rational arguments that supported this belief. How ridiculous to compare the study of theoretical astronomy to theology! The former, with time, had the possibility of yielding truth. The latter could only foment debates concerning the number of angels on the head of a pin, as it always has, *ad nausea*. If one needs religion as a crutch, so be it; just don't bring it into rational studies. Unfortunately, it was obvious that Steven fully intended to do so. This made me understand why Steven had chosen the Huichols as his alternative study: they had a simple path to their gods through the use of peyote. Steven could access that world subjectively without the lifetime of meditation and self-denial required by the Old World religions. He would show us all his alternative brilliance. Well, I thought, that will certainly be the day. Of course death would stop him, but it also seemed certain that his line of inquiry, if continued long enough, would implode from the sheer weight of ignorance.

The schoolteacher also pricked my interest. He had already admitted his attraction to her looks and demeanor. Would she figure in on Lacey's unraveling? Could this relationship have been the last straw to break the camel's back?

Apart from those items, though, the field notes did not come across as particularly interesting. Books about kinship ties and violent behavior have already been written by people far more gifted and experienced than Steven. I promised myself then to only skim the notes for background and concentrate on the letters, but on turning back to the notebook found myself compelled to read the very next entry, dated three days later:

Tutzingo 5/27

What a bitter disappointment! I am finding out the hard way that Indian studies aren't what they're cracked up to be. The trip into the mountains was spectacular, though. The cliffs rise abruptly from the north field, and the path follows their edge nearly all the way with few switchbacks. It is very rocky and very steep. The route takes one about 3000 feet above the valley before it begins to level off in the peaks. In spite of having had several weeks to acclimatize, I had to stop several times on the way up. The young Huichols zipped right along, of course, at a pace just below a jog and without any apparent effort, but they didn't mind stopping and waiting for me when necessary. These pauses were their cocktail breaks, for they had bought a half-gallon sized jug of local brandy while in town. They passed it to me at one point, and I sipped cautiously, waiting for the sting of kerosene or wood alcohol or some other poison, and was startled to find it delicious. It had a fruity, mildly sweet flavor that balanced perfectly with the fairly strong but smooth burn of alcohol. It was far better than the cheap sugary brandy I would sometimes buy for the holidays back in the States.

The boys had brought a burro along to carry heavier things, having traded meat and handicrafts for what they now had carefully wrapped and hidden on the donkey's back, and suggested that I ride for a while, but that wounded my pride. I determined to keep up with them no matter what, and was able to do so fairly well after we passed the steep beginning, and at points the pain of the effort was lost in the magnificence of the scenery. If the valley had been beautiful, the peaks and cliffs offered celestial delights. The visions were unlike anything I had seen before, not in the Rockies, not in the White Mountains, not anywhere. Here ledges would drop off, sheer, for 3,000 feet, and rest their massive, yellowish bulks on a perfectly green and gentle valley that was threaded through with the silvery cord of the river. On the other side of the river rose cliffs of equal magnitude, and with the perfect clarity of the dry air it seemed a natural thing to step to the opposite side, effortlessly. The feeling was so strong that it would occasionally send a jolt of fear through me, a reminder that it was folly to attempt to break physical law. The clouds matched the clarity of air, as white and ephemeral as could be, yet they also stood out as distinctly three-dimensional, making their dream-like quality impossibly real. This was probably caused by the perspective we got from being nearly level with the clouds and the crispness of the shadows in the crystalline air throughout the canyons, but it is difficult to say for sure, it was so magical.

The single path soon fanned out into a tangle of interlacing paths that had been made by browsing livestock. We would walk through a mile or so of tall pine and then would come to an open area that had recently been roughly logged, where the slash lay about in ugly bunches amid the bleak skeletal ruins of splintered tree trunks. In those stretches where the pine forest was intact there was little undergrowth, and since the branches of this species falls off towards the base, walking through them in the high altitude shade was like a walk in a cool park glen. The logged areas, however, were hot and dry and matted with thorny scrub that would make walking without a path difficult. When asked about the destruction of the forest, the boys would only say "cattle" with flat looks that didn't give away any feeling on the subject.

I had been told that the Indians make the trip to the village in six hours, but with me it took almost eight, and when we arrived the sun had already ducked beneath a peak that cast a long dark shadow from the pink horizon. Our arrival filled me with apprehension, but that was soon lost to the novelty of the situation.

For a good mile before we arrived, the boys had whistled loudly every few seconds with a hearty joy that contradicted the clear reason for making the noise - that is, as proclamations that they were residents and non-hostile. While this may be only custom, it made me more alert to my situation, as if danger could erupt at any second. But the village seemed very peaceful, and not all that different from Tutzingo at first glance. By the number and size of the houses, it was clear that the people lived in immediate family units rather than communally, although the houses were arranged in distinct clusters, perhaps through an order of extended families.

These structures were like those in Tutzingo, but cruder, often having simple piles of rock for walls rather than adobe, and haphazard bundles of sticks for fences to protect the little household gardens. There was a sense of dirt and disorder to everything, similar to Tutzingo but intensified as if by a fit of irrationality. There was a deer hide pulled between poles before a smoldering fire by one house, and a pack of incredibly thin dogs fighting over a pile of entrails at another. The village was disorientating, for it had the rudeness of a hunting camp, yet contained complete and permanent families.

Within seconds I noticed a building different from the others, one that was larger and more neatly constructed, composed of cinder blocks and with a corrugated metal roof. Despite its more perfect geometry, it somehow stood out among the lesser structures as a giant sore, and it was to here that the boys steered me. On the walk, the boys had assured me of lodging provided I promise to buy a .22 rifle for them later, but now they told me that it was necessary to talk first to the "director." Of course, the director lived in the "improved" house. The building gave me a dark premonition, and when a man clearly dressed as an urban Mexican came from the door, I was certain that something unpleasant was about to happen.

My sixth sense was not disproved. The boys presented me to the *criollo* as young hunters presenting a prized kill, and the skinning began immediately. The director didn't bother to shake my hand as he started his fleecing in perfect, city Spanish:

"I am told (By whom? When?) that you are a gringo scholar who wishes to stay with us for a while. Do you have papers from the Director of Indian Affairs?"

I told him no, that the consulate had assured me that all Mexican Indians were full citizens and were not officially separated from anyone else.

"Do you know how harmed these people would be without our protection? Yes, they are citizens, but they are not yet ready for the outside world. My mother is Huichol, and after the University I was given the task of protecting my people from the greed of modern humanity until they could become educated enough to protect themselves."

I assured him that I had come from a good university myself and was trained in such things, and had papers to prove it, but he stopped me short:

"Yes, yes, I am sure you are qualified. But what good will your studies do for these people? You will go and write a book and become rich and famous, and what will they get? No, to be prepared for the modern world one needs money." He stopped and rubbed his fingers in his right hand, and then used the vulgar word for cash. "*Lana.* You understand?"

I stared at him blankly, not willing to dignify with a response what was coming next.

"We would require a contribution of 400 pesos (about 100 dollars) for every week that you stay here. As it is already dark, for this one night, we would charge 100 pesos. In any case, you would stay in the official house. From here the village elders would determine your participation. We would not want to disturb the fragile cultural practices, yes?" All this was said in an unctuous, soulless manner that made me furious.

"Yes, and what?," I wanted to say, "That you wish to treat these people like babies while you shake down the tourists? That you control access for your own gain? That nineteen out of every twenty *centavos* goes into your own pocket?" It would have been pointless, however, since there was no extra money at my disposal anyway. The fee would have left me with nothing for food, clothing, supplies, travel, or for health. Instead I tried to practice discretion and said only, "You say these people are free Mexicans. Well, I have come as the guest of these men. Can you order them not to take me in?" I looked at the boys, who immediately stared hard at the ground. It was clear my hand had been overplayed.

The director waited a moment for my situation to sink in, and then spoke as the voice of reason: "You see, they know what is best for their community. Now, if you wish to make your contribution, I will show you where to sleep. Otherwise, you must leave." He knew that he had me, and could barely conceal a triumphant smirk as he held his hand out to the growing darkness, but he had underestimated my anger. It made me furious to see that he had brought the corruption of his country into the heart of the few people left who were not parts of this destructive chain of greed. I turned from him to walk into the night.

"Understand," he said, "that there are wolves out there, and bears. But worst of all are the bandits. We who know the area rush back before dark to avoid the bandits. They will kill you for a centavo." He shrugged and turned back to the house. He was so sure of my return that he did not try to negotiate a new price. If he had, he would have been two dollars richer, for doing nothing.

It was only fitting that one of the Indian "boys"- men, really, as they both had wives and babies, to my surprise – would stoke my anger. When the director left, they both looked at me again and told me of their families and how hard it was now to get fresh meat for the children. "You will get .22's for us?," one asked at the end of their homily.

"No," I told him, "you will not get your .22's. I cannot stay because your director is greedy and wants too much money from me. That is money that would have gone to your rifles. You have him to blame." It might have been instructional to add that they had themselves to blame, too: that they could have behaved like free men and taken me in. But my accented Spanish might have slipped past their rudimentary grasp like a ship in the night. Then, too, maybe they couldn't conceive of a gringo without infinite cash.

I left them looking puzzled and disappointed and returned to the route just traveled. It was much too late to walk back, but it was essential to get far enough away so that the captain couldn't charge me for an official stay. I had a flashlight, but wanted to use it only briefly so that it would be difficult to be followed, just in case the director wanted to use the opportunity to send out a few "bandits." The encounter had made me suspicious, and the enveloping night turned that into paranoia.

After stumbling around on what was hoped to be the right path for about three miles, complete darkness and weariness made me stop. I reasoned that this might be far enough from the village to sleep undiscovered in the bushes until the first light of dawn, and found a dense patch of brush to spread the sleeping bag under. Thoughts of rattlesnakes and scorpions curling next to my body for warmth competed with my intense need for rest.

It was not the fear, though, nor the creeping cold that made sleep so difficult to hold, but rather the noise that the Huichols made along the path. For about two hours into dark, groups of men slipped by with torches and flashlights glowing, all the while whistling their manic calls of return. It occurred to me that each whistle was a little different, and that everyone back at the "rancho" would know exactly who was coming and who would soon need a meal. No sooner would I nod off to sleep than another spray of lantern lights and whistles and woops would pass, leaving me to drift in a semi-dream that became more nightmarish with time. Night and sleep bring out the primitive mind, a beast that has no notion of courage or nobility, only of self-preservation. Fear began to overwhelm me. Images of murderous bandits, and then of murderous Indians flashed within as though they were without, armed and evil and very real. The experience demonstrated the burden our basic humanity places on our greater spirits. It is hard to be high-minded when alone and afraid.

It was during this state of half-sleep and terror, while lying curled and shivering beneath a bush, that a hand on my shoulder made me lurch upward and around in wordless panic. A truncated scream may have made it past stiffened lips before my eyes focused on the apparition before me. First appearances did nothing to calm me. It was a man-like being dressed as a Huichol but bursting with hair, dense mats of it that sprung from everyplace on his head. I leapt to my feet and stepped back slowly, getting ready for a mad dash to safety, when he spoke with words that froze my movements with incredulity. He repeated the words again in plain American English something like "be cool, man," which identified him unquestionably as a hip, younger compatriot. He was casual and unworried, which calmed me enough to join in a conversation.

He identified himself as "Trip" or "Tripper," an adventurer from upstate New York who now lived with the Huichols. He expressed concern for my safety from what he called "the greasers," hired assassins, or *pistoleros,* from the cities. He named them as the reason for the great caution of the Indians in their own territory. I asked him why they were here and who had hired them.

"They're fucking sadists," he said, "who make the Mafia look like a ballet class." He went on to say that the ranchers and natives had been fighting forever, but this was different. The new people were drug lords who had enough money to buy an army of assassins as well as half the public servants of Mexico. As he put it, "The pushers skim the forest off to grow their shit, pot and opium poppies. The animals that survive look for cover elsewhere and the "Huicholes" are left with nothing to eat. The bad guys keep taking more and more. An elder or shaman tries to persuade them to stop, and they kill him. So the Indians retaliate, and the bad guys send in the pros, the greasers. Just the sickest fucks. Cut your balls off and stick you to bleed to death ass first on a wooden stake. And no cops will touch them. They're too busy counting their *mordida,* the pay-off."

I was shivering with the cold and still trying to convince myself that all of this was real. I steadied myself in the surreal shadows of a flashlight and asked him about the ranchers.

"Hell, they're driving the ranchers out, too. Now the cowboys know how it feels. So they hire their own hit men. It's a battle of bad-asses, but it's no contest. They don't have the money the druggies got."

I asked him what he thought would happen.

"Fuck if I know. What are ya gonna do, bomb half of Mexico? Maybe it'll get to the UN, I don't know. I just pray and carry Little Bertha here." He held up an old double-barrel shotgun. He went on to tell me that he had first come for the peyote, to live a more sacred life, and had tried to keep out of the fight. He had little use for my academic objectives, saying that after I trip, "you ain't never gonna wanna bother with that shit again." He may have been closer to the truth about academia than he realized.

He was not subject to the fees of the director, "Carlitos," because he had arrived before the government had, and had married a Huichol woman in that time. Carlitos himself had some Huichol in him from his mother's side, but had grown up in a fairly affluent family in Guadalajara, where his father owned distribution rights to a popular brand of *malta* carbonated beverage. His older brother now worked the business while his father's connections had enabled him to buy this job, which Carlitos claims he does for the good of his people. Tripper claims he does it for money, working the angles and counting the time until a place opens up for him in his father's business. "But," he said, "Carlitos could be worse. He keeps out of the way. Doesn't help much, either, but what could he do against drug money?"

Tripper then invited me to spend the night in his house, which he admitted was infested with lice, but only "good, family lice." He lived about a half mile from where we stood and was on his way home himself after an unsuccessful hunt. He said that he had found me in the bushes because he could "smell gringo meat a mile away." Tripper is quite the character. I would not put him in charge of, say, the nuclear missile silos in South Dakota, or a school bus, for that matter, but he is *simpático* as a human being.

We arrived at his house about 10:00PM, and it seemed to be primarily a pile of rocks with some adobe patching. He brought me inside and threw an old wool blanket on the hard dirt floor to mark my spot to sleep. It took a few minutes to make out his wife, who was working silently by the faint embers of the hearth rolling tortillas. Later my eyes would adjust further to see that a girl of about four was beside her, and another of about two was asleep in the big folds of her dress. It was hard to tell for sure, but it seemed the woman was pregnant. Whatever their relationship was, much of it passed in silence. When we ate in the faint light of the rekindled fire, Trip would mumble a few words in Huichol and his wife would essentially grunt. The quiet wasn't cold, as it might have been in an American household, but it wasn't warm, either.

Next morning would give a better sense of life there. I awoke to the pounding of the mortar in the *metate* and a haze of smoke from the breakfast fire. She (Marta) was grinding corn for the tortillas while her little daughter cleaned the hulls from the meal. The house looked even smaller in the daylight, which cut through the abundant cracks in the wall. The night had been uncomfortably cold, being high in the mountains, and I woke at times in spasms of shivers, but now a gentle coolness only made the sleeping bag that much more snug

To make a quick appraisal of the house: within the twelve by twelve foot space was a sleeping section on one side, a hearth on another, a *metate* beside that, and all their worldly possessions, including a small pile of cheap aluminum pans, a plastic bucket and gourd bowls, a digging stick, the shotgun and a few machetes and other iron tools. From roof rafters enveloped in smoke hung bunches of corn and herbs and a large haunch of meat that had been thoroughly dried and preserved. There was no chimney for the smoke, leaving it to fly as it may through the cracks. The fire itself was set in a raised brazier of hardened clay that was banked against a wall. Two small walls of the same clay had been raised on either side to hold a charred sheet of metal over the flame to cook tortillas.

In this crowded little household Tripper was nowhere to be seen. On standing up, the smoke was so dense that it made me cough violently, which did not seem to register on Marta, who continued to pound the corn without expression. I stretched, coughed harder, and set aside the tied bundle of sticks that served as a door and ducked through. The first breath of clear air made me realize that a dim sense of claustrophobic panic had been on the periphery of my awareness. The blinding light of the early morning was a joy. Of note in the vicinity was a cow with withered flanks tied loosely to a bush, lazily snipping at some invisible flora. A calf was butting its nose against her udder. It took another moment before I noticed Tripper off to my right, sitting cross-legged in the dust, apparently in deep prayer or meditation. His head was slightly bowed and he rocked slowly back and forth with his eyes closed like a mother with an infant.

On return from relieving myself, Trip had opened his eyes to the world. After he recognized me with a smile, he motioned to a pile of rocks before him that had the rough shape of a house and told me that this was his *xiriki,* or altar. The sun shining upon him was his father *Tayaupa*, and between the two and the sacrament (peyote, no doubt) he claimed to have more religion than a Christian did in a cathedral. Mindful to not break his reverie, I asked him softly why he lived apart from the Los Zamorros rancho of the Huichols.

He said that, as he had no blood relatives there, his opportunities for good growing land were limited. While hunting was important symbolically for the men, farming was what kept them alive. He could live with the in-laws, but that carried a burden of its own, so they lived on the outskirts and did "OK." He said this with a nod while sitting comfortably on the ground in the warm morning sun with his legs pulled up to his chest and held by his arms. He looked odd with the mop of goldish-brown hair and a bush of reddish beard erupting from the traditional white, highly embroidered garb of the Huichols. He could have been a new age disciple at a Hare Krishna ashram in Woodstock. I was about to ask him if he found life here truly fulfilling when Marta came out through the door. Her dark eyes still seemed shrouded in smoke. In the universal language of hand and mouth, she told us that breakfast was ready.

It was as we ate, a few simple tortillas with chili and a dash of meat, that the nature of the cross-cultural marriage unfolded. Tripper continued in his mild ecstasy. There was no way to tell if he was chemically altered or not, but he was clearly savoring every bite of his sparse fare, closing his eyes often in what must have been prayerful gratitude. Meanwhile, Marta - who was most definitely pregnant - talked very quietly to her children, sometimes for no apparent reason, other times to send the older girl for something.

She was - it's hard to describe - empty yet full, blank but fulfilled. Tripper was on his heroic quest for God, while Marta took care of the things of the earth. Both seemed content in their own way. Maybe Trip's enthusiasm was due to the exotic location he had chosen. Certainly this life was nothing new for Marta. But it seemed they coexisted well in different worlds, like a river rendered by divergent currents and oxbows. They would flow together for a while, part, and then merge again. It seemed so natural that it may be the way of Huichol men and women in general.

I gave Trip the two dollars that would have gone to Carlitos, and said my farewell. He took the cash without a word and reminded me to stay to the south side of the intertwining paths before he turned towards the house. I had gone about a hundred yards when he yelled out, "Hey, Professor! Stay cool, man. Remember, keep to the south!"

I finish these notes in my house in Tutzingo, having arrived two hours ago. The warm beer sweating in its bottle on the cool earth floor never tasted so good.

Fieldwork now is in graver doubt than ever. There is a lot that could be done in this village, but the situation is still disappointing. It seems at times as if the whole world is closing in, becoming corrupt, all of a piece. It causes the same subtle but pervasive feeling of hypoxia that the smoke-choked hut had. But a secure bed awaits, and I give thanks for the good health and good life and good fortune that have been granted me.

Hasta mañana, ST

CHAPTER 5

The Wings of Birds and Bees

I closed the notebook with some astonishment. I did not like Steven, but still had unconsciously assumed that he was at least marginally competent. It was stunning to me that he had traveled all the way to his field site without having first procured the necessary papers, as silly as they were. There was little doubt that the process was only a layer added to government to provide another opportunity for bribery, but that is the price one pays for exotica. If Steven didn't have the money, he shouldn't have gone. It was shocking to realize that he apparently went with the hope that things would turn out for the better. This was obviously a byproduct of his theism, an irrational denial of the lessons of failure that had dogged his whole career.

The readings also had sparked an increased interest in his project. They had begun to show, dimly, what the vectors leading to his death might be. While they might eventually show that he was dispatched by a jealous husband or a drunken peasant, it was more than likely that they would prove he died in the conflict over the area's resources. How this would have happened in the confines of Tutzingo couldn't be ascertained – maybe it would occur at the hands of a corrupt government agent - but the mystery of it now claimed my attention.

However, if I had not forced myself to follow the story to this point, the very dullness of the characters would have left me with little reason to continue. Thus my problem with Suzanne. While the preliminary letters would call to her venal weakness for gossip, it was by no means certain that the rest of the transcripts would be as tempting. It was necessary that her interest be maintained so that she might help to repel Shari. The hook had to be baited with the right fly and then played for the duration.

Fortunately, it was Suzanne who first sought me, arriving, as it were, after the drop of the first cast. She couldn't have come at a better time. It was about a week after my last reading of Steven's entry, on the last day of March and the first day with a warm, south wind, and I had come to the office in the late afternoon after a long search in the library stacks. A lack of material had kept me from conclusively tying the origin myths of the Great Lakes Ojibwa with those of the natives of the Pacific Northwest, a pet project of mine, and after several days' work only a few scant graduate students' notes from the late 20's had been found that contained some morsels of relevant information.

I had arrived exhausted and lost in thought as to how the project could be made viable, and had dropped into my chair without my (by now) customary inspection of the premises. Immediately the oddest sensation of soft and hard flashed from my buttocks, as if they had just squashed a giant beetle, which caused me to leap up with instinctual fear. A look back at the chair revealed a substance that at first was incomprehensible. On the seat was something long and yellowish with streaks of red that glinted at a spot as with stainless steel.

Within a few seconds it became clear what it was: something from a crazed mind, a twisted bit of hate, something from HER. It was a banana, partially peeled, that had been skewered by sewing scissors. That part of the message was clear enough. What made me gasp was the nature of the red that covered the banana- by the dark clots, it could be nothing but blood. There were also, in the clots and along the edge of the peel, short, dark, curly hairs. This was clearly a fetish, a voodoo doll wrapped in a jumble of hellish symbols, all pointing to one end: psychosexual violence. Which was pointed, obviously, at me.

I had scraped up the mess and had been sitting on my desk (apart from that foul chair!) for nearly an hour, smoking from a pack of cigarettes that were kept for forced all-night tasks, when Suzanne tapped lightly on the door and entered. She seemed almost glad to see me until she noticed the smoke and coughed, waving her hand in front of her face.

"That's thick. I didn't know you smoked."

"I don't. Just when I'm tense."

"You, tense? What, like a rattlesnake before it strikes?" It was an insult, of course, but it had an easiness to it, like the jibes of a fellow thief rather than the protests of an offended victim.

I was about to tell her about this new threat when it occurred to me that this might give her too much leverage. She must be kept beholden to me. "I can't pull together my thesis for McClain's class. Two weeks wasted on a wild goose chase."

"If you smoke after something as small as that, you'll drop dead from asphyxiation before you finish your thesis. Put that thing out, would you? I want to talk about our, uh, deal."

My hand opened to the chair, and she took it this time, looking pleasantly in charge as she did so.

"Then we agree, Suzanne?"

"If it's fair. And legal, yeah."

"Yes, it's certainly within the moral parameters of our little world here. First: yes, I do have notes. And letters. Personal letters. They haven't all been perused, but I think they cover Steven's entire time in the field before he was promoted to heavenly emeritus status."

"You haven't looked at them all? I find that hard to believe."

Her smug familiarity was starting to annoy me. "I want to experience it closer to real time, to get the full flavor of it."

"Really? Empirical man searches for feeling?"

"Believe what you like. In any case, there is a large bundle at my disposal that you may read after me."

"No. Now."

"You can read along with me, if you insist. Not before. That's part of the deal."

"All right. After, I want them in my hands. For keeps."

"You've got to be kidding. Besides, they can be photocopied anytime."

"Where? You can't let anyone find out about your little treasure. And let's not forget about little Shari peering around all the copying centers."

"First things first, please. Ok, fine. I will consider letting you have them. On second thought, Lacey might ask for them some day, and I'd just as soon leave the explanations to you. But you have to pick them up at my place."

"Your place? Said the spider to the fly. That's too cheap, even for you."

"You flatter yourself. Besides, no one would rationally think that you might be seduced by my charms. What would you have to gain by that? Unless you are entertaining little fantasies alone at night, Suzanne?"

"Uh! You are a foul man. I simply didn't want to give you the pleasure of making me walk to peek at your spoils. Okay. But the ones we read go home with me."

"Excellent. I think we have reached a suitable compromise. Now, for your part of the bargain, all that is needed is a little acting, just a few stage whispers to set the scene. The primary actors will do all the rest."

"Oh, brother."

"No, it isn't all that novel or elegant. You know about that little tryst between Greene and me?"

"What a noble conquest!"

"No, no, listen. You might also know that Greene is Shari's advisor.

What I want - come on, listen – is just a little gossip about my affair with Greene."

"And you think her jealousy will cause her to leave grad school? Your ego is greater than your cognitive failure."

"Don't laugh, this isn't about my pride. It's about my ability to keep on breathing."

"I see why you brought up acting."

"It's not Shari's jealousy I'm counting on. Let's face the facts: around here, it's the brownie points that count, not emotional attachments. Everyone knows it, no matter how psychologically impaired one may be. No, what you will be whispering about is Greene's anger. Of course it's all fabrication. She doesn't give a damn about me. We were both using each other in the time honored way. No, this is for Shari. Tell your friends about my dalliance with Shari any way you wish, and then mention that Greene has found out, also, and is now furious. Not out of affection, mind you, but for pride, being two-timed by a grad student punk. Let it be known that Greene is out for revenge any way she can get it. Through anything or anyone associated with me."

Suzanne let her mocking smile loosen and thought for a minute. She looked up at me again as one professional to another. "You know, it has all the traditional elements: hierarchy, pettiness, innocent victims and revenge. You're right, it has to work. Shari will drop you like yesterday's theories."

"Exactly. The epistemology of our little world would allow nothing less. To continue a relationship with me would not only be crazy, but suicidal. Once you're in this box, you can't think out of it." My lips formed a sly smile of triumph, but Suzanne continued to frown in thought.

"I can do this, sure. But you are one cynical bastard. And I have agreed to work with your cynicism. That's not healthy."

"Cynicism is healthy when well-placed. It's an upfront recognition of reality. You're only lost when you take all this around us as normal and good. And you are one step above me on the ladder of righteousness.

By your disgust with both me and the system, you stand before the gates of heaven."

"Stop it. You think you're funny but you're not. What is wrong with you?"

She leveled me with a beam of indignation that should have been slashed by another dose of cynicism, but I let it lie. She must always think that she was the better of the two of us. The unconscious pride she had in her moral rectitude would be her leash.

I clapped my hands and stood up from the desk. "Ok, then, settled. We can arrange a time for you to come by my place, whenever you'd like."

"Now."

"Except for now. Make it sometime during the day when we have nothing to do. Maybe, let's see now, Wednesday?"

"Now." She was tracing the lines in the palm of one hand with a finger from the other. It was clear that she was beginning to think the deal was too immoral, making immediate concessions necessary.

"OK, OK. Let me get my books together and we'll take the North Campus bus. I haven't finished the first notebook yet, but there are several letters you can take, OK? That's the better stuff, anyway."

"That will work for today." She remained grim. Her faux camaraderie was preferable, but the bargain had been struck, leaving me with nothing to lose and everything to gain. It was as if the fates had granted me a clear path through their enigmatic web.

Suzanne rode with me for the letters. Her reaction to my room when she entered was comical, so typical of the fairer sex:

"God, this place stinks like musk."

"Of course you are intrigued. All the women are. True men stink, as the Ibe of Nigeria say."

"True men do not live alone in a little rented room."

"True men do not become academics. Nor do true women. Yet here we are. Life is a paradox." And there was truth in all that was said. While living with the northern Quebec Cree, I noticed how the men would reach down to adjust their genitals from time to time, and then smell their fingers. There is a fundamental fascination with the secret scent by all humans, and it is curious that women in our culture, who as a sex are so fragrant in that area, attempt to define their femininity through a lack of natural scent.

Yet Suzanne did not run away. She lingered with the pretense of disinterested distraction as she tried to absorb everything she could of me from my lair. We were academics, but also something else. It was only after the letters were placed in her hands that she snapped out of it and perfunctorily left the room. Immediately after, I spilled the unread papers out across the table, for more information of interest was needed as soon as possible. It was necessary to supply a reward each time she pushed the right button, as instant gratification had been proven to be the most effective way to manipulate animal behavior.

I picked up the plain red grade-school spiral, along with the next two letters, and compared dates. The first letter was from Steven to Lacey, post-marked four days after the last note entry read, meaning it had been written on or near the same day, counting handling time. I tapped the letter out of its envelope and found, with disappointment, that much of it was a rehash of the notes. It was not until the last few pages that a significant difference leaped out from the scrawl:

"I think, Lacey, that this is our dilemma, not just ours but millions of us from our cultural tradition. We feel that a couple has to be of one stream or the relationship is a failure, when more often than not the reverse is true: that genders follow different courses just as individuals do. It is enough that we, in good faith, follow the same valley and strive for the same destination through our differences. Tripper and Marta may not seem the ideal couple, but they live contentedly like two bubbles enclosed in a larger one. There is, really, no ideal couple, just something that works. One might think that a relationship must go one way or not at all, but that ideal may be impossible. Of course, it is also true that some people are simply incompatible. Do you think that of us?

Anyway, enough of that from me. Bitterness and disappointment have never solved anything.

To conclude my failed adventure with the Indians, the walk back to the village was torturous in more ways than one. It was difficult physically, as you might guess: what had seemed like a main path cut with minor divergences turned out to be a set of equal divergences. It was often hard to decide how far "keeping to the south" actually meant, for some paths actually veered down canyons that were all but shear. But with the application of the general rule of "south" and some common sense, the village was reached without disaster.

The most grueling test, though, came with the realization that the village might remain my home. While the sight of the little houses from the final cliff brought a sigh of relief, it also brought the weight of failure. Having to do this project on a shoestring has afforded little latitude. I did not tell the official at the Indian village that the papers he demanded were once pursued vigorously. You have heard the story: the man at the Mexican Consulate whispered that a $2,000 fee would be necessary to "process" my request to live in the field with the natives. There is no telling what other requests would have followed, with uncertain results. The odd thing is how these people, like Carlitos the director, often prefer to get nothing rather than something less, which is not the logical way of the greedy. They say that bribery is a tradition in Latin America because of the small pay that officials get, but this is only partially true. It is not just about money, but control: *cajones*, if you will. There is an inflexibility to this that is anachronistic. Like the Dodo bird, these people live on a precarious little island amidst a world that has evolved beyond them. They will become extinct, too, but not without first trying to bring all those around down with them like drowning men. And as they drown, they blame others, like us, for their misery. Many believe them.

Still, Tutzingo is rich ground for research and not without its advantages. A study of the co-evolution of the Indians and the village can be made, comparing everything from kin obligations to spiritual beliefs, as enough has been written about the Huichols for such an attempt, and the historical records on the Mexicans are infinite, thanks to the very bureaucrats that are now helping to pull most of Latin America down. Life is also easier in the village: there are actually a few things to buy at the store, and there are vehicles available for emergencies and to simply get away. And of course I speak the language and share a degree of cultural background with the people here.

Another thing, and it will be the last time this is mentioned: my arrangement places me in a fairly stable environment that would be easy to share. You might want to spend at least the summer down here. The altitude tempers the heat of the sun, making for perfect evenings. There is nothing more luscious then dangling your toes in the cool river while sipping a beer and watching the sun sink beneath quiet, wild mountains as their peaks hang in the clearest air you have ever breathed. I hope you will consider, one last time,

Love, Esteban

Ah, poor 'Esteban' was now begging. Manly advice for him immediately came to mind: "Steven, my boy, didn't you know that the last thing a woman wants is a man in need? Look at it with a socio-biological slant, if you wish: the man who whimpers for love is not the king of the roost – he is simply a man in emotional poverty, a loser by definition." If Lacey were the woman that Steven imagined, such behavior would only seal the loss.

My hand paused before the notebook. While the cause of Steven's demise had become something of an obsession with me, the monotony that undoubtedly dominated the bulk of his field notes was a detriment. A Mexican peasant village is no more interesting than a small town in North Dakota, except that North Dakotans have the money to do something different now and then. Drunken brawls and a few murders by cuckolded husbands could only hold one's interest for so long.

I passed over the notebook and picked up the next letter. This would most likely contain Lacey's response to our lonely hero. Would she decide to drag him along, just in case, as she had done so far, or finally dump him? Here she would reveal the sort of woman she was: either the confident independent sort, or the sort that needed her vanity primped, whatever the cost. And great cost it must have been for her receiving the moralizing treacle of this rust-belt slob.

The letter was postmarked from the USA with a date two weeks later than Steven's, an obvious response to his last:

Dear 'Esteban,'

I love the sound of that name! It sounds like a call to the round table and the noble quest, although so does 'Steven.' You have to admit that it gives you more dignity than 'Steve,' don't you? I know that this doesn't interest you, and am glad for that, but it is all for so little effort.

Really, it doesn't interest me much, either. I'm sorry for my last letter. I rethink it with horror and feel that I have been split in two, with one half fervently rejecting the other, like Dr. Jekyll and Mr. Hyde. Please excuse my moods. It is all very tense now, as you may understand.

Steven, it sounds lovely down there, and I would love to come (although I don't like the idea of rushing my toiletry because of pigs!), but unfortunately there is other work that absolutely must get done. You know that I am scheduled for exams at the end of fall semester and the reading list has barely been touched. It is very hard to concentrate so fully on my studies when the idea that it is all for nothing flutters about. It is possible that even the very enchantment that once drew me on will disappear in the layers and layers of theories and words. It makes me think sometimes that there is no point to anything. What is our time on earth compared to the time that planets take to spin around their suns, and that the suns take to rise from cosmic dust and flame out again into nothingness?

Excuse me if this depresses you. I write this only in the hope that you will understand a state of mind that makes commitment to anything difficult. Let me change the subject to something a little lighter: department gossip. Suzanne is still in her relationship with Bernini. It is obvious that she actually loves him, as one loves an idol. The last paper he published in American Anthropology was almost identical to the paper she wrote last year on Neanderthal-Cro Magnon miscegenation. I wonder how long she will tolerate this? It is so clear that she is being used, but she refuses to have anything bad spoken about him.

Barbara has gotten a three-year position in Fargo and is delighted. I am happy for her, but, my God, North Dakota! It shows you how desperate we have all become! Leidleheim arranged the connection for her, and we are all assuming for our own sakes that she earned this favor the honest way. It is hard to imagine how Leidleheim's wife can be so desperately jealous at those department soirees. But it is easy to understand why she pounces on the cheap box wine and stale Ritz crackers that always greet us at such functions.

Carol is six months pregnant now and VERY large. As we all thought, her 'artist' boyfriend has left her, but he has assumed legal responsibility for the child (at least until his first child support payments are due). She fully expected this to happen, and is very happy to be having the baby. She says that she has always wanted children, and at 35 and in our profession felt she would never find a suitable man for marriage. Given her position, it is infuriating to see those hoary retread professors who believe they can catch a young sprite anytime they wish, unencumbered by a biological clock. Unfortunately, they are right.

Please don't feel badly about your setback. Tutzingo sounds wonderful – every bit as interesting as the Indians. I know that you were eager to discover the insights of their religion, but suspect that you will find much of what you are looking for in disguised form in the village. You know that Christianity, especially Catholicism, has had a long tradition of angels and demons and miracles. Besides, in town you will not have to watch out for the "pistoleros." They sound like a nightmare, and nothing, especially our own uncertain profession, is worth that kind of danger. Please settle into your village and send me every interesting detail. You most certainly will do a lovely job!

My impossible stack of books awaits me. If I could only snap my fingers and have it done with! Please take care. Remember, you are only a visitor, and as such should avoid the feuds and schemes of the area. Good luck,

Love, Lacey

I had thought that the letter would reveal one of two types of woman, but the most obvious had slipped my mind: a woman who is falling apart. At least her collapse was not due to Steven but rather to the groundless void typical of the academic. It still puzzles me why some people are plunged into the depths of despair when they realize that nothing is certain and that all is a puff of smoke in the void. At one stage in our lives we realize we are not the center of the universe, and at the next that there is no center at all. It is a grown-up concept, but then again, that's what we are supposed to be. I am convinced that the whole desperate business of psychological trauma is only a melodrama of the immature, of those who have failed to pass a childhood stage. For some, they seek and find the necessary Teddy Bear in religion.

Steven's notes revealed that he numbered among the religious, which explains his arrogant complacency in the department, and the rationalizations of his failures in Mexico. It is my belief that death has the last laugh with these people - that in the end they stare into the yawning chasm and, finding no welcoming warmth of spiritual arms, expire screaming in their own little hell. Thus it is that those who live with a belief in hell die surrounded by the imagined horrors of hell.

The morsels of gossip offered up by Lacey gave little of value, save for amusement at the thought of Suzanne's reaction to her own portrayal when she reads the notes herself. Surely she must have known that Bernini was screwing her in more ways than one with his outright plagiarism, but the realization that others knew this should knock her down a peg. Or, one should say, knock her off of Bernini's peg. From that point on, it was certain that Bernini would be working solo. A woman may be scorned, but not publicly.

The digested letters were brushed roughly to the side in a pile for Suzanne to take. There was no desire on my part to read any kin studies, anthropology's monotonous answer to Biblical 'begats,' and several pages of this lethal laundry list now were quickly skimmed until the words 'Dr. Gary' caught my eye. I retreated to the date mark for the beginning of this entry:

6/21/80 Tutzingo

It's the first day of summer, but summer has been with me in effect for nearly seven weeks. It puzzles me now that so much is made of the changing seasons up north, for only a few months outside of summer are objectively pleasant. Here the weather is nearly always perfect, and it is simply true that the more perfect the weather, the better, although today has had some rain. They have told me that the short rainy season is just about over, although nature will always be unpredictable.

The word "unpredictable" reminds me of my talk with Dr. Gary yesterday. I had been in a small valley to the south that is invisible from the village, where Rafael has a large planting, and was writing up his agricultural methods when the sound of the plane broke the silence. The little valley is perhaps two miles away from town as the crow flies, but five tough ones on foot, and it took over two hours to finish up and get back.

I knew that he sometimes went on horseback to the Huichol *rancheria*, and thought that if I could accompany him there our association would make me a bit more welcomed. If not, some information could still have been gleaned for my comparative study. On reaching the schoolhouse, however, I found that he had already left, and that he was expected to stay in the government house for the night, a great disappointment to me.

Near evening, though, Angelica came to my house and asked if I would like to join the doctor for supper at the schoolhouse. It seems that he was met along the way by the Indians, and had been told that all that was needed were the supplies he was bringing, and he was able to turn back. Of course I wanted to join them. The doctor has been coming here for four years and must know as much as anyone about the basic facts of the Huichol way of life.

The meal was the best that has come my way in months, maybe years, including a fair amount of beef that had been smoked and spiced to Mediterranean perfection, served with tortillas. There were also well-spiced beans and fruit, including strawberries, and a pitcher of strawberry *pulque*, a mild beer made from cactus that is often flavored. We sat like lords at the teacher's table, with kerosene lanterns lit and Angelica as our attentive cook and waitress.

The attention embarrassed me - it was totally undeserved. The doctor, of course, was the picture of mercy and charity, and so was due this respect, but I did little more than teach a course in English on Tuesdays and Thursdays (Yes, I volunteered for this, more out of boredom than for ingratiation). My few protestations concerning her service were met with a slight but definite chillness: she made it clear that this was her job and any interference was unwelcome. How easy it would be to become accustomed to this service.

We men talked about the lack of resources in the mountains, about malnutrition and child mortality rates and infectious diseases until we both paused as the moon threw some silvery light across the table through one of the high openings in the building. I had meant to steer the conversation towards current subsistence strategies, particularly the one concerning temporary migration to urban areas and how this was affecting the culture at large, but Dr. Gary filled the unexpected vacuum of silence as he cleared his throat and said, "You know…" He trailed off until I responded, "yes?," and he continued: "You know, the Huichol still believe in their pagan gods."

I told him that this had long been known to me and was what had brought me here in the first place.

"Yes, and I suppose you find it fascinating. And beautiful. And it is, in its way. They believe in a cycle of life where energy is sacrificed by species of plants and animals so that humans may live. Humans, in turn, must give back spiritual energy so that these life-giving beings may be born again."

I knew of this, of course, and told him, "Yes, the cycle of the Corn King. Sir James Frazier wrote about that extensively. It is a broad belief among people everywhere. Many point to the similarities with Christianity. Some think the similarities with the Huichol beliefs are due to Christian influence, but I believe that they are there because we all share the same world and the same knowledge of our fate." I was feeling breezily philosophical, perhaps because of the pulque, but the doctor was of a more serious mood.

"A lot of the lost souls from the U.S. come here and seek their salvation in the archaic religions. I know you've met Jim (Tripper). But there are very sharp and important differences between our beliefs. For one thing, there are the demons. They (the Huichols) practice witchcraft, you know." For the first time, Dr. Gary was frowning.

I mentioned Christians and the witches of the Middle Age.

"Yes, but those witches were cursed, antithetical to the cause of the faith. This is not so with the Huichols. Dealing with demons is expected of the *mara'akame* (the Huichol holy man), even condoned. They do not care if he kills others outside the group, and even praise him for it. That is why I bring the Gospel, the Good News, to the people here. It is not that their beliefs are without virtue. In fact, there is more good in the Huichols than in many in our own society. But they miss the larger, truer words of Christ. In Christ, everyone is your neighbor, not just the man who lives next door. His was the first truly universal message. As long as you may use demons to slay others, no matter how remote, you are not living up to Christ. You will not enter heaven. Or maybe you do not believe in any of this?" This was not said as a dare, but as a compromise to the probability of my own agnosticism.

This was a question that had no answer in me. I have always felt that my belief was firm, yet could not say exactly what it was. My pause allowed Dr. Gary to pursue his point.

"The problem is that the modern conscience, like yours and mine, is individualistic. This allows for a broader base for humanity, one not tied to a tribe, but it also cuts us off from a sense of community. It is this sense of community that I love so much about these people. It is a paradox that will only be solved through Christ. Believe in Him and someday a new world will be made. In an instant. It is my belief that we must first bring the Word to enough people, a critical mass, so to speak. Then it will be up to us whether we accept the Word or not. It is then that Judgment may be passed, and a more perfect holy order realized."

I asked him if he believed in the Apocalypse.

"I believe in it any way it is intended. One way or another it will be fulfilled. Anyway, don't let me bore you. It's not my job to force anything on anyone, just to present it." The doctor, at once strident, was now almost penitential.

The conversation struck a chord. It came to me that both Pagans and Christians had their own routes to heaven and to hell. With Christianity had come individualism, as the doctor had said, and with that had come a freeness of thought. This had allowed for the development of the moral conscience, but also the progression of science. This is turn has led to the creation of our own tools for Armageddon. Was this, I asked the doctor, God's plan? And could anything be more perverse, or even diabolical?

The doctor answered my question by way of his personal story. He told me that his wife had died five years before, in spite of everything he could do, and he had become angry with God and asked for an answer. It was given him, he claimed, through a Mexican boy, an illegal, who was hit by a car near his house. He cared for the boy until his recovery, to shame God, but it was the boy's mother who surprised him. In spite of hardships and tragedies, she possessed a faith and trust in God that he had not thought possible. He said that her optimism made *him* ashamed with his own preoccupation, and in time he came to lend his will to the divine force. He learned in a manner of revelation that this world was brief, and its sorrows shallow before eternity. He found that the mother of the boy was a Huichol convert who had moved to Guadalajara and then come to (his home town in) Colorado with her Mexican husband to work on a farm, and then to the doctor's neighborhood through work with a lawn service. The doctor felt after his epiphany that he had been called to heal the Huichol, and to speak to them in the name of Christ.

"God," he continued, "took what 'was' to form something else that was better, as always. My pain began my life's work. There are sequences to things, the answer not being in any knowable link in a chain. The Jews, for instance, weren't chosen because of their DNA; they were chosen because of their cultural history and where they lived. This history made them accept Jehovah as they did, and their location involved them with the greatest empire of their day, Rome, which enabled the word of Jesus to spread as it did, and so on. So we see that the Jews were part of several steps in the world's spiritual evolution. And so the nations of today are made as steps towards the realization of God's goal. The Jews were not perfect, the nations are not perfect, and we are not perfect - we are all still evolving towards a higher order.

"As for technology," he continued, "we have yet to match it with our spiritual progress. But I believe that it is worldly science, and the horrors it has wrought, that will force our spiritual advancement for our own survival. Each is a link in the chain, and none the chain itself."

Our conversation wore down as the slight effects of pulque turned into a powerful soporific. Angelica seemed very pleased with our night, although she had barely eaten with us and had not understood much of our English. I noticed how thoroughly clean she smelled and wondered how she maintained herself so well in these conditions. Nothing but a pleasant odor of wood smoke and a touch of spice came from her, as if she were incorruptible. The fact of her son kept her from sainthood among the Latin men, but that very son would probably bestow on her such virtues within the same tradition. Such is our world, a tangle, a paradox whose antipathies cause movement to an unknown end.

ST, Tutzingo

He had a few more pages of notes for the above entry, but, with a few exceptions, they were only descriptions of quotidian life mixed with minor reflections on observations. Of the exceptions, it was mildly amusing to see that the facts had made him drop any pretense at finding cross or parallel cousin marriage patterns, or any patterns outside of prestige unions and incest avoidance (found among us all). His comments were also notable after discovering a father/daughter marriage:

"I have not only found few formal patterns for marriage, but am beginning to believe that they mate like dogs. The father/daughter marriage that I uncovered through genealogical charting was not acceptable until she gave birth. Then, as one informant said, 'what can you do?' In an isolated village like this, with no resident priest and a laughable absence of governmental law, everything is dealt with as a matter of family. A family that squabbles, for sure, and occasionally kills its members, but a family none-the-less."

I could picture Steven scratching his (lice-laden?) head as structure fell apart, causing him to curse the people he would, as all anthropologists must, come to "love and respect." After the discussion with the doctor, though, it was obvious that Steven was not quite the Holy Roller he had seemed earlier, although he was most certainly a believer.

On the other hand, what good were his feeble nods to rationalism when he could cave in to 'belief'? Empiricism must be thoroughly practiced to please the god of reason, a jealous god indeed. Had Steven lived, that god eventually would have reared its head through his thesis committee. It might have been better for him to have died.

On a personal note, Angelica still stood out as a potential mistress for Steven, but it seemed that she was holding out for something legal from the gringo, something she most certainly would never obtain. An affair of any kind, though, would provide another little tale that could be whispered in an ear, in Suzanne's ear, to resound like a shout in a cathedral.

With that in mind, I proceeded to seek out such a bombshell and skimmed the notes until an entry from June 25th titled "St John's Fiesta" grabbed my attention. Fiesta meant 'party,' and it was possible that even in Steven's dry hand something of interest, romantic or not, might stand out. But the first few words dragged on, and it came to me that there was work to do, sleep to catch and more work to do. The notebook was dropped that night and would not be opened again for two weeks, and only then because of the most compelling circumstances.

During those weeks, Suzanne became curiously distant. I thought that perhaps the writings she had received to date had not been up to her expectations, so I gave her all the letters I had read so far, as well as pages torn from the notebooks right up to the point of my last reading. The gossip on her affair with Bernini worried me somewhat, as anger or embarrassment might cause her to drop our bargain, but she registered no emotions of that kind, either. She refused to show even a hint of her old conspiratorial sarcasm, nor even the slightest acknowledgement that we shared in any conspiracy at all.

After a few days of this a worry grew that she had decided not to comply with her end of the bargain, and at last I confronted her point blank. Without expression she said, "Yes, everything is taken care of," and then went off to some other task as if she had just related to me that she had finished stapling the multiple-choice exam for 101. One could only assume that a combination of guilt, shame and anger had caused her to shut out the human source of her discontent, and as the days passed it seemed that she might be handing me the jackpot: that perhaps her practiced lies had thrown off the psychopath and now she was eager to forfeit the remainder of the papers, too, out of her misery. This rationalization was so convincing that she disappeared from my thoughts until those few weeks later, when she buttonholed me in my office on the tail end of a beautiful spring day.

"Hey, Solo-man, where are the notes? You're holding out on me. Don't think that I couldn't turn your little gossip war around in an instant." Now she was connected; angry, but alive again.

"It didn't seem to me that you were interested anymore. In any case, how do I know that you really did comply?"

"You should have thought about that before the deal. We're dealing in intangibles here, Solomon." I didn't like her using my last name, and she knew it and liked it. "But have you gotten any more scatological love letters?"

"No. Nor phallic calling cards draped with menstrual blood cooing promises of castration."

"Oh, you didn't tell me about that one."

"Yes, I sat on that one, so to speak." She gave me a puzzled look, and then pressed on to the point.

"Have you even seen her? No, you haven't, nobody has except in a few classes. She's missed the last two of Greene's. I saw her slink out of one like she was being hunted by a demon. I can't believe you had sex with….anyway, I hope you're satisfied. She's out of your life and probably out of the department. Now, where are the notes?"

"So that you might destroy the evidence of your little love triangle?"

"That's not even funny coming from you. I broke that up…"

"I *thought* the last letter would make you do that."

"I would have done it anyway. He's like every other man here – soft, shallow soil on a bedrock of pure ambition. Nothing could put roots in that."

"I wonder if his wife thinks so."

"She's as cold as ice, you know that."

"Why wouldn't she be? Anyway, it's nice to know there is at least a little depth of soil to me."

She turned from me wearily. "I said the men, not the larvae. I don't care about you one way or another. Just give your part of the bargain."

"Sure, sure. Saturday morning looks open, but not too early, though. I might plan on a hang-over."

"I want them now."

"Golly, Suzanne, are you this demanding of all your larvae? I haven't read a word of it in two weeks. You're all caught up. Wait 'till Saturday and they'll be plenty to give you."

"I'll read it with you, then, like you said before. We can do that tonight."

"Jesus, what's the rush?"

"I heard from Lacey. She's not doing so well. I don't like this deal about Shari, either. I want to dig in and see if there is something there to help. Don't believe me, but this is not about the gossip. It's stuck me that we're standing at a grave that's still surrounded by the grieving. Something decent has to be done." She stopped, as if to hide a catch in her voice. I almost mocked her sincerity, but stopped as well. She was serious, guilt-torn, miserable. Nothing would be gained by pushing her further.

"All right, then, you win. I'm about finished here. Let's go."

It had been my intention to ride the bus, but when we opened onto fresh air and sun, I had a burst of youthful enthusiasm and convinced Suzanne to walk back to North Campus with me through the arboretum. She dragged suspiciously behind until we passed the arboretum gate and got to the top of the hill. Below us was a steep-sided dell that had been scooped out by the last glacier, forming the best place for winter sledding in the area. Now, students lay on the side of the grassy-green slope, white skin exposed to the sun for the first time in months. Others flung Frisbees down below where the land flattened to the river. There was a stir of excitement in the air that called for wild parties, adventure and sex, and it tempted me to throw off the backpack and run down among the undergraduates. Instead I tossed a casual remark at Suzanne:

"The spring has stirred our rabble youth to frolic and folly. I could almost run down there with them myself."

"It is a nice day," was all she would say. I had somehow expected a surprising flash of poetry, but instead had gotten a terse platitude that rose only slightly above her caution, like the eyes of a frog that peak above the scum of a pond.

The expansive mood was still upon me when we arrived at the room, and I offered her a cup of tea. She politely refused and we sunk into an awkward silence until the notebook was retrieved. She was invited to read until the "St John's Fiesta" entry while I went to the bathroom and then made some tea for myself, which was sipped beside her while my eyes occasionally cast a look over her shoulder.

Finally she arrived at my finishing point. She remained in my chair while I sat on the edge of the bed with the notebook tilted over so that we could both read. It was an odd, even juvenile arrangement, but there would be no breaching our treaty now, whether or not it made sense. We began:

6/25 La Fiesta de San Juan

I stayed a little late at the store last night as the men got to buying rounds on the eve of the fiesta. At first it appeared that tomorrow's feast was to be the religious highlight of the year. They were, after all, an agricultural people, and San Juan's day signified the end of the planting season and the time of first fruits. It only took a bit to discover that St John's Day was more like our fourth of July than, say, Easter, an excuse for a party after the hardest work was done. The ceremony would prove to hold plenty of deep symbols, but the men, by and large, seemed more interested in the bacchanal.

After sleeping later than usual the next morning (this morning), I went to Rafael's for breakfast and found that he had already left to drink with "the others" at the garage. Since drinking with "the others" always involved the swilling of raw mescal, something far too harsh for me at that time of day, I circled broadly around town for the path that led to the Huichols and followed its steep incline.

Near the top of the first cliff the village appeared in full below, and there behind the schoolhouse could be seen a flutter of bright colors, undoubtedly coming from the cache of costumes that the "spirits" in the parade would wear. Events were not to begin until mid-afternoon, but the reminder of the festival in the bright clothes had me turn back anxiously to town.

It was noon by my return. A few women and children were hurrying about on last minute errands, but the village was quiet otherwise and I went to the store for a pop.

Before I could slip in, the "others" spotted me, and Chico called out in a loud and blousy voice for me to join them. Rafael had once shown me the bus radiator that was used to distil the mescal they drank, lead seams and all, and on my walk towards them my mind fought to conjure excuses so that I might graciously leave the party before enough could be imbibed to permanently damage my nervous system. They pushed the bottle in my hands on my approach and declared "for the memory of St John the Baptist" that a good long swig be taken. This was done with great theatrics on my part, with wincing and coughing to make it appear that more was being taken than really was as the men watched with slanted eyes and sloppy grins.

"Salud, Estebi!" chimed poor Simon, the man who had almost lost his leg to Chico's truck, as he raised a bottle from his seat on an upturned log, a cane at his side. He was already plastered. To his side was "Culito" (the little asshole), who was usually called "Cortito" (the short one) to his face. This was the guy who had 'married' his own daughter. It gave me reflexive shivers to think that we may have shared the bottle. When I asked Simon about his smashed leg, Chico answered for him, almost yelling,

"You can see that he is almost as good as new. We are prepared for the party of today. All our debts are paid off, no, Simon?"

Simon nodded, almost falling over: "Yes, cousin, it is true," he slurred, grinning vacantly from his stump. Chico continued:

"You must join us in our great sins today, for it is the season of growth, and Saint John will cleanse us of our misdeeds with his baptismal water." The men all laughed at this and I asked no one in particular what that meant. Rafael replied:

"We get drunk and notice the pretty girls, you know? It's that time, to eat fresh meat after a winter of the same old cornmeal." The men laughed again. Rafael added, "It's still best to keep one eye open, though, to not fall in the wrong hole like Culito here!" All but Cortito laughed even louder than before. Cortito's expression was chilling - a drunken party like this could go from joviality to murder in seconds. I interjected an academic question quickly:

"But you will honor the holiness of John the Baptist, too?"

The men laughed again.

"We will, we will, but we leave it to the women and children for now. Now is the time for men."

I asked if a priest would come.

"Yes, he will be here if the bus arrives, by the will of God. But don't worry, Big White Man, he will not steal any meat from you! Like all "patos" (ducks), he prefers the corn cobs in the crib." The men laughed until they cried. "Pato" is a derogatory slang term equivalent to "queer" or "faggot."

I sighed, grinned and threw up my hands as a sign of surrender to their outrageous behavior. This allowed me to make an excuse to run off and "write up my notes on the gardens." They protested until I promised to return later with a dozen beers.

I walked up the deserted street to the other end, and was headed towards the school when a sister-in-law of Rafael's, a half-sister of Angelica, flatly told me, "No, don't enter. The spirits are dressing." A cautious lean to get a peek caused her to say again, more rigidly, "No! It is bad luck for anyone to see them now." Since the last thing anyone wants is to be blamed for bad luck, which is never in short supply in this town, her wish became my command. There was nothing much else for me to do but to go back to the house and actually work on the notes, which I did, baking under the bed sheet that was needed to keep off the flies.

The afternoon must have stolen my senses, for it seemed that only an instant had passed before multiple strings of firecrackers tore me from a foggy sleep. My head ached from the heat and the taste of that single slug of mescal still lingered in my mouth, but the fireworks meant that the parade was on and that there was no time to lose. I was there, after all, to observe, not just to live, a fact that has often annoyed me. Sometimes it seems that academic observation actually keeps us from ever really touching the outside that is around us. Yet both "going native" and "going tourist" are fraught with distortions as well.

Once in the street it was surprising to see how few people were actually there to witness the parade. In such a town, all but the very old and the smaller children and their mothers must be actual participants. The actors had apparently gone behind the buildings to start the procession by the garage. The men had left their drinking, the town bus having taken that space. This meant that the priest must be there, and he appeared as soon as the procession began, his way cleared by children throwing firecrackers before him. He was dressed in a green robe and a sash with a brilliant, Aztec-like design and he carried a long candle pole with a lit lantern at its top.

To his right marched a man, (Tomás, older brother of Mando), also in priest-like regalia, who held a portrait of a bearded, biblical character, probably St John. To the priest's left walked Angelica's mother, La Dona Castaña, in a long blue dress, carrying a portrait that was obviously the Virgin. As I recall, there is a familial relationship between Mary and John the Baptist which must be checked later.

About twenty yards behind them were the spirits, the space between them and the priest maintained by more children throwing firecrackers. These "spirits" were obviously non-Christian, and either represented demons or spirits of nature. They were made up of both males and females from their raiment, dressed in everything from ornate tapestry to sack cloth and hooded by ingenious, oversized masks. Many of these would be familiar to museum-goers, including the long, white mask of the goat with outstretched spiral horns, as well as the black, oval face that often represents tree spirits with their colorful, leaf-like stripes. There were also sharp-horned devils, some of them painted red, others white with black beards, the latter looking suspiciously like Spanish conquistadors. There were still others with grotesque, pock-marked faces and grimaces of pain. Some appeared as eerie and tragic sufferers, like the ones with round, blank faces and round, black "O's" for mouths - the spirits of dead babies, possibly, a reminder of the hard times these people still live (see list and diagram on following page).

The procession ended at the school, where the priest stood out front and held a shortened mass. In the end, he scattered drops of holy water with his fingers, to bless the people. Behind him stood the spirits, and after the priest's blessing, the kids and the young mothers and everyone else who was not among them reached for the pots and cups and buckets of water they had brought and threw them on the spirits, who shrieked and scattered behind the buildings and walls into the fields and rocks and clusters of brush. The symbolism of rain and fertility and the displacement of evil and disease and premature death was obvious, and this made the comments of the men earlier about "the pretty young women" more appropriate. This was a time when people might break away from the ordinary rules of propriety and have sexual trysts, a reversal that is common among agriculturalists at the growing time of year. To make this more obvious, one old crone admonished that I run to the "montaña" with the 'spirits', saying, "you are a young man, go, go!" Another joined in, laughing, until their heckling forced me to escape and hide beyond the schoolhouse. There, thankfully, the spirits had either not returned or were well hidden.

The question remains: how is it that the "evil" spirits, who are banished to the countryside, are also responsible for the "goodness" of fertility and fecundity? Obviously, there is ambivalence here about the natural world and its processes....."

Etc, etc. There followed a rather standard symbolist explanation, with a pairing of items and events and times and whatever which Suzanne and I agreed should be passed over, at least for the time being. We quickly skimmed several pages of these notes until we came to normal script again, whose title was kept in parentheses:

June 26 (Personal Script)

Of last night: it is now apparent that several townspeople had set me up for the evening, including the old ladies, as well as the drunk men and certainly Angelica. She was waiting for me just outside the wall by the schoolhouse, behind the creosote bush where I had crouched to complete the last notes. Her mask was still on, which gave everything about her a dream-like air, and she came to take me by the hand.

There was a small depression nearby covered by more creosote bushes, and Angelica pulled me into it with a grip so hard that two of her fingernails drew blood. Her identity was immediately clear despite the costume. In the most curious way, I felt her, as one feels the presence of someone without seeing her. It struck me that I had been feeling her all along, with the urge of a natural desire that seemed oddly predestined, but had refused to acknowledge it.

How such knowledge travels is a mystery; perhaps our nerves are fired by pheromones or body language or other signals that are too subtle for the conscious mind. It truly felt like telepathy, though, and we came together without a word as if this had been a mutually accepted inevitability. It was very odd how dislodged from reality it made me feel, just as it engrossed me in the present as never before. Simply, the experience cannot be related without this sense of paradox. It is probable that my cultural persona was pared down to a more essential level, making me more "real" – more authentic – the less "me" it seemed I was.

The physical act of lovemaking was minimalist, too. I have long been used to the cosmopolitan way of love with long foreplay, but this was a mating as basic as could be. After pulling me so aggressively into the bushes, she became completely submissive and lay on the ground. She simply became mine, as if she were a body of prey after a successful hunt. This might seem boring, but the sense of power and control that this gave me was exhilarating, like one feels after reaching the top of a peak. I was master of the universe for a few minutes, a strutting peacock with his feathers a-flare.

Then it was over. After helping her to her feet and dusting off, we wordlessly parted, as if by some silent code. I then went to find the party of men that had undoubtedly regrouped somewhere in town to continue drinking. They, the original crowd and several others, were immediately found where they had been before, at the garage, some in regular clothes, others still in the lower part of their costumes (all masks were gone), and I bought the dozen beers as promised, then a dozen more. The late afternoon passed with tall stories of outrageous sexual exploits until the women called us to the feast near the school, where a drunken mariachi band had materialized. The priest was there, too, and people danced and sang, but stayed within the bounds of propriety. Even the weaving drunks, and there were several, carefully thought to turn their backs before urinating. It was obvious that nature had been put back in its place, back to the *monte*, and that human social life had quickly taken charge again beneath the kerosene torches.

After some dancing and a few shots of mescal at the dance, Angelica (now in her Sunday best) surprised me by suggesting we return to her home at the schoolhouse for something additional to eat. She had generally ignored me at the fiesta, causing me to assume (with much embarrassment) that what had happened was only incidental to the special day, and that subsequent memories of it must be kept to ourselves. There in the house in the wavering yellow light of a kerosene lantern, she brought me a large bowl of beans and chili and a *mantilla* stacked with hot corn tortillas.

The act of a young women giving cooked food to an eligible mate is recognized the world over as an overture for a more permanent bonding, and it was with some reservation that I accepted it. She nursed her son in the shadows after, then welcomed me into her bed for another tryst as her son slept in an open dresser drawer, the only furniture besides the bed and a chair in the room. The last I recalled was her smell of wood smoke and spices, before sleep rocked me in a cradle of peaceful domesticity.

I awoke to children's voices the next (this) morning and realized that she was giving classes! Escape was not possible through the barred window, and panic neared before I noticed another door beside the bed. This led to an open shed where she prepared her meals and hung laundry. My hangover was not as terrible as it could have been, but it made me clumsy enough to trip over the cooking fire and fall back into some bushes beside a window in the school. A few of the kids saw me and laughed, which caused me to lurch to my house at top speed. Much to my horror, several people were already out and about, but all said good morning as if nothing had happened.

Now I am sitting in my house drinking a cup of coffee and thinking of settling the sourness in my stomach with a few of Teresa's cold tortillas and beans. There is no telling how yesterday's events will change my status here in town. Everything is calm now, but time will tell.

One thing's for sure: life will not be as before. Fiesta or no, such actions are not forgotten in a small town. It also is impossible that the schoolteacher and I can ever face each other as we have in the past. The consequences could be unpleasant. But as nervous as I am about the situation, the thought of our time together calls up a great desire. Part of me knows that this must be kept under control while another insists that the reins be let go, that all is as it should be. And then there is Lacey.

Sorting this out will have to wait until later. First it must be determined if doing so is worth the effort, if there is still a choice.   ST

Suzanne and I looked at each other, stunned by what we had just read. My fingers had been pressed to my lips towards the end, and as they unconsciously moved downward, our hands accidentally touched. I was about to mention that Steven's escapade might have led to his entrapment when the touch caused a pressure in my throat not felt since undergrad. As my breath immediately quickened in response, Suzanne's movements seemed to change with mine. I tried to steal a quick look at her to test whether this was a product of my imagination when our eyes locked. There was a hard glint to hers that made me speechless. For once not a cutting quip or a sly joke came to mind. The tension climbed to an unbearable level and peaked as our fingers climbed up each other's arms and then went further as the force became like filings pulled to a magnet that could not be stopped by anything in the natural world.

CHAPTER 6

Now Sleep In It

It has always puzzled me why sex between two healthy young people should cause them to sleep, even early in the evening. It is not as if the endeavor were a foot race up Pike's Peak. I suppose that this occurs so that the male will stay with the female as a potential shield while she lies supine to allow the sperm easier access to the ovum, necessary in the days when our species was not as numbingly successful as it is today.

So I found myself with Suzanne, at an hour in the evening usually reserved for research or a late meal. Staring over her still form, the clock showed that we had slept for nearly two hours since the most inspired sexual experience of my life. It had all the passion and mystery of the first time without the guilt and the fear, at least at the moment. Suzanne's warmth now rose gently in the whisper of her shallow breathing. A final hint of dusk allowed me to see her softly, and I nudged the covers down so that one nipple, then the full breast stood out in view. Hers was of medium size, pointing to the outside, beautiful, as most breasts were.

Large, small, soft, firm, big-nippled, pointy-nippled, women's breasts were a marvel, a gift. Such they had always been for me since before the meaning of sex could be grasped, distinguishing me as a "tit" man who undoubtedly carried all the psychological baggage inherent upon it.

I leaned close to her and smelled, pulling in the warmth and perfume and lotion and hint of sweat and sex, and then the quiet scent hidden behind the others. This is the scent that rests in all fecund women, a slightly sour, milky odor that both fascinated and repelled me. It reminded me of love and pleasure, but also of capture and oppression: it made me want to grab and hold, but then to run and hide, for it also reminded me of the confining power of my mother.

I had to turn from Suzanne and sit up in bed in the dark, cheap student room that was now edged in the sharp light of day. I felt slightly nauseous, and wished fervently that this had happened at her place, or not at all. It brought back memories of the darkness and light of our home in Chicago, of the terrible panic of suffocation that would grip me at night in the cramped, stuffy rooms of our rented faculty house.

My parents were both academics, and they had made their respective specialties blend with their gender identities as well as their cultural and ethnic backgrounds. My father was a professor of economics at Chicago as well as a Jew, and he played the stereotype to the hilt as the cold, tight-fisted, severe father. He would have been a rather biblical character were he not an ardent atheist. His parents had brought him from Poland in the 30's, and had told him again and again why no relatives were left in their homeland. He had assumed, as many of his generation had, that a god who would allow such evil to befall his people was not worthy of adoration. A mere mention of belief would set his jaw in anger.

It finally came to me one day that he had never stopped believing in God, but rather saw him as a thunderous, vengeful being who commanded by fear rather than love. It would not be an understatement to say that he took his role as father from his concept of God. Fortunately, in a perverse way, he was also like God in that he was endlessly involved with projects other than me. Thus I was to be raised as most urban Jewish boys were raised: by a mother omnipotent in her own house.

The twist was that my mother wasn't Jewish. She was, in fact, as far from Jewry as one can be this side of New Guinea. It was funny that my father had picked such a counter-stereotype: a white-white skinned, freckled, plump Irish Catholic woman with red hair, green squinting eyes and a tongue inspired by the Blarney Stone. God, that woman could talk, and as my father would not, she talked to the walls, her paintings, her plants, her pots and pans and, when that was done, to me.

My mother taught art appreciation at Northwestern, not because it was necessary and not because it was her first love - that was painting itself - but because it gave her a vocal way to communicate. It was as if her solitary time at the easel had to be balanced by gripping the world with her words, as if she would lose everything without that. She used her words to explain, to familiarize, and then to bind. My father, as stern and quiet as a rock, was her human easel, an unforgiving blankness that must have reflected those quiet times before the canvas, a time that demanded skill and concentration and, the hardest thing of all, a well-spring of creativity that could only come through grace from the inexplicable, wordless darkness.

This need for grace must have caused her great trouble. As an academic, she could not be so naïve as to believe in an organized religion, but as an Irish artist she could certainly believe in the sprites and fairies of nature and in the great cosmic arbiter of fate. Thus her chat with inanimate objects was a chat with her gods, which I learned were used to hold at bay the black onyx of creativity behind her flightiness. In all this I would be her puppy, and she would dress me with her words and tie them in bows around my neck and then hug me in those great white bosoms chanting, "You are my great little boy, mommies little sugar, her warmth and comfort," and so, on and on, well into my adolescence.

I broke her heart one day when I was fifteen and had come back from school, red eyed, after smoking pot with the gang behind a pile of boxes by the alley dumpster. She had been alone and in need, and came to hug me at the door, which freaked me out, as we used to say, sparking me to push her away in disgust. She stopped talking to me after that, completely at first, and then later only to convey necessary messages. She loosened with time, to be sure, and slumped into a normal range by my graduation from high school, but I would never be her little sugar plum again.

My head slumped in my hands. It was all so asinine, everything, from our propped-up personas to our sense of love and duty. We as humans had a super cortex, a tool to make other tools that had turned on itself like a self-actualized robot to create imaginary things. The trouble is, imaginary things are so much easier to create because *they don't have to actually work.* This is a point that I had to make constantly with my idealistic acquaintances. We should be required to work with the world we have at hand, not with the imaginary ones we have been burdened with.

But with our cognitive abilities we may also remove the layers within us that have no practical function, or indeed may hinder a function. The structure will not collapse without them: this structure is, after all, an abstraction, and may float in the air as well as stand on the ground. All it takes to create this streamlined world is unfettered self-knowledge and a determined will.

So here I was, a practical man, stuck with a near-stranger in my bed that was no longer of use to me. She would expect a bit of imagined 'romance,' and society insisted that one comply, at least for a time, or be considered a predatory monster. Although we both gorged on the same sanguine carcass of desire, it was now expected that the remains of the corpse be turned into Valentine sweets.

The thought of the process made me agitated, which made me aware that I had to urinate. There were still too many people awake to walk uncovered to the shared bathroom, so I grabbed my London Fog and slipped out the door as quietly as possible.

On my return, Suzanne surprised me by not only being up, but by being nearly dressed as well. She gave me a glance as she pulled on her sweater, then spoke, turning away as she did so.

"I was hoping to leave before you returned. It would have made it much easier to forget it ever happened." She had finished with her clothes now, and was beginning to lace up her boots in a precise but hurried fashion. Her remark was surprisingly painful.

"Forget what? That was the best sex I've ever had. You can't say you didn't enjoy it." I tried to get her to look at me, but she continued with her boots, speaking to the floor:

"Save it for the undergrads, Solomon. I know you. You know you. That was a one shot deal. God, no pun intended. Like the one and only time one gets drunk on sloe gin fizzes. Let's let everything go back to business, shall we?" She tied her last knot with a tug and looked up at me on the final words. She was already all business, except for something, perhaps a hint of embarrassment from an exposure of weakness. I was surprised by her objectivity and should have jumped on her offer, no pun intended, but something else began to work on me: pride, perhaps, or something similar from an inner source.

"Suzanne, why throw away a good thing? The maxim of not mixing business and pleasure is not a law. We're smart enough to work around that, aren't we?" It struck me immediately how slimy that sounded, but it was too late.

"You bastard. I'm holding the door open for you. Don't foul this any more. We can meet at the museum for the notes. Now you can get out of my way. There's a bus to catch."

"Jesus, Suzanne…" Inexplicably I grabbed her arm as I spoke, and paid for the impulse with a painful slap from her other hand. She had to turn around to do so, and as I winced and held my face, she turned hers at me, one that was flushed red with tears streaming from eyes that showed a frightening emotional cauldron.

"Out of my fucking way, you bastard! It was stupid, stupid! to have

126

anything to do with an asshole like you. Just forget the whole fucking thing! Keep your goddamn notes, just stay out of my life!" She gave one more forceful look of anger and pain and tried to slam the door as she left. I caught it and yelled down the hall.

"Suzanne, don't leave like that! Forget how that last phrase sounded. I'm an asshole, you're right. Just…" The outer door slammed shut and ended my speech. The last words that she, and those who lived on the hall, heard were "I'm an asshole!" Someone somewhere exclaimed, "Got THAT right," but that was left behind as I hustled after her, through the first door, and then the next in my trench coat and slippers.

From the porch she could be seen striding past the parking lot, halfway to married apartments. There was no time to lose, and in an attempt to jump down the stairs, a flopping slipper caught on the faded and curled welcome mat. I fell onto the sidewalk, badly skinning a knee and my palms, swore, kicked off the other slipper and tried to sprint for the bus stop.

Closing in on married housing, my coat opened, exposing me in all my glory to the chill spring night. I quickly buttoned myself down as a scenario flashed in my mind of a child screaming, of me getting arrested, of the line up identification by the tearful child and parents, and finally of a life led as a convicted sexual predator. None of this was enough to take away the pain of my frozen bare feet.

When I reached the bus stop, Suzanne was standing under the florescent lights shifting impatiently from foot to foot beside a tired looking Chinese man. She turned just before I reached her, and she jumped in shocked surprise.

"What the hell are you doing here, Solomon? You're at the wrong shop for ego salve."

"Suzanne, I'm standing her in the cold with bare feet, naked under a trench coat like a demented pervert, and you think I'm worried about my ego?" My words caught both of us by surprise. What *was* I doing there? My mind seemed vast and hollow, thoughtless, burning and seething with raw emotion. Suzanne's look changed to one of puzzlement.

"What do you want, then? Tell the truth for once, goddamnit!"

"I don't want you to go. Please. It's not the.." A glance at the Chinese man made me self-conscious… "You know, don't leave. Not like this." Suzanne's look changed from puzzlement to astonishment as a small tear ran uncontrollably from my left eye. I should have panicked, but instead felt relief. My eyes held hers as my hands touched her lightly. "I don't know, Suzanne. It's something I don't understand. My heart feels…hollow. Open." It was incredible that those last words had come from me, but it was true; my heart did truly feel open. It was terrifying, a joy. There was a fear of being hurt, a hope of something new, greater. Suzanne softened.

"I believe you. You amaze me." The sound of the bus made us turn to look down the hill. "Ben, I should go. I have more work to do and all my things at home. I'll see you tomorrow, OK? After 101." The bus stopped and I stood there stupidly until she put her hands on my shoulders and kissed me lightly. "OK?"

"Yeah, tomorrow. Take care."

"You, too." I watched her take her seat under the bright interior lighting and inhaled the diesel fumes as the bus slowly gained momentum. I watched and waited for her to give me a last sign, a wave, a look, something, but instead saw her fading silhouette remain as unmoving as an etching.

As the bus disappeared down the hill, my emotional meltdown evaporated like morning dew. Damn! Damn, damn! She had escaped, barely scarred, and had left me an open pile of mush on the sidewalk. She had finished me off like a school kid with his first crush. Jesus, what had gotten into me! Why the hell had I behaved like a slobbering yokel! She had gotten a hand inside me and could now move me like a sock puppet, manipulate me through my shameful exposure.

Or so she thought. With my protective wall magically restored, it came to me that this situation could be turned around with a few words, with a slight-of-hand to create a double-entendre. She could be made to see that she was being manipulated by my feigned surrender, that she had been seduced and then tricked again with a play of emotions. Of course. Why the worry? This would be a piece of cake.

It then came to mind that this entire sequence had been inspired by Steven's essay on his dirty little sexual exploit with a native. Although it was ridiculous, the thought of his active agency kept playing with my imagination. The cold, manipulative hands of Steven could almost be felt from beyond the grave. It came to me against all reason that he was avenging my contempt for him by turning my strengths into weaknesses, and so forcing me to have contempt for myself. It was outlandish, but since the idea would not leave me, my revenge would have to come from having fun with it. Steven, this queer hallucination of Steven, would be shown that his "spirit powers" could not get the best of me. Imagined or not, even his ghost would know that he was a loser son of a bitch.

The retreat back to my room was made by walking on the sides of my feet, now in searing pain from the cold. Once there, I threw off the coat and jumped into bed for welcomed warmth and there instantly felt a lingering dampness where Suzanne had slept. Damn her. It would not be so easy. A turn of mind could not always turn the world.

After several minutes, after recognizing that sleep would not come in such turmoil, I decided to slip past my darker thoughts by reading more from the book of Steven. Perhaps he would disclose how his own little impetuous indiscretion had been solved. It would certainly be easy enough to pick up where we had left off: the notebook lay open on the desk to the very page where Suzanne had enthralled me. Several pages of garden plot sketches and lists of food products followed, however, before his personal musings began again:

July 2, 1980 Tutzingo

I am not quite sure of the date for the moment, and it is late. Things have moved very quickly and in ways not expected. In particular, the sequence of events that happened the day after the festival has put me in a daze. There was no precedent in my mind to help select a course of action, and it proved fortunate that, after sitting up from bed in a cloud of flies that hovered over and around my hangover, the growling in my stomach was left to determine the next move.

I walked carefully over to Rafael's in hopes of some leftovers and stood in the door waiting to be welcomed in. Teresa, his wife, was not discernable at first in the darkness of the house, but the sound of patting tortillas confirmed her presence. My eyes adjusted to find her squatting on the floor, flipping tortillas from one hand to another next to a daughter, who was carefully arranging them in a basket. Still, she would not look at me. Her silence forced me to speak:

"Doña Teresa, would you happen to have some old tortillas and beans lying about? The fiesta has caused me to sleep late." My words brought her face up, her look expressionless. Again, she was silent. I was about to speak again when she cut me off:

"Professor Esteban, of course you are welcome to what we have, but it is customary to seek daily food in one's own house." She remained intent on her work, again without expression.

"Yes, Doña, but you know I have no kitchen and always come here to eat, where the women cook."

"Professor, it might be that a woman cooks for you now." Her black eyes glittered. She might get a good laugh out of this later, but it was not amusing to me.

I murmured an "adios" and left, frowning, for nowhere. Of course it was obvious what she meant. They had railroaded me. The schoolteacher had been an acquaintance for nearly two months now, but we had never dated, never let any romantic intent be known to one another. To have everything turn on a dime like this seemed nonsensical, even dangerous. What could she possibly expect from me? She was certainly attractive, but did anyone believe that any sort of permanent union would be formed? There was also the relationship back in my world. It was a tentative one, but the world in which it was imbedded was not. This one was. It was improbable to the nth degree that life here could hold me, and it was nearly as improbable that Angelica could be embraced in mine.

I turned towards the rocky southern pass in spite of my grumbling stomach to brood, and in brooding became angry. It could be that this whole episode was an exercise in using people. The villagers wanted to use me, for my mechanical ability, for my literacy, for American money; and Angelica wanted to use me as a man, a substitute father for her child, a protector and provider for both the child and herself.

It was also expected of me to use them all in turn, Angelica for sex and domestic services, and the villagers for information for my thesis. It all seemed so practical, so much so that it also seemed immoral. What would happen the next year or the year after that? What would happen if Angelica's child got to know me as a father and then was abandoned? What if Angelica became pregnant? No one seemed to care, or to want to make protective arrangements, like marriage, for such possibilities. It is as if we could all avoid personal responsibilities by pretending that tomorrow would never come.

After walking about two miles from the village, fatigue brought me to sit on a small boulder that had warmed in the late-morning sun. As soon as my feet settled, something felt terribly wrong, for the right foot touched hard rock while the left something squishy and mobile. Before it could be moved there came a sting, and when I leaped from the jolt of adrenaline something followed my trajectory. Then I saw it, a coiled snake, tail rattling, waiting for another strike. My foot was completely exposed since I had (foolishly, it now seemed) taken to wearing sandals, and on the tender top skin near the point where the foot joins the ankle were two small, identical puncture wounds. Good Lord.

I began to circle around the snake to escape before realizing that it should be taken, to identify what type of poison it carried in the event that time remained for an antidote. The snake was not very big, and seemed more wary than threatening in its stance, so it was easy to crush with a small boulder. I carefully picked it up with a long stick and started my walk back. My legs were trembling, so much so that it was difficult to pick my way over the rocks. Faintness descended along with a cold sweat as I looked around in frozen terror at the landscape, thinking, "So this will be my grave. This is where I will die. What a waste." The idea came that life was pointless, a path without a destination, and my bitterness alternated with fear just as my pace alternated from slow to fast, as reason could not decide if it would be better to get back quickly for help, or walk slowly to slow the circulation of poison.

The schoolhouse, where the doctor stayed, where the only person of education lived, drew me towards its open door where the voices of the children fluttered like angel wings. They were just finishing class before the siesta. I stopped and took a calming breath, so as not to frighten the children, and held the snake corpse in the air just outside the opening and managed to ask, in a voice that was nearly free of quavering, if someone knew what kind of snake it was. A few of the boys instantly jumped up as Angelica's hands went to her mouth, understanding what had happened. Before anything more could be said, the boys began to laugh.

"It's a grasshopper snake! He eats the bugs and the mice! Did you kill him for us?" The whole class began to laugh. It became clear that my panic had not been as hidden as hoped. Angelica laughed as well.

"But it rattled its tail!"

"It is the little brother who pretends to be the big one. He shakes his tail against the leaves to fool the coyotes and little children." The bigger kids laughed even harder. It was hard to know which possessed me more, relief or embarrassment. Angelica acted quickly to end the spectacle.

"Come, come, enough! It's time for siesta. Pick up your papers and leave your pencils. Have more respect. We will see each other tomorrow. Go with God!" She turned to me again and was about to speak when a girl tugged on her dress. "In a moment, Maria. Now, Steven, it is lunchtime. Are you hungry?" The question brought the old pulsing of morning hunger through my distress, and I nodded.

"You are just in time, then." She answered a few more questions from her students and then motioned me to her room. It felt awkward, her place too small for me. She didn't notice, but moved outside to her hearth where smoldering coals had kept the beans hot, and returned with the pot and tortillas and a bowl of squash. She offered me her only chair, and I sat and ate while she did the same on the bed. We were silent until she started to giggle, then laugh.

"You were very brave, believing that you would soon be dead." Her smile was broad and open.

"It is lucky," I told her, "that I am not down in the river now scrubbing my feces from these pants instead of eating here with you."

We both laughed.

And so it happens that a new place has come to be my home. I have no idea, none, what the future will hold. It's clear to me that fate mocks "the best laid plans of mice and men." People's lives will be changed because of these last few days, and it is now my responsibility to try to make these changes be for the better. Although we are not in control of many things, we are responsible for our actions. Everyone here may live for the moment, but my background obliges me to keep an eye on the outcome, however that may be altered. For now, though, a time has been granted to indulge in a fool's paradise, if that is what this is. Lacey is still with me, still. There is nothing more to say on that.   ST

Oh, Steven, Steven!, I mocked him. You will soon have more, for there before me was a letter from Lacey marked only six days after his last entry. Of course it was written before any correspondence concerning the new "bride" could have arrived from Mexico, but it would set the tone for his future anguish. I felt fiendish, certain of a cruel twist of fate and relished it, still living as I was with the sting of my emotional exposure. To assuage my conscience, I feasted on the idea that with "the best laid plans of mice and men," the noble and the selfish end up in the same place.

Dear Steven,

It seems so long since I have heard from you! Of course you have your business to attend to, but I worry about you. I have thought about the drug dealers and the situation in Mexico in general and am afraid that your little village must be involved in all this somehow. Please, just steer clear of any complicity. Even if it seems a good thing, you don't know the connections of one person to another, and have no personal protection yourself. Remember that you are not in a position to change things, nor is that your mission. This may sound selfish, but keep in mind that you will be able to right the wrongs more effectively once you have gained some professional standing and prestige.

At home: Andy has been able to go back to Haiti for a few weeks. His change of status to full teaching assistant has allowed him to borrow some money from the credit union. It's so sad that he has to add further to his student loans, but no one in charge here has bothered to think of anything like that. It is also very clear that the job market has dried up permanently for our profession, and that the faculty continue to take in the number of grad students that they do only for tuition and cheap labor and to maintain the appearance of need for the full staff. No one bothers to consider that most of us will be tens of thousands of dollars in debt and have no place to go. This will not be a problem for me monetarily, but the situation may force me to suffer the humiliation of crawling back to the family enterprise. It's not that I don't love them, but we pride independence. My anxiety is such that, while sitting before this huge stack of books, it often occurs to me that I should stop the bleeding and find another profession while there is still time. Yet in that is defeat. It is all so hard, thinking like this, to settle down to work.

Of course, if it would be humiliating for me to go back to my own family, how hard would it be if we were married and you had to rely on your in-laws? I probably should stop now with that, I made such a mess of it the first time. This is not about my pride, though, but of the pride that any successful relationship must have in itself. But don't believe that you are ever far from my thoughts. Absence has made my heart more aware of the loneliness that you filled. If we could only live as we did, from day to day, but when we think of the future we must face its reality. I can only hope (would you pray?) that it works out. It does for some. Anna was able to get a job as a computer programmer, just like Carol, (her baby is a girl, a red-head like her. She was so lucky!) but they are archaeologists and have had that training. Anna's husband is just as goofy as before, but has received another promotion. Our future, it seems, is in technology, which will be run by idiot savants, the socially inept, along with the hereditary effete who have always controlled the national direction. One could hardly say that technical wizardry is leading us towards an evolutionary advancement in intellect.

The summer fair has been on this week, and it is just the mixture of delight and commercialism as last year. They had a food court with Thai dishes - you would have loved it! The same old black drifter sang "Day-oh" to apparently the same old crowd, who clapped and sang along just as we did, which made me sad. I miss you - can't you come back so that we could think of something else to do with our lives? Carol has made me think of having my own family someday, but it would be a mistake to do it the hard way. Nothing is worse for a family than insecurity, I believe, don't you? But nothing is worse for a person than isolation and loneliness.

That blackness touched me strongly after hearing the Day-oh man, when I saw Suzanne and Cindy eating ice cream by the social science building. Cindy had finished her exams last month, and was wearing a pair of wire antennas with balls on top, which are the rage with the college set this year, as if to show her contempt for serious thought. She told me that she has made up her mind to leave the department and join her fiancée in London. They have planned to marry, and she is going to "soak up England" for a year and attend her husband's symphonies. It seems even violinists have better opportunities than we do.

Anyway, her leaving, her situation, her attitude have all left me feeling the great emptiness of things again. Is it that we have no more purpose in life than to live somewhere, breed, and then get out of the way until death? We are not just tiny to the universe: we are tiny to each other, only one in four billion, most of whom live and die without any worthy contribution. Even if they did contribute, what then? What did man's first fire do but end up powering war machines and polluting factories? What did modern medicine do but cause overpopulation and additional misery? I believe that Claude Levi-Strauss was right, that our thoughts are built from opposition and contradiction, that we cannot remove ourselves from that structure any more than we can remove ourselves from the brain. But he forgot a more metaphysical component to this structure of opposition: that everything good in life will have negative consequences. This seems more an attribute of an evil world than a bipolar mind. If only I could believe in God as you do, for I now am beginning to believe in the devil. So much darkness without light is a terror that no one should have to face.

You see, we are all on fieldwork of a sort, aren't we? But mine is a fantasy, and I apologize for bothering you with it. You are living the hardships, not me. I just thought you should know a little of my present state so that you may understand my decisions, or lack of them. Forgive me. Be careful. May you return soon and safe.

Love, Lacey

Oh, Lacey, the poor little rich girl, what a wreck awaits her! It was both amusing and painful to follow her reasoning and her plight. Our intellectual heir to predestination, Claude Levi-Strauss (curiously a

Frenchman and a Jew), created a theory on human thought based on the structure of the brain – an iron-clad box that, for all of personal will, cannot be escaped. He based his theory on the apparent chaos of primitive mythology, noting that if we looked closely, there were common themes buried within them. For instance, the moon might be presented as female and the sun as male, or vice versa, but they would always work in opposition, and always, in one way or another, in a gendered fashion. The perceived contradictions cause action and a new condition from that action, but never resolution. Such is the paradox of life to the human mind.

This is all very unexciting until we dissect Lacey's dilemma. She saw the contradictions of life, but was stopped at the negative axis. By not completing the circle, she could only think that all things good end badly. She could not see that all things bad will eventually turn into the "good."

But these are not objective definitions. Nature does not care about your car accident or your winning lottery number. It does care about life, as the living wish to continue living. But life is just another tiny aspect of nature. In the greater scheme, nature contains nothing good or bad. It exists in every form without a higher reason or purpose beyond simply existing.

But for Lacey, nature did have a purpose, which was to cause pain. Without a great and powerful god to make sense of it all, as her ancestors had, her conundrum and fate were all very clear. As meaningful existence crumbled for her, she was only able to draw on a skewed nostalgia to entertain romantic possibilities and a fairy tale ending with Steven.

I knew that this would not happen. Steven would die before he would ever see Lacey again. And Steven had a new lover. It was not a question of whether Lacey would be crushed, but only how and when. When would she hear of his affair, and how? Would Steven come clean like a good boy scout, or hide his dirty little secret until she found it in his diary notes after his death?

These meanderings, meaningless as they were, worked to soften the humiliation of the night with Suzanne. They let me believe that worse things could happen, and also gave me confidence that my intelligence could turn my personal fiasco around. Certainly the turning of the cosmic wheel was in my favor. It had to be. If I was humiliated now, it would someday be Suzanne's turn.

Given such positive prospects, I resolved to stop my meanderings in Steven's lost life that evening to spend an hour or so in review for finals and then to sleep the last of this chaotic day off. Still, the notes and letters could not be shelved just yet. There remained a compulsion to know Steven's ruminations during the time that Lacey's letter of need and madness slowly worked its way across the border. It would not arrive until about two weeks past Steven's sin-filled adventure on the birthday of John the Baptist.

I decided to do a quick scan of his writings during those weeks to see if any more thoughts had been written about his dirty deeds, and if he had mailed those thoughts to Lacey. Nothing of that nature appeared until this entry made some ten days after the last:

7/12/ 80 Tutzingo

The doctor flew in yesterday morning, and stayed the night with us in the schoolhouse. Angelica once again treated us as sultans at meal, and Juanito, Angelica's little King John, made the model picture of a cherub as he sat on his pudgy rear and laughed to the sound of his shaken gourd rattle. I had not known that children could be such a joy. It must be how their parents survive all the trying times they put them through.

We talked about news on the outside, about the crazy hostage crises in Iran and the slumping economy and the general world entropy that has hampered the doctor's funding. I had not wanted to press him on anything about the Huichols, wanting to distance myself from my failure, but of course they came up. He first began where we had left off as we pushed the last of our beans around the plate with our crumbling tortillas. It was obvious that his memory is better than mine, regardless of age:

"I have been thinking about our last conversation, and feel it necessary to say that I hold the beliefs of the Huichols, in general, in high regard. The Lord has given all men a platform of faith on which to keep His light alive until they have been introduced to His Son and Emissary. I mean only to introduce Him to these people, not to pass judgment on them. Still, many from the outside come here thinking that it is people like them who have the answers to life. It was only my wish to point out this error."

He still spoke in a formal manner, but we both felt relaxed with one another. This manner comes, I think, from his conception of his mission. He is the emissary of the Emissary and must act accordingly. Keeping within the bounds of this formality, I informed him that it was not my belief that the Huichols had all the answers, but that they had some that we did not, adding that the Huichols have known of Christ since the 17th century.

"It's apparent," I ended, "that they consider their own beliefs more fulfilling."

"Yes," he agreed, "but it's often the case that the message is not brought at the right time or by the right men. Still, they have adopted many of the motifs of Christianity, and are certainly close to conversion. Did you know, for instance, that their sun god created fire as his intermediary? Did you know that they confess their sins to the fire to cleanse their souls?"

I replied, from my book knowledge, that their understanding of all this is quite different. The relationship of fire to the sun is roughly akin to that of Christ to the Father, as the sun is too hot to approach alone, but the sins they confess concern only those of a sexual nature, not the more egregious ones. This simple confession, in turn, is done to prepare them for the peyote hunt, where they will use chemicals to alter consciousness and enter the spirit world. These are not in line with

Christian belief.

He continued with some more arguably valid comparisons: "It is the *mara'akeme,* the priest, who talks to the spirits. The people do not have that strength and knowledge. Again, the priest acts as an intermediary for the people to God, just as with many Christians. Of course they conceive of these things differently. But you see how the structure has already been formed. The people have been set up for the true knowledge of Christ. They are thus in the position to accept him or reject him when He is brought to them in full."

With that we arrived at the fundamental mission of the Doctor, which was to spread the Christian gospel to everyone so that a final judgment could be made and the new era of Christ could begin. This time I told him just how awful and cruel that sounded. His reply was shot through with the steel of his beliefs:

"That is the talk of the modern humanist! You say that you are an ecumenical believer, but as is always the case, this points to little or no real belief at all. You see, this," and he spread his arms out into the shadows of the schoolroom like a prophet, "is not a game, not a class in ethics. This is life, which involves suffering, disease and death. It is a contract entered into in which there is no graceful exit through the flesh. There is either salvation from this world or an enduring torture within it until its harsh laws send everything back to nothingness. These laws were made by God, but caused by Man. Before man sought his own enthronement, he lived in the paradise of Eden. It was Man who brought on the curse of this hard life. All men, including the primitives. Thus all are subject to the fulfillment of His word, and that is that salvation shall come only to the believers."

I asked him a question then that has long bothered me: "Why would God set mankind up for such a fall in the first place? Certainly He could have anticipated the weakness of His own creation?"

His manner softened. "Steven, I cannot answer that completely, for no man can know completely the mind of God. But we have been let in on part of the plot. Man was given free will, which he selfishly enshrined above the will of God, thus ensuring his condemnation to this imperfect life that we live. But God, KNOWING OUR WEAKNESS, sent His son for our salvation. He sent Him knowing that we could never completely abandon our selfishness, so that He may take up our weakness. But it is up to us to believe in Him. That is all we have to do, just give up that part of our will. If we do that, Jesus will do the rest. But even this is too hard for most, such is this world. So I repeat: life is not a college philosophy course. Nor is it a campus filled with temporary acquaintances going their own way. We are all in this together, in the living book we call existence, written by the Creator's hand."

I asked him that, if the book is written already, where is free will?

"Surely you understand that all books that we can read, even The Bible, must work through the minds of men and as such must be inadequate. This is why I spoke of the 'living book.' Our destiny is written in the book of life. In this we actually bleed. You may recall that God had to bleed through His son for our salvation. So, you see, the ideas you have of "fate" and "free will" are still only academic, only products of the classroom. When prophecy is written in books, it seems so clean and mechanical. When it is written in life, on this earth in pain and blood and despair and hope, it is filled with the full will of man, even as the laws of nature prevail. Jesus knew His fate in the Garden of Gethsemane, yet He sweat blood while beseeching His Father that it might not come to pass. So it is with all our lives. We are made in the image of God, and may choose one path or another, but sooner or later we choose of our own accord the path that is etched from eternity in the sky and the sod."

He paused to let the depth of his words sink in. I looked through a window and tried to imagine this great path drawn in the white strip of the Milky Way that curved overhead into the mountains. Was his "we" a collective, or did he refer to karmic cycles, a Gnostic theory of rebirth?

He spoke again, low, in tune to the night: "We were made, you see, in the image of God, in the likeness of perfection, but we were corrupted through the evil of our original sin. Because of our sin, we will always have imperfections in all our designs, and because of our divine origin we will always discover these imperfections. Thus we are made to reach for more perfect systems, until we find our way back to Him. Such is the motivation that moves our story."

"Which moves us to Armageddon?"

"Which moves history. As far as Armageddon is concerned, it is with us now. It is always with us in our fight for perfection. Each life is lived with a sword to its throat, and each one must commit either to the forces of the Holy Spirit or to those of the world. For those who choose spirit, the fight is fierce and unending, but its reward is eternal."

"But with time comes improvement? On a global scale?"

"With time come improvements, and the misuse of these improvements. For instance, as we noted earlier, once we all thought in terms of the tribe. Now many think globally. But the forces that made this possible have also caused many to lose their spirituality, to become the humanists and relativists of our day. Such people may help others, but only physically. That covers just one aspect of our being, only a small part of our destiny. Material aid should be, first and foremost, an exposition of God's love."

It was late, and when the conversation drifted off, the doctor shuffled in his chair as if to leave. Before I could follow suit, though, he hemmed and coughed and brought up an entirely different subject, one that might lead to a great breakthrough for me.

"I've been thinking. You seem to have settled in pretty well with Angelica and Rey (Juanito). Around here, this gives you a measure of family status. Did you know that Angelica's father was a Huichol?"

"But isn't she the sister of Teresa?"

"Yes, more or less. You know how complicated these things can get. The point is, you now have some leverage with the Huichols. If you come along with me on my next visit, perhaps luck will favor you after all."

Of course this has given me hope for what had seemed impossible, a hope that has kept me up half the night talking with the doctor. We had discussed great things, but nothing is more fulfilling than experience. How different are the Huichols? What answers do they have? Are they fundamentally closer to the truth in their simplicity, or is that only a nostalgic wish of weary civilization? And what of peyote?

Before we went our separate ways, in beds now only one room apart, he added, "I think you'll be surprised at these people, in many ways. I think the most difficult thing for us to do is to look through the exotic for the truth. The new is often alluring, but the old is often the best."

The doctor will return next week, and we will both be bound for the high hills on the flanks of an ass. Whatever The Way may be, it seems to have answered my prayers and opened a path. Soon my entrees will be in Mountain Time.

ST

It pleased and even surprised me a little to see that Steven's betrayal of Lacey had been so easily shrugged off. Still, his conversations with the bible thumper were getting tedious. Steven had shown that he was not a Jesus freak, but rather the typical educated coward of today – a man who was too knowledgeable to commit to any religion, yet too afraid to break away from the nagging possibility of a god. What a monumental waste of time this was! Instead of diddling with unconscious longings for fetal bliss, Steven could have been asking questions about his future field site, about the difficulties ahead, about the power structure, about the government agent, so many things. My estimation of him as a self-immersed sentimentalist had, to this point, not changed one iota.

In any case, Steven's affair made me almost giddy over what he may have written Lacey in the next letter that now was in my hands, postmarked a week after the last entry. But there was work to do, and Steven and Lacey weren't going anywhere. They were dead-end history and only existed on a dark and dusty shelf, of interest only to the few of us who still remembered them. Steven's confession, or lies, would be tucked away for the following evening after the real world was served.

The morning that followed reflected in every way the betrayal that the month of April is in Michigan. Whereas we had all pranced in the Elysian Fields just the day before, now the skies were as somber and depressing and as cold as November. At first, this was fine by me: as I made my way through the solemn woods and gritty streets to campus, it helped sharpen the sarcastic wit that would be essential in the duel I had imagined would happen between me and Suzanne in the TA office.

What couldn't have been divined then, though, was that the depressing regression of the season was an omen, a clue, a telltale part to of whole. It wasn't that my fight with Suzanne would go badly, but that it wouldn't happen at all as expected. Reality imposed its will on me like a smallpox epidemic on an American Indian shaman; no amount of dancing or praying could change the outcome.

I had just slid my backpack off into my hand to reach for the door of the TA office when through its small window came the sight of The Girls huddled in a tight circle around Suzanne's desk. I paused for just a second and drew in a deep breath: apparently, she had recruited her friends for the attack. This did not surprise or bother me. In fact, something of this nature was expected, and it took me but a moment to gather my wits for the full assault. This was the way it should be. Her presumed conquest of me would be turned into a humiliating defeat before the audience of her friends.

On entering the room, I was thus poised to ruthlessly swat down the first volley that would certainly be coming. Instead, my opening shot, an ironic "hello," elicited nothing more than shrugs. Only Suzanne looked over, and her glance of horror and sorrow brought me to a complete stop. Another quick look from her reflected an additional expression of deep, indelible guilt. After taking a few seconds to reorient my thoughts, I asked what the hell was going on.

Cindy turned her face to me briefly. "It's Shari. They pulled her from her room at four this morning. She's in the hospital." She turned back dismissively to face the circle, as if this were somehow a women's thing, forcing me to aggressively intrude.

"What, then? She swallow her tongue or something? What? Anyone want to tell me?" While this was meant to convey breezy contempt, another glance from Suzanne made the words sound cheap and false. I hoped this interpretation was only in my own mind. Suzanne looked up and focused on me with the intensity that comes from summoning an iron will. She paused in deathly silence before she let out a deep breath. The girls glanced at one another, then to her as she took another breath and spoke.

"The people in the apartment next door heard her screams. They said she sounded like an alley of fighting cats."

"How could you know what they said?" Some of my combativeness still lingered.

"The janitor saw the ambulance and heard them talking to the police. He saw them take her out, strapped to the stretcher. He said she was snapping and struggling like a wild animal, her eyes glazed like a madman. The sheets were soaked in blood. The EMTs said she had been found stabbing her arms and legs with a kitchen knife."

"No shit!"

"It's not funny. She went into shock and had to get a transfusion. She's in a coma now. They say that even if she does come out.."

"Isn't that a little dramatic? A shock caused by blood loss. She'll be as fine as can be."

"..if she does come out, she will need several months of psychiatric care."

"No kidding. No surprise there." By this time, all the girls were fuming at me. Their attitudes were so theatrical that I couldn't reframe from coarse sarcasm.

"Hey, you all knew that she was nuts from the get-go. This place drives even the sane nuts. She didn't have a chance."

"Maybe if we had treated her better." Anna gave a cold shrug and turned toward the others to ignore me. Obviously my little tryst with Shari had now become the primary cause in their minds of her disaster. They had made me an accomplice to attempted suicide.

"Oh, come on! Who could have known that she was an emotional cripple? You know, it's not as if she were wearing a prosthetic device or a breathing machine. Let's be…"

Suzanne cut me off with a snap of the whip. "Stop! This isn't about you or your feelings. Someone we know has almost killed herself and we are shocked and horrified. Why don't you just go back to your office and get on with your little myth project? Why don't you just lock yourself away with your beloved, yourself, and let the rest of us live real lives?"

"Suzanne.." I gave her a hurt look, something that ran so contrary to my earlier plan. That had been to play the slick mastermind, the triumphant playboy who had run circles around her game. Now the situation called for a diversionary retreat, a feint to draw out our connection, our ties from the night before, to dare her to be so cold as to deny them.

"Not now, Ben."

I looked dejectedly at the floor, turned slowly and went to my office. Perhaps my pouting would complete the baiting of the hook. The elicited guilt would cause her to respond. I counted to myself, 'Five, four, three, two,' then the door opened, right on time.

"Ben?"

"Come in."

Now where would we go?

CHAPTER 7

Wrestling the Spirits

"You were such a cold bastard out there. It won't change what you've done, you know." Suzanne's pretense at anger was betrayed by her pallor and trembling voice. She was shaken and guilt-soaked to the core.

"I think you're more worried about what *you* have done."

"Don't mention last night."

"That's not what I meant, but why not? What was wrong with it?" Again, I surprised myself by taking the role of the victim. An intuitive impulse insisted it was my best offense.

"You're avoiding the point," Suzanne squirmed. She was trapped, but it was important not to overplay the fact. It was a time for subtlety; to let myself believe a little in my outward expression of vulnerability, to allow myself to believe, a little, that I had cared about us and was now dejected. It was this vulnerability that would control the focus.

"I thought that we had broken through the ice, found a little warmth through our intimacy. Now you have joined someone else's personal disaster to your own circumstances. What has she got to do with us?" I held my hands out, palms up, to convey an open sincerity that my tone of voice must have contradicted. The overall affect worked to confuse her and take the edge from her unformed accusation.

"Let's not....let's not talk about that now, OK? Someone has nearly died because of my pride. You played on that like a cat with a mouse. Down deep, you are responsible for this and yet you joke about it as if it had been a fraternity prank. For a minute, yesterday, I forgot who you were. Was that your plan, too?"

At this, something cracked. It had all been so under control. A pretense, an edge dissolved and left me to fall into a buried aspect of myself that had no guile. "You think any of this was planned? There was only one plan, the one you know, to save my ass from what I hadn't planned. This Shari - she approached me, not the other way around. Her psychosis wasn't apparent until after. Don't tell me you haven't been hurt in the long run by an impulse for pleasure."

"Don't use that against me."

"I'm not using anything." My mind started to work clearly again. "I'm just pointing out the facts of life. Last night wasn't planned, god knows. Your presence in my room was at your insistence, remember? And what happened after that was the furthest thing from my mind. Tell me, are you into some kind of intellectual S & M? Do you think scheming each other is foreplay?"

"You're getting off the issue..."

"No, I'm getting to the relevant issue, the one we can do something about. The rest is mental masturbation and self-flagellation. All about self." I looked down and took a breath. There was a pause, a regrettable pause, in the effort to maintain self-control. "I came in here today thinking of bright new possibilities. Now you throw this freak incident in my face. So it makes me wonder: why didn't you look back at me from the bus? That was a brush-off, wasn't it? That was your little signal of triumph, wasn't it? Your little victory dance."

She seemed truly puzzled now, taken off her issue. "You noticed that I didn't look back? There was the kiss - wasn't that a clue?" Before I could answer defensively, she regained a confidence that startled me. "You've been thinking about this all night, haven't you? That's you, isn't it, Ben? You're just an insecure little boy longing for his mother's breast! That's what this is about, isn't it?"

Even with my best poker face, the bright flush on my face made everything appallingly clear. There was no other defense but anger. "Oh, good, good, throw a little pop psychology at me to excuse your carelessness. If I go out and stab myself, will it then be your fault? Give me a fucking break. Listen, you want to call it quits, fine. But don't come with this shit. You call me plotting. Maybe it's you who could do with a little honesty."

"Ben." Her assessment of me was obviously set, unshakable, pitying. The fight would have to come from the trenches now. My humiliation caused an anger that could barely be held as she continued. "I was dishonest with Shari and it may cost her life, and almost certainly her career. It was my fault, but it wouldn't have happened without you. Last night was a complete surprise, and I felt something, really. But now, with all this, maybe we should wait…"

Something moved me to leap from my chair and grab her shoulders. I had slipped into that strange world of instinctual action again. "There's no need for this. Nothing has changed since last night. Only Shari knew about her psychological problems. I merely followed the law of expectations. This shouldn't change anything." Her smell made me want to pull her closer. I was near to losing control. She pushed me lightly away.

"No, not now. Not until I can fit some things together. You're a complicated man, Ben. Tell me, really, honestly: why are you in anthropology? Why not in business or a technical field? Why would you do something that takes so much work and time and gives back so little?"

That sense of bizarre spontaneity continued to exert itself. My face flushed again. "I want to find how people connect. How we make a society and a unity. I want to find the key to empathy." The words came as if spoken by someone else. They were a surprise even to me, but to Suzanne they must have shown like the key to my soul. She put a hand on my arm so tentatively that it seemed she expected an electric shock.

"You want fellowship. Respect. Love." Now she flushed. Nothing this embarrassing, this humiliating, had happened to me since freshman year of high school. "Of course. The physician must first heal himself. There's hope for you, Ben, but maybe it's best to wait. It's a tough time of year."

"Then go fuck yourself." I snapped back with a vengeance. "You know? You've known me, what, three years? Then you fuck me and scrape it off your shoe. Then go fuck yourself."

"It's just too much work now, Ben."

"Go. The letters stay with me. Deal's off. Fucking crazy Lacey wants 'em, you can tell her where to find 'em. It's her own goddamn fault."

"We can talk later." Suzanne was backing out of the room now.

"Go talk to your fucking friends."

"Later." She closed the door. I almost threw a book after her in my fury. Both my pride and a playmate had been lost in one fell swoop. The same old combination as usual, goddamn it. I soothed myself with platitudes that had proven their worth: 'Women are like busses, one by every minute; there's plenty of fish in the sea; in a year, you'll wonder what the excitement was about.' All true. But why did getting laid so often end up like this? It would take a while to smooth out my feathers, but it would get done. I'd start that night. That night I would cool things would off with a good read about Stevey's problems with his own neurotic love interest.

As much as the escape into someone else's life was needed, though, it was exam season, and there was so much work to do that it was not possible to return to my room until near midnight. Several hours under the numbing pulse of fluorescent lights had left me exhausted with my eyes barely able to focus, but a balm was essential. It had been a day. Whiskey might have worked, but a hangover couldn't be risked. Thank god there was good old Stevey. As soon as my shoes were off, I dug into the pile and pulled out the next letter, the one so eagerly anticipated. I hoped Steven would not let me down.

Dear Lacey,

Some luck at last! The doctor friend I have mentioned has decided to help me move into the Huichol rancho. We leave tomorrow and it is my hope to stay on awhile, so you may not hear from me for several weeks. The long delay in my plans has made this even more exciting somehow, as if the rancho were a long-parted lover. It is probably wise to take full heed of that analogy, for desire often covers prohibitive imperfections. Life in the mountains can be difficult, and I will be a lone outsider. It cannot be imagined, even for a moment, that all will be pleasant or easy. Still, halleluiah!

It also has come to mind that the months spent in the town have been more than useful. It is often the case that fieldwork is considered only from the researcher's immediate perspective, which may be confined to a small village or island. Of course, most people are not isolates, either by accident or design, and to see them as such distorts the overall picture. My stay in Tutzingo has given me a tremendous advantage in this regard, for I have not only learned of the connections they have to the rest of the world, but also of the sense the people here have of themselves and where they fit in it all. I think this sense will have considerable relevance in understanding the Huichols, as Tutzingo is their nearest and most immediate contact with the global community. It is impossible to guess, though, whether they will see Tutzingo as a desired model of this greater reality, or as a cautionary tale about the empty ways of modernity. I often hope that the latter perspective prevails.

Not that this village is so bad. There is a sense of completeness, especially among the women, that is enviable and so needed in the world. It is as if each woman forms the center of her family's universe, which to them IS the center of the universe, a world of eternal renewal. Certainly the goddess lives among them. But many of the men, particularly the young, feel cramped and insufficient, left out of the great and glorious rush of history. These are the ones who are trying to supplement their livelihoods with "alternative" crops (and the ones likely to be beaten senseless by the big-time traffickers- welcome to the real world!), whose frustration sours the whole sense of community here. Still, the children are refreshingly free, every one of them being amongst relatives who share responsibility towards them all. It is a vast improvement on the fearful parents of our nation who increasingly shelter their children from the community as they recall the sad faces that haunt their milk boxes every morning.

Which moves me to your thesis from the last letter concerning the dichotomous nature of the human mind, and the evil and pointlessness that is its ultimate product. You know, my own sense of the sacred comes not from the Sunday sermons of my childhood, but from an abiding sense that there is something greater within me, something that even intercedes at times with my normal life trajectory and steers me to a better (or more appropriate) path. This is a belief, a sensory belief in a way, which is shared by millions. This interceding power is called the Overmind by some, the Archetypal Mind by Jung, and the Greater Self by many mystics. It is a not a "feeling" alone, although that is often all one can say about it, but it is a sense that, at some level beyond our ordinary selves, the contradictions are made whole and pain and meaninglessness are superseded by a greater good. Yes, there is "good" in this world. Ultimately, I believe, creation is good. Evil, in one way or another, stems from partial perception, or disunion. Creation is separateness, but at bottom it is united. It is hard, but the answers lie at the perception of this union. And I know all of this through that "sense" of the Overmind that usually does nothing to alleviate my own stupidity and self-made misery. However we may be directed, we are given a long leash!

On leashes and family: I don't mean to open an old wound, but it's time to be frank: if you keep waiting for the perfect time to start a family, you may wait forever. You say that you are miserable being alone, but still insist that you don't want to "do things the hard way." Don't you think that this is what you're doing already? You are no longer an unformed, uninformed teenager. You are now responsible and have specific knowledge and skills. You can make it, even if things aren't perfect. It's what many in the world call "life." Lacey, maybe that's why you're so depressed – you're searching for a perfection that is forever hidden behind reality, and in so doing are missing life itself. Couldn't my best attempts at loving you be enough?

That's too harsh. It is intended only as a potent metaphor. But you have to admit, you have given me some reason to be harsh. I have begged you to share my imperfections, for better and for worse, and you have rejected the offer. That may have been wise in my case, but imperfections are a part of life, as are the circumstances that often flow from them. You will not find fellowship to combat your unhappiness until you can tolerate the uncertainties and imperfections of the world. It is my opinion, and it is a humble one, that your unhappiness stems from a lack of faith. Not in a particular god or religion, but in life. One has to have faith that, with all these imperfections and uncertainties, life still has great promise. Further, one should understand that the world is radically improved *just by one's faith in it*. The opposite, fear and distrust, only make more of the same. Life is often dichotomous, but the overall process is positive. You have to believe in that, for with that, you will live life and find that, in the end, life is good.

So much for my inestimable wisdom. Forgive my inarticulate groping. It is done only in the hope that you will realize how much you really could have. While we may never live together again, it is still my concern that you use your great gifts to improve the human lot beyond our own years. I know that you can do this.

Must go and pack. Tomorrow another adventure begins! Will write when possible,

Love, Steven

I put the paper down with mixed feelings of resentment and awe. On the one hand, his escape from further humiliation at the hands of a woman galled me; on the other, his sudden flash of deftness (as it simply must be) with double entendre and emotional manipulation left me in stunned admiration. Without an iota of confessional guilt, he had made their entire situation sadly her fault, brushing off any obligation on his part by fixing on her glaring personal errors. By accentuating her guilt and concealing his own affair, he kept alive his option for a possible renewal of their relationship. And if, for some reason, she found out about the affair or he took strongly to his native paramour, the fault again would be hers, giving her no right to confront him with the wrath of a woman scorned. He had made it clear that he was off the leash through her, rather than his, volition. Beautiful!

A glance at the letters showed that only a half dozen or so remained, with all but two of them written by Lacey. It was possible that in the next Lacey would reveal her final loss of stability when she realizes that she has been served her walking papers. Perhaps she would also guess that Steven has found another woman, of whom he would not speak, for his personal affairs were no longer any concern of hers. Perhaps she would wait a few weeks for a letter from him, would nervously restrain herself from writing, then finally blurt her problems over the page like a small child sobbing over her dead puppy. In desperation she might proclaim her love and beg for his hand. This and more was possible, even probable, given what was to become of her.

As for Steven, I could see him removed, unconcerned, living with his Indians and returning to his village girl for sex and tortillas on alternate weekends. He would write once, a long letter about his work, and end,

154

saying nothing about love, nothing about 'them.' She would fall off the edge, intimating it in a last missive, whereby Steven, now only concerned for her out of pity and his sense of manly duty, would offer her a brotherly shoulder to cry on. Perhaps he would slip in the name of his new object of desire, to end the torrent of troubles she sent scribbled in her pathetic hand. Or perhaps he would reiterate his love as he felt the end of fieldwork approaching, so that he might take up with her again, his ticket to her wealth assured through the oldest trick of love, the slight-of-hand of hard-to-get. Emotionally frail, she would have given him what he wanted with gratitude.

In the end, though, we might only find that she simply heard of his death and fell apart.

Of course, nothing could be known for sure without further reading. As that last encounter with Suzanne had proved, there are few certainties in life and none in the volatile chemistry experiment that is sexual relations.

It would not have taken me long to read the answers to this cliff-hanger, scrawled as they were on a few pages within the frail airmail envelopes that lay on my desk. Oddly, however, the temptation was not enough. In fact, only one more piece would be read that evening, and that from the notebook. Hard as it is to understand in retrospect, the remainder of the story, of the mystery, of the death, would be left to collect dust for the summer in my tiny little room while the semester wound down and I went off to work on an archaeological dig in southwestern Ontario. It wasn't that there wasn't time: all the pertinent information could have been gleaned in one light weekend. No, the story had been let go because the motivation to continue had been lost. What importance was there really in aging department gossip? What importance was there really in a defunct couple who would never again enter my life? More importantly, what reason was there to care about something that no one else now cared about? The truth was that my zeal for the papers had largely been spurred by the game that they had put in play. Now, for all appearances, the game was over. With summer, Suzanne and everything else would be left behind for the painstaking labor of mapping a Paleolithic Indian site as it emerged centimeter by centimeter from the earth.

The following is the entry I read that night, the last I would touch before the long summer interval removed me from the grime-smudged notes and letters that had led to my pain and humiliation:

August, 1980 Los Zamorros

In the last month, I have never been so busy and yet so idle, so excited and yet so bored. This curious dichotomy comes from two things: on the one hand, everything is new. From language to work patterns to social relations to quotidian rituals, all is beyond my current abilities. Life is also physically challenging. One morning might find me weeding corn or picking off slugs from the squash for hours at a time, straining my back beyond endurance. On another I might be pushing myself in the hunt, moving through steep mountains and cliffs for twelve hours or more, not returning to the rancho until well after dark. My spare, fatless and sugarless diet leaves me more alert and always hungry, and my weight has dropped so much that I feel as light and jaunty as a teenager (except on the really big mountains). In fact, the newness of everything makes me feel very young and fascinated as the young are with everything.

On the other hand, when time here isn't spent on something, it's spent on nothing. There are only my few books and no electronic entertainment nor peers to discuss the latest theories. There is no beer or rum to share with the men as in Tutzingo, where we would talk of women and things of the world. In fact, here I can only use signs or rudimentary parts of language to indicate the most prosaic of things, and it is probable that, even if my language skills were perfect, we would still have little in common to discuss. Information there would be, but that would come from a question and answer situation, not a genuine dialogue. It is personally lonely here, which leads to the ultimate source of boredom: oneself. I have quickly learned that the stream of consciousness is a short reel, replaying again and again with only minor variance. New thoughts are produced by active engagement, and the only active engagement now available is with the page before me. That, too, is of limited satisfaction, like any self-stimulation. The thrill of life comes from the meeting of differences. At this point, my meeting with differences is constant but unintelligible, like the viewing of a foreign art film. Or, to extend the metaphor, like trying to satisfy one's desires with nude photographs.

My welcome here is also ambivalent. Carlos, the Indian Affairs man, was not delighted to see me arrive walking between a mule and Doctor Gary. He gave the sense that his power was being challenged, even superseded. He has a low-level sinecure, while the Doctor brings real care and material free of charge, giving the bureaucrats extra pocket change from the money allotted this sector. He doesn't stand a chance against him. By extension, this has furthered his resentment towards me, and perhaps put me in the camp of the religious, who are hated in Mexico by many men of education and by almost all those in government. In this land it has long been the fashion of the elites to shift recriminations from themselves to the Church (as well as to America), which they blame for robbing the nation of its great ancestral wealth. In the halls of higher education, this resentment is combined with a loose Marxism, giving a theoretical coherence to its skewed view of ancient history. Although I have explained to Carlos that Dr. Gary is not affiliated with the Catholic Church, this does not matter. To him, God is a fantasy cooked up by the rich to enslave the poor, no matter what institute presents "Him." This, combined with Carlos's pride in his Indian ancestry (when useful) and his abstract hatred of gringos, makes the Doctor (and me) an especially hard pill to swallow. But he needs what Doctor Gary has.

The Indians, on the other hand, love the Doctor, but are entirely ambivalent about me. I had brought up a bag of goods for them as initial presents, and now dole out a few things and a little money for information, which they appreciate. The Doctor has also given me charge of some of the medicine (further embittering Carlos by eroding his power, even though Carlos refuses to apply topical ointments), both these things giving me use value. But I am still an outsider, a pale version of the "Spaniards" who have for so long drifted in from the surrounding area to kill and steal from them. They are also frequently annoyed by my questions, which must seem either stupid or overly personal at times. I speak like an overgrown infant and know next to nothing about living here in the mountains, about how to grow corn and hunt deer and treat the landscape. My ignorance robs me of any wit or entertainment value, except for my numerous pratfalls and poor word and grammar choices, which elicit a good laugh now and then, although not enough to balance my invasive presence. This makes me about as welcome as the Three Stooges would be in an American home: good for a few laughs, bad for co-residency.

Considering all this, then, being here is pretty good. While the locals don't love me, they don't hate me, and the lifestyle is oddly suitable in spite of the pitfalls. While I may sometimes fidget with boredom and long for a connection with the "real world," the peaceful simplicity of this world is growing on me. There is the lack of trucks down-shifting and of jets flying and the darkness of night, the stars so bright and numerous without the ambient light. There is the brightness of day, the air so crisp and pure that the sun makes everything sparkle or shine, including the air itself, as if it were a sheet of purified water. There is the stilling of breath in the mountains which leaves space to hear the farthest stir of wind in a pine or the scurrying of a packrat in dry leaves, tiny notes that embroider the pulsing undertones of the Sierras.

There is also the simple beauty of life in my hut, a little mound of mud and sticks that was abandoned and is now on loan. It is on the outskirts of Los Zamorros, closer to Tripper than to Carlos, far enough away that the domestic conversations of the locals are inaudible (although I couldn't understand them anyway). This is so perfect in the morning. Because there is no electricity, most go to sleep shortly past dark, which has me wake at the first touch of dawn when the day and I share the fragility of the newborn, as tender as the inner membrane of an egg. We grow together in silence after a small fire is built for warmth and tea, the day brightening just as the first sip is had. The Huichols value the morning, too, and one will rarely hear the clang of a metal pot or cowbell before the day is ready for it. As the tea steams, I sit on a small stump near the fire facing the open door and the luminous horizon, my chilled feet curled in my sandals on the earth floor. This earth, the smoke from the fire, my hovel of sticks and mud, make me feel a natural part of the day, as welcome and familiar to the world as the rising sun. I feel I belong, as much as the crows or lizards or squirrels who share my love of light and warmth.

It's made me think: why is it so different here than in Tutzingo? The technology is about the same for both: light is expensive and sparse, only a few have radios, neither have electricity nor traffic and so on. It's true that the Huichols are higher up in the mountains, with a thinness of air that grants different sensations, but both are isolated from the jumble of large populations and machines. No, the difference seems to come from attitude. The Huichols at times can be a pain, as some of the younger ones stop by now and then to ask for things, but overall they are content with what they have.

In Tutzingo, they are not, even though they have more and are all but free from famine through government and donor produce. Tutzingo is tied to the outside not only by a rickety old bus, but also by affiliation. They feel they are the country cousins of the masses in Guadalajara and Mexico City, as naturally entitled to global life as the city people. That they do not have what some others have is seen as a lack, as an unfairness that must be amended. While this gnawing need is not as strong in the younger women, and is absent in the elders, in the young men it is overwhelming, causing many to plan for a life in the United States to make their fortune. It would not surprise me to find in twenty years that Tutzingo has become as deserted as a nation in time of war, with all the young men gone and the town quiet and withdrawn like all towns that lack the dangerous energy of breeding-age males. It is my bet that, as usual, many or most will never come back.

The Huichols, on the other hand, see the outside world not as their rightful prize, but as a threat to their way of life. Most here resist the pressure to meld with the wildly evolving hoards of the megalopolis. They want it to go away. And it is more often the men who resist the most. They feel that they have been singularly blessed with the true knowledge of the world, that which comes from spirit, which can only be contaminated by contact with the outside. Thus goods, like the .22s the boys had wanted, may be desired but not at the expense of the prevailing ethos. As for the women, perhaps they wish for labor-saving devices such as washing machines that are now taken for granted by much of the rest of the world.

But this is a minor consideration. The greater one is that, by in large, most Huichols want to remain as they are, forever. Malnutrition is often obvious, meat-hunger is prevalent, and death through disease is a part of everyday life. The goods that they have are simple and pathetically few. Yet they prefer their life in spirit to all the food and goods that they might imagine they could have. It has struck me more than ever how ironic it is that Doctor Gary feels he must evangelize them. It is obvious that they live closer to the ways of the early Christians than every 'born-again' from Kansas to Wisconsin. It is true that many of their ways are not typically Christian, including their supposed promiscuity, and their xenophobia is hardly brotherly, although understandable. Still….

I asked the Doctor about this on his last visit a week ago, and part of his answer was expected: he feels he must evangelize so that the coming of Christ will bring salvation to them. The other part gave me more to ponder. He put it like this:

"They get their happiness from the demons their witch doctors conjure through the use of peyote. I cannot see how any good could come from that in the long run. But let's say I'm wrong; many sorcerers among these people are receptive to The Word. But still, their religion makes them turn from the perfect love of Christ. Even if some of the spirit forces they encounter are angels sent from heaven, these cannot bring them the eternal joy of Christ."

I told him this sounded like a tautology - that one first had to accept the goodness of Christ before one could actually receive His goodness. He laughed and said,

"There is logic, and there is what it real. Let's just speak of the Indians. It is not all good for them. They run in fear from the bad spirits and evil sorcerers of their world. And, more importantly for you, their world is a little one. It can't last much longer. It is better that they are prepared for it by me than by hustlers."

He was right in that, although it is certainly possible that their world could be protected from the outside, at least from its full brunt. However, given the state of the world in general and Mexico in particular, it is more likely that Jehovah himself would come rumbling down from heaven with his horsemen and columns of fire than the government would protect the Huichols from the greedy and corrupted.

Heading back to Tutzingo tomorrow for a few days, for supplies and to see Angelica and Juanito Rey. It's funny how I miss Rey. He's not my flesh and blood, but still, little kids have a way to make you love them. Must be a trick of evolution, or more likely, a calling from the spirit world. What else but inspired love could have anyone put up with the needy little buggers?

Tripper keeps insisting that we take peyote together. I'd prefer to do it in a Huichol ritual (if at all), but have had no invitation from them. What to do about peyote has been on my mind from the first, but no clear decision has come. It would undoubtedly give an insight into the Huichols - and maybe into myself - but there is also the risk of insanity. It still seems the best bet to wait for the right context. We must see what comes. ST

For Steven, the plot was thickening. Given that he was on the verge of flinging himself into the psychedelic revolution, it might seem puzzling that I didn't continue reading the notes that spring. In fact, it may have been this experimentation that killed him – death by a leap from a cliff to end the torments of demonic hallucinations. But the scene with Suzanne in the office had shaken me more than I cared to admit. It was now clear that it was not business that kept me from the papers, but my own puzzled unhappiness. My loss of control with Suzanne had formed a seismic crack in my cool academic façade that needed the quiet of a methodical archaeological exploration to heal.

Time would prove, however, that this tremor had been minor compared to the earthquake that awaited me upon returning to campus in the fall. If that future had been known, I might have leapt from a cliff of another kind by fleeing the ivied walls forever, to lose myself gratefully in the grinding monotony of commercial labor. Instead, I returned from the fading northern sun and the dirt of the dig to find a soap opera made especially for me.

I had come early to the TA office the day before classes to ensure my continued occupancy of the back office and had recoiled at the sight of the girls clustered and gossiping in the main room. Spotting Suzanne caused a sudden flush that quickened my effort to squeeze past the flock with a minimal amount of verbal contact, for the tone in the room made me suspect that Suzanne had disclosed our affair to my disadvantage. On being noticed, I readied for the barbs and snubs that were undoubtedly coming, but instead was met with something entirely different: silence. Everyone but Suzanne quickly looked elsewhere, not to hide contempt, but to avoid something more personal and intense. Suzanne forced eye contact, which was broken by me with a downward glance, a move that unwittingly solved the mystery: Suzanne was visibly pregnant. I quickly counted the months on my fingers: mid- April to May to …September.

That would be about 5 months, pretty much on the mark for her condition.

Still in shock, I clung to hope. Perhaps she had run out quickly for another man, to wash away my taste, so to speak, leaving in doubt the paternity. Maybe she had someone just before me, or, more likely, a steady squeeze- maybe the Neanderthal?- on whom she could lay the blame. She certainly wouldn't want to pick me if she had the choice.

On the other hand, why did the girls turn away? The alternative was unthinkable. I determined to nod curtly at Suzanne, brush past her into my office, and let life continue as before. Halfway through the nod, though, Suzanne touched my arm and forced another look that froze. When she spoke my name, it was clear the worst was to come.

"Ben, we have to talk." The tone was like a summons to the principal's office. It was over for me. With a mixture of anger and confusion, I simply couldn't fathom Suzanne's carelessness. She was well educated and a feminist, as all university women claim to be. Why was she not on birth control? And why the hell had she not gotten an abortion? Carol had at least told her boyfriend that she wanted his child at whatever cost. What I knew was coming seemed simply a slap in the face.

When the door to the back room was closed behind us, my righteous indignation could not be contained:

"Now, what the fuck is this, Suzanne? Don't say what I think you're going to say!"

"What? That it's yours?"

"Shit! And? And what? What the hell were you thinking? We have one little roll in the hay and then you dump me. OK. I lived with it. But what the hell is this? You don't have to go through any of it!"

"Were you asleep in biology class? And no, I couldn't just kill her."

"Oh, it's a girl now?"

"Or him. It doesn't fucking matter, does it?"

My anger had finally hit the mark. Good. No more of that smart-ass women shit. She was gathering her own fury.

"I was just doing you the favor and letting you know. My mistake. Forget it."

"Oh yeah, huh? And all your little girlfriends will forget it too? And the faculty and, what the fuck, the goddamn president of the United States? What the hell were you thinking? You know, they got a nice little clinic for this sort of mistake right down on State Street. If you needed to borrow some cash- no, just needed cash, no strings, you could have counted on me. Hell, still can, right?"

"Fuck you! I already told you no. Forget it. Forget everything."

She turned to leave in a huff, but I leaned against the door.

"Don't you get self-righteous with me, Suzy Q. You dump me then expect something from me? Paternity payments? Will the papers be served? Why didn't you tell your little friends it was some hometown sweetheart and leave it at that? Now you've got me with blackmail, right? These immoral tenured deviants in our department will go all gooey inside about the baby, you know, suddenly all concerned despite the little bastards they trail behind them in their serial marriages. If I don't pay out, I flunk out and you know it."

"I did tell them, asshole!" She was tearing up now. Excellent.

"Tell them I wouldn't pay up?"

"Tell them that it was a friend's from home. Like they believed me. They know something happened between us last spring. It was pretty obvious the way you moped around." She was back to her senses, biting her lip and looking fiercely defensive. I felt a surge of hope.

"No shit? Oh, I can make them believe you. I can mope around about that, too. Yes, and moan that you had another, one you cared for so much that you now carry his child. Yes, I am crushed." The more I thought of it, the more possible it seemed. "So that's the plan, right, Suzy?"

"That's Suzanne, you bastard. You know, I was going to tell you I hoped we could---well, forget it."

"We could be an item again? Oh, give me a break! Where were you these last, let me guess, five months? A little late for me to believe that."

"You were out in the sticks all summer, asshole." Her defense had turned to offense. I spoke quickly before her words held weight.

"Uh-huh. You didn't think of finding me through the archaeology office, huh? Listen, suZANNE, you gonna play it my way or work me over for financial crumbs?"

"Get lost. I thought maybe there was something in you, but I was wrong. Shit, and how!" She pushed me – hard - from the door and stalked straight out of the office. The girls looked back at me accusingly.

"Hey, she had another boyfriend, OK? Show's over. It's none of your business." I closed the door hard, but not before my look of anger was crossed with a brief, almost tearful look of sorrow. That'll get the hens clucking.

Still, much as victory had been salvaged from defeat, the day passed with a glumness that could not be shaken or understood. Suzanne had to be given credit; she was always one step ahead of the game. She managed to slip it in that she had hoped to rekindle our relationship. It most certainly was a lie, but it had irritated a misgiving that had arisen at the sight of Suzanne's rounded belly, a nagging voice that kept telling me that it was mine. Mine, mine.

To which I kept replying, "so what, so what?"

After a morning of this tripe, the notes came to mind as a balm, a cool breeze. The night to come would be a good time to fall into them, into the lives of others known personally, whose stories had endings more disagreeable than my own.

That evening, the September sun still hung wearily above the horizon when I propped myself in bed and found the passage that had been abandoned some long months before. It was eerily dated the very same day as this, only one year earlier:

September 12 Los Zamorros

At last I accepted Tripper's offer, with the added bonus that several Huichols also joined us. The experience was so different from expectations that it is difficult to describe, if such should be attempted at all. They say that the visions you receive are personal things for you alone and should not be shared. But I feel it is my duty to write them down before the feelings are lost or are cast into doubt, trusting that any secrets revealed will be kept from the wrong hands. A future self may one day read this as well, one that may be quite changed, but one that hopefully will be reminded that each life remains of one piece, that what 'once was' remains in what is now.

First, however, the cultural and social context of the "journey" must be drawn. This is not only necessary for a broader understanding of the experience in general, but also for a greater understanding of myself *by* myself. Such insight might help to critique and correct the impressions so far written of my hosts.

To begin with, it is difficult to assign a proper place to Tripper. His name brings up images of Cheech and Chong doing the waste-head comedy routine, and his appearance and vocabulary does not help to alter that impression. On the other hand, in reality he is nearly always sober, is a serious husband and father, and has delved deeply into the meaning of his life's experiences. But he is also peripheral to the community, as alien here as he would be in an IBM boardroom. It is probable that he would be on the edge no matter where he lived, and he agrees, as he once told me that he was the "universal shaman," with some pride. His relationship with his wife still puzzles me, for whatever reason.

In any case, a week hasn't gone by without him insisting we take peyote together, something he assured me would broaden my life immeasurably. He maintains that the Huichols use a variety that never causes distress, which seemed unlikely to me until I saw a ten year old child choking some down. I quickly pointed this out to the mother, aghast, and she only laughed lightly, shrugged, and went back to her *metate*. After questioning several of the men, who together made one complete Spanish speaker, it became apparent that this is not only permitted, but encouraged. Anyone can take peyote anytime he wants, which some do at least once a week. This surprised and disappointed me, wanting the majesty and pomp of ceremony with such an event, but truth is truth. I knew from my readings that they did have intense ceremonies including peyote, and realized that it might actually be better to get to know its effect in a routine setting. It was also this casual approach, especially regarding the children, which convinced me that an episode with Tripper might be manageable, if not enjoyable.

The preparations for the event were minimal. Tripper told me to go without food and water starting the night before, explaining that this was how the Huichols avoided the nausea that was typical for those who used it in the States. I told him about the child, though, who undoubtedly had not prepared himself, and Tripper made a caveat: the Huichols typically ate very small amounts of peyote for recreational use, just enough to get a nice glow that subtly changed the perception of the world, to one that whispered the sacred. This information caused me some concern, as it was apparent that he planned for us to take a large quantity. Just how much would that be? His reply:

"A shaman's dose. You gotta have a vision. This is your virgin trip. You don't carry any baggage yet. This can be the really important one."

This sent a shiver of fright through me, and I told him that it would be unlikely. He laughed and responded, "we'll see." And damned if he didn't snooker me into taking enough to link arms with the shifting realities that are exposed or created by such toxins.

So it was fortunate that I fasted that night and morning, just in case, before arriving at Tripper's an hour after sunrise, as told. He was seated cross-legged before a small fire, surrounded by amulets and crystals and the other things that made up his "xiriki," or personal altar. He was singing lightly, his head down as if in trance, and I was able to make out some Huichol words in his song, 'Tayaupa' and 'Tatewari,' which are the names for Father Sun and Grandfather Fire respectively, two of the most important deities in the Huichol pantheon. Oddly, it is to Tatewari that they pray for beneficence. The sun is too powerful, a dangerous source of energy that has to be appeased. The fire, however, warms them and gives them light at night and cooks their food. It makes sense in that way. Throughout native Mexico, the sun has had to be appeased in some way, which brought the ancient Aztecs and Mayans to offer to it thousands of beating hearts. The Huichols are not so "civilized," thank God.

At the fire, two young Huichols, Jerome and Lazarus (Lazarus had been with me that first trip up), stood by us, hands filled with peyote buttons, joking around as if waiting in line for a Saturday matinee.

It was difficult to get over the contrasting sense of amusement and profound seriousness. It was obvious that the boys were on a casual lark, escaping for a few hours the daily drudgery. Tripper, however, was downright melodramatic, and I wasn't sure how to treat him. He was obviously acting as a *mara'akame*, or shaman, whether or not he was recognized as such, and it was hard to decide whether to kid him about his role or give him the lead. When he looked up from his chant to reveal the round blackness that his eyes had become, the later course was chosen, as he was clearly so high that he, at the least, took himself very seriously. Even the boys became quiet as he clutched a cluster of ceremonial arrows and pointed to the four directions of the Earth, then to the center in the fire, and then bowed his head again in a murmured chant. This was repeated five times in as many minutes, at which time Trip sat upright and pulled two large peyote clusters from a woolen bag that hung by his side, a beautiful thing embroidered with the outline of a blue hummingbird. He held the cactus before him for a moment, as if blessing the host, then motioned me over with a slight movement of his head. The boys went off to the side again, laughing as they popped a few cactus buttons into their mouths before wincing from the bitterness that I assumed.

My assumption was more correct than imagined. Tripper had me sit to his left side by the fire and then handed me the cluster of buttons. Although I had thought to have only a few, as the boys had done, the act of sitting before the fire brought on a curious suspension of ego, as if my personal characteristics and will had gone to rest in some corner out of the way. What was left, my awareness, simply fell into a vacuum in space where it was drawn along as if in a sealed tube. One might say the pull was irresistible, had there been anything within me that wanted to resist. Instead, I simply took what was given me and ate the absurdly bitter plant until there was nothing left. This was followed by a silence that was both a deep recess of peace and an anti-chamber for great movement, like a womb before the first contractions. A small corner of my mind could still taste the horrible bitterness in my mouth and worried, "what have I done?," but something else simply brushed the voice aside as if it's complaints were the cries of a baby with minor colic.

The world remained normal until I noticed that my attention seemed to be floating on a soft buzzing in the ears that gently lulled it on a magic carpet of sound. I looked around. Tripper's head remained tilted toward the fire, his mouth moving in quiet chanting or song. His body was buried in a large wool blanket that had been quilted with yarn of startling colors, making bright fluorescent visions of deer and corn and cactus dance together in a scintillating shock of visual energy. We sat on the dry, sandy ground before Tripper's hut, the irregular clearing hemmed in by small rock ridges from which sprouted stunted pine and grass and scrubby, thorny bushes and cactus.

From our location one could catch a glimpse of a huge ravine about a quarter of a mile away, a sight that was now a wonder of puffy white clouds that hung so high in the sky, yet stood at nearly eye level from our altitude. The sun was rising bright and clear and hot in the thin crystalline air, now dancing on the highest crest in that bit of horizon not obscured by pines and masses of rock. The boys broke the reverie with another laugh before they ran to some unknown destination. Except for

Tripper's mumbling, which now seemed more like the soft undulation of waves, I felt alone. Not lonely, but alone and clean, pure before the eyes of the world like a prophet in the wilderness. After staring at the sky beyond the ravine for an unknown length of time the idea came that it would be good to get up and walk to its edge. As I started to rock forward to move my stiff legs into a crouch, a clear, high voice sounded over my left shoulder.

"Wait for me!"

I turned around with a slight start and saw someone, or something, that should have made me scream in horror. Perhaps that distant voice in my head did. But the rest of me took it in as part of the normal flow of life. It, perhaps a "he," was a gnome, a "little people," a cross between a leprechaun and the classic bald-headed, earring-wearing genii made popular by the detergent soap. The little genii-gnome stood no more than three feet high and wore, besides his earring, purple silken pantaloons that flowed as if in a continual breeze. He was also, it is almost embarrassing to say, green on every part of the skin that showed, from the face whose countenance wavered from baby to geezer and back again in one glance, to the bared child-like chest and tiny feet. His teeth were all white, setting off the intense redness of his tongue as he spoke. His presence enthralled.

"Well, what are you waiting for? Let's go!" Again, his voice was too perfect, high and vibrating like a Munchkin's from the Land of Oz. Then, with a grin that finally brought on fear, he bounced around the tops of rocks, from one to another along the clearing towards the valley's cleft until he fell from sight somewhere near the edge. Each jump plucked something like a chord in my chest, as if he had gut-hooked me and was pulling the line, but without pain. I pushed myself to my feet, suddenly nearly frantic to find him, and fell against a jumble of jagged rocks as my numbed legs refused to obey my will. The blood rose from the scratches on my hands, whose sight sparked a tremendous surge of power that pushed me to top speed along the broken ground with no thoughts, no wall between me and the blood running through my heart to my legs and lungs. The ground passing beneath looked like camera shots made from a moving, bouncing jeep, and the rhythm froze my attention until something said, "Look up!" It was a fortunate warning, for this brought me to grip a knotted bush that clung to the edge of the cliff three thousand feet from the gorge floor.

"Over here!" The gnome pulled my attention to his little green form as he balanced impossibly on one foot atop a pinnacle set some fifty feet out from the cliff. He then spun on that one foot and swung the other leg quickly around, twirling like a discus thrower to gain momentum before he hurled himself towards another pinnacle another fifty feet away. He made it with ease, flawlessly landing on one foot, his arms raised out like a soaring bird, while the tugging at my guts became so strong that it made me gasp. With this, though, came the realization that his leaps had not really been jumps, but pulls, as if strings were yanking him into the air. As he turned to jump again from his pinnacle, the strings came to view, wavering like a mirage, appearing as a fine, gold and silver belt of cords that led from the gnome into space. As he jumped, the cords flexed like a series of elastic bands. I knew from my readings that I was not the first to witness these strings. Carlos Castaneda, the peripheral anthropologist and trickster, had mentioned them in his books, and the Huichol themselves had a word for them: *kupuri*. What had been most impressive about them, however, was not the sight, but the feel, as if the stings had been those of a giant harp whose music reached deep into the heart and very guts and made them dance to their vast, rubbery vibrations.

The gnome then literally pulled me from trance again, as he actually tugged at my hand. This made me jump and yank my hand back as if it had rested on a hot stove. At this he gave a brief but loud laugh, showing again the bright red of his mouth that evoked such inexplicable fear. He stopped abruptly and spoke.

"You will have to learn to jump someday, you know." The grin had dissolved into pursed lips that made the hair stand up on my neck. Then again, there was a sense of compassion in his words. I could only stare mutely.

"Fear is for those who believe they have a choice. You must know better. You must either follow the road made for you or die huddled and cringing by the side. Either way, there is still no choice...." His voice trailed off before he leaped straight from the ground to land on the tips of the branches of a gnarled old tree. He balanced there for a second, and then skittered along the tree tops like a cartoon being run at double speed. His rapid, jerky motions almost made me sick. I had to sit down or risk falling from the edge of the cliff. The sense of nausea continued until something inside loosened, then separated.

What seemed at first to come from my stomach, an intense floating sensation, settled in the center of my chest, as if in my heart and lungs. With this came a sense of suffocation that made me take a great, panicked breath. With the new air came a surge of feeling that mounted like floodwaters until something in me painlessly broke, like a soft earthen dam. Tears streamed as a torrent of great, wonderful love for everything, for the sky and air and sun and mountains, the trees, the gnome, Tripper, Angelica, Rey, Lacey, even the university, everything, rushed through every cell. The thought, the certainty, arose that fear had imprisoned me by its creation of self-incrimination, of doubt and shame and sin. Without this fear, this impurity, it was easy to live in God's Land through love. I laughed through my tears with the realization of how shallow my life had been, at how simple everything was, at how pure and true our lives could be. There it was, always, before us all: just play the strings of your destiny and let your song carry you through life on a wave of shimmering bliss and joyous wonder. What stupid, dead worlds we have confined ourselves to!

At some point an internal impulse had me stand, wipe the dirt and tears from my face and turn back from the cliff. Although my sense of self seemed to have returned to normal, a tremendous energy and dexterity remained that caused me to nearly skip back along the rocky path. This sense of "self," while me, was now scrubbed of gloom and care. All around, colors shimmered brightly, and everything had an undertone of truth, of divinity. Apparently, the big part of the experience was over, and what was now being experienced was the reduced affect that the Huichols so often sought. It was clear to me then why the Huichols remained in poverty with their old ways: what use was all the junk of the world compared to this outer beauty and the inner sense of the sacred?

I trotted into the opening expecting to find Trip at the fire, but instead found the small plaza empty with only a small spiral of smoke remaining as proof of a former presence. This struck me as extremely depressing, and a sudden vacancy of thought brought me to sit before the ashes in a simple attempt to find some warmth. The sun was now at mid-noon and the heat of the day at its greatest, but it was necessary to hug my knees to fight off rising shivers. An instant of time had moved me from elation to despair, and now it felt as if a dark pit was looming, one in which there was no hope for escape. The terror of it was so absorbing that Tripper's voice brought a shock that made his words at first hang without meaning.

"It's not so easy, huh? It's not supposed to end this way, but it's not always controllable."

My eyes had been pressed against my knees, and now his image came as a blur. As the sense of the words came, it seemed uncanny that he knew my thoughts, but still, it also seemed quite natural.

"It was so perfect, so simple. How could it change so suddenly? Why would it?" I looked seriously at Trip for words of consolation, but instead he puzzled for a minute, and then brightened with understanding.

"Oh, you're talking about your trip! I was talking about going to sleep. Just conked out. What happened to you?"

My vision of him cleared, revealing his rumpled hair and a face still laden with the effects of a deep afternoon siesta. "You tell me. We're now *hikuritamete,* tripping brothers."

He shrugged, then turned to say something in Huichol towards his hut. A few seconds later, his wife came out with an amber bottle of local brandy. She had the same flat expression as usual.

"Go on," he said, "you look like you need a spot or two." He held the bottle out for me and at first it was difficult to judge its distance in space. I took a small sip, then a larger one. He was right. It was just what the doctor ordered.

I told him about the gnome episode, and then focused on my turn to despair in hopes of peeling off the blackness that now oppressed me. Tripper took a big drink from the bottle and spoke as if he knew exactly what my problem was.

"You expected the reality of your high to last forever. You thought you had overcome life. When you started to come down, you realized that there was no permanent escape. Just temporary shifts in perspective."

I asked him why the better perspective couldn't be permanent.

"You are what you are. I've had so many trips, I got this down cold. You see, reality is both essence and perspective. Essence is – who knows? We can only know things by contrast, and contrast is perspective. So in life you get a certain perspective more or less handed to you. Then you take peyote and get another perspective. When the chemical wears off, you get your old perspective again. Neither is 'essence,' neither is the immutable truth, so one simply turns from one to the other. "

Trip handed me the bottle, but this was waved off as I argued that essence, truth, had indeed revealed itself to me. Now, it was being unfairly replaced by my old limited perspective. It seemed a matter of divine punishment rather than the dueling of alternative perspectives.

"Ok," he said, "you're right in a way. You saw *more* of it. You saw a bigger picture that took in more of the essence. But you live what you live." He stopped for a moment, apparently pained by thinking. "Let's say you're a coyote, see? And one day a sickness or something you ate makes you see things from a crow's perspective. Now you got more of the truth. But next day you're still a coyote. The rest is like a dream. You aren't living that other perspective, and in time you can't even feel it anymore. The best you can do is to take the insight as true and change yourself then and there on the spot as much as you can." Tripper took another swig after a deep sigh and continued.

"We come out of ourselves to see a greater reality. This coming out is the ecstasy of the ancients, the communion with the gods. When we step outside, we become one with one or some of them. Knowledge and glory falls to us like an infinite series of tumbling dominoes."

A vision came to me then of knowledge as an eternal process, stretching from the beginnings of consciousness to its infinite horizon, from its maker to the made and back to the maker, like an eternal Socratic lesson. Yet there *was* Truth, pure essence somewhere within us. I had felt this, and was about to tell this to Trip when he made a summation:

"You know, Steven, at bottom it's about beauty. God, knowing there are gods and maybe even a God of gods, makes life beautiful, and knowing beauty brings us to the mountain of the gods. It's all about finding beauty in life."

As he finished, Marta came into view off to the side. She was cleaning the baby's behind with a cornhusk, wiping with brisk, efficient motions. Her frown was deeply set. It then occurred to me with the certainty of peyote insight that in the beginning she had looked to Trip to make her happy, not with his love, but with his connection to America.

Not everyone was content here, as I had first thought.

She had wanted to become a rich woman of the world. It came to me then how she starred longingly at the jets that sometimes passed, how she marveled at them as they glinted silver in the sun, and how she dreamed of riding them like the goddess rides the wind. She had dreamed, too, that her babies would grow into powerful people who bowed to no one because they had everything they could ever want. She had given herself to this man with all her hopes, a man who instead had become a Huichol, and not a whole or competent one at that. She was thankful that he didn't beat her when he drank like many other men, but she would have taken his blows and more to ride high over the earth on silver wings.

CHAPTER 8

Steps and Stumbles

The last entry left me unexpectedly morose. Steven, clod that he was, had lived something of a life for a while, even if he had fallen into delusional mysticism. Yet even that had been tempered by his realization that some of the Indians saw the old ways as dead ends. It seemed like his life was coming together, at least as far as was possible for his talents, while mine was flying apart, all hell breaking loose because of crazy or irrational women. I had become my own clown, hoisted on my own petard, betrayed by my own pleasures and, much worse, by my own schemes. It was not enough that my social set would shortly conclude that the responsibility for Suzanne's foolish predicament was not mine, nor that the birth of the child would not result in ruinous child support or any other penalties of obligation. No, not enough; for she would always be out there, holding the truth like a sword, forever ready to wield its power. The woman who had burrowed into my vulnerable spot could reappear anytime like a cicada grub released to life again from its 17-year slumber. She had dug into me and could resurface whenever the impulse struck.

Needless to say, the TA office was now avoided whenever possible. Every now and then I would catch sight of Suzanne's increasingly wide hips or recognize her waddle, and would turn in the dark hallways or crowded sidewalks to disappear into the anonymity that a massive university provides. Little could deliver comfort, much less the increasingly distant relevance of my purloined papers, but I continued to read them, on and off, seeking an end already known, like a captive of a daytime soap. Bored with the last entry about the "trip" and desperate for something to push aside the darkness of that semester, I again turned to the letters. To my surprise, the postage dates showed the next to be written by Steven, shortly after his little dance with the gnome. It had been my assumption that Lacey would now be in pursuit and Steven in tactical retreat. What had gone wrong? Had Angelica dumped him? Was he preparing for a victorious return? I opened the letter and hoped that more than some theological ramblings would greet me:

Dear Lacey,

It often feels that you are with me in our letters, so I count it as very fortunate that another may be sent again. I came back from the mountains yesterday to buy a few things, including a rifle in Hueuquilla, if the right man to bribe can be found. It seems the Mexican government so mistrusts its citizens that it tightly restricts their right to rifles (but not shotguns- their range is so limited), and yet anyone with a little money can pay an official for the necessary paperwork. So, ipso facto, we have a Hamiltonian government where only those with capital might own the machinery of power.

Anyway, the rifle (a .22 repeater) would be for my informants, all of whom swear that game is too scarce to try and bag with bows and arrows now. From what I can see, though, it is the rifles they already own that have cleared out many of the bigger species. These, along with our new neighbors, the "alternative" crop farmers who kill animals to reduce crop damage. However, it seems unlikely that deer and boar would forage in cannabis and poppy fields. Then again, maybe they are like horses that get purposefully drunk by gorging themselves on windfall apples. Perhaps our mammalian brethren are not as different from us as we think.

Of alternate consciousness: a hippie ex-pat with a Huichol wife got me to take a large amount of peyote last week. I had no desire to, and had only planned on trying this once in a ceremonial setting, but he was insistent, and when we finally sat before the fire for the endeavor, he projected an almost magical quality that did not allow "no" for an answer. (His name, by the way, is not related to his drug use, but comes from his being the third in his line. He admitted to the moniker "James Andrew Sikorsky III," no relation to the helicopter producer. He is no preppy. His father runs an OTB office in Albany. James has hinted that his dad's work is often "way off-track," or illegal.) The experience was not as expected, and perhaps I may never do it again, but it did give me a possibly applicable revelation.

First, as to the unexpected. From what I have read (primarily from Barbara Myerhoff), seeing colors and getting mystical feelings are par for the course, but the extent of the hallucinations came as a surprise. On that, skipping the details, a spooky little gnome appeared who made spectacular, death defying leaps from rock to rock, suspended by a matrix of shining strands that looked like spider webbing. He also gave me 'words of wisdom,' which warned that I must "take the leap" at some point, which may seem like a metaphor for all sorts of things in life, but I felt he had something more specific in mind. Perhaps the hallucination was from an unconscious aspect of myself that understands something that my waking mind refuses to acknowledge. Maybe a cancer is forming in me, or an incurable strain of hepatitis, or something else that is precipitating a 'leap' into illness? Or, even more frightening, might this truly be a portent of an actual death-defying leap to come, however impossible such prescience might be?

Things can get strange when you're a stranger in a very strange land. Really, though, it is most probable that the "gnome" was an aspect of myself insisting that something in my life must be faced that has been avoided in the past. What this might be has given rise to an introspection that is perhaps unwise. Yet shouldn't we know the truth about our lives, ourselves? Or might it be better sometimes to sweep some things away, like sordid affairs engaged in before marriage?

So, in pondering this, how are you? Are you still troubled by a feeling of lack of purpose? As I have warned myself, this form of introversion might become a kind of shovel that can dig a very deep trench. Oddly, however, my psychedelic experience has given me something of a solution for that. It came after the gnome had disappeared from the cliffs as I was returning to the campfire. It was a realization that "being" was the answer to purpose. If we open ourselves, being becomes complete and perfect in and of itself. There is no need to feed the poor in Calcutta or discover the cure for cancer to be fulfilled. That might be what we are called to do, but the doing is not what saves us. What is needed to open the gates of Eden is to have complete faith in the eternal spirit. We gain this through a constant adoration of the essence of creation. That is very hard to do when depressed, but if you could make the effort, who knows?

While this 'revelation' might sound like fairy dust, it does explain a few things. For one, it explains why the Huichols, almost alone, resist modernity and the outside world so fiercely (with some exceptions, to be sure, including Tripper's wife). The experience of "being" given by the cactus makes all else seem petty. With it, even a life of material poverty would seem so much more than a life of affluence that is spiritually flat.

This explains the downward spiral of many religions of conscience in the western world, doesn't it? You have said yourself that your family was bedrock Episcopalian until this century, when everyone stopped believing. Why did they stop? Wasn't it assured fulfillment of physical needs?

As the physical nature of the world became more dependable, so the spiritual became less, until God became nothing but a human symbol for compassion, a philosophical abstraction aimed at reducing physical suffering. With that, many lost sight of the subtle essence of the universe, the spirit.

What people still don't realize is that without a divine source for our base, nothing is "self evident," not even compassion. We could easily turn into a culture where once again the big fish eat the little fish. But I stray.

So, what else could these religions of conscience become but a relief agency? With only a vague notion of God, with no solid belief in heaven and none in hell (God has become the ultimate relief worker), what else would it exist for? With that, why should we not simply donate to the Red Cross, or better yet, pay higher taxes and sleep late on Sundays?

But Lacey, this advancement came at a huge price. It left the question(s) about the meaning of life unanswered. It is my belief, now stronger than ever, that without the sense of God in a religion, it withers and dies, along with its followers. People must be shown that there is a real thing, an experience of God open to everyone, an experience by which everything else becomes mere background. In fact, it is my belief that we all are aware of the divine, deep down, and it is this knowledge that makes so many in the wealthy, materialistic cultures so depressed. There, people have plenty of everything, but all that is nothing when compared to an experience of God, or what may be called (ecumenically) Pure Being. The more they are fed the religion of material compassion, the more they are led from the spiritual, causing them to long for it all the more strenuously, and to search for it where it cannot be found.

Perhaps, then, this is the cliff I should jump from? The one that drops us into pure belief? Perhaps this is an answer for you, too, although to tell you to "go jump off a cliff" seems a little rude. Seriously, perhaps if you dedicated yourself to the belief that everything is suffused with goodness and sacredness, you would be given what is needed so much by us all. Just as important, you might also know purpose, which, I am coming to believe, is twin to a reverence for life.

Of course it is hard to maintain reverence in our world. It seems as easy as breathing for the Huichols, but for us it is nearly impossible. Nearly all our forms of knowledge and discourse, especially the routine, lead us in the other direction. Our ancestors altered our perspective with the seed of their want, which grew into the tree of mechanical knowledge, and they plucked the apple and ushered us into the new age of increasing technological wonders and decreasing wonder in general. Is this not the Faustian bargain? The sense of reverence is the pearl of great price and worthy of our greatest effort, regardless of our ultimate success. While it is certainly best to reach our goal, which has always been spiritual paradise, just the reaching gives our lives meaning and ultimately nullifies pessimism. To know that it is here, to believe it is behind every bush waiting for us, can only ennoble. But to believe in only the body can only bring death to the soul.

Anyway, after returning from Hueuquilla, I will leave again for Los Zamorros. The doctor is supposed to come, bringing with him his assortment of salves and sermons. It is so beautiful sometimes up in my little shack, living by the sizzle of the night fire and its smoky plume, watching as it floats high into the black sky towards a sheet of stars whose clarity is a stunning revelation for those of us from the fog and smog and light of the Midwest. It is fitting that our industry would cover the shock and glory of the stars with its pollution just as it has shifted our perception from the glory and awe of life. The nights here have convinced me that no one can remain a materialist before this sparkling entrance to eternity.

Not that all is perfect. It is often exhausting living as an eternal outsider and eternal source of amusement. While I no longer attract a constant crowd, it is still rare when at least someone isn't staring at me, taking mental notes to share with his clan for nighttime amusement.

It's also a pain not having easy access to water. We don't have a broad river to use here, but rather a part-time stream that often retreats into little sinkholes that cannot be used for bathing for the obvious reason that one can't drink bath water. So washing water has to be scooped first into a pot, and it is such a nuisance that, save for my face and hair, I often let my body go as nature dictates. This is not a sweaty climate, but it is dusty, and exposed portions of my flesh have become deeply stained by the red-brown soil, marking me as a creature of the earth. The simple diet and the smoke from the fire seem to keep body odor down, but that is a personal opinion, and one gets used to one's own smell. In hindsight, perhaps it is wise that you do not plan a visit.

It also seems that true friendships might be impossible to form among the natives. Everyone else is so embedded in their genetic history and in the land that I am little more than a passing oddity. No one is rude, but no one is *simpatico* either. Such things take time for adults, it is true, and there is Tripper. He has become as good a friend among men as I have had since high school. For all his four years here and his marriage and his children, he, too, will always be an outsider. Of course, he says he would be one anywhere, and this is probably true. His loose ways would ordinarily have kept us apart as well, but the circumstances here have enabled me to see that he is a sincere man with the courage of his convictions. His wife is another matter, but that is not of great importance. Here, men and women are production units, running like businesses back home, and they keep to their own gender for empathy and entertainment. This, along with the local mysticism, is something that Trip has mastered as well as any Huichol.

Excuse me – the bus is starting and it is time to go, although, in truth, the schedule isn't always tight around here. One never knows. On Fridays like this, the bus driver often stays over for several beers before he takes a siesta at his *casa chica*, his mistress's house. But now, with the engine revving, it is possible to assume that his pleasantries have been completed. Keep reaching for the stars. And if you find someone, I will understand. If he brings you to a better place, I will be glad for you. Please write when you can - anything that's on your mind.

Must run, your friend, Steven

What, Steven, no "Love"? Still, his words of care were mixed so adroitly with his off-hand referral to an outside relationship, to his own self-pardon, that he earned my limited admiration. How much better for him than me, who had so thoroughly botched the Suzanne affair. Who would have thought that Suzzanne's stony countenance on the bus had *not* been a dismissal? Who would have thought that our fling had *not* caused her torment and regret, that a seething self-contempt had *not* compelled her to drag me down with her? Who would have thought that she *would* have unprotected, fecund sex? And who the hell would have thought that she would decide to have the baby? Just as inexplicable, she had also let go of the notes, the letters, the whole Steven-Lacey thing as if they had been nothing, mere distractions in her more eventful life. Which they, in fact, really were: nothing more than bits and pieces of cheap gossip.

All this led to one inexorable conclusion: since it was impossible to believe that Steven was superior to me in cunning, yet still soared above his women, it could only be that Suzanne was gifted with a peculiar genius. And since her wit clearly did not match my own – how could I ever think that? - this genius could rest only on a superior grasp of social life. While Suzanne's thoughts on religion or spirituality were unknown - no one in my field but Steven admitted to any such beliefs – it was clear that her priorities were not contingent on immediate gain. She, in short, had principles. I had tossed those away long ago after reading *Das Kapital*, and had felt liberated because of it, unchained by a morality that had been fashioned by a society intent on maintaining its class system. Yet it seemed, of the two of us, that Suzanne had come out the better for her scruples, in spite of the hardships she faced, the ones I never would. It was me who seemed to be wilting in misery while she stepped more and more briskly into a world unknown except for its demands of sacrifice. I could not conceal my contempt for such complacency, but could not hide from the fact that her belief in something beyond herself had somehow given her an advantage. I had even developed a grudging respect for her.

It was most likely this that gave me the desire to seek her presence in the office, even though something would have to be offered for the exchange. That she probably would accept nothing meant only that there would be nothing to lose from the endeavor. However, just what might be gained wasn't quite clear. Could it be that my dormant conscience needed to be assuaged? A look within, to my relief, revealed that it was not this weakness of self-imprisonment that drove me. It was, rather, a need to satisfy the curiosity that Suzanne's approach to life had elicited.

At that moment, though, I decided to proceed to the next letter, this one from Lacey. There was still considerable suspense concerning the precise time of her thorough mental dissolution and the particular event, if any, which had acted as the final catalyst.

The envelope slipped from its bow. It was smudged, as if by soot, and a faint odor of smoke rose from the pages:

Dear Steven,

Thank you for your last letters. I am sorry that exams have kept me from a more prompt reply. The third and last of the exams was finished just yesterday, and I still cannot believe it. They seemed to go well, all in all, although nothing is certain here, as you know. For now, my relief is mixed with a sense of loss, as if all this study has created a huge space in me that is now vacated, an empty hole that needs to be filled. I could get to work on more grant proposals, but am just too exhausted by papers and theories and thinking in general. It would be nice to wear a pair of those silly little antennas on my head like Cindy and eat ice cream in the sun, but all the business of autumn is upon us, and daylight is growing shorter. It feels, in fact, as if my normal life is sinking with the sun, the fear and darkness growing ever greater within as without. I know it is not uncommon to feel depressed after a big event, but this has been growing for some time. The fear of the dark place within makes me feel sometimes that I am going crazy. This is not said to worry you - I am certain things will right themselves in a few weeks or months, as they normally do, but I have brought it up in consideration of your experience with the gnome.

The truth is, Steven, from my current perspective I can only understand what you have said in abstract form, and there have been so many abstractions in my life lately that what is really needed is something real and simple to hold on to. What the "gnome" said about overcoming fear sounds good and true, until it is experienced personally. What you have deduced about belief and meaning and reverence sounds great until the attempt is made to implement it. While you mean well, remember that you are talking from a platform of health and optimism, where everything seems possible and glory is just around the corner. When one is in a dark place, one sees only doom and gloom. The world does not appear as if it is ultimately good, but just the opposite, and the best one can do is posit that life is meaningless and absurd. That is so much better than branding it evil, as it all too often seems to be. Honestly, I think the nihilists and existentialists are working feverishly only to convince themselves that they stand at the entrance to a circus rather than to Hell.

I believe you about the Huichols and their commitment to a sacred view of life. But they apparently need alkaloids and isolation to maintain this, and even then, as you have said of Tripper's wife, it may not be enough. You mentioned that it is impossibly hard to keep a sacred view in our world, but that it is enough to constantly try, as the effort is itself a part of the sacred way. Once again, it sounds good, but this does not work for the dispirited. Believing in God or Jesus is precisely like believing in Santa Claus: once maturity lets the secret of him out, there is no way of stuffing it back in.

You are right about the pride of knowledge. I willfully cast off my spiritual beliefs as a teenager to join the ranks of my more sophisticated peers. But what appeared to me as logically superior then is now magnified many fold. At some point we may *want* to believe in Santa Claus, but we could never do that, this side of madness. Just as certainly, though, the fear of the blackness also seems to lead to madness. And having no way out leads to madness. Yet the realization of the absurdity of the situation gives no relief.

I envy you your sense of "Pure Being." I have heard of this before, but still don't know what it means. If it hadn't been you who said it, I would say it is just nonsense. Still, how can one chase something with all one's heart that cannot be seen or definitely known? I do recall the feeling of sacredness in church that touched me as a little girl, and similar sensations have come in quiet natural places, but those sensations were more like something called "peace." At this point in my life, peace alone would be enough. But to gain even that I would have to drop everything, my whole life, and live in the woods or a monastery, neither of which would suffice for long. A life of non-doing would eventually make me just as miserable.

Please don't push new romances at me. Forgive me if I suspect you may have ulterior motives for this, but it would be hypocritical to point fingers. Our situation as it now stands is my doing and does not allow me to be jealous. Please have a free conscience, whatever may be going on. This may sound cold - I do hope you will be around for better days - but it would be selfish to hold you for a day that might never come. It is also impossible for me to imagine becoming involved with someone new right now. My worry is that I have brought you harm, and might bring you more. While my need for you has grown, it is best for everyone that I become well first. Signs of my mental illness have had somatic repercussions, one being so unbearable that it is painful to relate, but it is important that this comes from me first: I have developed an obsession with plucking at the hair on the top of my head. At first it appeared related to exams, but it has become worse, if anything. There is now a clear circular bald spot at the whorl like a monk's, which might be only an annoyance to a man, but is an unspeakable shame to me. I not only cannot will myself to see the world as a holy place, but can't even stop myself from creating this horror. I feel less and less in control of my normal functions, let alone supernatural ones. Revelations like yours have become only distant dreams.

It would be a solace if you were here, though, although my friends, particularly Carol and Suzanne, have really come through. Carol is truly amazing. Even with her new baby, a part-time job, teaching and her thesis, she still finds the time and the temperament to deal with me. Her affirmation of life raises my own maternal instinct at times. It is a powerful force, perhaps a woman's special bond with what you call "Pure Being," but it is wrong for me now. My current neuroses should not be allowed to spill onto a child. This is what my mother did, toss out her own version of fainting and reaching for the 'vapors,' and I can only thank God for my father, when he was home, and Maureen (the cook) when she was sober. It occurs to me now that I have become my mother except, thank God again, there are no children around for me to damage. Why, with all she had, weren't we enough? Why couldn't my brother and I have evoked that great instinct in my mother that has so empowered Carol, with all her financial problems? I am so afraid that it is a disease with genetic links, and that no prescription can ever relieve me of this madness.

It sometimes makes me cry to recall your sweet proposal, and how lovely it might be to have a family of my own someday. It is all through no one's fault but my own. I am so sorry. I am also sorry for troubling you when you are the one living with the hardships and uncertainties. Please, take care of yourself. My friends and family are here to support me through this silly crisis. Write when you can,

Love, Lacey

Bingo! It was clear that our little debutante was well on her way to the emotional equivalent of a back-alley dumpster, although the process was not proceeding as suspected. It had seemed obvious that her demise was to come from Steven's confession of his affair or an academic disaster or the confluence of the two. Instead, what had driven her mad was simply the steady beat of loss, of loss of purpose and meaning. All along, the correspondence between the two concerning such things had elicited a mixture of scorn and bewilderment from me. What was wrong with them? Everything was cut and dried. You lived life and died. From ashes to ashes. You made of life what your circumstances, ability and will permitted, then laid down and died. What horror could there be in this "darkness" that is existence? It is our home. Consciousness is the great fluke in nature, the kink in the dance of atoms and quarks, but it is temporary, shaken out quickly to allow the random collection of the laws of matter to continue. In fact, self-reflection may be present only in our own little corner of the universe, significant to no- thing but us, as short-lived and meaningless as a shooting star. I felt like grabbing Lacey, slapping her and screaming, "Live while you can, you pampered fool!," until my current circumstances admonished me. While they would never make me tumble into a meaningless void, a void that had no place in my mind, life hadn't been so pleasing of late. Similarly, while the madness of self-mutilation could never find purchase in me, I had developed the embarrassingly adolescent habit of daily masturbation. And as with Lacey, the idea of starting up another relationship just then, no matter how shallow, was out of the question.

With this last thought in mind, it occurred to me that it had come time to pay Suzanne that visit. It was mid-noon Wednesday, the time when Suzanne would be coming off her Paleo-genetics 201 class. I briefly considered going to her apartment, but it was out of character and hinted too much at a pining desire to resume some sort of acquaintance. No, the office was neutral territory where no pretense was necessary. If she rebuffed me there, I could simply shrug my shoulders, blame her obstinacy, and move on to some sort of work.

I walked down to the university, passing over the river on the old train trestle and up through the arboretum where Suzanne and I had walked that warm spring day the April before. It was cooler now but more glorious, if anything, as the array of colorful autumn leaves on display could only be found on a property designated for a maximum presentation of species. As crisp and blue and clear as the day was, the only others sharing this final wealth of the year was an older couple walking their dog along the river. The manic energy of the students was missing, now confined to the dorms and classrooms and quads. This struck me as deeply sad, conjuring the feeling that life had somehow passed by, and I quickened my pace to bury myself in the crowds on the sidewalks and staircases of central campus.

My arrival among the masses did bring some relief, but the urgency to get to the office and talk with Suzanne persisted. This became so pressing that by the time I had raced down the hallway of the social science building and opened the TA door, my nerves were jumping as if poised for a formal presentation. While slipping off my coat, I shot a glance around the desks but could not see Suzanne. The others ignored my presence. This was not unusual, but now it annoyed me. Someone would now have to be approached to inquire about Suzanne.

I did so casually with Anna, and she unexpectedly snubbed me.

"What do you care?," she sniffed, then turned back to her work, pretending that she wished me to go away. It was obvious, though, that she desperately wanted to speak, to deliver a sermon, and needed only the proper opener, a verbal submission on my part. It was painful, but there was no other expedient course.

"Hey, I want to know. We're grown-ups here, aren't we?" At this a flush of self-righteous anger came to her face. She took a long breath and turned, slapping me with a look of contempt.

"We're taking a little interest in something that is purportedly none of our business, aren't we?"

I began to protest that it was Suzanne alone who concerned me, not whatever else she possessed, but she cut me off. "They, she, is in the emergency room, if you have any interest. She nearly miscarried last night. And, no, she didn't ask for you, and why would she?"

It shocked me to hear that she had gone to the hospital, but I had had enough of Anna's passive aggression. "You can take your little gender-solidarity indignation and cackle all night with your fellow hags for all I care. I only asked about Suzanne and was hoping for a little civility. Let bygones be bygones and all that."

"And calling me a hag is going to do that?"

"Let's stick to Suzanne. I don't give a rat's ass for your opinion. It is clear that your only joy in life now is pretending that you are somehow superior to me. Perhaps you have finally awoken to the man you married."

"At least he's a man. You are a rat, ass and all. And the only thing bygone around here is your ability to trick another woman with whatever small charms you may have, not that I could ever see any."

"Ooh, hisss! The cat is playing with the rat! Oh, save me, save me!" I gave her a look of feigned terror, then rolled my eyes.

"I'm afraid it's too late for that. Did you hear that Shari might be coming back next semester?" Anna searched my face for signs of panic, but I honestly could give her none. Shari was now nothing but a fruitcake from a season past.

"She really must be fucking nuts to come back here. Hey, enough already. So what's up with Suzanne now?" My unexpected anxiety for Suzanne and the baby had been hidden long enough and now the time had come for serious information. Thankfully, Anna shifted into her professional demeanor and complied.

"She's not out of the woods yet, although they do have it under control."

"What's 'it'?"

"Pre-eclampsia. It's like an allergic reaction to the fetus, where the mother's blood vessels constrict and shut off the oxygen and nutrient supply to the uterus. It also causes dangerously high blood pressure in the mother. They would have induced labor if she had been another month or so along, but now would have been too dangerous for the fetus. Although they sometimes do it for the life of the mother."

"So…."

"So she'll probably be OK for now, but she could have another crisis. They have to be very careful with medications because of the baby."

"What's her room number?" It seemed that Suzanne was out of danger, but I thought a visit might be essential anyway. It would raise my profile with a minimum of effort. Anna, however, had not moved over to my side by a long shot.

"I don't think you should go. You two aren't on the best of terms, and I doubt your sudden appearance would have a beneficial effect. What's the point? It seems to me that you'd be doing this for your own image, not for her." She sliced into me with a flat look that would not allow finesse or maneuvering. As often happened with 'things Suzanne,' though, something unexpected, apparently genuine, popped out of me.

"Let's be straight about this. You know this might be my child. What happened, the way it happened, could make anyone upset. But I want to make sure they're OK. There's more in this for me than you." I was suddenly grim, determined, and a little angry. Who made her the gatekeeper?

"Maybe on the physical plane you do. All right, if they'll let you in, she's in Room 413, section B. Let us know about her, OK? And if she asks how you got the number…"

"I got it at the desk, OK? Jesus, Anna."

I had hoped to get a little work done but now had no recourse but to go directly to the hospital. This annoyed me outwardly, but the same nagging something that had made me rush to the office continued to push, to lead. The source, its nature, was unknown, and a spontaneous thought wanted to call it destiny, although I did not believe in a 'calling' or divine inspiration. Objectively, we were born with such and such abilities into such and such circumstances, and acted according to the meeting of these predispositions with the physical environment. Such it was with me, undoubtedly, although it still felt as if some magical spell had enthralled my will to redraw my path. The strange compulsive feelings that directed me first to the office, and then to the hospital, could no more be denied than instinctual urgings in the primitive beast. It, things, seemed out of my hands.

It was not until I entered the emergency room that my forward momentum was checked by the pervasive, subtly evil smell that all hospitals have. The odor of disinfectant only underscored the underlying smell that it had been intended to mask: the smell of death. When we think of instinct, we must think of the nose, for it and it alone stirs desires and fears unfiltered by cultural nuance. It is the smell of a woman that readies a man to touch, and it is the smell of the hospital that readies him to run away from the undeniable presence of disease, suffering and rot. Placing a mental image of Suzanne in these smells seemed wrong, perverse. Every base instinct called for flight, to let the world re-form itself into what it should be. The world of the hospital was one that teetered frighteningly on the edge of *terra incognita.*

Still, my compulsion pushed me from one desk to another until an attendant was finally able to direct me to the room with the same number that was clutched in my sweating fist. Once there, actually standing before it, the door seemed too innocuous and anonymous to open onto Suzanne and her crises. Biting my lip, I tapped lightly on the plastic faux-wood veneer. A soft, unfamiliar voice answered.

Peering around the door, I was shocked to see the withered buttocks of a gray-skinned woman just as the nurse-orderly lifted her from the bed by the legs with one hand and wiped her clean with the other. Nausea roiled through me as the idea flashed that this was Suzanne, now made ancient and infirmed by the baby and the disease it had caused. Fortunately, before sickness led to panic, her same soft voice rose again from the tired but still pretty face of a dark-haired woman in the adjacent bed. She looked different in many ways from recalled images of months past, but she still shone with the essential qualities that marked her as Suzanne. I swallowed my horror and walked stiffly to her bed, brushing aside the largely symbolic curtain. My mind slipped into its Suzanne mode.

"What, Suzanne, you so desperate for attention you had to come here?" Although the discomfort behind the forced humor must have been obvious, she laughed helpfully. It was clear from the slight dullness in her eyes that she had been sedated.

"I thought coming here would be the only way I would see you." She was still smiling, going along with the joke with no accusatory look. She held up her left hand by my side.

"I'm happy you came. It was almost all for nothing, you know?" I quickly grabbed her hand to stop the direction of the conversation.

"Anna told me. I'm glad you're all right. We'll take your classes for you."

She nodded and turned her head from me, then looked back, catching me by surprise. "You're so uncomfortable here, aren't you? You're always hiding, hiding from the obvious. That's why the girls like you, you know. You're like this little boy who pretends to be tough when he's scared. It's so cute and brave. It just screams out for nurturing." She held my hand tighter. There was no way out save for silly humor.

"It's just a plot to get the womenfolk. You don't have to worry none 'bout me." I expected a cynical smirk in return, but the drugs had brought out her emotional side like a bottle of sugary wine after the high school prom.

"But I do! Now I have two boys to care for. He's a boy, you know. That might be why I almost lost him. Bigger antigen reaction. Like father, like son." I kept looking for signs of hostility but could find none. She was shooting dizzily from the hip.

"Suzanne, I never ran from you. You never once got in touch with me after. I just thought, you know…"

"Oh, but you were gone. And you didn't try to call. Remember, you accused me of making a fool of you? Ben, look, I really am glad to see you, but you try to hide. From life. From death. From love and loss.

From all the obvious, inevitable things, Ben. They're the things you can't avoid."

"You can avoid love."

"No you can't." She let my hand go and turned slowly away again, to my relief. We sat in silence for a full half-minute until I spoke as a precursor to my leaving. Things were going in unexpected directions, to points unknown, and that was not good.

"So, when they letting you out?"

"Tonight or tomorrow morning. They just want to make sure everything's settled down."

"So, everything's all right, then? The baby's fine?"

She nodded and turned towards me, holding my hand again. "You don't have to worry, Ben. You don't have to do anything. I'll be OK. Carol and Anna said they'd come by if I needed help, but I don't. I'll be ready to go in a few hours."

"You sure now?" I had slipped my hand from hers already and had moved beyond the range of the curtain. The compelling drive that had gotten me there had gone, leaving me dangling like a panicked climber in the middle of a cliff. My legs couldn't move fast enough. Her answering nod barely registered. I backed out and began to turn at the door when she spoke.

"You can come visit me if you want. At my place, I mean. No strings. I just would like to see you now and then."

After mumbling a vague assent to her invitation, I made it down the hall to the elevator as fast as possible without breaking into a run. I breathed the pestilent air as shallowly as possible until the lobby floor was achieved and the imprisoning doors were flung open to the tinted light of a crisp autumn evening. There, over the ambulances and octogenarians in wheelchairs, hung a wisp of high clouds that had been transformed into a dramatic slash of pink and purple by the sun that squatted on the horizon like a rubbery egg. The long shadows of the trees spoke of the darkness to come, giving even greater cause to rush to the bus stop to find my ride home. I did not want to see any more people. Night had become a looming threat. At home, I would bury myself in my work and wash myself of the day. Nothing was more desired than to be back at my place, back with my studies, back with my old concerns and plans.

Still. Once home, after hours hunched over my desk, after hours spent pealing one page from the other in my thick books, separating the great minds from the vainglorious, a pressing need arose to make a human connection. It was late, and there was only one convenient location available for chatter. I opened Steven's notebook to the next personal entry.

October 2

Two occurrences should be mentioned from the last few weeks. The first happened the morning before we left Tutzingo for Zamorros again. The doctor had not shown up as expected, and I was packing some final "bargaining chips," goods used to exchange for information, on our departing caravan's mule when his plane sounded in the valley. Of course everything was stopped for him. The two of us have not only developed a mutual system of aid - I carrying things and dispensing prescriptions, he giving me the support and prestige necessary to do my work - but we have also entered into a friendship through a dialogue about faith and life. So it seems, anyway, although it might just be that the need for intellectual conversation has convinced me of a mutual personal affection. Angelica, for instance, is smart but limited by background and averse to spending cognitive energy on invisible ideas. Tripper is of the other extreme, *too* engrossed in the invisible, with every conceivable fantasy as real to him as the feet on his legs. The doctor, though, is a practical man who has come to his ideas and devotion the hard way. As he told me, he had once been a "physician" of the body, a flesh mechanic as so many doctors are. Life and death had changed him. With my own background in the social sciences, I felt we walked on similar paths, yet were drawn in many ways to different conclusions.

When we met at the plane, a discussion started almost immediately, one that reiterated former themes that would (once again) prove relevant for my investigations. In fact, something close to an argument started with our first handshake. His grip seemed a little lighter than usual, and he gave a quizzical look that mixed concern and reproach in one glance. I asked him, flat out: what was the matter?

"I've heard that you used peyote with the hippie." He said this with another glance that was now pure reproach. He turned his back and bent to arrange his bags and boxes. Moving to help, I told him that this was true, and that it had been a deep learning experience. He was not placated.

"I've known of young people coming down here and jumping off cliffs from that stuff. It's a toxin manufactured by a plant to keep animals like us from eating it. It does not hide this fact with its horrible taste. I thought you would know better." He continued sorting his things, unnecessarily. It was the first time he had lectured me like this, and it was hard to contain my annoyance.

"Gary, this is my profession and these are my chosen people. It was necessary to experience the substance that is so central to their lives. I had hoped to do it with the shaman, but he hasn't even let himself be known to me, if there is one. But nothing can take away the beauty of the experience. You must know something about that after so many years here. And you can't believe that these people are simply self-destructive." We now had packed everything and began to walk towards the school. After a brief silence, he settled, thankfully, into a pattern of respectful debate.

"I don't question your right, but only your judgment. Obviously you have survived, and I hope you have come to understand the danger in taking this substance. Regardless of my own prejudices against it, I hope you will not put yourself in that kind of jeopardy again."

We had reached the school and paused to drop the materials in the shade towards the back. The class was in session but Angelica insisted on welcoming the doctor into our cooking patio and began preparing coffee. Our departure would wait. We filled the air with small talk until we were settled in, sitting on ancient wooden chairs before the remains of the breakfast fire beneath a light canopy of thatch. Angelica handed us our cups and left, leaving me to handle the serious turn of mind that had overcome Gary since our meeting. He came at me, like a cryptic first move in chess, with a question.

"So tell me, what was so special about your experience?" He would clearly continue to condemn any drug use, but I determined to answer without guile. More and more, it has dawned on me that life is best served by understanding, not by winning. The colors and the gnome and the disturbing warning came to mind, but they, the visions themselves, had not made the core of the event. Concentrating on the overall experience rather than on the spectacular helped my thoughts arrive at the kernel.

"Behind the whole experience is experience itself. You feel that the world is alive and full of purpose. This purpose is not yet to come, or already past, but *now*. It gives you the certainty that NOW is a miracle, a treasure to cherish." I settled into my chair and *café con leche*. Gary frowned into the last wisps of smoke that rose from the fire to vanish in the hardening light of the morning.

"So you believe the Huichols have a superior method of relating to God through floral toxins?" He continued to frown and stare into the fire pit.

I told him carefully that this was not my point at all – rather, that this experience had been special; that divinity had been felt in an immediate way, not from above or outside or from a sermon or domed cathedral but from within, as if I were complete, worthy of grace. "How," I added incautiously, "could this be bad?" This brought a flush of anger to his face that caught me by surprise.

"Do you think any of this is new? Don't you think the Apostles were aware of chemical reactions that mimicked revelation? Don't you think that Paul or Christ Himself would have recommended these substances if they might bring us closer to God? Haven't you thought about this, and about why we were given the DNA we have in the first place? You say you felt complete, but how complete were you if you were seriously disoriented by a drug?"

We both took a breath. After a while his normal color returned and he shifted again into a discursive mode.

"Let me put it this way: how do you really know that you had sensed divine being? If you were to have adulterous sex, for instance, you might feel love at the climax, as if the affair were self-evidently correct. Facts on the ground, however, would almost certainly prove you wrong. There would be guilt, jealousy, broken families and perhaps violence. Only the selfish man or the stupid one would say that the feeling of the moment justified the action at large.

"You must be aware by now of the pervasiveness of sorcery both among the Huichols and the *campesinos*," he went on. "Even these people recognize that sorcery is wrong. Where does this dark force come from? Did you know that the most malevolent sorcerers of the Huichols are failed mara'akames? Did you know that the evil ones get their power from peyote visions too? You see, this sort of experiment with individual sensations and "inner truth" is dangerous and unpredictable. You, alone, have no idea whether the "good" you experience is really good in the divine sense. You have no idea whether the 'god' you experience is really God or a demon." A slight shift in the breeze brought us the strong, delicious odor of tortillas toasting over a wood fire from the next house, and as the doctor breathed in deeply, I used the pause to jump into the breach.

"But you know as well as I do that the formal religions, the coherent and codified religions of large social groups, have been responsible for some of the great evils of history. To go by the group and not personal feeling is easily as dangerous as going with your own feelings. And as you said, the Huichols know all too well that sorcery is an evil. Their sense of right and wrong may not apply to those outside the tribe, but within it is strikingly similar to the Christian view. They know the difference between an experience of good and one of evil."

He took another long inhale, relaxed now and unperturbed by my argument. He had obviously heard all this before.

"Personal revelation informs a personal vision of the world, one that is necessarily less adequate than one sanctified by scores of the brightest and holiest throughout the centuries. More important still is that the great faith of the West is based on a singular genius, a prophet of unparalleled insight. Yours can only be that much less than His. As for experience, He welcomes you into His own through faith. This is not only important for the end result, but for the process, for to have faith, you must give up the belief in the supremacy of the personal ego. When that is eliminated, then selfishness and evil are eliminated."

I replied that when the ego is eliminated, false prophets might gain control and perpetrate horrors.

"Yes, but that is why we have a code that is not constructed from personal ecstasies. Following the New Testament, the Catholic or the Episcopal or Methodist church will not demand that you drink poisoned Kool-Aid."

"But the charismatic might."

"My faith is Presbyterian, but my mission is non-denominational. We pray for the experience of God within the fold, within the faith. Besides," and he broke into the first real smile of the morning, "we come as a group to spread the word. The Huichols, too, have a coherent society, and have bound the peyote experience primarily to tribal continuity. Unleashed onto the world without sufficient background, it would produce far more Charley Manson's than would the preaching of John Wesley. Chaos. Chaos. Mainstream Christians do not stand for or spread chaos. And that is another point. Established religions can have tremendous social impact. They can unify in ways that ecstatic experience cannot. And it is only this unity that can confront the pervasiveness of evil in this world."

It was difficult for me to pull all the strands together. If one never got beyond faith, if one never experienced divinity, why would one stay with faith? On the other hand, if one did have such experiences, should those of Moses and Jesus be given greater weight because of their antiquity? And wasn't it possible that these ancient revelations had been or could be manipulated to serve the status quo, or to create a new secular order? On consideration, it seemed to me that personal revelation held the greater promise for truth and redemption. Organized religion could too easily be used as a tool to subjugate and control the masses. I offered this opinion to Gary, to which he gave this tempered reply:

"You might be surprised to hear that I agree with you, to an extent. Personal experience of the divine is tamper proof and God's greatest gift. But how can we know it is truly from God, especially if it is brought about artificially? In organizations, power is often accompanied by corruption, but it is only through organizations that the power to save the world might come. Our Christian faiths, codified for everyone, follow the standards set by the wise and faithful and most of all, Christ the Lord Himself. This serves to legitimate and unify all who come under the roof of His moral righteousness. If we join His cause, we can bring the faith to all the nations. A unified Christian world would be much safer and saner and healthier in every way. That, I believe, is part of God's design."

"And this design," I added, "includes Armageddon and the Second Coming."

"Yes, and that is another discussion. But before the final judgement, we will have a reprieve, a paradise on Earth for the repentant. I can't tell you exactly what the promised paradise would be, besides a life of peace and joy with God. But it almost certainly must be brought forth by our compliance with the great commandments to love our God and our neighbor. It could mean a time of healing brought by our faith, leading to a joyous ascension. Or an Earthly paradise made by humans from God's blueprint. Either way, it enforces the point that we must actively work for the coming of paradise. If the divine is reached through drugs rather than the will, what good does it do? How could it fundamentally change us? We must willfully submit to the Savior. It is our hearts that must first be changed before the world is changed. Ultimately, there can be no other way."

And so the door was closed, each of us unmoved from our beliefs. It is not that I think him wrong, but rather uncomprehending: without having had my experience, how could he judge? It seemed to me that peyote did not distort or create, but amplified and personified what was already there. Still, he did accentuate some of my own misgivings. That circle of speculation, however, must be left for another time. More relevant is my recent encounter with another man of 'god.'

A while ago I noted that there had been no indication of a Huichol medicine man in the area. That changed last week, however, and the reasons that he had remained unknown to me have become clear. For one thing, he is not from this rancho (Los Zamorros), but from the next one over, "Xipate." While it is still formed by (extended) family members of Los Zamorros and is no more than a few miles from us as the crow flies, the problem of proximity comes with the terrain. We are not crows, and to get from Zamorros to Xipate requires a walk down four thousand feet of steep rock, then a walk up another four thousand feet of steep rock. Even for a Huichol, this is not the sort of thing that is done on a whim. Coincidentally, this fact explains in part my hallucination of the gnome. Just imagine how wonderful it would be to be able to leap from one cliff to another in this area. There certainly must be a great deal of frustration in being able to see a place with ease but to reach it only with great effort. How this tribal desire made its way into my subconscious, though, is still a puzzle.

Back to the main point: as silent as one is supposed to be about one's experience with peyote, mine got around (through Tripper evidently; no one else was told) with such amazing speed that children were jumping up from behind rocks and shrieking with laughter within a day in imitation of my gnome. More disturbing still were the dour looks the older people began to give me. They would come alone, or by twos and threes, especially the women, to stare, not as before but in a way that made my hair stand up.

When asked, Trip told me that a vision like mine meant that I had received a calling. He said that normally only the mara'akame receives visits from the spirits, meaning that my position now is something like that of a bomb with an unpredictable timer. When asked if he had told anyone of my experience, he promised that he hadn't mentioned it to a soul, not even his wife. That brought to mind her presence by the fire, and the question: had she learned English through my conversations with her husband? To me, that seems as improbable as the gnome.

And still the people kept coming. Very old people, like babies, look remarkably alike, but there are so few elders here that it was easy to pick out one who stood before my hut who was not from Los Zamorros. When I asked in my bad Huichol where he was from, he replied in perfect Spanish that he came from Xipate, pointing to the adjacent mountain. I noticed then that he was not really all that old, perhaps fifty, but that the power of the elements had baked and creased him like an ancient, exposed cliff. He wore such an assortment of animal bones and charms that he clicked when he moved. After several more uncomfortable minutes of staring, he got to his point. He was the first of the many gawkers who had admitted that he had a point. He told me that he was the local healer and spirit guide and that he had heard of my experience with the gnome (he called it the "hikuri") and was interested in hearing the story himself. He also mentioned that he had purposefully avoided me before. He said that many crazy North Americans and Europeans had come through the local towns looking for shaman wise men. He told me that he found them "loco" because they had no appreciation for the wealth and stability of their own backgrounds and the dangers of the path they pressed to follow. He knew they did not have the commitment, usually created by a dire need, which directed most to his profession, nor the slightest knowledge of Huichol and peyote spirits.

I then asked him why he was bothering with me. Surely other crazy *blancos* had taken peyote and had crazy visions. He replied with an unsentimental analysis:

"It is not the man but the vision. The little *duende* you saw was the *hikuri* speaking, the spirit of the peyote. Why it has chosen you, I cannot say. No man can know in entirety the thoughts of the *hikuri*. You do not know them at all. But they speak to me through you, and so I am here. So we must plan a sacred journey to Wirikuta. So you must come with us. Do you drive a car?"

It's funny how often we are deflated, after thinking we know better. How many people say, "I never win anything," thinking that God has singled them out as losers when, in fact, very few people can ever win anything of value. It would break the system. Yet we continue to see ourselves as special even when that special-ness is manifested in bad luck. At first, the visit of the shaman made me feel like the anointed one, especially since he claimed that the visions I had were not supposed to come to someone from my background. Then he revealed that his interest in me really came from a need for a car. What had seemed to separate me from other gringos merely resulted in my being used as a gringo.

From accounts of the trip to Wirikuta, or what Barbara Myerhoff called the "Peyote Hunt," it is known that this is a sacred journey that the Huichol shaman and his group should take every year in the late fall/winter period to respectfully harvest peyote. It is also considered a sacred journey to the tribe's roots, and special places along the route are paid homage to, such as the site where the first man and woman appeared, or where the fire and sun spirits emerged, or where deer developed a relationship with Man, and so on. This is a hard, dry journey of about 300 miles into the northern desert that has for centuries been done on foot, the whole taking about forty days. In the past few decades, though, the journey has increasingly become a motorized one. I'm not sure if anyone now does it the hard way. Apparently Horacio, the medicine man, didn't, and now he has found his ride. My little vision probably means nothing to him.

Actually, it is better if it doesn't. The tremendous good fortune of being invited to the apical event of Huichol life has come my way for only the price of a microbus rental, and it is better not to be part of the story. It should take place in December, right around Christmas. Gary might well be appalled at the pagan way I plan to celebrate Christ's birthday. But God's creation is most certainly big enough to accommodate the myriad highways we find to journey back to Him.

CHAPTER 9

Away in the Manger

Suzanne was released from the hospital the day after my visit, although I did not witness that event myself. In fact, an entire month passed before I would see her again, and then only because she herself came down to the offices to thank us and wish us a happy Thanksgiving. My inattentiveness was not due entirely to callousness, but also to the cause of her gratitude: we had been working double-time to cover her classes since the emergency. Her doctor, a Lebanese, must have received his degree from one of his nation's medieval universities, for he had ordered her confined to bed for the duration. As things had since settled down, she was now allowed to take short walks, and had shown up to not only thank us but to inform us that she would be back for the rest of the term. This last had not been approved by her doctor, but had seemed logical to her, as teaching was far less demanding then carrying nearly eight months of baby up and down the sidewalks and corridors. The girls flocked around her like petals around the bud.

This, for once, was a great relief to me. While it may not have been entirely my fault for not visiting, an odd sensation was summoned on seeing her. I had known guilt before, but in most instances it had come to me as a child when caught with hands in the cookie jar. Now it appeared unexpectedly, chiding me with rude recriminations for having left her alone, especially since she had pointedly invited me to her apartment, and I struggled to reason away this discomfort while hiding behind the books on my desk. In truth, since the impulse had touched me to see her that day, it had never entirely abated. Guilt had arisen again and again like a force of nature, but in its wake it always trailed a stench of revulsion. Her condition was too mammalian, too needful and sanguine. While the sex act was hardly antiseptic, it brought an intensity of pleasure that was its own reward. But need brought obligation, and in its tacit admission of weakness, it concealed a strength that bent the will.

This situation brought to mind the time my mother had the hysterectomy, when I took the "EL" from the university, clutching the dirty cold steel hand rail by the bench as the grit and grime of the dark February day snapped by. No one smiled. The most content were those who hid behind magazines or earphones, removed from this unwanted collection of witless faces that in minutes would melt away like dirty snow in a gutter.

After arriving at the hospital, I found her lying in bed in the same kind of torpor, and with the same need and dazed acceptance that would one day envelope Suzanne. The musky scent of the convalescent bed had mixed with the vapors of bathroom cleanser and the hint of urine. I did not ever wish to face my mother's sense of need again, the dumb proof of our bodily limitations and intellectual vanity.

With that, it came to me that my guilt was the reaction to the wrenching struggle between social compassion and self- preservation. This alleviated my discomfort considerably. Still, Suzanne was not simply an idea, and with her rising like the dead that day in the office, some sort of rapprochement had to be formulated. Once again, though, as had become so customary, Suzanne surprised me as she breezily, even happily, broke the ice by calling me first to her attention.

"Ben, is that you back there hiding in your books? Are you afraid that my condition has cursed me with an appetite for masculine flesh?" The girls laughed and snickered, leaving me no choice but to defend my dignity by pretending, to no one's belief, that my attention had been lost in studies.

"What's that? Ah, Suzanne, glad to see you up and about! So you've shrugged off that auto-immune disorder?" I stood then and leaned casually, showing polite interest, in my doorway.

"It's not exactly auto-immunity. The baby is its own free agent."

"Much to the chagrin of Women's Lib."

"Ha, ha. No, nothing's been shrugged off. I've just been lucky. And it's near the point where the baby would survive on his own, if he had to come out."

"A "he," huh?"

"I told you that last time. Yes."

As usual, I had taken her good mood and turned it into peevishness. What concerned me, though, was that she had remembered our last meeting so well. I had assumed she had been too medicated to remember, or would have been too embarrassed to admit that she remembered. Until now, it had also seemed a safe bet that her affection had not been genuine.

"No one told me that you were doing so well. I didn't want to bother you, just in case. You know my presence isn't exactly a balm on your gentle mind." The girls became still, watching as the relationship that they pretended did not exist revealed its hidden text.

"Ben, just do as you feel. You're terrible at emotions, so you might as well wing it. You couldn't do worse."

"Perhaps we should have a dinner some time to relieve your gestational cravings? On me. As the expression goes, that is."

"I'm not sure whether your generosity should be accepted as a study of the rarest of behavior, or rejected for its freakishness. Perhaps you'd better call first." More tittering, of course, just as it occurred to me that I did not know her number. Before the reflex could be stifled, I publicly asked for it. Cindy "oohed" like a 13- year- old hearing about her friend's 8th grade crush. Suzanne laughed too.

"You're resourceful, Ben. I'm in the book. Besides, I didn't really mean it, about calling. Surprise me." She laughed again and turned back to the circle. Her profile revealed that a recent gain of weight had given her a slight double chin that looked as soft as angel food. It surprised me to find that the thought of touching her buttery form was arousing, as if a tribal archetype had whispered from the base of my skull. This was immediately followed by another voice, one with which I was more familiar, that advised me in no uncertain terms to run. Run, you idiot, you're off the hook now, run!

I harrumphed in my most distracted scholarly manner and closed the door. Instead of feeling saved, however, it came to me that a channel of inquiry had been opened that had to be resolved. Thanksgiving was in two days, and Suzanne's plans for that holiday had gone unspoken. If she were to stay here, my inattention to her lonely state might cause more scorn from the girls. It was not that the scorn itself concerned me, but rather what caused the scorn - that they might think of me not as a womanizing cad, which was perfectly acceptable, but as a man who was afraid of a woman. I myself did not know which might be closer to the truth, but it could not be known to the outside world that the feminine art of emotional warfare could fluster me. The door had to be opened again.

"Oh, Suzanne, by the way." They all stopped talking instantly and eyed me suspiciously. "I presume that you're going home for the holidays. Just in case, though, perhaps Thursday would be the right time for that dinner." I said this with the flat good manners of the Victorian gentleman, and waited to hear her thank me, but, alas…. Instead she asked her own question.

"And your parents have done the wise thing and disowned you?"

"Maybe they have, but I wouldn't know. Travel's a mess now, and there will be all of Christmas Break. I was going to have my own kind of Wild Turkey for the holiday and then do a little puttering in the stacks. Exams next semester, you know."

"Then I'd love to join you! My mother has confided that Dad has sworn to kill the bastard, (pardon the term, my son), who has dishonored me, so I'm waiting to let things cool and see them with a fait accompli. Oh, except I know the co-ops. I think my place would be better. We can split on the turkey and the cooking. I'll get the fixin's and you get the wine. That sound easy enough?"

It did, all too easy. Suzanne's voice was sincere, but her eyes were laughing. In fact, I had never heard so much laughter in a room that was now without a sound. The gamble had been taken and lost.

"I'm just a hot-plate kind of guy. You might want to keep me at peeling potatoes."

Then good ol' dependable Anna chimed in again.

"Oh, no, we are all brilliant here, aren't we? Take this as a learning experience, Ben. Heat up a can of peas! Feel the awe of stuffing a turkey!"

"I would like to say something about stuffing, Anna, but I'm sure you'd take it the wrong way. Then again, maybe you'd take it any way."

"At least I own up to liking turkey."

"Either you're referring to your husband or you can't say what you mean."

"I mean I take responsibility for my appetite." I was on the verge of rejoining about the apparent growth of her appetite when Suzanne broke in as referee.

"Wait, Anna, wait! You can't argue with him like this. You already have a husband!"

"Every peg has its square hole," I had to add, drawing the beginning of a snarling insult from Anna that was thoroughly and finally extinguished by Suzanne.

"Fine, fine. How about 10:00 then?"

"In the morning?"

"Unless you want to start at 10:00 on Wednesday. Of course in the morning. Could you get the turkey? I don't think I should carry it upstairs right now. You have to get it today to thaw by Thanksgiving. Is ten enough for my half?" She produced a ten-dollar bill from her coat as if it had been waiting backstage, right on cue. Could she have played me that well?

"Oh, no, I've got it."

"We'll ante up on Thursday, then. You can leave it in my fridge…"

"No, that's all right, the co-ops have a walk-in I can use. Wine or bourbon or both?"

"Neither. That's for you. I thought you'd need, you know, want them. Whatever you want, but you have to make it home alone."

Anna got in the last shot. "That's a relief."

I ignored her. "Alright, then, *vin de bourbon*. I'll keep in mind that the bus stop must be found all by myself." Suzanne handed me her address as I winced inwardly, recalling the mess that had been made at another bus stop. No, the mess had been made before, in my bed. The bus stop had been the universe's critique of that disaster.

With the door closed behind me, finally, my smile dropped instantly. I had just made a very, very bad mistake. Another mess in the making. Suzanne drew these out like a poultice drew out pus.

The turkey had been surprisingly awkward to carry. Even though I had gotten the smallest one at the supermarket, at 14 pounds it was too big for my backpack. It had to be carried in front like a frozen, detached potbelly, and the pain in my lower back intensified with each step from the bus to the co-ops. Worse was Thursday morning when it had to be heaved to and from the bus, then lugged around several blocks of sordid student housing until the small, rusted numbers on Suzanne's building revealed themselves on the second pass. As I walked inside and then up the stairs, bottles clinking on my back, it became obvious that the heat came with the rent. It was overly warm in the stairway and probably a hothouse in the apartment, at least comparatively. The school and the co-ops had accustomed me to permafrost throughout the cold months, and already anything above 65, especially after first coming in, made me sweat uncomfortably. I was mad that this would betray my nervousness unjustly, and when Suzanne opened her door, the blast of heat made me gasp.

"Ben! What's wrong? I mean, at the moment?" She was dressed lightly in a pink-flowered summer moo-moo, a pregnant and barefoot Polynesian mistress awaiting her mighty hunter. I told her about the heat and complained further about the weight of the turkey:

"And why don't they grow little turkeys for today's independent households? I've broken my back for more leftovers than we can ever handle."

"Don't look to me for sympathy about carrying a back-breaking load. Or include me in today's carefree lifestyle. Put the turkey in the sink and the backpack on the couch and take off that coat. You're going to soak through in a minute." I could smell nutmeg and thyme in the air and knew that much of the heat came from an oven working in the small area of a one-bedroom apartment. As sane women always do, she had made her plain little hovel into a comfortable living space. There wasn't much, just a table and chairs and sofa and some end-tables in the living room, but they had been fixed amid little things like drapes and kitchen knick-knacks to a warm and hospitable affect. It had long escaped me how I, along with most other men, created apartments that were colder lived in than empty, made hard and unforgiving like a mechanic's garage.

I stripped down to my civilian clothes and felt the air against my wet shirt with gratitude. It was understood from the start that this day would call for booze, and I pulled out a half gallon of cheap California wine from my pack, sliding it from the cushion of my surprise bundle of papers. The bottle of bourbon was left for later.

Suzanne arched her eyebrows in mock appraisal. "Ah, Chateau de Cheap. A fine vintage. I'm glad for once to be on the wagon. And what's that? I hope I'm not so boring that you had to bring your work with you." She had noticed the two manila envelopes with their edges poking like horns from the pack. I took them out with flourish and dropped them onto her coffee table.

"Should we begin, then?" I said with an exaggerated accent, immediately plopping on the sofa before she could answer. "These, if you will recall, are the axis of my original sin. What got us together in the first place, if you think about it." I dumped out a stack of letters from one envelope and slipped out a tattered red notebook from the other. Suzanne stood dumfounded, and it was only then that the poor timing of my exposé became clear. I quickly looked for a glass, found none, then twisted the aluminum top off the bottle of wine. The silence crashed like a fallen chandelier in mid-swig.

"You idiot! Is this your version of 'winging' it? God, you are so stupid!"

I wiped my mouth on my sleeve as calmly as possible. "Easy, easy. I just read something recently that you might like to hear. Well, not 'like,' but find of interest." My hands opened out to her out like those of an oiled Arab merchant. It was oil on flames.

"This, these stolen lives! You used them as a weapon of blackmail! Just the thought of it brings out all the reasons I should hate you. How will you ever do fieldwork? They'll kill you within a week! Have a brain, Ben." She walked as stiffly as her widened hips would allow to the kitchen. I took another large mouthful of the sugary wine and turned towards her. She was tearing open a package of stuffing.

"That's all over, Suzanne. You should know that. It's just that there's something here that might be significant to you. I read it last night. There are no ulterior motives." This was not entirely true. The papers had also been brought to keep the conversation off ourselves.

"You mean you haven't read everything yet? What, you're still figuring out what 'See Dick run' means?" She had poured a can of chicken broth on the dried breadcrumbs and was stuffing them down the turkey's orifice with a little too much vigor.

I brushed aside the insult, hoping we were now square. "You know, that's part of the thing about this. After our little spat last spring.."

"Your little tantrum."

"Yes, yes. After that, I lost interest myself, and then went off for the summer and didn't touch any of it until, um, we met up again. It turned out that the date of that next passage was the same as its re-opening, one year removed. So I've been keeping up with them now at a more or less parallel chronology. They have a coincidental resonance that has become a little spooky. It's almost as if their lives and ours had been choreographed together." The next slug of wine tasted almost good. The apartment seemed to take on a more festive atmosphere. Suzanne had finished sprinkling salt and herbs on the pale bird and now spoke to me in a normal tone.

"Would you lift this into the oven? Oh, and could you pull out the giblets from the neck? They're still a little frozen in." I took another drink and sauntered to the kitchen. I put an arm around her waist, or rather on her waist. It was shocking to feel how large and tight it had become. My other hand was used to pull out the clotted organs as she responded flatly with a brief question, as if she were only making small talk.

"So, what kind of parallels could Steven's life in the mountains of Mexico have with yours in the dusty halls of academe?" She moved from me and opened the oven door. I had to shift the top grate down a notch to make the turkey pan fit and stupidly grabbed the pre-heated metal with a bare hand. I jumped back, almost lost the bird and swore a string of expressions usually reserved for the wharf. Suzanne gently took my hand when it was free and hid a laugh behind her concern.

"It's just red. You might get a few blisters. I'll get some ointment."

"No, no, it's all right. Just have a seat. I'll cool it with this wine."

"I can believe that. Serve well chilled indeed." We returned to the living room where she nestled on the end of the couch away from the papers, and I returned to my seat besides my large bottle. At least things were civil again. "So, go ahead, tell me what's so important about these papers. Enough to almost send you to McDonald's for Thanksgiving, you should know."

"Blasphemy on such a day, Suzanne! Anyway, the parallels aren't always exact. It took reading into December of last year to find the clincher. Still, it's pretty close. I'll catch you up to speed until November, and pick it up there." I then told her about Lacey mentioning the beginning of her obsessive habit, about Steven's trip with the gnome, about his discussions with the missionary and about his coming journey to peyote land. The journal was then opened to the entry for November 23rd, only a few days off from our own little feast. "So, here he begins:"

Los Zamorros, 11/23

Some good news and some very bad news. The good news is that I'm being let in on the spiritual dimension of Huichol life. As a future traveler to the sacred land, a *hikurit`amete,* chosen by the priest-witchdoctor himself, it is necessary to learn the ways of the true world beneath the world so as not to cause calamity by error on the journey. This inner view of the sacred might be called Platonic, since they claim that this shared material universe is only a shadow of the real thing, which they alone understand, but this would be an inexact comparison. Their mysticism, if that is the word for it, is not an intellectual exercise or even a cause of the will; it is a way of thought that reveals a deeper reality they take for granted, the way a carpenter takes for granted the planes and angles of a house that are unknown to the layman. It simply is. Of course, this alternate view could never exist so naturally for me. One must be born into it, unless one is high on peyote, but even then one must eventually submit to the "superiority of natural chemistry," as the doctor would say. So it is that I will take the cactus again during the journey, but not otherwise. It may accentuate certain inclinations of the spirit, but for me, my given form and faith must come first, as they will be all that will endure. It would be unwise to create a spiritual dependency on a drug that is both hard to get and illegal in my native land.

To return: it is impressive to hear the respect in their voices as they talk of the five colors of the corn children, or of their grandfather fire or grandmother rain, but their sense of spirituality isn't the same as mine. For the Huichols, the corn that I see and the corn that they see are visually the same, but to them it is different because they not only see the corn, but the story behind the corn. In this way, the world is full of spirits, even as they live among them in ordinary things.

Still, we must understand that Indians are made of clay just as we are. As I wrote above, this is not to say that they think the same. They have a different mental map that tells them, for instance, that the stars are the faces of the gods, while ours tells us that they are distant suns set into infinity. Both involve abstractions that are no more rationally realizable for us than for them. They also have spiritual specialists who may truly live in this mystical world, but others who do not, just as with our holy men.

The truth is that, by and large, most of them skip through life more or less as we do, with one notable exception: their "communion host" packs more punch than ours. This may well make their spiritual beliefs more grounded and unshakable (this because the peyote is embedded in the whole spiritual fabric for them. It would not be as indelible for us.) Still, it seems that they return to a profane sense of being after intoxication, just as we return to ours after a sublime walk in the hills.

Perhaps bigger, more lasting secrets will come at the hands of the mara'akame. Regardless, fascinating insights come daily in the learning of the ritual.

The bad news: the tensions of the competing groups here in the mountains have reached what is hopefully the crescendo, as they have resulted in the pointless death of one of our own. At first I had assumed that the outsiders would go away and spare us, or that talk about them was exaggerated. In hindsight, this was only wishful thinking. One can fiddle while Rome burns, but it burns nonetheless. So it was that fate had me be among the first to find him.

In my defense, it had been impossible to tell for sure that any disagreement was actually on the hot plate. I had noticed that there had been a sudden abundance of meat, and had been told when asked that it was "Spanish deer," a joking expression for cattle. This occasional theft has been going on for decades, probably for centuries, and it did cause periodic trouble. Still, it had become something of a dance over the years, where the rancher would send some vaqueros down to angrily demand recompense, which would be dickered over until no one was really satisfied with the grudging terms but no one felt wronged enough to use violence. So it was so much more shocking to find him splayed out as he was.

The funny - no, creepy thing about it was that I had been on my way to visit the mara'akame on the other mountain. We had met again about a week after our first encounter and I had asked if he might teach me the rituals of the "journey," whereupon he invited me to come to his house for a few lessons. This month is the best time for visiting, as it is harvest season and most remain by their gardens. Everyone said that the path was "fácil, liso, Señor Pelo" (some of the young men call me by that nickname, meaning "body hair," for obvious reasons), but it seemed prudent to get a guide. José, who along with his cousin Lazarus had accompanied me on my first ill-fated trip to Los Zamorros, still wanted his .22 and agreed to take me for a small fee.

We started out in the near-dark of early dawn, and had reached the valley, about six miles down, when a startling high-pitched scream sounded from where José should have been, about a quarter mile ahead. The hair was still up along my back when I reached Jose, who was standing stiffly by a large bush holding what appeared to be a bloody deer leg in his hand. Everything stood still for the longest time as the scene sorted itself out bit by bit, until at some point the meaning of the situation became clear. A human body had been dismembered and the remains had been strewn around the vegetation like toilet paper, sections of entrails swinging from this branch, a hand or part of a leg on that rock. It was still early in the morning and cool, and the steam rose from the larger piles of offal, meaning that this had happened recently. Fear flickered in me like a distant flame, hardly noticeable in my numb state, until I heard the words that José had probably been saying for some time.

"His head, Señor Doctor. His head. They took his head." He was holding onto the hand at the end of the arm, which he told me he recognized as that of his cousin Lazarus who had gone hunting that morning. I looked around stupidly for a head until it came to me that a born hunter like José would have done so already with a thoroughness beyond my meager skills. I then asked rhetorically if we should leave *pronto*, but he shook his head, apparently not frightened at all, displaying only a look of loss and sorrow.

"They're gone, doctor. They've left for their farm with my *primo's* head."

I asked, shocked, if the ranchers often did this after cattle were killed.

"Those are not their shoes (he was pointing to the horse prints). These are the *narcotraficantes*. They have taken my cousin's head to their farm." He then looked at me in a manner begging for clarity and asked, "What do the Spanish do with Indian heads?" He thought that I, being from that world, would understand this grotesque custom. I told him that I had no idea, but the reason was obvious: such things are done to terrorize, to demoralize with fear. It surprised me that a Huichol didn't understand this. I had thought that tribal peoples everywhere understood the tactic of terror. Apparently, a real bush war hasn't occurred for so long that they, at least the young, have forgotten how it's done. That the "Spanish," had never forgotten gave me a moment of shame.

I stood for a while amidst the gore while José gathered what was left of his cousin's bags and amulets and clothing, and then we returned

217

up our mountain. The news in the village was met with a silence that expressed either horror or resolve (or both). Several men then left for the trail, some to return with all the body parts and others to go where we had intended to go, to the other mountain to visit the shaman. I was no longer up for it. It was not the physical strain, but the emotional shock.

That night, this shock turned to fear, and for the first time I wished for the relative safety of Tutzingo. After a very bad sleep, the morning was a waking nightmare, but through the fog came the conviction that it was necessary to go to Xipate, and José again volunteered to guide me. He was going anyway, as were all the men, and although he disappeared ahead of me after the first mile, the trail had become plain enough with all the travel that I was able to reach the foreign rancho by early afternoon. The scene that greeted me was startling.

Because of the shaman, Xipate had a *kalihué*, or religious compound with a large central hut for ritual activities. The houses here were also drawn closer together, so that the whole resembled a genuine village with a main street and a true center. The compound was at the far end, the east end, and there were perhaps 150 men and women and children crowded around the outside, with an unknown number inside, the women with small children hanging around the fringes, nervously turning their heads and occasionally peering around to get a glimpse of the 'sanctum sanctorum.' The way between them and me was deserted except for the skinny yellow dogs that slouched before the empty houses and bared their teeth with my passing. I proceeded with caution, slowing to a crawl when the high-pitched voices coming from within the *kalihué* struck with force. Besides a few small children, no one had noticed me until I was nearly upon the crowd, and when one, then several women turned, they screamed and nearly scared me out of my wits. Few outside of my own rancho knew me, and the sight of a strange white man walking up from behind with a shotgun shortly after a grizzly murder was cause for alarm.

The men turned then, first those on the fringe, then those in the crowd, their machetes rising above their heads in a wave like breeze over grass. I quickly said in Spanish, then in my best Huichol, that I was with Marcos, the nominal leader of Los Zamorros. The tension fell noticeably when a voice, probably Marcos's, shouted from within, saying something with my name in it, and more so still when Carlos, the director of Indian affairs, stuck his head out and motioned me to the front of the crowd. Where the arm of the central government was in all this had been unknown till then, and now it seemed probable that the army had been radioed about the situation before this meeting.

The readiness for hostility was palpable as I passed between the blades that were lowered only slightly, the flush of battle still in the air, and it was obvious that without proper control, this situation could get out of hand. Upon reaching Carlos, he grabbed me by the arm and ushered me inside where we stood about three rows back from the center. Here Horacio sat in state in the '*uueni*,' the official chair of the shaman-priest. The men in the front were arguing among themselves too rapidly for me to understand while Horacio sat quietly, as if daydreaming, with a clutch of colored arrows pressed to his temple. Carlos told me that he had called me in for my own protection, as the people were indisposed towards outsiders at the moment, and also because of my gun. A loud shout went out from the men in front, quieting the rest of us, and then they went back to their parlay. I asked Carlos if the army would come.

"They might, but not to help us."

I was incredulous. "You mean they might come after the Huichols for defending themselves?"

He shrugged, trying not to look ashamed. "Money has many *comandantes*, no? But I have not called any in the army, only my chief in the agency. It is up to him." He changed the subject abruptly. "Look, they are arguing whether to plot revenge or call the officials. See how they are looking at your gun. The *brujo* (witch doctor) believes he can hear the advice from the gods through the arrows that act as antennae."

"Will the people do as he says?"

"They'll do as they feel. They do not have the same sense of law and order that we *racionales* do. But his word is the most respected." He paused, knowing the question in my mind. "I have told them that my superior has been given the true details of the case and that I am waiting for his advice. I have also told them that they should not count on any help, which they knew already. I have promised to give their side in any official inquiry."

I bit my tongue and breathed deeply. I will never get used to the lack of even the hope of justice through government in much of the world.

As the thick air filled my lungs, the sting of the smoke that curled before Horacio drew me back towards the center. The lodge was several times larger than the average house, which still did not make it very big, but it was impressive by comparison and it exuded a certain sense of mystery. These structures were purportedly round in the past, but this was rectangular, with a floor of packed clay and a lower wall of adobe like the other houses. Here, though, the ceiling was considerably higher, and the upper walls were fashioned from reed matting, which allowed the light of day to splay across the floor in the patterns conceived in the weave. Our priest sat in the middle of this light, obscured occasionally by a trail of smoke that danced on and off in the shafts of light until it disappeared through the openings at the opposite ends of the walls where the roof peaked. The ceiling interior was black with soot.

Horacio's brightly woven clothes and dangling amulets and bags made him appear the perfect image of the primitive medicine man, particularly now with his eyes rolled up and his head nodding against the arrows. He sat this way for some twenty minutes more as the men argued, waiting without urgency for the conversation to wane. When at last there was silence, the men looked at each other one more time, then at Horacio. It was another few minutes before he spoke. I could not understand enough to make sense of it, and, ten minutes later when he had apparently finished, I asked Carlos for an account. He shrugged, unimpressed, as he had seemed all along, as if this, too, were in vain.

"He spoke to the family of Lazarus, bewailing their loss and proclaiming the need for justice, then spoke of the automatic weapons of the drug lords. He told them how Lazarus had run into one of their poppy fields when hunting on Huichol land, and how it was not right that the people should be punished so for simply hunting for their families on territory that has been theirs since the time of the gods in Wirikuta. He said it would be unwise to send a warring force against them, as they had such powerful weapons, but that he would send his own spirits who would claim justice. He told them that he would gain special power this next month on the sacred journey, and he would use this so that the people would not be bothered again." Carlos set his mouth firmly to hide what he thought of it all. I asked why my gun was deemed essential if they knew no war party would be assembled.

"Oh, one will be. His is only advice for the people. You are from Marcos's village. They are counting the rifles of their rancho and their relatives as he speaks."

"But I can't go on a war party."

"Then they will ask you to loan the gun. Legally, I would advise against it. Personally, I would advise you to go back to Tutzingo until the heat is off. There is no way that you can win in a situation like this."

For a moment it crossed my mind that his advice was aimed to finally get rid of me, but what he said rang true. The officials would hang me out to dry as some form of foreign mercenary if I were to participate. They would hold me co-responsible for any action taken with my gun if it were loaned. And if the Indians asked for it and were refused, they would see me, at the very least, as unsympathetic to their cause. As it was, I had not seen Angelica and Rey in a month, and their company would be a balm to the horror and sense of danger that had enveloped my life all too suddenly. So, as the men broke up into smaller groups, I made the decision to leave the mountains first thing in the morning for at least a week, and return before the sacred journey with whatever goods possible to fulfill the people's needs.

This is the best that can be done for now. Before returning to my hut to write these notes, I told several people of my plans to see my family in Tutzingo and to hunt along the way, letting everyone know beforehand that neither my shotgun nor I would be available for any revenge killing. This makes me feel a bit cowardly, and it's true that such violence stirs fear in me, if simply from lack of experience in these things, but this problem, even by Huichol standards, is not my business. I am neither family, permanent resident nor tribal member. My absence will also take out a potential witness against them should they accomplish anything. So I go, not entirely comfortable with my role as both insider and outsider, suffering the constraints that have bothered anthropologists from the very beginning.

It tears at me regardless. When we left the big meeting for home this afternoon, we were all of us a unit, 'Huichols.' I had walked in front with the men down the hard rock trail, united by a common tragedy. Now I am abandoning them to their fate just when times are getting tough. Hopefully they will understand. Still, it is possible that what respect was gained will be lost by my return.   ST

Suzanne was silent as I put aside the notebook and reached for the packet of letters. These slid out halfway before the one previously placed on top could be sorted from the rest. I was removing the pages from the envelope when Suzanne spoke. Her quiet solemnity carried a warning.

"I can't believe you have continued playing with this thing."

"Oh, you would prefer to 'let the dead bury the dead,' is that it?"

"Something like that. It might be better if you read the New Testament in its entirety, too, instead of stealing enigmatic little quips for your arsenal." Her words stung more than I would have imagined. Things had been going so well. My old shield and sword were raised.

"Grandpa Abraham might not like that. The goys already have stolen one Jewish prophet. He would be outraged if they stole another." My hands continued to smooth out the pages for the reading.

222

"Oh, you're a prophet now? Then why couldn't you foretell my own outrage at all this? Ben, it's downright creepy the way you keep up with this thing."

"Suzanne, please, there's a reason for this. I have mentioned that there is a synchronicity in all this, and ...how to put this? ... It almost seems that there is meaning in here for us, as if these words still have an active agenda. It's an irrational idea, but it's hard to read all this and come away with any other conclusion."

"It all concludes with his death, is what it is. And that letter, it has to be about Lacey one way or another. She's alive, Ben, and suffering. Either finish them all now and burn the lot or send them off to her, whichever. Still, there's no true point to all this, is there?"

I had hooked a glass from the kitchen and now poured a tall one from the jug of fruit from California's lesser vineyards. My plea had been framed well, sketched enigmatically and poised unalterably at the moment of truth. She would see that this was no silly little game. It was time to pause for a light moment before the hammer struck.

"Just a little wine won't hurt the baby, will it?"

"Maybe not, but why bother? Besides, it won't be long now, will it, little Willard?" She patted her abdomen affectionately.

"Not fucking Willard, please! It's the name of a horror movie, and for good reason."

"And you should care how? No, of course it's not his name."

"Now you're doing the Jewish mother thing. You forget, my mother isn't Jewish. Maybe I never told you?"

"I know everything about you, Ben."

"Then you play with me. And I'm the sick one? But I'm not playing with you. Just have patience and let me read. You'll be forced to concur."

"OK, set yourself up for failure. Despite appearances, I'm all ears." She leaned back into her chair, her great belly rising up in her lose dress like a bubble in a vat of gravy. I had to force myself to concentrate on the letter.

"Ahem. All right then."

Dear Lacey,

I'm sorry for the anxieties that are plaguing you, and think some wisdom from the missionary doctor here might be of help. As it is, it is only luck that allows me to write to you now, as I had planned to stay in the mountains for at least another few weeks, but this luck was caused by the worst misfortune. Please don't be alarmed, as I am far from danger, but a murder of one of the Indians by the drug growers forced this change of plans. The field site had to be abandoned temporarily to avoid involvement in something that can only be played out between the people who live here. The whole situation has brought me a good deal of anxiety and guilt. I would like to help my hosts, but know that the interference of a gringo would only hurt their cause, as it would be proclaimed by their enemies that the trouble was due to Yankee imperialism. Believe me, only *Díos* can count the number of thugs and thieves in Latin America who have hidden behind that claim.

Such it is that a sense of failure now bedevils me. Making matters worse, I knew the murder victim and was with the party that found his body. Death like that has a chilling effect, shaking us from our customary foundations. Still, it worries me that the situation hasn't disturbed me *enough*. Could it be that the deceased isn't quite human to my mind? This is how they probably think of me, but my compassion is supposed to be more expansive.

So you see, you are not the only one caught in an emotional snare. This has not brought me to pluck a tonsure in my scalp as you have, but if it did, I would see it as proof of the depth of my feeling, something I should have more of. You have also discovered in your misfortune that you have true friends in Carol and Suzanne. You see that even with our personal flaws (it still gives me the shivers to picture Suzanne with Bernini!) we might be worthy human beings.

As for your feeling of being "empty" and fearful, that probably is tied in with your mental exhaustion. You have had questions about faith before, but this deeper depression coincides with your great stress. The grit of the field, with real dirt under your fingernails, should relieve you of a lot of your confusion. I know that fieldwork has opened my eyes, especially through the doctor who I have often mentioned. He is a proselytizer and as such relatively stiff and narrow-minded about religious beliefs, but he has seen and heard a lot in his life, and lives his faith with courage and conviction. This lends value to his words, which brings us back to my opening sentence.

We had been comparing the merits of the knowledge given through peyote with those given by traditional religion, when he expressed an interesting perspective. He believes that the exercise of "faith" is the strongest possible expression of individual will. Will, free will, is at the core of the Christian concept of God, a true paradox in that this god is omnipotent yet has chosen to give to humans something that places them out of his control. The greatest exercise of free will is faith. With the gift of a savior that Christians believe God has given us, we don't have to start from the bottom up, or be perfect or healthy. We just have to will our belief in Him.

Compare this with the peyote experience. The advantage of this drug is that it works powerfully, all the time. With faith, on the other hand, you only know if it is working if get positive results over a long period of time. The disadvantage to peyote, though, besides the possibility that one might have a psychotic episode, is that it does not include the will. Things seem to be shaped for you rather than collaborated with you. You might get lasting memories, but they probably will not be as life-guiding as experiences brought about by your own will.

Forgive me for sounding like a healer in a revival tent. It's just that, with all of us sooner or later, surrender to The Power is the logical tact. We cannot always have control of our destiny, as each is only one actor among many others and many things, so what, in the end, is there to lose? You say that faith takes optimism, but that is not true. It just as likely takes desperation. It is when we find that we are powerless to stop misfortune that we look for help. And that is what faith is: a belief in a power that will help us. It is not a complex thing, only one act of the will.

Words - I don't know how much good they can do. Perhaps if you understand the concern beneath them they will have greater affect. In any case, congratulations on exams! What a grueling ordeal. All life seems to pass from milestone to milestone, each believed to be the toughest that life can give, each followed by another more difficult still. Surely, though, the doctoral exams must top them all. Of course, we can still look forward to struggles with our dissertation committees, but how bad could they be? (I say this tongue in cheek, of course.) In any case, fieldwork is infinitely more satisfying than fourteen hours a day of reading, reading, reading. You should have come…

Which brings up our last correspondence and relationships. Succinctly, then: no, I am not trying to push you into another's arms, and, yes, I am hiding something. I am currently involved in an intimate relationship of my own. It was not planned or hoped for, and there are no future plans or hopes for it one way or another. It just happened, and what will become of it is impossible to say. I would not have mentioned it at all but for your intuition of it and my need to retain your trust. If you can still hold to this trust, then, trust that my feelings for you have not changed, but only that time carries all things on its current. Where it will bring us in the end is unknowable, but it may be said with fair certainty that I will return someday, soon. What that will bring is hidden in our hearts and in fate itself. Perhaps our time apart was meant to reveal what is hidden and so bridge the divide between us. Although our past is gone, a future lies ahead. Wherever that leads lies in our hearts as well as in our hands.

Have confidence that your bad times will end, and, at the very least, make that confidence your faith, for that will make it true. Understand that others love you, and that the fits and starts of your career will be less and less important with time. Go out and have some fun. I will let

226

you know of my "journey to sacred time" as soon as possible. This will be my "fun." Please take care, until we meet again,

Love, Steven

After reading, these pages were folded quickly, my eyes held to the task. The climax to the presentation, the point of this whole exercise, was about to begin, and I felt a need to hurry before Suzanne lost the sense of mystery and fate that the letters hopefully conveyed. I stuffed the letter back in its envelope and reached again for the notebook, but was stopped by the painful finality that weighted Suzanne's voice.

"Ben, that's enough. You've been carried away by this obsession and I don't want to be dragged along. It's indicative of your problem that you can't see how morbidly sick this all is. You're intruding on the dead and the ill through an act of theft. This is the closest to sin that I've been in a long time and I've had enough. You make me feel dirty."

"Oh, me again? Of course it wouldn't be the mention of Bernini that's responsible for your self-disgust, would it?" My tone, the words were shocking to my own ears, but the wine had separated my tongue from discretion. More words wound their way from my anger though my wine-soaked belly like a slithering viper. "Then again, maybe I'm here because you got knocked up by that Neanderthal and now you need someone who's legally available. Maybe the real sin is in that sordid affair you had, which you are now compounding by your little work of seduction today. Maybe people who live in glass houses..."

"You bastard! The utter gall!" Suzanne had turned bright red, a flaming, doughy firebrand of anger. Tears dropped to the floor as she pushed herself from her chair. "You are a sick bastard. To think I let you in! To think I wanted you close to my child! Get out! Out!" Her glower stilled the room, making everything hang for a moment like an arrow at its highest trajectory. My attention settled numbly on the darkening of the smock over her breasts, her emotions apparently forcing lactation. I scrambled clumsily for my papers.

"Yes, take your filthy shame out with you! Don't you ever dare…" Her effort had made her double over from shortness of breath. I instinctively grabbed her arm to steady her, but she yanked it away and hit me with astonishing strength across the face with the other. "There, you bastard! Get out of my house!"

There was no possibility of a response. I absently grabbed my backpack along with my papers and nearly fell through the door. It slammed, as if by a ghost behind me. It was not until the chill air on the street had done its work that some thoughts began to stir again.

The first was consolatory: today, after all, had gone about as well as could be expected. When had it ever gone well between Suzanne and me? How could anyone think that a pregnancy that was, possibly, from my volition could bridge the chasm of differences between us? It was clear what this little dinner was about from the beginning - Suzanne was trying to be the modern single mother, intent on letting her child know its father, basing all on the assumption that we could be calm and reasonable. This idea made me laugh out loud. She believed that she could use trendy psychobabble to cover her humongous mistake. She had allowed herself to get pregnant by a man she could only detest – me - and then clung to the absurd notion that she could fix it all by being friends.

There had been a more certain and sanguine solution to her error. It was called "abortion." That is the spirit of our age, after all. That she believed her mercy towards the fetus might bring her happiness was simply juvenile. A future of toil and limited romantic possibilities was as certain for her as the rising of the morning sun.

The swollen crack in my lip began to throb. Anything with salt would make it sting for a week, including salted turkey. Fourteen pounds of it, gone to waste!

My thoughts then settled on the stolen papers, on Steven's blind march to his fate, on his Victorian-like admission of indiscretion and eternal devotion. On the other end would be Lacey, who would read one disappointment, then another, the cracks growing wider as the bad news trickled, then flowed to her mailbox. There was the death, of course, the last straw, but what would she have done if she had known all the facts? What would she do if she were told them now? These facts were meant to be revealed to Suzanne this afternoon, but the curse of the writings, the insistence on placing everything in its time, had worked its magic again. I rarely made a blunder like the one with Suzanne. Even I had to admit that I had been an asshole.

After some boozy musing, I came to an inescapable conclusion: such a mess could only be the fault of Steven's ghost.

The last weeks of the semester spun into Christmas Break in the usual frenzy. It was easy to get lost in the work, as we had to continue covering for Suzanne. She had had a relapse of her condition that very Thanksgiving afternoon, and after her release from the hospital was ordered to do nothing but relax for the remainder of her time. The girls knew without my saying a word what had happened between us and went out of their way to cast dirty looks and ignore me. Except for a slight sense of guilt over the ruined turkey (an article had appeared in the paper, accompanied with pictures of fire engines, about the smoke that had poured from Suzanne's apartment and the fate of the bird that had been forgotten in the rush to the emergency room), neither the girls' taunts nor the original fracas itself bothered me. I had little time to think beyond my scholarly chores, and felt little responsibility for my relationship with Suzanne when the thought did arise. While it may have all been the fault of Stephen's ghost, it was she who had made the decision to rig an ersatz paternal relationship. Remain friends? Are you kidding?

Apparently, Suzanne had emotionally disassociated herself from me as well, for the news of her labor did not reach me until the very morning that it occurred, and that came only through eavesdropping on the feminine clutch gathered in the outer office. When they saw my straining ears, they even stopped talking in a genuine but belated attempt to distance me from the event.

These things hadn't mattered to me at first, neither the birth nor the snubbing. I pushed my door closed after the girls drew the curtain of silence and went back to correcting exams for nearly an hour before the same nagging urge as before began to rise. It was contained successfully for another hour, but finally the effort to control it made working impossible and I gave in to the impulse to visit the maternity ward. It was not something that promised any pleasure, and my intention was only to sit in the waiting room until after the delivery and then leave without making an appearance.

Once there, however, the hospital staff proved to have different priorities, and deciphering my complex relationship with Suzanne was not one of them. When I arrived at the ward and asked them about Suzanne, a nearby nurse pointedly asked me if I was the father. This question caught me so off-guard that I said "yes" without thinking of the consequences, whereupon she hustled me into a nearby room and handed me a paper hospital gown.

"Take off your clothes and put these on. The operation will start in a minute."

Her manner had me dutifully undress as I fumbled for clarity. "What operation? What's happening?"

"You haven't been told? You know of her condition, don't you?"

"Yes."

"Well, it has led to the constriction of the arteries in the umbilical cord. The baby is literally being starved to death."

"Jesus, will it be OK?"

"It should. We just have to get him out with a C-section and get him on a feeding tube. Quick, I'll bring you to the delivery room."

My head had barely pushed through the opening in the paper smock when she pulled open the door and began to power-walk down the corridor. I tripped over my feet to catch up, no more in control of my life now than a drunk in a Tijuana taxi. We came to a partially opened door all too soon, where she led me to a shiny stainless steel table irradiated by a bright light, under which blinked Suzanne. She seemed a little stunned but otherwise gave no sign of alarm. Her belly had been exposed and marked with cut lines, the surgical instruments readied at her side. They gave me a seat by her head, where she recognized me with a dreamy smile, as if she fully expected - and wanted - my presence. I gave back a nod and weak grin and felt her hand touch my wrist.

"You're late. But you made it to the grand finale." Her hand slid lightly into mine.

"Had to finish correcting your damn exams. You've got a bunch of morons for students." She began to laugh, then winced. I saw with odd detachment that they had begun to cut. "You feeling anything?"

"No pain. Something." She looked away and concentrated on what must have been some very strange sensations. I looked back in time to see a gray-pink pile of innards - intestines, umbilical cord, embryonic sack, one or maybe all – and marveled at how they raised not the slightest revulsion or nausea. The nurses brushed off some of the blood and guts, and somehow a skinny, wrinkled form emerged, his eyes and nose tightly shut as if preparing for a high dive. The doctor patted him lightly while a nurse pried his eyelids open and quickly dribbled a few drops of liquid into his sudden look of astonishment. A new world had been born.

I squeezed Suzanne's hand. "You were right about one thing. It's a boy." His tiny penis stood up like a brittle twig as they briefly let her hold him, and then took him aside for measurement and inspection. I trailed after them.

"He's probably lost a pound in the past week. We'll put him on a glucose IV until he gains some weight. 5 lbs, 8 ounces, not too bad." The doctor felt over the head, moved his hands in front of the eyes, and generally probed, finally declaring him OK and sending him off to neo-natal care. A nurse asked me twice about circumcision, which was rejected twice, it being nothing more nowadays than a useless expense, and then

231

she asked me for a name. This had never come to mind before, but I answered instantly, "Abraham." The thought that every Abraham from the very first might be rolling in his circumcised grave never occurred to me. It just seemed right.

I walked back to Suzanne, where they were cleaning and suturing and preparing her to lie by the tiny baby with the giant name. "I have just consecrated your child to Yahweh." This brought a sudden expression of concern to her formally relaxed face.

"What have you done now, Ben?"

"You now have as your son the father of all the tribes of Israel. Abraham." She began to laugh again, then stopped with a wince.

"Make sure it's not spelled with an "I," you know, the Arab spelling. It would kill your father, wouldn't it?"

"The only thing that would kill my father would be the adoption of the gold standard by the Federal Reserve. No, the name came clearly from the Burning Bush."

"Is he all right?"

"Fine. Just needs some calories. They're going to take you to him now." On cue, they suddenly appeared to help Suzanne onto a rolling bed and wheel her into the hall. I walked besides them.

"Thanks for coming, Ben. You're not the rotten bastard that you seem. But what you said on Thanksgiving, that was mean."

"The wine got me drunk on an empty stomach and made me defensive about my forbidden hobby. Besides, there was one more entry I really wanted to read. I'm sorry." The last words were harder to say than the operation was to watch. She nodded absently.

"We're both fools. But I'm not sorry for Abraham. What was it that you wanted to read that was so important?"

"It doesn't seem so big at the moment."

"Tell me. Whatever." With all that had happened, the anesthesia and adrenaline apparently had reached a brief balancing point, making her sound even more normal than normal.

"OK. Remember how Steven finally confessed to his affair with Angelica? How skillfully he brushed off her importance to him? Well, it turns up later in his notes that Angie's pregnant! You gotta love that. Dated at January 2, just a few weeks shy of a year ago. Coincidence?" I grinned comically, but she turned from me with a frown.

"Abraham was supposed to be born that day, before the problem. But how awful that must have been for Lacey!" She began to cry. The balance was gone and I feared the drama of a post-partum depression.

"No, he didn't tell her. This news was only in his notes, not any letter to her. She probably was too upset to read them after his death and doesn't know about this still. But that's the surprise, you see? The story's not over. It's living through us. Oh, hey, here we go. We're here at the foot of the miracle."

Suzanne dried her eyes and looked back at the ceiling. We had just come through a set of doors and now they rolled Suzanne next to our child. Her frown broke into a smile as she cradled him in her arms.

"Hello, Abraham! Mommy loves you!"

CHAPTER 10

Test of Faith

Tutzingo, Jan 7

A ll things considered, since the mountain communities had to be abandoned anyway, it was fortunate that my exile fell on the Christmas season. It has been good to see Angelica and Rey - more on that later - and lots of fun celebrating the long journey to Bethlehem taken by the *Tres Magos*, or Three (wise) Kings (one being little Rey's namesake), which dwarfs our holiday season by going from Christmas all the way to El Día dos los Tres Magos on January 6. The pre-industrial Europeans had a knack for creating holidays of excess and revel, a tradition that is carried on heroically to this day in lands where time punch-clocks are unknown. While Tutzingo is too small and poor for anything really big, Rafael's family (with the help of my rent money, which I still pay to keep the house) was able to put on a pretty good feast, with some fireworks to boot, and the others always had liquor and special treats on hand. A young bull and a cow were slaughtered, and the abundance of meat struck me as a welcomed bounty. The sense of meat deprivation that everyone has here now affects me as well.

I also have not had such a binge on alcohol for years, and can honestly say that it will be good to get back to a more sober life. Still, it has made for some memorable times, the greatest being those spent with Angelica late at night around the hearth next to the school, where we sat by one another in our (mine, usually) semi-inebriated states and stared into the fire. It was sharp and clear every night, enabling us to watch the stars move with the rotation of the earth through the mat of twigs and thatch over our heads. We would listen to the sound of drunken singing off in another house, or to the crackle and hiss before us in the small glow. She told me what little gossip had gone on in my absence: which women were pregnant by whom, which wife had been beaten, which young man had left for the States, the state of the war between Chico's and Simon's families. My own news of the death of Lazarus did not particularly disturb her, for, as she said, one could always count on death and struggle in the mountains. This attitude, that my experience was not unique, has convinced me to return to the mountains shortly. Hopefully whatever lust for revenge there was has been worked out, preferably in a non-violent fashion. Violence is a game the drug lords will always win.

The biggest news came after New Year's, at the height of village inebriation when even Angelica got noticeably tipsy. Mexican country folk are not very demonstrative of romantic affection, except for the culminating act, but an abundance of that good brandy unleashed the warmth in her bosom, and that night she lay by my side hugging me before the fire. She openly talked of love, of our love, which we confessed to mutually in the liquor's embrace. It was then that she told me of her suspicion that she was in the family way. With a little questioning, she revealed that it was more than a suspicion – Dr. Gary had verified it just two weeks before, her being into her third month now. This was taken in good humor then, leading to one of our more passionate nights, but the next morning, with the *resaca* (hangover-literally, the undertow of a wave, very poetic and apt) and the painful light of day in my eyes, anxiety mounted over the turn of events. I chastised myself for being surprised by the outcome of my behavior and for expecting that she, because of her education and sexual experience, would have taken the necessary precautions. This was still backwoods Mexico. What destructive selfishness had gotten the better of me?

It was not that there was any confusion as to my future course of action. The conflicts of sexual need and personal obligation had tormented me in my youth, the coarser of the two often vanquishing the other. In time, though, experience taught me that any pain given up for another would be rewarded many fold. This became all the more striking in graduate school, where the unhappiness of a faculty member could be measured precisely in proportion to the size and selfishness of his ego. Some believe that a code of honorable conduct is a self-imposed shackle, but if it is heartfelt and not mere empty form, it is really a vehicle of freedom. Instead of being bound to the pleasure or advantage of the moment, it frees one to find one's greater self. So it is clear what must be done concerning Angelica.

It is not at all clear what to do about Lacey. No promises have been broken, and we have discussed the possibility of romance with others at length, but her emotional condition keeps me from bluntly informing her. What has happened with Angelica might prove a good thing, but my relationship with Lacey holds me back from celebratory thoughts. As I write, I am rocked by feelings of guilt, shock and joy. Yes, this will be a good thing, it must be, but what to do about Lacey?   ST

Tutzingo, Jan 9

The Doctor flew in on the afternoon of the preceding entry. He was able to spend time with his family over the holidays, but it is probable that he would have avoided Tutzingo during the fiesta in any case. His feelings are understandable, given certain inevitable circumstances - for instance, a few days ago a girl claimed that she was raped by a boy who had been drinking all day, and now the families are negotiating between marriage and payment – but the holiday reverie causes no more outrages than everyday life over the long run. For most of us, this is a time of amusement and communal affection.

In any case, it was good to see him. He hedged around Angelica's condition ("What, Steven, would you do if you were confronted by certain obligations down here?") until I told him that I knew of that "certain obligation" and had come to responsible terms with it. He was relieved, happy, and surprised all at once (surprised that someone from my generation understood responsibility. A sad reflection). He knew as I did that the village as a whole would be pleased with the situation. They have an unrealistic but sincere sense of the importance of my nationality and education, so Angelica will be seen as marrying up. And the single men will not be robbed of a prized mate, as she (by their standards) is damaged goods, useful and prestigious as her position is. It is, then, a win-win. The only sadness in this is for another not here. Professionally, I have awaited the doctor's arrival for his advice about the situation in the mountains. What was needed first and most, though, was his opinion on the very personal matter of Lacey.

This had to wait until I could accompany him on his rounds in the village. Angelica understood a little English, and it was important that she not misinterpret what was said. We first went to the house of Tomás, the cousin of my landlord, where Gary had to treat his 9-year-old son, who had a horrible-looking canker on the side of his mouth that kept him from eating. The doctor recognized the wound immediately, saying it was from a worm passed from pig excretion to hands or food and would take the dedicated use of a noxious ointment to kill it. He also told the mother to mix corn meal with powdered milk for the boy until he could chew properly again. On the way back we stopped at a flat rock, where I seized the opportunity to confess the complications of my relationship with Lacey. The serenity of the crisp morning beneath the dew-bright mountains made it easy and true. The doctor proved to be a conscientious arbiter.

"I can see your problem. Ideally, a woman becomes a man's wife when they join together, but you have done that with both, confusing the issue. That is one of the great problems with today's license - the laws of God to man can no longer be applied with ease.

"Saying that, you have defrauded no one, made no promises that have been broken, and now have a much greater moral responsibility to Angelica. Lacey has come to her situation through her own volition, flawed as it was, which has caused her great misery. You are an accomplice, but now have a duty to move along another path. You cannot be tied to past sins if they cause you to continue to sin." He paused, looking into the brightening sky as if searching for the right words, then turned to me.

"I think that about does it, don't you?"

I had to agree. But that has not absolved me from my part in the misery of another. It has not erased the genuine affection, even love, which I feel for Lacey. This has caused a pain that will never fully disappear, one for which I was solely responsible. It may be that Gary is right about the young today; that our carelessness with sex and love has increased our sorrows, but it seems to me that sorrow has never been a stranger to the world. Perhaps wisdom only comes through holding sadness in one's heart.

Yesterday, the day after our talk, we had our now-customary dinner discussion. There was a subtle shift in the doctor's demeanor, to that of a guest in another's house. This made me realize that, for the first time in my adult life, I was now truly invested in a society. The ensuing sense of pride was quickly overshadowed by the thought that social respect did not come cheap. Hardship and struggle were sure to follow. But these must be shrugged off as the inexorable agents that they are - for how else can we move on through life?

After a moment of awkward adjustment to these mixed sentiments, the pertinent questions about the drug dealers were laid at his feet. His answers were not reassuring.

"No one here can predict what will happen, because the villagers see this as a new thing. It's not gold or serfs or women that the new invaders are after. The greatest similarity this new exploitation has to the history of the area is the need for land. Even this is peculiar, as the drug producers want the land that is the least accessible, for obvious reasons. Because of these differences, Mexicans at large don't count it as a big problem. In fact, many of the more unscrupulous believe the drug trade may be a boon to the area. In any case, it's a disaster for the Indians because of where they live.

"For us, though, it's easy to see that this will result in the enslavement of the people, just as all the incursions of the past have. The drug dealers don't believe in drugs, but the money it brings them. After their first million, they don't want the things that money can buy, but the power it can buy. For that, there is never enough. So we can predict that their operations will continue to grow with their power, and that their power will grow with their operations, and so on. This will eventually affect everyone adversely. As they claw for more power, the power of another will come to mean less power for them. Soon they will need to crush everyone around them."

His assessment was convincing. Surely that was the way things had gone in the past in this country. Drugs or cattle, it always came back to land and power. Everyone wanted to be king. This brought up the question concerning the dangers of returning to the field site. For this his answer was less certain.

"No offense, but you have proven to be a 'nobody' over the past months, and that's good. You're obviously not a CIA agent or an undercover reporter. I wouldn't think that they would bother with you during your short time with the Indians. But that horrible thing with Lazarus...I don't know what Marcus will ask the others to do about it, or what Carlito's input to the government will generate. It's also not clear how involved the DAI (Department of Indian Affairs) is with the drug money. Most likely, the Huichols will perpetrate some act of retribution to restore respect, and the DAI will be bribed to look the other way when the gang retaliates. When either of these things will come to pass is hard to say. One would have to be on the inside of both of those worlds to know. For now, you can only go on intuition. Pray for guidance. You also have to realize that you are responsible for more than yourself now. You have to think about that."

This had not occurred to me. My plan has been to return to Los Zamorros and, at the very least, stay for the Peyote Hunt. This is the golden opportunity for the highlight and success of my thesis. Quitting now would force me to refocus on Tutzingo, with all the baggage of peasant studies that it implies. This is not my passion. Now I must sleep on it, and pray for guidance, as the Doctor said. Joseph Campbell recognized that God has many masks, and perhaps the Doctor's and mine is the same God in different guises.

His concern and advice are well taken in any case. I am not alone anymore. Already my new role tests my faith. Perhaps sleep will open a pathway for my prayers. ST

These are the notes that I had been so eager to read to Suzanne that painful Thanksgiving. After that debacle, the rational decision was made to finish the last scraps of this pathetic story during the holiday and then toss the whole thing to the wind, but the bitterness and anger of that day had me put the papers aside once again. Their theft had brought nothing but disaster, leading me to think against reason that they carried a curse akin to the mummy's tomb. Every action brought about through them created another wall in a maze, and every step forward seemed diverted by inscrutable caprice. Although the words had once fed only a sordid and meaningless hobby, they now had become like the incantation of a necromancer, unleashing a diabolical force that increasingly formed the winding path to my future. It was undeniable that the latest of these obstacles, the – our - baby Abraham, had been created by the papers. As with everything else wrought by the papers, this obstacle, this insipient human child, created an uncertainty that brought the willful mind to its knees, prostrate before the black and horrible obelisk of fate.

Suzanne could no longer in good conscience be avoided. She had just given birth, and the caesarian's effects could last a month (the first caesarian had killed the first patient, the mother of Caesar. Things were simpler then). Although she had friends and even parents who were anxious to help, I, the father of the baby, would be expected to make a heroic appearance now and then. It was all so awkward. Did Suzanne expect to form a husband-wife relationship with me, or keep me as the divorced male presence and provider? If the latter, should I choose fight or flight? If the former, was there any choice at all?

There were no answers to any of these questions simply because what I wanted for myself was unknown. One thing, however, was known for certain: my acknowledgement of paternity had been carefully recorded at the hospital, making it all nice and legal. Suzanne could get from me whatever the courts could squeeze out, which might be every damn cent I would ever make over subsistence. Being friendly was the best defense. Perhaps an exhibition of my better qualities would keep her from resorting to the slimy clutches of the ambulance chasers. Deadbeat dads have little sympathy with the courts these days.

A preliminary offensive was devised. I would go to the hospital again, quickly, before she and Abe were released. Hospitals always serve as dramatic backdrops for showing how much one cares, no matter the real feelings. To miss my chance to perform might upset Suzanne and get the unbalanced hormones of recent motherhood racing in the wrong direction. A bouquet of flowers, virginal lilies perhaps, would serve as my entrance card to her good graces.

After a day to let the pair rest and bond, I gathered the necessary resources and boldly walked into that pit of stench and death into which little babies are now born.

I arrived at a good time, when Abe was taken off the feeding tube and allowed to grope at Suzanne's breast. He was still thin, but the wrinkles were gone and he had considerably more energy. A flush of awkwardness came to me as he sucked at her nipple, reminding me of how little I knew of her flesh myself. While we should have formed the classic portrait of a proud father watching his son nurse, it seemed more like that of a Peeping Tom at the bedroom window. With an effort, my gaze was shifted to her face, which showed a curious combination of weariness and peace. I put the flowers by the bed and tried to speak, but could not find words. Suzanne quickly filled in.

"How nice, Ben, to bring the lilies of the field! Spring has come a little early this year."

"Grown in Mexico, I expect. Abe looks like he's picking up."

"Now there's fine poetry. Nice to see you, too. Who shamed you into this visit, now? No, forget it. I'm glad you came. Yes, he's doing very well."

"So, when you getting out? Plural you, that is. Ya'll."

"I'm out already. They kicked me off the list the day after the birth. They let me use this bed for face time with Abe. See? I have everything on but my sensible shoes. And my blouse." This must have raised a blush, given her next words. "Ben, you're downright bashful, aren't you? You've been put you in a horrible position, haven't you?" Her face showed concern but her eyes laughed, as they so often did with me. She made me feel like a shuffling little boy. I reached for wit, but could only squeak.

"You have to admit, it's not like we know each other. Well. In a way..."

The eyes still laughed. "Ben, stop and think. I once told you to be spontaneous with your feelings, but I take that back. Way back. Think what you want to say to a convalescing mother who is so in love with her little boy."

"Uh, yes, you make a winning pair! Smashing, really."

"Only a pair?"

"With a proud father, that makes three. We make a smashing, uh, triumvirate. Like the Roman Empire, Pompey and Cassius and the other fellow. Like the Father, Son, and the Blessed Mother. I would say Virgin, but that would be presumptuous on my part." A sense of self was coming back. Suzanne did know how to break the ice.

"Yes, that's the Ben I know. Always graciously insincere. Although your rested look is puzzling."

I asked why that might be.

"Because I know how worried you must be over your acknowledgment of paternity. Think about it, though. You weren't told about the delivery, weren't asked to come, and weren't asked to sign a thing."

"But I did sign. That's makes a difference." Oh, how stupid that was! In a flash her suspicion of my worry had been confirmed. She did not act surprised.

"I'm glad you did. I somehow knew you would. But this has never been about trapping you for anything. Trust me. You're as free as a bird."

In a cage of conscience, I thought. That beast was becoming more active by the day now, trembling into wakefulness from its long slumber in a hidden cave.

"I know," I lied, "it's not that, but us. It's uncharted territory for me, and as such, uncomfortable. Am I to be the doting uncle? Or is there a chance at romance?"

"I don't know. Is there?"

"Ladies first." Once again, Suzanne had maneuvered me into a discussion against my design. How did she do it? And it sounded like I had started it, too.

"How convenient are manners now and then. All right. Sure, why not?" She winced suddenly as Abe began to paw and suck at her like a desperate runt in a large litter. I grimaced for her and wondered when he would grow teeth.

"Ouch! Looks like it hurts."

"Love often hurts." She smiled with mock piety. "Well, what do you say? Have you the courage? If you don't..." She shrugged and adjusted Abe as they both maneuvered for a more comfortable position.

"Ah, love is a challenge to my courage now?"

"What do you think?"

"I don't think we'll ever be Ward and June Cleaver."

"Ben, they're fiction."

"No shit."

"Then what's the point? We'd be who we are."

"With the magical catalyst of chemistry. Alchemy. Do we get gold out of lead?"

"A family out of three would do. Gold and lead are both cold and heavy."

"So the nursing mammal speaks. The mother seeks rough browse in winter."

"If you're a fucking deer. Look, Ben, I'm not begging. You hadn't the balls to suggest a relationship, so I took the lead. If you're not interested, being a distant uncle would be fine."

"I said doting."

"We're academics. We move. Distant would be fine." She turned back to Abe, scarcely hiding her anger. As usual. It was always my fault, of course, but how did she make it my fault? Surely this constant antagonism was a bad sign. Perversely, as seemed to be my stance with Suzanne, this assurance of doom made a decision leap to my mouth before it could be muzzled.

"Hell, why not? It's the three of us against the world, right, kiddo?" For the first time I touched Abe and noticed the clean, slightly sour scent that surrounded him like a halo. He kept at his meal, but Suzanne looked at me in genuine astonishment.

"Where the hell did that come from?"

"I don't know. Really, where anything comes from around you is a mystery."

"I've noticed. You can take it back."

"Especially now. When do we share the wedding bed?"

"You are the ardent groom, aren't you? We might want to wait until my abdomen can be touched without eliciting a three-alarm shriek. And we might want to get to know each other a little."

"Jesus, dating? If it's like our first, I'm all for it."

"Wise ass. I like you because you're pathetic. What if I find you're the bastard everyone else says you are?"

"Then have someone else's baby."

"Who knows? Just kidding. Let's take it as it comes, all right? Let's try spontaneity one more time. Now with a goal in mind. An inclusive goal."

I agreed with a nod and left with a kiss to Abe's head. It was all baby powder and sweet and sour mother's milk. The lump in my throat allowed only a wave goodbye.

There was no use pondering how she did it. I walked out of the tomb of death into the brittle air floating in a warm inner pool, dazed out of thought, comfortable and uncertain. In another cavern another beast stirred, one that was feared but wanted. It was bigger than conscience. The waters of a warm pool caressed its lair.

It didn't take long for my feet to grow cold. By the time the last exam of the semester was graded, the impact of this new situation had dropped down into the real world. My life was cherished as it was, with its books and risk-free ideologies, and it now struck home with a certainty that everything was about to be blown to pieces. It was a certainty because the forces of destruction came from within as well as from without. But since dwelling on the interior forces of those awakening beasts was intolerable, I focused only on the numerous external threats. Christmas break was upon us, leading to all sorts of open time that was to be spent in the rich smells of a library niche. Now much of this time would be spent communing with mortal flesh.

There would be mutual soul-searching, needs and flaws probed and massaged, all manner of interpersonal exchanges made that passed for relationships these days. Just as bad, it was probable that the "in-laws" would pay a visit. Since "Papa" had promised to break the neck of the bastard who had knocked up his little princess, it occurred to me that his violence could be used as an excuse to visit my own family, something I was suddenly almost eager to do. This put me between a rock and a hard place, promising me only the relief of misery that comes from the lesser of two evils.

As this was the Christmas season, a brief flicker of hope sparked momentarily in a forgotten place in my brain. It was a prayer for a miracle. Not a very grand one, not a gift of a palace or a cave of riches nor a heeling of limbs. It was a prayer only for a simple regression in time, and not a long one at that: only about nine and a half months would do.

It was well after dark by the time the last grades were recorded, and my office light let out a solitary glow. I turned this off with a sigh and walked into the silent corridor, empty of life save for my footsteps. The door opened to the outside glare of light in blackness, and with the clicking of the lock from behind came the customary sting of the winter wind that howled through the greasy canyons and streets of the city.

The streetlights hummed in their alien glow as I approached an old wreck of a house, a cheap imitation of a classic Victorian. A jumble of blinking Christmas lights on the porch threw erratic bursts of colored flame into the shadows, illuminating rusted chairs and bicycles and hockey sticks and a foul-looking sofa. This was a student rental, probably all male, the lights a paltry poultice for the wounds of winter. It occurred to me that these lights were as ephemeral as the beer-enhanced camaraderie of the resident bachelors who so strenuously sought to mute their howling loneliness and fevered dreams.

Loneliness, however, could be one's best friend. It had been my fondest desire to stay at the co-ops for the holidays, nearly alone with my thoughts and work. The vision of the 'in-laws,' though, drove me almost to panic, forcing me to plan a trip home to Chicago, a place that could be tolerated for one night, or two or three at most. The problem was that I needed to be lost for several more, but where? There were my old high school chums, but they were married now, living in atmospheres of feminine domesticity that elicited mutual boredom. As usual, for me vacations weren't vacations, but problems to solve.

This particular conundrum clung to me on the journey home that night, but no plausible solution had been reached by the time the door to winter's darkness had been closed and I had entered my dusty little room.

It was a relief to be back in this safe haven. The sight of the cheap single bed and institutional desk helped me drop my cares. There were four weeks of winter break before me, each fraught with personal hurdles and littered with mounds of books to read for exams, but for the moment I was free. This was a night for celebration, and for that, the remainder of the notes and letters, everything of a personal nature in them, would be read, lock, stock and barrel. They had been allowed to grow into myth, had through witless amusement been allowed to chisel destiny from mere coincidence. This myth that had been forged by my imagination would now be dispelled in a piece, just as science had thrown off the phantasms of religion. Dull passivity had brought me to the doorstep of superstition. In one illuminating step, the belief in the agency of Steven's ghost would be vanquished.

I prepared a cup of tea in the communal kitchen, recognizing others only by a grunt or nod, then settled back at my desk with the folders. The next envelope in line, one from Lacey, was tapped out of its casing. This could be pathetic. A thought arose for an instant: should my heart that was so recently buoyed by holiday cheer now be subjected to her self-absorbed whining? Moreover, was it even decent to learn her thoughts, knowing what she did not, that her erstwhile lover had become the property of another?

This hesitancy made me laugh out loud. Of course I would read it. This damn clot of papers had brought me into an affair and the inescapable clutches of social obligation. Why should they be given even the slightest sign of courtesy?

I slipped out the letter from its smudged confines. The first page was marked by a thumbprint that smelled of gun oil:

Dear Steven,

I don't know whether to thank you for your sage advice or damn you for your healthy sanity! Of course, this conflict is born from envy. Do take heart that I am feeling much better, and can actually understand the possibilities of faith. Leaving school for the holidays was like lifting the lid from the coffin. My old, retrograde house is so much dearer to me than the glittering halls of knowledge. Still, even my home would not have been enough in the worst darkness. I now understand what people from the past meant when they believed they were damned. When you are suffering in a certain way, it does seem at times like only an eternity of hell can exist for you. But thank God that it is not everlasting. You were right. Thank you and the grace that delivers hope for the new possibilities.

Still, do not misunderstand me. Your carefully worded news about a new relationship has not settled lightly. I forfeited any right to bind you to any promises, and there is no need to apologize for your current affair, but it makes me angry and frustrated with myself. From what you write, you are having relations with a local peasant woman. If I understand rural Mexico, this can only mean that she is either recognized as your wife, or as a 'woman of the moment.' Since you have stated that the relationship is indeterminate, might I infer the latter of the two? This is nothing new in the history of my family. My whaling ancestors left for years at a time, and the colorful tales told of them in the late hours confirm that they were men with ordinary weaknesses. The stories often recount the dangers that may attend the way-faring life. Please be careful. Sometimes these dangers affect the ability to have a family later on.

Perhaps you can guess from my words that relationships and family have returned to mind of late. Your words of concern were a greater balm than you could imagine. Suffice it to say for now that I look forward to your return with increasing impatience and expectation.

There is a problem, though: I have not signed on as TA for next semester yet, as my mother has proposed a winter in Italy for the two of us. From your descriptions, the sun and hills of Tuscany share qualities with your little valley, and as such you might understand my attraction to Italy in the face of another grim Michigan winter. On the other hand, if you were to return soon, the winter would be of little importance. Please inform me of your plans ASAP; another winter in Michigan without you would be like a long, long night without day.

As to the extent of my rehabilitation, you may have noticed my regained sense of humor, and, were you here, you would certainly notice my new growth of hair. It will take a year before it has thoroughly blended in, but its newness is like tender shoots of spring reaching for the sun. In this euphoria has come an examination of my faith. While your theological scholasticism helped to get me on that highway, I have found my own truth on a less exalted byway. In my misery, the relationships in my life were left untended, yet they endured to pull me through.

Perhaps it is a "women thing" that our greatest connection to life comes through the affectionate embrace of others, for we find that there is nothing better outside ourselves than a true friend. Our connection to the infinite is made in the same way - through the intimacies of family. From the initial spark of life, we are successors to millions of other sparks that have led to our kind, the acts of creation of our primitive ancestors blossoming in us with the expression of love and the glimmering of our Creator.

So you see that belief does not have to be abstract and stoic. Instead it may grow from the love of friends and family. So you might understand why a woman, with this more practical connection to the divine, might be more careful in her choice of a mate in which to contribute to eternity.

But, equally, you might understand why, once she has decided, she does not so easily change that decision.

So I am healing, and well. You were right, in your own way, that my sickness was due to a lack of faith, which in turn was caused by forgetting who and what I was. Now, things could only improve by your presence. Please let me know your plans. You will be recalled in my prayers,

Love, Lacey

Oof! Even with my seething contempt for this couple, whose correspondence had come to curse me, I had to feel pity. Her very recovery, based on family and relations, had caused her to make a positive decision about our benighted working-class hero, whose death later could only throw her into a pit of madness. In a way, Steven's discourse on his deity had proven to be the better of the two: while his version of the lord asked only for blind faith, Lacey's asked for love. What, then, would become of her without the focus of her love? Steven's faith, as archaic as it was, could never die. It could be lost, but as long as there was a fool to trace it in his mind's eye, it would, in its fashion, live. Love, as we all know, is a chemical aberration that may die long before the object of its affection. Just as the barbarians of the Old Testament counted their spawn like a lineage of cattle, so the eternity of the flesh could be as cold in its continuity as the most detached philosophies of men.

I had to commend Lacey on her detachment. Spurned and yet ever bright to reclaim what was hers, she proved herself a member of her class as well as of the intelligencia. Such a frozen heart in Suzanne might have saved me from the paternity trap, but such a cure would most certainly be worse than the disease.

The thoughts on her discourse were dropped to prepare for another, a personal entry in Steven's notebooks. By the date on the heading, he would not have received Lacey's letter at the time of the writing:

January 17 (in the new year of our Lord) 1981

Perhaps the formalization of the date will fix it in my mind. In the mountains, time loses its numerical significance. Fortunately, I haven't had to write any checks lately, although that might change. Los Zamorros has undergone a dark metamorphosis since my return, and a check for a fast ticket out of here might be advisable. With the peyote walk coming so soon, this is meant as a joke, but recent observations have made me nervous. The men walk with their rifles or with bows and arrows everywhere now, even to work in the fields. They have discussions that are whispered or stifled in my presence, leading to a distancing of the people from me. They are clearly pulling into themselves as a unit, circling the wagons for the trouble they anticipate. They are not willing to wait for it to come back to them.

I met Jose not long after returning, and noticed the soot and grease mixture he had put on his face as a sign of mourning for his cousin. On questioning, it turned out that this 'mourning' was really a ritual meant to hide his spirit from the vengeance of another spirit. He pointed out a new string of items he wore with his other ornamentations. They seemed to be withered seedpods, and I asked him to specify what they were made out of in the interest of the botanical aspects of Huichol magic. He grinned with pride as he told me: "The fingers of the enemy who killed my cousin."

A closer look verified this, although one seemed out of place. When asked, he laughed and said "the other finger of my enemy," and then touched his groin. Having witnessed the viciously mutilated body of Lazarus, I had to nod in sympathy. In retrospect, this reaction frightens me, for it shows how easily outrage can lead to savage revenge among the primitive and civilized alike. Regardless of the horror, this brutal act of revenge filled my heart with satisfaction.

I have made it a point since then to ignore the signs of conflict around me, for fear of becoming too involved. Work has proven to be

251

my greatest shield, and with this in mind, a question about the long, steep road to Xipate was asked. My mission was to find if the peyote journey was still on for the time planned (a week from this entry), and the effort was rewarded with a strong affirmation. In fact, Horacio was more determined than ever that it should proceed. When asked why, especially with the greater possibility of an ambush, he answered:

"What is happening is because the world has lost its balance. You think that the sun and moon and earth all move according to laws of science, but we believe differently. We believe that all things are held in moral *brazos* (arms, or spiritual platforms), and when human beings push away from them, disaster falls like stones from a cliff. It may be that the very sun could come down from the sky and burn us in flames. This would happen not to punish us, but because its place in the heavens has been disturbed by our wrong behavior.

"So, I tell you, it is important now that we hunt for our ancestors, to find them at the beginning, in Wirikuta, and so become them and live the stories of the beginning and set all things right. We must first sit before the fire until all is forgiven between us and then proceed in harmony. We must bring the time of law back to us by living it. This will restore the proper balance in the world so that all things become beautiful."

I asked him if the vengeance his people sought was wrong.

"How can I say what is wrong when the balance is disturbed? What happens is right for the time. It is just that the time is off-balance. It is the Spanish who caused this state of affairs. They do not even see it, and have no idea how to change it. It is up to us. So we will right things next week. You will get the van?"

I told him the arrangements had been made, then asked him if he thought that balance could always be restored.

"We always have. But there are so many (outsiders, non-believers) now. Who knows? One can fix a house and fix a house, but someday it will have to be brought down and replaced. Maybe this is the time? But I cannot say. I do my work and let the world decide." With his distinct and formal Spanish, his words seemed very wise and somehow chilling.

His emotional and prophetic presence was so powerful that it probably triggered the dream that struck me last night. It was the feeling as much as the imagery that made such an impact. While only the outline of the story remains in memory, the impression that it reflected a greater reality remains, strong and unshakable. As I sit on my mat before the fire, goose bumps rise just thinking about it. It went something like this:

I was walking in the night, in a barren, rocky place with cliffs like those around me now, when the path that was traced by the light of the moon came to a darkly sparkling sea. To my left and right the rocks lay low so that one could walk to the shoreline, but before me rose a mound of piled rock about thirty feet high, topped by a great level slab. The middle of the pile was rent by a large black oval that was clearly the entrance to a cave. At the sight, several people who seemed familiar to me climbed down the rocks by the sides of the entrance and eagerly encouraged me to pass through with them. It was obvious that I was the only one ignorant of the situation, and as we slipped down a dark path to go deep within, I asked one of the men what this was all about. He answered as we reached a small chamber with a roughly flat floor. "It's an initiation, Steven!"

The others became more excited at that and laughed as I stumbled about in the darkness. A small fire was then lit on the floor, illuminating in the flickering light the sides of the chamber that had been etched and drawn with ancient symbols. The others lit torches from the fire and held them before the markings, bringing out the details of the geometric patterns and astrological signs as well as archaic depictions of people and animals and were-animals. One person after another then joined in a slow procession, sticking close to the wall in single file. I realized my place with them and followed in the back of the line.

We circled the den once and then left by an exit opposite the cave entrance. We had to clamber up a steep slide of rock, with those holding torches somehow managing to do both. We arrived at the flat space on top that had been visible from outside, and my "friends" (for that is what I felt they were) laughed and stomped their feet until we were all clustered together on the flat stone. It was a bright, clear night, like the kind we have here in the Sierras, and the Milky Way appeared thick with stars despite the moon. The ocean glimmered beyond the hedge of rocks that surrounded us. I could not see over them to the water directly below, and it seemed to me that we were higher than the thirty feet estimated earlier. There was only one route out from our platform, one that ran directly to a ledge that apparently dropped down to a sharp mass of rock from the full height of the promontory. I assumed that this ledge was a look-out until one of my friends yelled, "Let's go!," dropped his torch and ran full speed for the cliff. He jumped off with a "whoop!" and disappeared. Another did the same, and then another, until the last told me it was my turn. I told him that it was crazy to kill myself like that, and refused to go. He laughed and said, "You have to have faith. You have to believe. God will take care of you!" He said this with all sincerity, then ran with abandon for the cliff and disappeared off the edge. I strained in the dark for sounds, any sound, the sound of voices or groans of pain, but heard only the rhythm of waves. I looked to the stars again, and then to the dark glittering water and felt a rush of courage mixed with desperate desire. A decision arose that made me act at once, bringing me to run full hard for the ledge, not caring for myself but only for the momentary triumph of victory over fear. Right at the edge, when it was too late to stop, when my feet had already left safe land, a deep finger of water that pushed in from the sea appeared, nestled in the rocks below. I splashed into it without harm, not even touching bottom, and swam to my friends who were all laughing on a nearby rock.

Upon lifting myself from the salt water into the warm night, revelation poured in. The words of the ancients arose before me as lamps unto our destiny, lighting the way past evil and ignorance, enabling us to find the pure power within and so cast aside fear. "Live thusly," they intoned, "live from the soul with a joy unbounded by trepidation. It is with such faith in life that we gain wisdom, for such faith places us in the heart of the universe, in the infinite ocean below an infinite sky. We will not fear the rocks, then, for no rock awaits a man of faith. His leap into life will always end in the sensual depth of an ocean pool. He cannot be crushed and annihilated on a rock. His faith will always bring him to a safe landing, allowing him to emerge in the joyous space of fellowship and the wonders of creation."

After sitting with my friends, one bid me to walk with her, a beautiful dark-haired woman, down to the shore to board a small wooden sailboat. Our friends cast us off, waving and rejoicing as we left for another shore whose lights could be seen glittering in the distance. As we sailed, she held a small dark-haired boy in her lap, and his young eyes marveled at the water and the night. I then became him, cushioned and warm and safe in the lap of this woman as we glided towards a destiny of glorious promise. I woke then, with the same manner of contentment of the boy I had become, and felt peace and certainty in the process of life. The revelation seemed so vital that it could not be confused for anything but the truth.

Now in the shadow and flicker of my lantern, doubts invade. What was left of this glorious promise for the slaughtered Lazarus, or for the miserable devil whose fingers and penis now hung from a Huichol belt? It seems to me now that my dream was an ideal, the final reduction of creation to the bare bones of eternity. Yes, in the long run, the suffering and horror that infest this world mean nothing. But they mean everything in our present lives. This ideal should not let us run from nobler desires out of fear, for we all die in the end, but we cannot ignore our pain and terror now, nor, it seems to me, should we. Recognition of suffering produces acts of compassion. Without acts of compassion, faith is as smoke.

On second thought, fear and doubt did play their roles in the dream. The revelation would never have come without terror. My boat to paradise would never have sailed without the faith and courage, without the supreme act of will it took to defeat the fear of death. So fear was essential for victory, and the fear was the fear of pain as well as that of death. As fear could never be real without significant objects to fear, pain and death may well be necessary for salvation.

Perhaps this is true not only in my dream, but in all the great dreams that are the myths and religions of Man. How many versions of the martyr, or the sacrificed hero, have been generated in our long history? The essence of the martyr was most memorably captured in James Frazier's phrase, "The king is dead! Long live the king!," in reference to the "corn king" who must die to make way for new growth. Such metaphors have been linked to agriculture, and to the cycle of seasons. There is a need for suffering. Life must make way for more life, and for life to have value, it must fear death and suffer at its approach. To overcome this fear with the ultimate sacrifice makes the hero and gives us courage. So we grasp the martyr. But there is also something else.

In one of his books, C.S. Lewis talks of the crucifixion of Christ and, after many comments, remarks that, in the end, the crucifixion may simply be beyond us. That is, for whatever we take it to be, God may have reasons beyond our knowledge. That is, great sacrifice may also be crucial in the design of the world for reasons we cannot fathom.

This is appealing because it seems obvious that we who cannot understand our own personal lives cannot possibly understand the meaning of existence. The wise have always linked suffering with wisdom, but there always remain more questions than answers. So it is left to us to find reason and example in the words of the wise, as well as to acknowledge the unanswerable with courage and to act with faith.

Wisdom, courage and faith: the revelation of the dream.

With all that, it is unlikely that my dream will have any practical effect. It is not thought that moves clouds but clouds that move thought. With that I go to bed. Hopefully, the next entry will concern the far more interesting events of the Sacred Hunt!   ST

It should not have been surprising to me that a doomed man might receive a mystical warning of his death, as Steven's dream seemed to be. My Grandmother had called my mother just a week before she died of a sudden heart attack, complaining of a yellow mongrel cur that would stare at her from the deck through the big sliding door, and then run off. This had been going on for a week at the time of the call, and she had found that no one in the neighborhood had a dog off the leash, or even a dog of that description. The night before she died, she called my mother again, now frightened, to say that she had just seen the yellow dog, and this time he had not run off when she approached the door, but instead had jumped from the porch, stopped, then turned to bark. Every time she walked a little closer, he would step off a little further, stop, and bark again. She had the distinct impression that the dog was calling her to follow him. This terrified her. My mother promised that she would drive down the next morning. When she got there, an ambulance had already packed up Grandma's body. An EMT said that the mailman had seen her lying on the living room floor. What gave all of us the willies was that as my mother went to her car to follow the ambulance, she saw the yellow dog come from behind the porch. When the ambulance left, the dog chased it for two blocks before he turned out of sight at the corner.

Such is our retrograde link to superstition. It is so strong that I still could not shake the feeling that Steven was talking to me, maybe even playing me to be the fool. Perhaps, I had even thought, all of this was made up, a spoof. Yet he had died, and he had written of a dream that foretold a leap and passage to another world. Some otherworldly breeze touched me at the thought, and an eerie tingling ran along my spine. This was quickly squelched by hard reason, which showed it just as likely, more than likely, that the events in his life of the past month or so had led him to his dream. In that context, Steven's transmogrification into the little boy bespoke an embarrassing psychological need to crawl back into the womb. Such, as Freud said, was the impulse of all the religiously inclined.

The matter settled, I flipped through another few pages in the notebook, skimming the observances that Steven had made of rituals for the dead (related to the disposition of Lazarus), until another personal entry aroused my interest. This lay surprisingly close to the end of all the writing, only a few sheets shy of the endnotes. This meant that his death was very near, although some letters, probably postdated after his final entry, remained in the folder. Could Lacey have continued such a desperate one-way correspondence for so long? The answer was only a few words away.

I was about to proceed when a knock on the door surprised me. This was followed by a monotone voice that informed me of a phone call, which was worrisome. Calls to me were rare and usually came from my mother for the purpose of imposing some tiresome obligation. Of course this is what it had to be. With a sigh I settled into the attitude always reserved for my mother and walked down the hall to the phone. To my continued surprise, the voice that answered was not hers.

"Ben? This is Suzanne."

"Suzanne?"

"I'm calling from the hospital. Listen, they need the extra bed now, and Abraham is ready to go, and they'd like us out, as in now."

"Why the short notice?"

"Babies keep on coming, Ben. The point is, I need some help. I'm tired and hurt from my stitches and have some baby things to bring over to my place, and I'd really appreciate it."

"Oh. I could call a cab for you."

"My father has offered to drive, but they've just arrived and must be tired from the trip. I told them I had a friend who would help."

"That would be me, right?"

"Oh, Jesus, Ben, forget it!"

"No, no, I'll be right down. Your call was just a surprise, that's all. Cancel that idea of the taxi. We can take my car, such as it is."

My mind raced to find some way to maintain an emotional distance. While the possibility of a sexual relationship had warmed me earlier, the grim truth of her needs and the demands of her situation now filled me with the pressing instinct of flight. Perhaps the car was a good idea. The old beast had not been started since October. If it would not start now, I would call back, apologize, get her a taxi and wash my hands of it. Surely they wouldn't kick her into the street until then.

Her reply showed that she had observed the peculiarities of my car before.

"I've seen that thing you have. Don't you have to push-start it?"

"Sure, that's why the taxi, but I'll keep it running outside. No fear anyone will steal that piece of shit. Oh, one thing. What's this about the parents? Doesn't your dad have a vendetta out for me?"

"Oh, that was a moment of passion. Besides, would he kill the father of his flesh and blood grandson? Besides, number two, he doesn't know who the father is. I told you, no strings. To him, you're just a friend in time of need."

"I'll be off in a minute. Just gotta put some shoes on. Give me your number just in case. You know the car."

"OK. If you're not here in half an hour, I'm going anyway. Be here, though, please."

"Sure thing. Bye." It was not a sure thing, and as my shoes and coat were donned, it began to snow. This would make things more difficult, improving my chances of failure considerably.

In the parking lot, the car was still where it had been thoughtfully positioned, heading downhill, looking wild and mangy in its coat of leaves and powdery snow, and at its sight an old hope rose in spite of myself that it just might start. After the door protested its unexpected disturbance, I turned the key to "on," (it had been left in - why not?) put it into neutral, then stepped out to push from the side. I jumped back in as it reached speed, pushed in the clutch, jammed it into second, and popped the clutch. It rumbled ominously, slowed to a near halt, then caught fire. The clutch was quickly disengaged and the engine revved triumphantly. Abraham would be delivered to his home in my chariot after all.

After a treacherous drive with bald tires on new snow, the car was parked in the loading zone in front of the hospital and left running with a hope and a prayer. I made it to the maternity wing, and was unexpectedly pleased at Suzanne's relief to see me. Abe was handed over, and he lay in my arms on the walk to the car, my body stiff and clumsy with this strange cargo. I felt no kinship towards him, yet could feel the tugging of the fatherly tradition as my shoes walked in the steps of thousands of other men who had carried their living seed from the ward in just the same way. But there the recognition stopped. The lives of those poor trapped bastards were not mine. This ran through my mind again and again, more for courage than from conviction.

We found to my surprise and delight that the car was still idling, which instilled me with a momentary flush of optimism. As we settled in and drove off, though, a sense of doom spread over me like spilt ink on a blotter, its stain expanding with each passing city block. By the time we reached Suzanne's apartment building, all hope within had been eclipsed, covered now by the dark penumbra of a wrathful fate. I helped Suzanne from the car in silence and then placed the squirming little fellow once again in my arms as we made our way up the stairs to the old, paint-flaked door of his new home.

Suzanne was slowly pulling herself by the banister behind me when I neared the last step and turned to ask her for the key. Before the sentence could be completed, the door opened, bringing my eyes around to behold the hairy nostrils of an aging Mediterranean man.

CHAPTER 11

Last Prayers

It went, as with all things "Suzanne," as unpredictably as could be expected. Her father was gruff and shrewd, as ruthless as a fighting cock in the ring with an inferior opponent, or with one cruelly hobbled, as was more appropriate for my position. Though I had only done what most men would have done in that moment of passion, his systematic unveiling of my part in the act of creation would place me in the role of the moral penitent before the lawful "keeper of the gate." This not only made a mockery of our society's espoused liberation from such possessive patriarchy, but also nullified Suzanne's guarantee that I could remain a passive bystander in her life.

His initial appearance should have been warning enough. The old man's raucous growth of black facial hair, despite efforts at shaving, accentuated his swarthy cast and bull-dog frame. Now a successful stockbroker, his scarce grasp of gentility underscored his start as a pipe fitter and industrial welder. He spoke before I could say a word, so loudly that I nearly tumbled down the stairs.

"Ah-hah! I see a stranger carries my grandson to the door. Suzanne, who the hell is this guy?" He deftly slipped the baby from my arms and looked only at Suzanne when he spoke. She was painfully struggling up the last steps behind me.

"Papa! I didn't expect you 'till tomorrow." She wheezed slightly and pulled on my arm until she stood gasping by my side. I thought this made us look too much the couple and involuntarily shrugged.

"I wasn't going to sit in the hotel while my daughter staggered into a vacant home from the hospital. A man doesn't leave his women in distress." There was a slight but undeniable glint of maliciousness in his robust humor. I intuited then where this was going and sought to excuse myself.

"Well, it's a pleasure to meet you, too, Mr. DiMandova. And there you have it, Suzanne, home nice and safe. It's time to get my heap and its bald tires back to the ranch before the snow gets too deep."

"No, no! Come in! I brought a special vintage with me, and wish to repay you for helping my daughter. The snow is turning to slush now, anyway." Mr. DiMandova pulled me by the elbow with his one free arm so forcefully that Suzanne and I found ourselves inside the apartment without effort, as if we had ridden a conveyor belt. The door, though, remained open behind me, and I strained for my freedom. There was no doubt that his vintage was the Grapes of Wrath.

"Slush is just as bad. Got a hole in the driver side floor that shoots it right up into my lap when she hits a pothole. Gotta go, Suzanne, see ya." My hand reached at where the doorknob should have been but only grabbed air. A split second later the door slammed, even as Suzanne and I still remained between Mr. DiMandova and the exit, as if her father had the benefit of telekinetic powers. I went to protest again, but was made as putty.

"Enough, now, the weather will only get better. Have a seat, uh, what's your name, young fella?"

"Ben. Solomon."

He handed Suzanne the baby as he grabbed me again by the elbow and levitated me towards the kitchen table. My eyes begged Suzanne for rescue, but she flung me to the lions.

"Thanks, Papa. It's time for his feeding and sleep. Thanks, Ben. I'll leave you two, now. Don't drink too much, Pa. You have to drive back to the hotel."

"We Italians know how to drink, Suzanne. Ben *Solomon*. That sounds Italian." He turned to me again as he let go my arm and sat at the small table. A bottle of wine was already open, hemmed in the middle of the table by two slender glasses. I remained standing with one hand tentatively on the chair.

"Jewish. It's the Sephardic influence. There might be more Spanish in my family than anyone would care to admit."

He gave me a deep, mock frown. "I'd say there's more Protestant in you than Spanish. You sure you're Jewish?"

"That would be Catholic, Mr. DiMandova. My mother's Irish, although neither of my parents is religious. It's just ancestry." My fingers slipped partially from the chair in the subtle anticipation of departure, but Papa would have none of it.

"Just ancestry! There's such a modern waste of the past in that. Sit, have some wine. I insist." He poured my glass near to the brim, then did the same to his. "Sit! Don't tell me that youth has no time for cheer!" I could have told him that, yes, we had time for cheer, and winding discussions, and even frivolity, but not for lectures from an ignorant and unwanted instructor. With loud vocalization, however, the floor was his.

"Ancestry, yes. How woven yours is, huh? From a far corner of Europe to the Near East. Suzanne's mother is German, so she is no stranger to diversity. My parents met in Detroit, their parents from different villages back in the Old Country, which was something back then. It's such an important thing to know your ancestry, don't you agree? Well, how couldn't you, being an anthropologist and all? Half your work is genealogy, isn't it?" He swirled his wine, sniffed it lightly, and took a sip. I followed suit. He seemed to be enjoying this like a pool hustler in a factory-town bar on payday. He didn't seem to care that I had smelled the trap. He seemed sure of his control. Well, my Suzanne, we would see who was Papa around here.

"Actually, that's true with the people I study, the Algonquin, but that's because of their formerly rigid clan structure. Today, we are judged primarily by our dispositions and the fruits of our labor. I find this both more satisfactory personally and more evolved for humanity at large." I put my nose back in my glass to sniff the finish. It was indeed a fine vintage.

It was obvious that Papa wasn't impressed by my refined sensibilities as he pounded twice on the table and laughed with the self-assured joy of mockery. "You don't believe that crap for a moment, do you? Do you think all those Kennedys deserve to go to Harvard? Do you think the young Fords deserve to run Detroit? Do you think that the colored man who's going to steal your tenure track position is more fit than you? Ancestry is who we are, kid. You can take the raw material and mold it in different ways, but society will determine the worth of the raw material first. You're better being born related to the Rockefeller's, even if you haven't inherited a dime. And you're much, much better off knowing WHO you are born from than not. Look at the colored people again. Since LBJ gave them a welfare ticket, half the kids don't know who their fathers are. Without knowing who they are, those poor bastards aren't going anywhere, affirmative action or not."

The man had sliced into his argument like a butcher on a beef flank. No, he was not a chess master. He was an assassin. I hoped to dull his blade with a stab at a sense of inferiority I assumed he had for his relative lack of education.

"Please, Mr. DiMandova, 'they' are insulted by that term now. They prefer to be called "black." And surely you can't condemn them for being the victims of malicious prejudice and overall oppression in this country?" I gave him a sharp look of vicarious offense. It was like rain on stainless steel.

"So, ancestry *does* mean something, then? I thought individual merit ruled American capitalism? Now how about this: how about we cut the crap and you tell me just who you are? Just who might YOU be related to around here, huh?" He finished his glass and glared at me with unmistakable sadistic pleasure. I carefully measured the distance between myself and the door before speaking.

"I'm Suzanne's friend. We started grad school together. It's a bonding not unlike that of soldiers in the field." My speech was cool but I could feel sweat forming on my forehead. Papa raised his blade again.

"You don't look like a fag. You try to talk like one, but I don't think you are. So tell me why a man with an interest in women would be chosen above a woman's girlfriends for the baby's homecoming? Am I just shouting in the dark here? You got an answer for that, bub?"

"Well, yes, we are playing with a possible romance here, yes. This is something relatively new, however, and we scarcely are in the position for a commitment. I believe Suzanne would second that." That last bit of truth helped me catch the waver in my voice.

"Yes, very good. Now, do all academics pirouette a dozen times before they get from point A to point B? Would you have started this romance, say, nine months ago?"

He held me like a rat in a cobra's gaze. "Yes, I guess it would have started about nine months ago." My words came out like an admission to a childhood theft before the teacher. A chill went through me in anticipation of what might follow. Papa seemed to settle down at my forced honesty, but such calm was usually the pause before the coup de grace.

"So let's just leave it at that, shall we? We know the score now, which was known anyway. The birth certificate still sits on the dresser in the room next to us, Mr. Solomon." He gave me a moment to hide a wince. "It's at least nice to know that you are honest, when pressed.

"And you, sir, are a son of a --- an olive grower. When pressed." My turn from anger to sardonic humor was from self-preservation, not wit.

"Hah! Yes, an Italian pressing his olives for virgin oil. Cleverness is not the finest of qualities, but it is a quality." He steadied his eyes on mine. I paused to fill my glass again and took a quick but deep drink. He waited, and then spoke in the steady tone of absolutes. "Now there is truth in virginity and in virtue. Both share in some qualities and diverge in others. I know that my little girl is a grown woman and has done what she has done from her own will. I do not claim to understand her in everything, nor condone all her actions. In fact, the news of her condition was infuriating, but it settled in with time. Suzanne probably knew it would. After all, now we have a grandson. And she knows that the child will not go hungry as long as we are around.

"I suppose you had not planned any of this," he continued, "and were surprised to find that your happy love song ended on a serious note. That's the way men are, and women, for better and for worse, have fought for and won the right to meet men on a level playing field. Which means I don't blame you for this. I don't particularly like you, but I don't blame you. And as you will probably never earn enough in your profession to cover anything but the bare essentials, I don't expect you to support your 'surprise.' In fact, it is my hope that you will get out of the way for another, better man in her future. Except for one thing."

"Ancestry?" The wine was giving me a familiarity with his tough demeanor. I felt more equal to his terms. Besides, the ending was beginning to look happy.

"That's right. You should visit your son regularly and let him know who you and your family are, so that he might know who he is. Remember his birthday and holidays, you know? If you do that, you will at least be a man who might earn some respect."

"From you or from society in general?"

"It doesn't matter, does it? I suppose they would be one and the same. I don't propose a father-son-in-law love fest between us. In fact, when Suzanne does meet the right man, it would be preferable that our families at large kept a respectful distance. Just let, uh, Abraham know who he is. That he's not been dropped on the kitchen floor like a mongrel pup, capiche?"

"It's the least I could do."

"And the most. Really, it's all that any of us want." Papa pushed out his chair and poured a small amount of wine into his empty glass.

"I propose a toast."

I stood up after him, feeling vaguely dissatisfied. My cup was still half-full. "Certainly."

"Good. 'To my grandson, Abraham, may he live up to his name in the embrace of our Lord, and may his future be prosperous and full of love.' And he will certainly have love from us."

"Here, here!" Before I could finish drinking, he continued.

"Thank you, Mr. Solomon. Now it looks like the wind has changed. The slush is starting to freeze. You'd better get going." He was still projecting a portrait of benevolence, but it was beginning to crack at the corners. I should have left immediately, but the thinly veiled disdain he had expressed for me was starting to burn somewhere deep inside.

"Oh, no, that's all right. The weather will only get better, as you said. I'll stay here for a bit and make sure everything's OK. You go get a good night's sleep at the hotel." I could feel my anger breaking through the façade just as his dislike for me quivered at the edge of his good humor.

"No, no, I insist. My car is in fine repair for winter. Besides, you have no experience at this baby thing, do you? No, of course not."

"Really…"

"Everything will be fine. After a mother, a dedicated, um, grandfather is best. I'll get the stairway light for you." He crossed the room quickly and opened the door, smiling the whole while. A dedicated grandfather, my ass! It was a wise thing that he did not attempt to carry me out the way he had hauled me in. I was nearly snarling.

"But it's getting late, Mr. DiMandova. You should leave nights like these to the young."

"I have stayed up many a late night, young man. Providing for my family has given me more stamina than the hardiest of youth. Don't forget your coat." His smile was dropping as fast as his undercuts to my character. In my anger, I could have turned on him without fear, but found upon consideration that I had no foot to stand on. I had taken no moral or financial responsibility for my son. No commitment had been made on my part to the mother besides an open-ended date. Indeed, all that remained at the moment was a vague promise to let Abe know about his family and a simmering hatred in my guts for the tough old dago who was pushing me out the door. I roughly grabbed my coat.

"All right, then. I'll have plenty of time to 'help out' once you're gone. Have a pleasant visit." I began to brush past him when he gripped my arm with the force of iron.

"Don't go messing up my daughter's life any more, understood? You got a freebee on this one. Only one strike's allowed in this game."

"Is that a threat?" I pulled my arm away and stepped forward to the stairs. "You know, Mr. DiMandova, no one likes being treated like a "colored" man. It causes resentment."

"Act like a white man and get treated like one, Mr. Solomon. Drive carefully." He shut the door firmly but without anger. Why should he be angry? He was the man on the inside.

The practical thing to do was to let the whole episode drop. Papa was a bastard, but his words had let me off the hook - again. The right things had been done as far as I could see, even if for the wrong reasons, leaving me free to skate. My hands were washed.

My pride was another thing. Back at the car, a rehash of the conversation tore into my guts like a swallowed fish hook while I scraped the ice from the window; gnawed like a weasel while I pushed the old junk to a start; and ground like a grist mill while I slid along the barren roads. The resentment grew to open hatred of the old man by the time I reached the parking lot and had me plotting revenge on the walk to my room. Fortunately, the sight of the bed made me realize my fatigue, and with that, the weight of fury fell like a load of bricks. My nerves were trembling, and I remonstrated myself. What was the point? My freedom and fortune remained intact. I had faced the worst and walked away as unencumbered as before. Why should pride hold sway when my precious freedom had been guaranteed?

Still, I was shaken. The old man had known how to push the buttons. What was needed was a literary nightcap to sooth the nerves. One last glass of clumsy prose from my former classmate, Steven, would do the trick. Perhaps his shallow tale would even come to an end that night. This, it occurred to me, would be apt, as both our lives, so to speak, would be completed in a way, a stage of struggle ended. I sat on the bed, took off my shoes and flipped to the next personal entry in the notebook:

26 de Enero

There is so much to write in so little time! I have excused myself from my *hikuritarame*, my companions on the Journey, saying that more "necessities" must be gathered for the long drive into the Sonora Desert so that this addition to the notes can be made before particulars are forgotten. It might be a while until I can write again.

The gathering around Grandfather Fire for the initiation of the Journey had more of an effect on me than I had supposed. As Horacio drew blessings from the 5 directions, the cardinal points and the center, making a cross over the fire, I felt the same separation from the profane and deliverance into the sacred that had come to me years before when we made the sign of the cross at church. Just as at my church, this was a signal of what was to come, for the ceremony would arouse the sacred again and again in many ways.

For instance, a special radiance was lent to the arrows Horacio normally used to communicate with the ancestors, as these same arrows were (are) to become pivotal in the hunt for peyote in Wirikuti. These arrows are the spiritual counter-part of hunting arrows, just as peyote is the spiritual twin of the deer. These later elements, deer and peyote, have been intimately connected since the "Beginning Time," as both are essential in maintaining the Huichol way in the world. Because they are seen as different aspects of the One Way, peyote is hunted just as the deer are, only with spiritual arrows rather than with stone or metal points. And just as the Master Spirit, or force behind the physical manifestation of the deer, must be appeased before a normal hunt, so the Master Spirit of the peyote must be appeased through this ritual. It is in this equation of substance and spirit, and of the "now" and timeless ritual, that the past and present and the spiritual and the material are pulled together to form a greater design. This design, this aspect of cosmic truth, creates a portal to the spiritual realm for participants. It is this coming together of time and matter and spirit in an all-inclusive experience that gives us the radiance of the sacred.

We also experienced the union of souls. The other world of spirit was opened again when a knot was tied for each of us on a cord as each confessed his sexual sins publicly (I brought up some embarrassing episodes from my dating life) and the cord was burned, just as another was made for our ritual life. In the flames was not only the expiation of our carnal sins, but also the actualization of the words of Horacio that accompanied the burning: that we were no longer simply humans; that we were now of one accord, the embodiment of the ancestor gods.

The overall ritual, the coming together of everything, has aroused in me a great longing, a type of atavistic nostalgia that has been explained away so inadequately by empirical theorists. It has brought me back to childhood, when the world was personal, when my classmates were my tribe and my neighborhood my territory, each as close to me as the notion of self. It is in this time that we experience the beginnings of all things; this is the time of Eden, when everything is known intuitively, before our dissecting intellect is sharpened to cut us off from our origins.

I believe that I now better understand what the Huichols seek in the Journey: the very essence of creation, the beginning when all things shown with spirit and all things great or small were of infinite significance. It has come to me, in a vague way, how this Beginning Time is ever present, how creation is not simply the initial spinning of the ball, but a constant force of spirit, a never-ending creation of beauty and power that burns like a fire in the black night.

It is hard to control the ecstasy! To continue: before I left to write, everyone was sprinkled with blessed water. This same water was added to a touch of cornmeal and stirred with a candle lit by the flame. This is the meal that will form the dough from which our tortillas will be made, this being the only food we will have on the Journey. We will be denied salt also, given little water, and allowed little sleep. We are to abstain from sex and selfish thoughts. Horacio has exhorted us to lose the stupor of greed and gluttony and free ourselves to become the pure spirits we must be to enter Wirikuti.

In a moment we will begin the walk to Tutzingo, where we hope to find the van delivered as promised. Although there is no question that things will not go according to plan - they never do in Mexico - I feel somehow unconcerned about it, certain that what is meant to be will be. I cannot tell if my sense of trust and my heightened sense of the sacred are simply due to fasting and sleep deprivation, or if there truly is a great new spirit among us. Might not the experience be proof enough?

Speaking of privations reminds me of a conversation I had with Gary about the issues of pain and suffering in Christianity. There is not much time, but I will write what time affords. The issue seems more and more relevant as the ceremony continues.

It had come up with a discussion of religion in Mexico, and how the people here cling to the image of the bleeding and agonizing Jesus that adorns every church wall. I had guffawed without thought at this primitive mentality, but was rebuked by the doctor.

"Tell me, do we no longer have pain, disappointment, sorrow and death? Of course we do. But you know what we sophisticates, we moderns, have done? So that we might better worship our modern technology for the material comforts it has brought, we have banished death and disease and fear to little rooms out of sight and sound. We thus are freed to feel superior to those of the past who dwelled with their infirmities and mortality. In the process, however, we have also thrown away the greatest truth that self- reflection grants us about life, which is that all things of this world die, rot and turn to dust. More to the point, we have disavowed ourselves of the vehicles that we have been given to overcome death, which are the very same experiences of pain and suffering and fear that you belittle."

I told him that it was only a reflex, but to him, that did not mitigate my blasphemy in the least.

"It is a reflex of the modern world, for that is the only way it has to shake off the truth – to throw it off reflexively before it can be examined."

I asked how pain and such could lead to truth.

"We have answered that, haven't we? When you disregard suffering, you focus only on the enjoyment or the concerns of the immediate material reality. The state of suffering and fear takes away the importance of baubles, or of anything else but its alleviation. With time, however, we learn that there is no palliative for the condition. Or, rather, that there is only one cure: spirit. So it is that one-day, we realize from these negative conditions that there is something greater, above and beyond our limited forms. It is at the door of suffering or impending death that we are forced to consider that which is beyond our transitory world. That is when we are able to find spirit. If we lived in a world where all this was understood, we would not have to confront the worst of suffering, which is the loss of spirit. We have forgotten this to our great peril."

In spite of my dream "revelation," I rejected his argument strongly, saying, "From my experience, suffering and fear are more likely to make us angry or resentful about life. How would this response bring us closer to spirit?" This posed no problem to him.

"The suffering you observed may not have been enough. Let me put this in another way: suffering is like the massive waves of a terrible storm at sea. If you were caught in them, you would indeed suffer in the worst way: you would be brought to the terror of death. Yet - and picture in your mind the tall black walls of water rolling out of an endless ocean under a chaotic sky - think how this horrible grandeur would also show you how insignificant your being and power are in comparison. An experience like that breaks the lie of the ego while showing the power that exists around us. It makes us think: who made the waves? How much more powerful is the creator than this, His raging sea? And who shields us in daily life in the palm of His hand against such forces? This is how pain and suffering and fear bring us to spirit: we see how protected we were before, we realize how powerless we are now, and we are brought to see how good and great God is."

Since then his words have brought many other questions to mind, such as "how do we trust in an afterlife through our suffering?," but I can now see that once you are brought to the "spirit" threshold through the seriousness of ritual, fasting, pain or fear, the benevolence of spirit becomes self-evident. It is like the internal journey to the dawn of creation we just shared a few moments ago at the fire. It is at this point that demands for proof and cause must be dropped and the fact of the experience must simply be lived.

Maybe that is the difference between those who are spiritual and those who are not: at some point, those of a spiritual bent can accept an experience as it is. Maybe, then, the Huichol life *is* more spiritual than ours; maybe, because of the Journey and peyote and the myths and metaphors of the language, they really *are* as far ahead of us spiritually as we are ahead technologically. Maybe the doctor was right when he said that we have lost something very big in our move to modernity.

It is time to go, they are calling. I will write whenever possible, but will first live the experience, this of a lifetime.   ST

For the first time after reading one of Steven's essays of "enlightenment" I could not be completely cynical; the touch of fingers on paper told me that only a few pages remained in the notebook. His journey, his hopes, his loves, everything was about to end. For some reason I found it odd that he did not confess a presentiment of his demise, for, at least in hindsight, his dream was clearly just that. Then again, he was always the optimist, and probably saw in his dream not darkness, but a new and beautiful spiritual life about to unfold. He undoubtedly understood that the dark-haired woman and the little boy were his own Indian mate and child-to-be, and the ocean journey one to a brighter future.

Normally, the demystification of someone else's dreams gave me deep satisfaction, but this time the inspired and clear vision left me cold. To see that his bright and spiritual view of life might only be a veneer that hid the dull and bitter truth of existence saddened me more than anything else. Gloating after winning a long battle for intellectual dominance is the great joy of the academic, but it dawned on me with a shock that this time I wished to be proven wrong. Something in me wanted to be handed the proof of a miracle from some greater and more perfect force that would confound hard reality. My disappointment made me wonder if something had changed within me. Had the events of the past year, particularly of the last month, made me soft? If so, would this be for better or for worse? Had this delving into other's lives, this that had handed me a woman with my child, burrowed even deeper? Had it found in some interior darkness a sputtering candle whose existence had not even been known?

Lost in such thoughts, I didn't know how many times the communal phone in the hallway rang before it caught my attention. As stated, I usually left it for someone else to answer, as calls to me were as rare as hens' teeth, but Christmas vacation was upon us and only a few in my building remained behind. The odds now leaned to me. It could only be another request from Suzanne. No strings attached my ass.

I plucked the receiver from the wall and spat out a sharp "hello." It took me by surprise when the voice that answered back was my mother's, the one that should have been expected all along.

"Benny! How are you? I called to ask what your plans are for Christmas." She sounded unusually cheerful, as if she had been given an increase in her medication. I reminded myself that I must cull reality from any manic swings she might have in the conversation.

"I thought I'd stay here and work, Ma. Exams are coming up. I was thinking of driving down for a day around New Year's."

"I thought that's what you might say, but listen to this!" I could almost hear the bells sounding behind her voice. She was flying. "A friend of your father's has a place out by Vail and he's going to be in the Caribbean this year. We've been invited to stay the whole week! Wasn't that nice of him?"

"Oh, you must mean Jim Thornman. Yeah, Dad wrote me about that. He said he got a bunch of his clients into metal commodities just before the Hunt brothers' silver hustle. I'll bet he made Mr. Thornman a bundle."

"Yes, and he has been kind enough to show his gratitude. Anyway, we're flying out Christmas day, as no one else is going then, and we'd like to buy you a ticket to join us. We could get you one right out of Detroit so you won't have to do any driving." Pleading saturated her voice as if her entire upswing of mood depended on my answer. Of course I would say yes - this was the saving grace that was wished for the day before, and later was better than never. But it was my custom to dig around the family plot before a commitment

"What about Sheila? Is she coming home?" I hadn't seen my sister in five years, ever since she married the Iraqi pilot and moved to an apartment in Samara. That country was now kicking up serious sand with Iran, and even though the US was backing Iraq, travel was restricted by its iron-fisted dictator, Saddam Hussein. There was more to it than that: her husband, Fayed, was now on active duty and the family would not allow her to travel, not when he might need her at any moment. It was also certain they suspected she might leave the country and not come back, with or without her two kids. I knew all this but couldn't help myself from mocking the romantic idiocy of my self-righteous sibling.

"Oh, God, Benny, you know she can't! It's just so awful there now, just from what she's permitted to write. God only knows how awful it really is."

"God has nothing to do with it, Ma. Sheila was "in love," and nothing could stop her from her lunacy. She'll return from there after her divorce, sadder but wiser."

"Oh, no, Benny, I don't think he would permit a divorce. Women don't have the same rights in the Mideast as men. It's hard to tell what she wants by her letters, they're so stilted. I don't know what we're going to do." I could hear her façade crumble as she spoke and knew it was time to put an end to it. It was difficult to stop mocking the romantic notions of the women in my family, but the validity of their view of the world was no longer in contest. Life had proven that their dreams were just shadows of an illusion. Just in case of backslide, though, it was still necessary to force their sentimental delusions to dance naked, humiliated, on the stage every now and then.

"It's all right, Ma, she'll work it out. She's got our help if she needs it. Anyway, sure, I'd love to come. You bring my skis, or should I rent?"

"Oh, I'm so glad, Benny! We'll be together for the holidays just like we used to. I'll call back tomorrow and let you know your flight. And let's just rent, OK? We don't want to carry all that."

"I'm kinda broke. Could you front me some money?" This was a tough one. While mom played the flaky artist and dad the realist hard-ass, they both were of one mind when it came to cash. Things, flights, anything they paid for first was OK, but to hand over actual cash brought a panic to them like a solar eclipse brought to the ancient Mayans. I had learned to enjoy the ritual. It was hard to stifle a laugh as she stuttered.

"Wait, Benny. I thought you were paid this month? I have to ask your father. We just had to buy a new hot water heater, and you know your father's problems with hemorrhoids, doctors are so expensive now. And you have no idea about property taxes yet, but the corrupt Chicago politicians are about to send us all downstate, or to Missouri for that matter."

"Oh, forget it, then. Save your money. I'll drive down this spring maybe, sometime after exams. There's too much work to do here, anyway." I leaned against the wall, waiting for her to finish extracting that painful tooth.

"Benny, we can't pass this up! You have nothing? How much? Oh, forget it, we can get you what you need. Your father's in a good mood after his department awarded him the senior chair. He gets more time to work in the private sector now, and, I think, yes, it will be all right." She was panting from the exertion. For all the anxiety it caused, I couldn't figure out why she bothered with me. She had been put through two crises in just that many minutes. Even we cynics had to admit to the existence of at least a pinch of parental affection.

"Great, Ma, thanks a bunch. Christmas day, right?"

"That's the day after tomorrow, don't forget! I'll call you tomorrow, late morning, OK?"

"Yeah, great, I'll see you in Vail." I hung up wondering if my ticket was yet to be bought, as an open seat on a little-traveled day to save money, or whether it had been bought in advance, causing her to panic at the thought that I would decline the offer and waste the money. No matter, the ticket freed me from Ann Arbor for a week, more than long enough, certainly, to avoid another run-in with the 'in-laws.' It gave me the shudders to think of a meeting with Mrs. DiMandova. If the Mr. had been shrewd, than the Mrs. was more than likely to be catty, a quality I placed somewhere between the attributes of Hitler and Richard Nixon.

Now, with that problem out of the way, nothing stood to ruin my enjoyment of the tragic tale of Steven Tressle's pilgrimage. I settled back in my chair and held for a moment the few thin pages left in the diaries. Such a fragile trace left of a life force. I found myself taking a deep breath before focusing on the first page:

Jan 25

Was it disaster or glory? Who can say? I have heard but never realized. Battle changes everything. What I thought it was is not. It was kill or be killed, but killing – Oh God, maybe it was the ritual space we were in. It was so sudden. It is clear now how death comes for creatures of the world - so sudden, so fast that lightening seems slow.

I had walked behind Horacio and my companions, trying to join with them in the response to his song, a beautiful thing like the fall of water over stone. We had been moving at a very rapid pace for at least four hours, putting us more than half the distance to Tutzingo. The memory comes still, so peaceful. I was so entranced, a being out of time, a brother to all nature and man. The first shots were not even heard, just the sight of one man, then another falling. The colorful embroidery on their white shirts grew like living flowers and I marveled at it briefly until the realization came that they were bleeding to death. My reaction to it stuns me now, as unexpected a thing as could be imagined. My mind seemed packed in cotton except for a response mode unknown to my life, one that lay beyond surprise and compassion. Because of the recent troubles, we were carrying our weapons, mine loaded with deer slugs, barrel open for safety. With the deaths, something within me snapped the gun shut with precision and swiveled to locate the sound of the shots. This same something jerked the gun to my shoulder at a hint of movement and pulled the trigger, then unloaded the other barrel at another movement.

Howls echoed as one man fell through the brush, then another. My hands reloaded quickly and fired again and again, reloaded, fired, reloaded. It was as if I were shooting skeet, ready, focused, taut, beyond fear or feeling, until Jerome pulled me down behind the rocks. Two of the others had rifles, and we kept firing as the five of us crouched behind a ridge. I remember resting my hand briefly on a rock just as it exploded into a shower of piercing slivers and chips. There was no feeling at the moment, but blood oozed and then flowed in bubbling throbs between my fingers. It came to me that an M16 round had the speed to smash bricks on impact, and understood that our assailants were using modern military equipment.

My injured hand went numb and throbbed as I mechanically followed the others. We were running behind Horacio, who was moving with impossible speed along the rocks and down the side of a cliff, stopping long enough so that we might see him. At the cliff I found that my left hand could not grab, so I cradled my shotgun and climbed with the right as we dropped from one ledge to another until we landed on the lip of a flat rock. Before us was a cave that was hidden from above. I followed the others in, blind at first, and instantly felt the coolness and a womb-like sense of refuge and peace. It took several minutes to adjust to the dark, and in that time a sense of self returned. My hand began to hurt like blazes. I shook all over, not from fear, but from exertion. We all listened when Horacio spoke:

"We have lost 'Kwaxi' and 'Tateima'(names of ancestors that each of us has assumed for the Journey) from our sight, but they still remain at the beginning of time for ever. We cannot stop our journey now, anymore than we can stop the journey of the sun. They are one and the same. We will wait for nightfall, then crawl past the enemy along the cliff and come out at the "puerta" by the lizard rock. They will not know to find us there We will finish this matter on our return, when we have brought back our power and balance. You, Tsata (this is my ceremonial name) have killed cleanly. You are a 'first person' and clear of any stain. We will only have to protect against the 'Tatusti'" (the evil sorcerers).

He then lit a candle that hurt my eyes, revealing a well-worn floor and a curved wall covered with paintings of deer and people and spirits.

I could sense then that our enclave was ancient, maybe as old as Man in America. Horacio fell into a chant that brought a peace that still remains as I write, one that somehow modified the pain of my hand. In fact, I must stop writing now to refocus on that zone before the intense pain returns. The question remains with me, though: where is my horror and remorse for killing?

An answer keeps coming that is hard to believe: I liked it. The battle, that is, and the victory in the death of my enemy. Until now, I have only known the lament of the Vietnam debacle, of the horrors of war and its insanity, and have always agreed with that assessment. But why is this real violence so fulfilling? It does not feel like it comes from a desire to slaughter, but from an eagerness to test myself against evil. The exhilaration is powerful, yet remains frightening, as if the self that I know might be overrun by a demon that has risen within me. Still, in between the pain I am eager for the next confrontation. It is confusing. It will take some time to understand this.

Who are our opponents? Are they military, ex-military, or have the drug lords merely bought the illicit weaponry from unscrupulous dealers? Being Mexico, I suppose, it's all the same thing. When we come down from the mountains, we will deny everything. Only the relatives of the dead will know that something that 'never happened' really did.

I must concentrate on the chant. My hand hurts like blazes. Something is shattered. With God's help I will write again. ST

Onward Christian Soldier! How perfectly that was said, how clearly the call of the crusader to war! This turn was not surprising in the least: his incipient zealotry was apparent from the start. His was the classic case of a man of reflection who could not reflect clearly upon himself. For this, I have always sneered at their self-righteousness and taken for granted their inevitable fall from grace. Those who claim to live in a higher realm never notice their feet below. When they do feel the grit of earth, they are shocked and appalled. The rest of us, on the other hand, know what we are from the start.

Once again, though, I could not revel in my gloating. I admired Steven's courage in spite of myself. Introspection, a cold judgment of my own being, found nothing nobler within than the laughing hyena, courageous before a weakened prey but ready to run at the sight of the lion. Did this insight make me wiser, or simply more focused on inner faults and deficiencies? Were courage and commitment in others only romantic illusions, or had my cynicism been merely a device to protect myself from my own lack of such virtues?

I did not want to dwell in that uncertain land of speculation for long. It was a muddy swamp in which there was no firm ground. Instead, I flipped the page of the notebook and found, as had been surmised, that the last words of Steven had finally been plumbed. As a mock "farewell" rose reflexively to my tongue, an emotional tension clenched my throat. This, too, was quickly swept from mind with a sorting of the remaining letters. Only two had not been read, the first from Lacey to Steven. The contents, a single sheet of paper, fell from the envelope with a single tap on the torn edge. It occurred to me that Steven probably had been dead on its arrival, meaning someone other than the intended reader had opened it. What this little note said was beyond pathetic:

Dear Steven,

I have accepted the TA position, as you have not written since my last missive, and hope that you can now tell me when you will return. If you need money, for a flight or whatever, please let me know. I was able to extend the lease on my old place, so everything will be just as it was before you left, a comfortable and familiar home. Is it possible that you might make it back before spring? These wretched months of winter will be hard to survive without you. But a correction in the letter is in order: there is one thing at our home that has changed.

I have discovered what the meaning of "want" is. It has been defined in our time as a grasping desire, but in its pure form, it was meant to express a need for something that would make one full or complete. I have spoken before of a woman's deep ties to her ancestry, as this is the feminine path to the divine. It is all about connection, of the miracle that hides behind passion and its loss and its deviations and its diversions. It's about the one continuous line from woman to woman, how each has loved the life that would come from her and go beyond her.

What is changed, then, is the very notion of my being. It is now clear that the trap of the masculine world of cold ideas has kept me at a distance from you. It has reversed my natural priorities and almost forced me to pay for it with my sanity. Turning from this phantasm has allowed me to understand that I can love you without reservations, without caveats; that I can live as a force of life, not as a projection. That I can say "yes" to our love with a joy unclouded by misgivings.

Please write as soon as possible. There will be no peace in our apartment until your words arrive,

Love, Lacey

Another man would have felt sorrow for this situation, but I could not hold back a feeling of nausea from the sickly-sweet aftertaste of hypocrisy. The coincidence of his admission to another love and her change of heart dispelled the fairy-tale notion of romance from the situation. Here was a woman on the edge, absorbed in herself to the point of self-mutilation, who suddenly found that her useful tool of a man had been taken by another woman. How could one not see that her words were only reiterations of Steven's philosophic and romantic notions, turned against him as a trap?

Regardless, it was over and Lacey was, as far as I knew, still curled in the fetal position in her family mansion. What interested me was the final letter. It was not stamped or postmarked, only labeled "To Lacey" in large letters, and in all probability had arrived with Steven's notes and letters in the package from Mexico. Its seal had not been broken! The sender could only be one of three people: the doctor, Angelica, or Tripper. Logic dictated the first of the three. Would, for instance, Angelica have known of Lacey, and if she had, would she have bothered to write to her rival? Or would Tripper have put himself out for such social niceties even if he had known of Lacey?

I stopped my guessing game, slit the seal and pulled the letter from its envelope. On the opening page was a hand-written heading that took a moment to decipher: Gary McMahon, M.D. He had added his address as well, and it surprised me to find that he was from Denver. It crossed my mind that, somehow, coincidence was again pulling me into this drama against any wish on my part. I ignored the chills that ran up my spine by returning to the letter and its content:

Dear Lacey,

I am not sure if Steven ever mentioned me in his correspondences, although I know he wrote to you frequently. Please let me introduce myself in my own clumsy way. It has been my pleasure to share this forgotten area of the Sierra Madre with a man of Steven's caliber. My job here is to minister to the poor and to the Indians, both in body and spirit, and when word came that an anthropologist had moved into the neighborhood, I prepared for the worst. We people of faith have often had bitter clashes with the intelligentsia in the field, but Stephen soon surprised and delighted me with his open mind and heart that yearned for God, although he did not define Him exactly as I do. It was, indeed, this difference of definition that made our conversations so interesting and our friendship so animated. Even so, it was his willingness to help and his sincerity that impressed me most. I know that whatever has been and will be, the fate of Steven is securely and lovingly in God's hands.

This is true now more than ever. Forgive me, but there is simply no other way to put this: Steven is no longer among us in this world. I know that you will deeply mourn his loss, but please take heart and know that he understood well that death in this life leads to a greater life in our Lord. He knew, as he once said, that this world is like a man born with one good leg and one bad: that every step one takes forward is matched by another that sidesteps or goes backward. We are born into a world of inevitable frustration, hardship and sorrow. We must hone our will so that when we are made perfect again, we are able to walk, straight and forward. I know that Steven even now is striding towards the eternal glory that he rightly deserves.

Even in his worldly demise you may take comfort that his end was as noble as his intentions in the rest of this life. I was not there, but Jim Sokorsky, a man often referred to as "Tripper," was able to gather the facts. He lives among the Indians and knows their language fully, and as he was a good friend of Steven's I have no reason to doubt his story. In brief, he says that Steven was undertaking the "Journey to Beginning Time" (or the Peyote Hunt) with six Huichol pilgrims when they were ambushed by the enemies of the Indians of the area, a group of narcotic traffickers with whom they had shed blood before. Two of the pilgrims were killed in the fight. Steven was severely wounded in his left hand, but not before he was able to kill several of the bandits, giving his companions time to escape the trap. He was able to make it with the other survivors to a secret cave on the side of a cliff, where they hid until they were tracked down near nightfall. At this point, the criminals attached explosives to the end of ropes so that they might swing them into the cave. Sooner or later they knew that one would go off at the right place and kill or maim everyone within.

Below is a portion of the account in more detail, as told to Tripper by Jerome, one of the six pilgrims:

"We were all afraid, for we could do nothing about the explosives. They were set to go off with fuses, but we could not bat them from the cave, for that would make them explode as well. It was twilight, and even with their electric torches, we had hope that we might escape when true darkness came. We prayed and sang to Tatewari, who steadied our nerves and made us brave each time the flashing death came into our sanctuary. For too long this went on until Mother Night covered us with her blanket. We knew the Spanish could not follow us then in our land, and we prepared to leave. Our mara'akame [a kind of priest or shaman, this one named Horacio] was the first to peer out when a bullet thundered into the rocks only a breath away from him. The dark ones had placed a killer on a small ledge that allowed him a clear shot at us. How he could see us we did not know. They continued to swing the explosives, and we felt that our lives were lost.

"It was Steven who saved us. He raised his injured hand to us to show its uselessness. It had now turned the color of late dusk and had grown many times its size. He told the mara'akame that he could not climb to escape with us, but that he could be of help. He said he could shoot at the killer while we escaped. After that, he hoped they would think all were gone and leave him to heal. It was a prayer only, but we knew that we would all be dead if we did nothing. Horacio agreed, telling him that he would come back later in the night and help him sneak from the cave if our enemies were still there. We all agreed to this, and raised our rifles to fire so that Steven could reach a boulder to hide behind and punish the assassin.

"We rushed out together, Steven towards the gunman and we towards the *puerta*, and he was blessed to kill the Spaniard with his first shot. We rushed for the path, but José was hit in the shoulder by another villain who had guessed at our route. We were surprised and helpless. We knew an automatic weapon was pointed towards us and felt certain that we could do nothing to keep from becoming food for the earth. It was in that instant that the cave flared with fire, knocking us to our feet. An explosion had gone off within, and the force blew everything out into the open night in a flash of lightning. The others only heard the second explosion, a smaller one, but Horacio and I saw everything in the white light of the moment before we were blinded by darkness.

We saw Steven fly like a raven from the rocks, his legs spread wide and back like wings, and we saw the flame from his shotgun and the dark shadow of the killer as he dropped his rifle. The blackness that followed was darker than before from the greatness of the flash. There was only nothing and silence. I felt I could not move, but the mara'akame whispered that we should grab one another by the shoulder and follow him. We were as silent as the turning stars, and we heard only a shout, then a few more, until we were too far away to be found.

"It was a long climb to the puerta, and we were surprised when Horacio said that he would then go back as promised. We had both seen Steven fly from the cliff, and unless he had remained a god [from the ceremony and peyote], only the raven that his soul had become would remain. But as he was now given to his destiny, it would be beneath the mara'akame to throw aside fate for safety. We were told to wait for him until sunup and sing the story of the great flood and the new earth that arose from the waters that gave us our lives. We were grateful for the light of the rising moon, but shuddered in fear as it darkened with the redness of old blood. It spoke to us of death, and we feared that Horacio was now lost, too, and that soon we would follow him.

"It was mercy that delivered him to us before we lost our courage. He must have flown with the wings of an owl, for he was back before the pure and silver morning light, holding in his hand the bag that Steven always carried. His breath was slow and deep like a panther's and his eyes shown with light like mirrors as he told us what he had seen. It was all part of the miracle of our journey, and I feel forever blessed by these, his words:

"'I moved with the power of the first being, without effort or hindrance, and found myself shortly in the rocks above the cave. The evil men had already gone, although I could still smell their horses, and I saw that they followed the trail from which they came, blind to the way of our passing. The moon had risen, as round as a baby's face, but I could see that she was hurt and shortly saw the wound spread with the north wind, from this side to that. I cried the prayer to her brother the sun and heard in reply that she suffered for the work of the gods, that she danced a dance as old as earth itself, of the giving of her life to her

286

children, just as the mother earth had given herself to yearly death to save us from the flood, just as we pour out our sweat and youth so that our children may live and grow. And I saw that Steven had flown from us a god, and had died for us as he would his children, and had joined his star in the heavenly family, a star beyond the moon, the moon who will always dance her dance of the deathly wound and the return of brightness and life.

"I saw that he had shucked the small world of man for the eternity of the gods, that he had not left us as most do, limping, old and pitiful, but instead filled with courage and life, to join in the eternal song of wonder that is creation. Surely he had left the cave of our ancestors in a blaze of light like a baby who is born into the bright sun. I saw that he walked in a path made for us, to show us that a new way is opening, that even the Spanish and the English might join our journey, and we theirs. How this may come is not certain, but it has been opened and walked and we will see. It has been laid before us in the way of the gods, and we will see.'"

"So our mara'akame spoke to us, and I cannot understand all his words and ways, but it is true that our journey went so well, that the buses along our journey came at his whim and went with his way, that the land of beginning welcomed us, that our priest said it was a journey filled with the most power, that we were all pleased when we lit the last fire on our return and burnt the cord of our binding and returned to our regular life. And Horacio then said a prayer for Steven and told us one thing that was not glad to us: that the new times would mean the end of old ways, that the deer were leaving us along with the forests and our seclusion, that with a greater world and greater wisdom would come the sacrifice that must always accompany new life. And so we left with sadness in our joy, as Steven's death was the sadness in a greater tale."

Lacey, I don't know how much of this you understand, or how much we can believe, but it is a certainty that men were killed and that Steven is now held as a great and brave man. Having known him for several months, I am not surprised that he should have made the ultimate sacrifice for his comrades, and you should hold as true that his greatest attributes defined him in the closing of the book of his life. I know that Steven was not a strict adherent of the Bible, and he mentioned your questioning also, but we can be assured that if any man among us deserves His heavenly reward, it is Steven. Still, of course, we are sorrowful for his passing and he will be missed, but it should come as a great comfort to think him with his Holy Father now forever, far from the troubles of our imperfect lives. I believe this with all my heart, and hope that you can as well.

I will be in my home in Denver for the next four months, and should be around more often than not given the circumstances of my advancing age, as well as the escalating troubles in the Mexican mountains. Although you may know nothing of me, I feel that I know you well through Steven, and welcome you to call on me whenever you feel the need. All of Steven's papers and letters from Los Zamorros and Tutzingo are bound together here and left in your care, as his father is dead and his mother, as Steven told me, is not well. They are solely yours and you may do with them whatever you please. I hope that you read them first before discarding, as he surely has left something of worth behind in them, but that is entirely up to you. It is understood that you will be mourning and perhaps might want to leave things alone for a while. I am so sorry for your loss.

Please consider me your friend and contact me whenever you feel the need,

Sincerely, Dr. Gary McMahon

P.S.: Although I have had the Indians scour the area, Steven's body has yet to be found. It is a wild land of cliffs and canyons, but it is still odd that signs could not lead expert hunters to his remains. As a traditional Christian, I hold my breath at such news, but I assure you that everything has been done to locate him, and any news of his remains will be sent immediately to you. Please have faith and take heart, GM

I finished this, the last of many letters and notes in what seemed an eternal saga, with more wonder and less scorn than anticipated. Of course the little adventure tale was more superstition and fabrication than truth: no one gives his life so readily, especially since he had at least a few moments for reflection. More concretely, no one could retain the composure, much less the consciousness, to locate and shoot a foe while being ejected from a cliff by an explosive charge. It is most probable that a lack of agility, from a wound or not, had left Steven in the rear, and he was caught by the explosives and blown unconscious into the void. His silence under those circumstances may have been taken for bravery. As for the rest, it is my understanding that the "journey" they were on required continual doses of peyote, allowing them to see what they wished to see. And as for the style of the report, my god, I sincerely doubt that the Indians spoke like those in Longfellow's *Hiawatha*, regardless of a poor or sweetened translation.

Still, his body was not found, giving a hint of mystery to the story. Of more significance to me, the doctor had emerged as an accessible witness to Steven's adventure. For some reason, like readers of books or fans of film, I wished to have a connection to the story, something that would ground it for me, make it a more personal reality. While pursuing this connection through his acquaintance would have been far too costly and awkward under normal circumstances, the flight to Colorado allotted me a surprising opportunity. I could pay the good doctor a visit before motoring out to join my parents in a stranger's home in Vail for a good, old-fashioned Christmas.

First, the doctor had to be contacted for an arranged meeting. It had occurred to my sense of humor to arrive at his door unannounced, as a stranger brought to him by Providence, but that left his presence to fickle chance. I thus followed the path of prudence and courtesy and dialed the number given on his letter to Lacey. After several rings, a young woman answered, somewhat out of breath. The whine of a baby and the monotone of a young child's voice clashed in the background. The woman identified herself as the doctor's daughter, and had me wait on the line while she found the man of the house.

Doc Gary's voice was blandly pleasant in our introductions, but hardened when my connection to Steven was mentioned:

"You said your name was Ben Solomon? I never heard Steven mention you. How did you get this number?"

I told him that I was a friend of Lacey's, and that after her collapse of nerves, I had searched in her papers for a key to her emotional disturbance.

"Wouldn't that be obvious? The death of a loved one? How did you get hold of her private property?"

The old man was being an unexpected curmudgeon, but the petulant demands of pedagogues had dogged me my whole life. Lying to them had become second nature. I replied that she had not told us of the death, and it was only through the examination of her discarded letters and papers that we had learned of it, opening a new corridor for her rehabilitation. It was my mission now to find if there were any other details lacking that might aid her psychiatrist and other care givers in her recovery. I then asked him if a brief visit might be arranged for this Sunday, as I would be in Denver on separate business. He ignored my request.

"What mental illness does she have? My God, is she comatose? I can't believe that she has refused to tell anyone about Steven. I must call her and set her straight. I'm sure she can be brought around."

I explained that her care givers preferred that she remain secluded and that they had already dealt with the problems they knew regarding Steven. They were now working on recharging her depressed spirits, but they still thought it possible that some critical piece of information might be holding back her progress.

Doc Gary stopped me short. "This sounds preposterous. My letters to her were meant only for her, and your story raises the suspicion that you are a spy, maybe even working for the narcotics traffickers. But all right. I suppose since you already know my address that a planned visit could do no more harm. Yes, OK, Sunday early afternoon, for a few moments. Please don't be offended if you are not invited to Christmas dinner."

I thanked him, giving my sincerest voice of youthful gratitude, and then thought to call Suzanne. The purpose was not to discuss the doctor's disposition, which was meaningless to me as long as my foot was in the door. It was to analyze the doctor's unexpected use of a plural noun, "letters." That the call might also be used to show concern for her or my son was a voice forced into the back of my mind.

When she picked up the phone, the noise of her heavy breathing and the crying of the baby sounded much like the noises that emanated from the doctor's phone. It was all so depressingly uniform.

"Ben, how delightful you should call before Christmas! I don't suppose you've found the courage to dine with your son and his grandparents this Yuletide." When she stopped, I heard a rhythmic thumping and guessed that Abraham was being bounced on her hip.

"Gotta pass, darlin.' My own *parenti* have insisted I vacation with them in a robber baron's condo in Vail. I anticipate the smell of sulfur already. Bubbling from the hot tubs, no less. No, what I have to say is, I finished the cursed papers and made a little call. It's about Lacey." The background noise went flat, as if holiday joy had been snuffed out like a votive candle. In the space of silence I told her about the doctor's letter and my call to him in Denver.

"Yeah, it seems a good use of time to visit him since I'll be in the area. Just why, I don't know. Maybe to see if they found the body. One thing bothered me, though: he mentioned his "letters" to her, and there was only one from the doctor to Lacey in the package. What do you make of that?"

Her silence continued for an uncomfortable time before she answered, "I thought we'd leave this alone, Ben. Those papers have brought nothing but grief. Except for Abraham." There was silence again as I pondered how this statement might be worked to my favor. She beat me to the punch with a question. "Speaking of offspring, what ever happened to Steven's child? Honestly, I think it better to leave everything alone, but if you're going to ask about something…"

Another short silence ensued before I practically smacked my forehead with my hand. "The baby, you're right! Although that's one can of worms, isn't it? I don't know how Steven's mother would take it, or if some Mexican gold digger or what's-her-ass, Marta or whatever, might try to get some blackmail from her."

"Her name's Angelica, Ben, and I don't think she'd fleece anyone, or could legally, with Steven dead. But it's raising the issue, you know? This might not be good for Lacey if she found out."

"Who knows? Look: after Lacey left, any letters to her would have been forwarded to Massachusetts. I'll bet the doctor told her everything in another letter. Why else would he write it, except to add something about the body or a baby?"

"What, they couldn't find the body?"

"I'll show you his letter. No, and the doctor thought it might mean his corporeal resurrection. The fucking lunatics who represent America in the hinterlands, huh? Anyway, he's the key. Takes one to know one."

"But why, Ben? Why do any of this?"

She was right to question me. My motives weren't for the good of a possible baby - it hadn't even come to mind. As for Lacey, she was just another academic gone off her rocker. Experience had taught me to feign pathos in such situations, but it had become increasingly difficult to lie to Suzanne.

"To tell the truth, it's a voyeur's striving for realization, like a peeping Tom drooling at the thought of touching what he watches. Just call it a hobby."

"At least you have attained some self-knowledge. It's creepy, Ben, and it's been wrong from the start. Just don't fuck anything up this time."

"It's just for curiosity, nothing more."

She sighed and began to breathe those short breaths that meant Abraham was being rocked again. "Anyway, are you coming over before your little expedition? Abraham's too young for any presents, so you don't have to spend a dime."

"Your stereotyping of us Jews shocks me. Is this a date or a visitation?"

"Would you come for a visitation? Wherever it leads, Ben. Again, don't act spontaneously. Think first."

I promised, and kept my promise while visiting the following evening, and was even given a nice little send-off from Suzanne after the kid went to bed. It wasn't discernable if my little flight of ecstasy was from "love" or simple need, but we both parted assured that, if disaster were to strike us again, we had been blessed that Christmas Eve. I left on my flight for the mile-high city the next morning, eager for the slopes and for a few holiday ornaments of gossip from the evangelist physician. He would not disappoint me.

CHAPTER 12

New Paths

My taxi fare escalated through each successive phase of the city, from the cluster of high rises in downtown Denver, to the thin wood shacks of the poor in the old sector, to the brittle new honeycombs of the middle class on the outskirts, and finally to a tony cluster of opulent villas in the western foothills. We rose above the sparse short-grass prairie to a sloping enclave made green and rich by water stolen from depleted mountains or the ravaged Colorado River. There, glass glittered between the pines and aspens, reflections from massive windows held by heavy frames of wood and stone set like soulless eyes in the over-sized houses of the professional elite.

It was comical imagining the devout doctor preaching of chastity and poverty from his castled estate in the hills. If he proved to be rude, I would ask him when he planned to give up his silk and brocade for sackcloth and lepers. I basked in the smugness of the cynic who criticizes the good for not being better, this as we slowly cruised the smooth arcs of a broad avenue. His number and house appeared shortly, easy to find.

Having no idea how my reception might go, or of the time that would be permitted for my stay, I asked the taxi driver to remain until such information could be gleaned from my reluctant host. The driver, a Muslim from Pakistan, was more than willing. This being Christmas, he said, his services would not be in demand until later that night when the drunks would call to be transported after their holiday bacchanals. His matter-of-fact statement brought pictures to mind of the staggering and retching that would accompany the festively inebriated, and as I tapped the big brass knocker on the door to the big, chalet-style house, a sly smile remained on my lips. How pleasant such Christian behavior must be for our missionary!

The door opened almost immediately, and the sharp look that flashed from the elderly man standing there chased any notions of cynical satisfaction from my mind. Without asking, he waved the taxi away, commanding my entrance as he did so. After another penetrating look, he turned his back and strode militantly down a long, darkened hallway without a word, myself numbly in tow. No sound or portal offered itself until we came to a large, wood-paneled den. He quickly moved to a seat behind a scarred and cluttered desk and motioned me to sit on the other side without looking up.

We sat down in unison before he spoke, his head still facing the desk blotter: "Now quickly, what questions did you have? Ones that might help with Lacey's rehabilitation?" His voice was calm and even, but there was no hiding the anger. It was obvious that any slip in this game would put the conversation in jeopardy. To compose myself, a mantra continued to roll through my mind stating the fact that he had no power or meaning in my life. Taking a short breath, my opening words were then cast.

"Oh, nothing distinct. What more could be ascertained from that one letter? It might be important to know if Steven's remains were ever found, for one thing. Besides that, I was hoping that you might think of something yourself, something that we would not know."

"One letter? Oh, you mean from me?" he asked. "Yes, I found out that she did not receive that first one. But," and now he looked at me, anger cooled, the blue of his eyes shining clear and sharp from the lines and pouches of age. "I suppose, then, that you have read the rest of the package? You know, the other letters and notes that she left behind?" He had set a trap, one that was unavoidable. But what, again, was he to me? What the hell?

"Of course. We read what we could, but missed your other letter. Perhaps it was waylaid in the Mexican post. It wouldn't be the first time." It was obvious that the charade was up scarcely before it began, but I would play the hand until his call. Why not?

"Then perhaps Steven's notes told you about his Mexican wife? Maybe you read somewhere about their coming child? Would any of this surprise you?"

"Why, yes, he did mention those things in the notes. Far too disruptive for Lacey at the time, we all agreed. But perhaps raising that again might be appropriate now, yes. Whatever you would like to say about it." It was now blatantly clear that he knew me to be an impostor, but he could do nothing of consequence. Whatever surprise he had planned, I thought, would have less impact on me than he could imagine.

"All right, Mr. Solomon. It is probable that any information I could give you could be found elsewhere. So all right. Would you like a glass of Christmas cheer? I think we could use one, don't you?" He was already opening his desk as he asked, pulling from it a clear, unlabeled bottle of golden-brown liquor, sealed with a whittled cork. His hands shook slightly, and a trace of yellow could be seen on the skin and in his eyes. Jaundice - from a bad liver? Caused by what? Malaria? Alcohol? Was the old man a fraud, a closet alcoholic? I shrugged in assent as he set up two crudely-blown glasses.

"This bottle is only taken out twice a year, on Christmas and New Year's, a wonderful brandy from Tutzingo. It's a secret how they make this, so much like a drink should be. The cups were made there too, using a bellows and a straw. I think the old style glass contributes to the drink." He slowly poured the brandy into our cups. It flowed thickly, almost like syrup. "Go ahead, give it a try."

I thought for a moment that the doctor had slipped something into it, perhaps to make me talk, as he did not proceed to drink himself, but only stared expectantly. Again, though, what was there to lose? I took the first sip gingerly and noticed the mild flavor of ripe peach spiced delicately by alcohol. I took another, and tasted the exquisite balance more precisely. This was an outstanding drink, one where the alcohol preserved the fresh fruit flavor. Overwhelming sweetness was not needed to cool the bite of alcohol, as it seemed a cool condiment itself, like peppermint. I gave the drink its just praise, at which we both lay our cards by the side for a moment.

"Even that little glass is too much for me now. I let the smell escape into the room and watch the curls of vapor in the liquid, but the pleasure of the drink is lost to me, as all things become with age. No, it's not because of my religion – Jesus drank of the vine, and moderation and control have always been the key - but because of my liver. Parasites, from many years in backwoods Mexico. At my age, an attempt at a cure would be worse than the disease. After having seen a lot of people die in a lot of ways, it's almost a comfort to know how I will go. Barring a violent death, that is." He brought the liquor to his nose, and the hardness in his face faded to soft reminiscence. We were in remission.

"Do you expect a violent death?"

"Yes. No. It's possible. Look at the motion in the glass, see? That's the stirring of the alcohol, seen only by its movement among other things, like the wind brushing the leaves. That's how it affects you, you know, rising from the stomach as vapors that penetrate the tissues and the lungs. It's an invisible thing, a spirit that can have the most astounding, or disastrous effects." He quietly put the glass down and looked to a window, which I half expected to be shrouded in velvet drapes or drifted with newly fallen snow. Instead, only soft winter light brightened the panes. His words opened a line of thought.

"Doctor, did they ever find Steven's remains?" I thought this question would return his frown, but instead it seemed to make him lighter.

"You know something? They didn't? The Indians promised me that he had flown to the stars, so maybe they didn't look as hard as they could have. Maybe they wanted to believe too much in their story." He looked briefly at the lopsided bottle. "You know, that brandy, the secret to it? I have heard it whispered that its greatness comes from its processing by the phases of the moon. Of course this could not make a difference, yet here it is, the proof in its unique quality."

"So what you're saying is that believing may make something so?" I had to hold back a smile. The butch-haired post-structuralist feminists would be delighted. The doctor, surprisingly, did not agree.

"No. I'm saying that believing in something that is, or was, is coming closer to the truth, even when you can't understand how it could be. For instance, you might say that Steven could not possibly rise physically to the stars. Yet there is no sign of his body. All manner of reasons could be postulated, and I have raised some myself, yet to everyone involved, the body is gone. The ones who were there saw him take wing. The one who was last at the site, who specializes in these things, set forth his opinion on the matter. Now, would it be more correct to claim that his body had become lodged in some deep canyon somewhere? Beyond the knowledge and skill of the Indians, beyond the noses of the coyotes or vultures?"

"That would be my guess, Doctor. Science has yet to verify a disappearance, let alone a sublimation of a human body to spirit." Arguments similar to his had been tossed out in my classes before, and all had been annihilated by practical reason. But the Doctor was a man of faith, which could make one childishly stubborn. Still, rambling inanities often led to useful information. I listened intently, for meaning beneath the words.

"Yes, yes," he waved a hand dismissively, "I am well aware of the scientific method, just as you must be aware of the counter-argument: what good is observation if one is only willing to believe that things will occur only as things have always occurred to one before? Nothing new could alter one's special vision of reality, then, could it?

He continued: "Perhaps you know of other weaknesses of the scientific method: that it is made to deal only with those events that may be reproduced in a lab for universal verification. Yet we know that some things, for example, the emotions of hatred and love, cannot be tested, yet exist nonetheless. There is also the possibility that the wrong questions might be asked concerning an event, and that an alternative experiment may verify or explain it. Yet... Mr. Solomon, have you ever had a revelatory experience? Not necessarily of God, but of something? Perhaps you have found an answer to something without conscious thought?"

"Ah, you mean the "Eureka" experience?"

"If you want to call it that. Now, let's say something comes to you that you cannot tabulate later, that you cannot explain by your ordinary means."

"Given time and experimentation? That's a big concession, sir."

"Not really. Big ideas seem to move around like balloons. Recall the near- simultaneous realization of the theory of evolution by Darwin and Russell. And what about the dream of the DNA double helix? The logical impossibilities of quantum mechanics? Some of these realizations have since been 'filled in,' but some are still trying to be grasped.

"So let's continue: imagine an enormous flight of thought - let's say someone comes up with an idea that leads to faster-than-light travel. Let's say it works, but no one can ever figure out how it coincides with the accepted qualities of the universe."

"That is a mountainous concession."

"Oh? Did anyone really know how gunpowder worked before the Enlightenment? Did anyone know why cowpox protected us from smallpox, or how moldy bread cured an infection? Dissertations were made depending on the beliefs of the day, to be sure, but they were beliefs that we now realize to be false."

It suddenly dawned on me with incredulity where this was leading. "Please don't tell me that you are going to jump from cowpox to the Resurrection. Of Steven, no less!" My contempt was impossible to shield. This seemed to delight the Doctor, who had taken on the posture of a sporting man in his element.

"Mr. Solomon, I postulate that you know nothing of truth." There was a hint of menace in that statement that echoed our taught beginning. It seemed that the contentious evening with Mr. DiMandova was about to be replayed.

He continued, now with surprising animation. "You do not only *not* know the answers to the old questions concerning *how* we are here, but it is my guess that you won't even consider the question of *why* we are here. For to admit to any reason beyond chance would demand that a God, or at least a spiritual realm existed. And to do that, you would have to admit your ignorance of God and thus your ignorance of the cornerstone of our universe."

I regained my composure. I pushed forward my trump card.

"Perhaps God cannot be proven to *not* exist, but I would have to reject the Resurrection, even on your own turf. The tribes of my ancestors had a little spiritual knowledge of their own, and I cannot so casually discount their beliefs, or lack thereof."

"Oh, a Jew? Not a practicing one, I take it?"

"Part, by blood only."

"Well then. Yes, it's true that we shouldn't deny the wisdom of our ancestors. But sometimes we must break with them. This is why Jesus exhorted men to leave their families and follow Him. Ancestry is noble, but often immobile. It carries truth within the unbreakable ties of the blood, but it also limits us."

"But this brings us back to the mad prophet. Why should I believe the apostle Peter above my father? Why Paul above my grandfather?"

"Because your ancestors had reason to believe in Peter. The New Testament follows the Old, and foretold His coming. The old just wouldn't give way to the new. People flocked to Jesus, so much so that the Pharisees and Sadducees had him crucified. That's a fact. He must have had some power to bring down that wrath. But I know that won't convince you. It always comes back to faith. And what is faith but trust? How could we believe anything, or learn anything beyond the simplest of experiences, without trust? We'd be like wild children abandoned in the forest. After a certain age, these children can never learn to live with humans, never learn language, can never feel compassion. Without first having trust, we can learn almost nothing."

On those last words the mood in the room changed as perceptively as a change in temperature. The doctor's eyes fixed me again, as hard and penetrating as they had been on our meeting.

"Yes, trust, Mr. Solomon. Without that we could not have civilization, or any culture, or mankind as we know it. It is the essence of our lives. It is a shame, then, that I have no trust in you, for you seem to have potential in spite of yourself. Excuse me for being so direct, but it's time to lay the cards on the table, don't you think?"

"Continue." The return to harsh reality came as a relief.

"The call from you was suspicious, for several reasons, and I even feared that the drug growers were tracking me down through an American agent. I called Lacey again because of this suspicion. She told me who you were, nothing but a casual professional acquaintance. We talked of Steven's death and about other things – other very important things – that I had mentioned before in the later letter. But I was assured that no one anywhere near Boston ever got a look at the first. Now I know that it was never opened – until it came into your hands."

I again reminded myself that the doctor could have no effect on any important aspect of my life. "So what's the harm done?"

"A whole lot. Betrayal, humiliation, mistrust. You are not a child. It's sad that I have to remind you of these things. But it's not the end of the world, you're right. Your part in this is minimal, after all."

"My part? Dr. McMahon, my presence here stems only from idle curiosity. I admit to an innocent deception, but otherwise I'm only a peripheral observer after the fact."

"Oh, no, Mr. Solomon, you have chosen to become part of the story. You have entered this world without an invitation, but are nonetheless a part of it now. You see, there are no happy endings or tragic endings in life - there are no endings at all. We may believe we can set things apart in tiny containers, but everything bleeds into everything else, forever. As for you, I have a request to make, one that I cannot believe you would refuse."

"Perhaps you do not know me very well."

The doctor ignored my remark. "As you know, Steven left behind an expectant wife. I use that word because that is how they thought of themselves, as married. She gave birth to a girl some four- plus months ago, named Laura. After Petrarch's lady muse, of all things. I was told he had discussed this name with his wife before his death. Anyway, his death created a situation for Angelica, as you might imagine. For one thing, she was now a single mother of two, in a traditional village where both children had no paternal relatives. Her chances of finding another husband were nil, and her resources and time were stretched to the breaking point."

"So she abandoned the child? That seems…." I wished to deprecate her character but had no chance.

"No, she didn't, not at first. The women of Mexico are no strangers to the harsh realities of their gender. Besides, Steven was not just some boyfriend to her, as I have said. She understood that she had a holy obligation to the girl.

"No, what happened proved the cruelest test. You see, my health has become brittle, and with the additional problem of the war now being raged in the area, I have all but stopped my flights. It was the battle that involved Steven that touched everything off, like a match to tinder. It was just a matter of time, though, and it just happened to involve Steven."

"The Indians don't stand a chance against big drug money, do they?"

"It's not just the Indians. It's the cattlemen, the police, the army, the villages. It is Mexico as it really is, hidden from the view of the world. It's money, but more than that; it's traditions, alliances, land, power, race. It's the chaotic, furious engine that has always driven Mexico, sometimes for better, usually for worse. It is the spirit of the land, but it also is very personal. That's where the problem arises.

"You have read the description of Steven's end that was given me by way of Tripper? Frankly, I find it hard to believe that Steven was the only one, or even one of the people to have killed the narcotics criminals. But it would have been a good thing to blame the killings on a man who was already dead. We are not dealing with massed soldiers from different nations at war, but sets of relatives at war with their neighbors. This is more Hatfield and McCoy than World War Two or even the Civil War. This war is highly personal and filled with the vindictiveness of injured neighbors with the added twist of the Mexican tradition of *venganza*. In addition, it is not only important which group killed those drug thugs, but who among the group. Vengeance is demanded not only against the Indians as a whole, but also against the attacker himself. Being dead is no obstacle as long as the deceased left behind a wife or children. The greatest perverse joy for them would to be to trample out the seed of Steven for all time. I think you must now understand. Angelica has another child, and no place else to go."

"So you were given Steven's child, the girl?" I was now drawn into the dialogue, lost to any ulterior purpose.

"Yes. For now. It was my idea. Steven and I had talked quite a bit about family, and in this way he had let me know that Lacey was the person closest to him, and the most capable. They had never ended their relationship, no matter the circumstances. It also was apparent that the cost of a child would be of no great concern to her. After the birth of Laura, the death threats to Angelica began in earnest. This is what motivated me to send that last letter to Lacey, where the possibility of adoption was raised. After receiving no reply, I accepted the baby myself two weeks ago, on a quick flight for the holidays. Until your call, the lack of response had convinced me to end correspondence with Lacey. Perhaps she hated the thought of the baby, lamentable but understandable. But your call, bringing me to call her back - you see, you have made yourself a part of the story, even against your will."

He did not say this in a mocking tone, but with unchanged seriousness. A thought came to me of ancient prophesies, of how they worked regardless of intention or foreknowledge, and I shuddered. A mocking tone would have been preferable.

He continued. "Of course, Lacey's description of you allowed me to figure out your part in this immediately. It would have meant nothing to me if it weren't for the state of Lacey's health. I found her to be rational and compassionate, but felt something lacking. When the birth of the baby was mentioned again in my call, she again assumed a congratulatory tone, but nothing followed from that except her expression of remorse for Steven. Her reaction, and her condition, was such that the thought of her taking the baby was abandoned."

"Perhaps you gave up too easily."

"You may not understand. As a man who believes in prayer, I've come to find that Providence provides a sense of intuition. Lacey's case puzzled me as well. It is not in my nature to give up so easily, but my prayers guided my decision in spite of myself. Now, talking to you, I understand why. You have come as the messenger." This was said in the matter-of-fact tone that signaled finality, indisputable truth. In me, however, it brought only an end to my patience, to my deference to musty piety and the magical mysticism that had been thrown at me like a filthy horse-hair shirt. It was time to push back.

"Let's stop right there, shall we? You said you had a request that I couldn't refuse, in all decency. First understand that you overestimate my sense of guilt. Without your unbelievable suggestion to Lacey, this whole situation would have been dropped and forgotten. With that clarified, what exactly is it you want of me? Or should I be putting my coat on?

"Oh, no, Ben! You weren't chastised so that you would submit to my request. The disappointment and anger were genuine. You have misunderstood me, and it's my fault. Please forgive me. No, I have assumed that you would acquiesce once you heard, not out of emotional blackmail, but from compassion. It is only that you might help find a good home for this child. It is a straightforward request. I ask only that you call Lacey to remind her that Steven's child needs a home. If not her's, than someone else's. That's all."

Looking at the Doctor as he finished, his demeanor appeared to change from that of a ruthless strategist to one of a devout and sickly old man. It was now impossible to tell which one was the real doctor, and which was only a strategic projection. The only thing clear in my mind was his request, which now seemed pathetically anticlimactic. I took my hand from my coat.

"That's all you want? You know my acquaintance with Lacey is only marginal. It won't carry any weight."

"That's probably true. I was thinking that perhaps your co-worker Suzanne's words would. Lacey mentioned that they were good friends."

Suzanne's name sparked a flash of anger that surprised even me. "How did her name come out? How did a conversation about me turn to one about her?"

"It's nothing, Ben. Don't be upset. Lacey mentioned Suzanne as someone she could trust, and when your name was mentioned it came out that the two of you had a relationship. She didn't go into details about it, but girlfriends have always talked about things, haven't they?" He looked at me apologetically, understanding and forgiving my youthful emotions in one expression. I decided to let it go until Suzanne and I could talk. Yes, we would certainly have a little talk soon.

"So the upshot is that you want Suzanne to twist Lacey's arm to relieve you of the baby, right?" I had picked my coat up at this point and put it on my arm.

"No, nothing like that! Just for her to bring up Laura's need. That's all. I don't want her to take her against her will. That would do no one any good."

"Then why don't you take her? It looks like you have the finances." My eyes took in the wood paneling and built-in bookshelves with exaggerated motions meant to convey the detection of hypocrisy, but my remark only brought out a long sigh.

"You may not believe it, but I would love to raise her as my own. But I am a widower now closing in on my own death. I will not be around for another ten years, let alone twenty-one, and whatever time remains will not be filled with the vigor necessary to raise a child. The love is there, Ben, even the need. If a miracle would only give me the energy! My son is single and off somewhere in South America, and my daughter is already a mother of four and expecting another. She has offered to adopt her, but I shouldn't allow the burden. It's my hope that a loving connection can be made by someone who is in a better position to take her. This is only a hope, not a demand." He seemed even smaller and more helpless than before. It occurred to me that if the doctor was playing a game, he was playing it masterfully. It is, after all, not how the conflict is waged, but about the winning.

"All right then, I'll talk to Suzanne about talking to Lacey. I wouldn't expect much, though." My ironic grin and shrug was met by a gracious smile. He continued in good humor as he slowly led me down the hall. On opening the door, we were met by a cool rush of air that carried with it the hint of snow. We shook hands.

"Thank you, Ben. I feel certain that God will find her the best home. I will pray for you and for you and Suzanne's success."

He waved briefly, then left me standing on the steps. A taxi pulled up at that moment, and the coincidence startled me until I saw the same Pakistani driver. It must be that the first wave of the Doctor's hand had been interpreted to mean that he drive around while waiting, and this second wave a command to return. After all, the driver had little else to do. I warned myself to keep from watching for miracles. The Doctor's superstitions were contagious.

It disturbed me, though, at what he meant by our "success." The Doctor had appeared so fluidly layered that anything could have been intended. It would not matter in this case. If he were hinting at a permanent relationship between Suzanne and me, there would be little chance for success. Apparently, my occasional mistress had kissed and told. I couldn't wait to talk to her, but not for the reasons the pious Dr. McMahon would have liked.

The taxi driver dropped me at the bus terminal, where I immediately scanned the premises and quickly located a phone booth. Stepping inside, I fiddled absently in my pockets, imagining my revenge, until I found a single dime. A collect call from a bus stop would be just the thing to brighten Suzanne's day.

The booth was two blocks from the stop, its glass broken and phone book ripped from its chain, but the phone itself seemed intact. The long series of numbers to connect me to Suzanne were misdialed twice before I heard the reassuring pause. I was maliciously pleased when she answered on the third ring and accepted the call. She seemed happy. There were voices in the background, probably her parents at dinner. Abraham was also squealing his presence. She started with her own questions.

"Ben, have you seen your parents? Did you talk to the doctor?" She called back to her mother to see if Abraham was wet, or just hungry. My anger rose with every stalled second.

"Are you finished now? Good. No, I haven't gotten to Vail yet. I'm at a bus stop. Yes, I did talk to the doctor and found out a few things. For one, you've been blabbing about us for several months without telling me. Well done. You could give lessons."

"What the hell is this one all about, Ben? Can't stand someone enjoying Christmas?"

"Ah, good, bring on the anti-Semitic jabs. He told me that you talked to Lacey recently. That you mentioned our special relationship to her. I hope you mentioned it in the past tense, for that's certainly where it is, if "it" could be said to have been anything at all." In the ensuing silence I felt certain that the cold truth was setting in. What pretense could she make? The baby gurgled before she talked.

"I have to feed Abraham. There you go, sweetheart. OK, I'm all set. Now, what is this shit you're trying to give me? That I'm a traitor to you and all mankind for having spoken to Lacey about us and Abe? Oh, and by the way, I wasn't referencing your ancestry. You're just the type of asshole to ruin a good time, that's all." Abraham cooed and gurgled again. I could picture him greedily pressing at Suzanne's breast. My righteous anger was eroding quickly.

"Don't try to worm out of this!" I struggled to bring back my righteous anger. "So, how much did you tell her? No, let me guess — everything, right? How I had left you in the breech after I knocked you up. How you have struggled courageously despite my egoistic rejection. How 'woman power' has brought you through. How you will face the future bravely without me. Oh, please!" I set back then, waiting for the screams and tears, but heard only a few words said away from the phone, to the baby, before she addressed me. Her breezy retort was infuriating.

"Oh, Jesus, Ben! Is it always about you? You may find it hard to believe, but your part in all this was barely mentioned. Does she know that you're Abe's father? Yes, but that's not exactly a secret now, is it? There is nothing on Earth that would have convinced the girls otherwise. Does she know that I see you now and then? Yes, but who doesn't know that too? Look, darlin', just what kind of dirty little secret do you believe we're keeping?"

I searched within myself for an angry response but found nothing. I could only sputter.

"You could have told me you'd talked to her. Don't tell me you can't see the subterfuge in this." Again, the only reply for several seconds was a soft gurgling. The emptiness forced an unwelcome self-examination, one that found the object of interest, me, looking suspiciously like an asshole. The sound of her voice again was almost welcome.

"It was in the summer, Ben. Do you remember the summer? Do you remember my exact place in your heart last summer? No need to go all mushy on me now. As for the birth of our son, she has other friends. Cindy and who knows who called. I suppose they should have asked for your permission too. And it might just be that you'd know a little more about your world if you condescended to a little interaction with the little people now and then."

"There was some interaction last night."

"Yes, Ben. I remember the depths of our 'conversation' last night all too well. It's just the meaning that has eluded me." As fast as lightening, she had changed me from victim to predator. God, how could she do it? I sought refuge in the doctor's mission, something that had not crossed my mind until that moment.

"Fine, fine. Merry fucking Christmas. Forget it. Oh, and give my love to Papa, that dago son of a bitch."

"You Christmas angel, you!"

"Yeah, yeah. What I really called about," I lied, "was this. The doctor wants you to let Lacey know that he has Steven's daughter and has hopes she might take her for adoption. Can you handle it?"

"He actually has the kid? A girl? Does Lacey know already?

"Yeah, in a letter. He called her again a few days ago. The baby's name is Laura. He thinks the news needed time to set in. He mentioned that she needed a home and got squat from her. Myself, I think our little ice princess is showing her true colors." My joy returned at the prospect of a new victim for my anger. It helped assuage the pain of losing to Suzanne, once again. There was more silence, and when Suzanne finally spoke, it was with dead seriousness.

"She didn't care? I can't believe it. Tell me what happened?"

I told her the story, of the war and vengeance and the desperate mother, the whole shebang. Suzanne remained intense and focused. It hadn't occurred to me that her nurturing instincts would be so aroused.

"I'll call her right away. Something serious must be going on with her."

"Wait 'till after Christmas, Suzanne. Don't keep her from her talks with old Uncle Cedric and walks with Daddy Gotrocks as they wander around the estate. Wait 'till the family pride has cleared out before you call and let her plant her cold ass on you."

"This isn't a joke, Ben. This is the life of a baby. I'm calling her now. Either she needs more help than she's getting, or she's not the friend I thought she was. Either way, we should know."

"I can end your suspense right now. She wasn't your friend at all. None of us in the department are friends, are we? We're all goddamned egomaniacs, arrogant fucks who want to be the one and only philosopher king. But you knew that, didn't you?"

"The department's one thing, Ben. Life's another. Your problem is you get the two things confused. OK, if you look at the life of some of them, what you say is true. But we're - yes, we - we're not going to go down that road. Not if there's going to be any future between us you don't.

As I fought to recuperate from a stunned silence, she continued. "But I thought Lacey knew better. I know she does. I have to call." There was another pause, then an afterthought: "You OK?"

There was nothing left to tell her but "yes." She was on a mission. It struck me that Mistress Lacey might be about to meet her match, although she probably wouldn't even notice Suzanne's working class moralizing. I thought then to remind Suzanne of the myopia of the chronically wealthy, and was working up a few choice words for the Northeast elite when she excused herself with a "Merry Christmas" and made me promise to call the next day.

When we hung up, it took a moment to recall where I was. Only one person was standing at the bus stop, and it had started to snow. I didn't know how long the wait for a bus would be on the holiday, or if anything would stop by here at all. I wandered over to the Plexiglas shelter and saw from the posted schedule that a bus would come, but not for another hour.

That gave me an hour, then, to think about what Suzanne meant by "we." No, it was obvious what she meant, right off. Hers was an open invitation, an expectation, even, nestled in the belief that I would change according to the rules of domesticity. Family first. Obligations. Implied, it would be assumed, was Love.

The ride to meet my own family, my parents, went quickly, in spite of the blowing snow. I wondered where the love was here, among us. Where had it ever been, Dad? And under what conditions, Mom? It dawned on me then, with a sense of finality, that I didn't know a thing about myself or about life in general. That if life worked as I thought it did, it wouldn't work at all. There would be no Mom or Dad waiting for me at the chalet, and no son on this bus. The incongruity of it all made me lose a sense of personal volition, and I could only bring myself back from panic by thinking of the snow. It was cold and dry, falling quickly on a heavy base. It promised to be the best Christmas skiing in years.

CHAPTER 13

A Basket of Reeds

There was a curious difference this time in the Colorado highlands. I hadn't been to Vail in ten years and it was apparent that with each year, as with all things now, more of the proletariat and adolescent punks had washed up on the slopes. In truth, I was no better, just another vermin tourist carried on the same filthy tide. No, the difference was in me. The dry clear skies over the mountains were embroidered with a sense of expectation, a premonition of something intangible yet thoroughly life-altering. Whether for better or worse would not be revealed, although a voice kept telling me cryptically that it meant neither, that it was only a change. This caused me to reconsider the feeling again and again. Any change, in my mind, had to be either good for my plans or not.

This portent expressed itself quietly and profoundly like a vast but subtle change of hue. I skied with the same mediocrity as always, yet took more time on the curves and stopped more frequently to catch my breath and take in the view. When warming myself before the fire, the drinks went down more slowly and my attention went more to the flame than to the snow bunnies hopping about in full heat. When my dad grumbled about Carter's stagflation and the loss of American competitiveness, I listened politely, even with a touch of real interest.

My mother's disjointed remarks were allowed to flow without interruption, until a surprising stability ensued that allowed her to speak cogently to me for the first time since junior high. It was a marvel unto itself how much pleasure could be had in spite of moderation and tolerance. Not that it was great fun, but it was pleasant. It then struck me what had changed, what that something had been that was hovering in the air: maturity. This would have caused me to run in horror had not my complacency been so rooted. What was it that Suzanne had said?

This is not to say that outrageous personal indulgence was now behind me. Surely, even as the perpetual frat boy has to moderate his carousing and pranks with insistent age, he still falls into his old ways now and then. So it was that week that the first traces of maturity would prove delicately fragile, like the first light snow of the season even as it promised more. The old ways would constantly stir waves that would upend my newfound serenity. This started with the first promised call to Suzanne.

Paradoxically, the call was put off until the end of the second day at Vail so that my absorption of the carefree scene could be enjoyed before it was torn asunder by the uncertainty of our relationship. Succumbing to obligation, I tried first to call her using the chalet's phone, thinking that Dad would pick up the tab, but found that his rich bastard acquaintance had arranged for all long-distance calls to be routed through the lodge desk. Assuming that my name would not be on his list of creditable guests, and too embarrassed to ask my father, I slunk to the bar and fumbled in my pockets once again for change, then laughed at myself for the pretense. My fingers determined how many drinks could be had with the coins that slipped between them, then dialed 'O.' Suzanne cheerfully accepted the charges.

The first business was to ask about Lacey.

"So, did you give our little Puritan Primrose a ring?" My voice trailed off as a sex kitten swung by with an ass jammed so tightly into a pair of Levi's that it begged for release. I missed Suzanne's first words and asked her to repeat them.

"Jesus, Ben, are you calling from a bar? What's that playing, 'Dust in the Wind'? I thought that was only for drunks at closing time."

"There was no choice. Cheap bastard owner put a hold on long-distance calls. So what was that you were saying? Oh, and how's our sweet little rug rat?"

"I can't believe you asked. Must be the paternal hormones. He's fine, just fine. What I said was that I talked to her. She didn't say much, Ben. I told her about the girl and her name and that she needed a home, and she said she had heard that already from the doctor and continues to feel terrible for her. She mentioned that she would be leaving with her mother for Italy, at last, and would not be able to be in touch until spring. She hoped that I would keep her up on the girl's progress through the post."

"Did the bitch actually use the word "post"?

"What do you think? Ben, I was stung. It didn't come to me what to say until she began to say good-bye."

"I'm shocked! What's next, night following day?"

"Come on, this is serious. Anyway, I had to come right out and ask her if she would consider adopting her. It was like kicking a beehive."

"So she unloaded on you, huh?" Tight Jeans walked by again, and I gave her the thumbs-up. She smiled. Could be the old magic was still there after all.

"Not like you think. She started to cry, and when she tried to talk, she went into hysterics. I had to hold the phone away. She finally calmed down enough to be understood. She said that she couldn't think of this clearly now. It made her hate herself and the baby and the world all at once, one part accusing the other. She said part of her felt an obligation, another a love for what was part of Steven, and another hatred for the proof of his affair, for this impossible demand, for the woman who got to have his child, and for a God to have let this all happen. She said she had fallen off the deep end again, and was back to plucking her hair. She said it took her all morning sometimes just to walk out of her room. Ben, she's a wreck. I don't see how she could care for anything if she can't care for herself."

"A real basket case, huh? You think it's real? She could be brushing you off with a little cheap acting."

"If she's acting, she's too good at it to be sane."

"So that's that, huh? I tell you what: you call the doctor and let him know the score. He doesn't like me very much."

"Not like my Prince Charming?" I was surprised and glad to hear sarcasm return to her voice, which was surprising in itself. Unfortunately, she quickly returned to the subject. "Really, Ben. She told me to call her Tuesday, before she left for Europe. She would try to calm down and think this through. I don't have much hope."

"I already told you that. Listen, even if her illness is real, it's still based on *her* problems, *her* confusion, *her* fear. It's always the same with these people. They've been number one since day one and won't change for one day. Let her go."

"I'll call the doctor, but I'll tell him she's thinking of it. You don't know. There might be fate at work."

"Not you, too, Suzanne! Not my tough-minded paleoanthropologist! Next you'll be rooting for William Jennings Bryan! Just admit that the doctor's scheme is half-baked and let him find another family for her. He's got all those swank friends who would probably like to have a little Mexican maid-in-training."

"You know that word, 'asshole,' Ben? Don't forget it. Self knowledge is a valuable thing."

"Assholes? Hey, you can't live without one. And I mean it. This is the doctor's gig. We had nothing to do with Steven. Hell, I even hated the son of a bitch, from afar. It seems to me Doc should set the kid's mother up here in Los Estados Unidos and let things lie. He should also check on the health of Steven's mother. Find out if his sister has a steady job. Or just pay a *coyote* to get the mother and the other kid across, for Christ's sake. There's been a lack of thinking going on here, and I resent the resultant mess being dumped in our laps."

"It doesn't matter from the girl's perspective, does it? When life is put before you, it's all about how you handle it. And don't forget who uncovered this whole story in the first place."

This made me wince. Still. "You put it all up as a morality play. 'It's all about how you handle it.' From whose perspective? God's? Is that what you're saying now? Because I know how to handle this thing just fine."

"That's a lot of crap and you know it, Ben. It's about time you woke up. You may be an asshole, but you've got a man attached to it. It's about time you stopped scratching that asshole and took a look at whose doing the scratching."

"Ah, a saint AND a poet! Our relationship is just one big adventure of discovery!" There was no moan or a sigh this time, just a deep breath meant to finish the conversation.

"I'll make some more calls and let you know in a few days, maybe Wednesday. This isn't a joke, Ben."

"Call here early. I'm leaving then in the afternoon. And make sure one of your calls goes to the doctor. I have a feeling he's going to be heading for the adoption center or Mexico. Which he should have done in the first place."

"Abraham gives his best."

"Shalom. Call early."

"Merry Christmas."

I hung up with a melancholy foreboding. This was taking an ominous direction. I looked up from the phone and found Tight Jeans sitting alone at the bar, nearly in front of me. It seemed Father Christmas was delivering gifts after all.

Suzanne didn't call too early that Wednesday; it just seemed like it. I had come across Tight Jeans again, Grace, of all names, at the bar the night before, where she had been watching her college football team struggle courageously and finally win with a Hail Mary. To me, watching football was less interesting than watching an anthill, which actually had a purpose, so I allowed myself to join in doing shots of tequila to break the boredom. As luck would have it, the drinks along with the thrill of victory put her in a loving mood, and we found our way to her bed where we writhed and panted halfway through the night. The effects of the liquor enabled us to go through every position we collectively knew, with some innovations thrown in, before I found a numbed release and she found wordless peace in an alcohol-induced coma. It seemed as if only minutes had passed between the time I had staggered back from her place to the chalet and the ringing of the phone that dragged me unpleasantly from oblivion. The smell of alcohol and sex and bar smoke made me want to crawl out of my skin.

"Suzanne?" My raspy voice sounded like a Chicago blues singer.

"Ben? Is that you? Tough night, huh? Well, I have news."

"News, huh? Do it quickly so it's less painful."

"No, it's actually good news, I think. You might agree after you stop screaming and think past your ego."

"With the soul, right?"

"Let's not push things too far. Anyway, let me finish, OK? Lacey can't take Laura now. Really, Ben, I agree with her. She's still very sick, and even if she wasn't, she obviously doesn't want her now and, really, has no moral obligation to take her whatsoever. It's a tough thing for a sane person, let alone someone who is struggling."

"Struggling to spend as much money in Tuscany as she can."

"I said 'let me finish,' for God's sake! Here's the thing: before Steven left, he got life insurance through his research grant. He got the whole face value, $100,000. He named his mother beneficiary. The Doctor found those papers with the others and he checked things out. Steven's mother died a month after Steven, before she could get the check. And wait, here's the kicker; the contingent beneficiary was Lacey."

"Christ, the rich get richer, huh?"

"Listen! She's agreed to give the money to whoever takes the girl. Someone responsible, that is." This made me freeze instantly like a chicken on the chopping block.

"Rich WASPs like her never give a thing, Suzanne. A hundred grand's chump change for a clean conscience and it's not really even her money."

"Oh, like you'd give it away? Since when have you found a conscience? Ben, she doesn't have to do a thing. Would *you* raise your girlfriend's child from another lover?"

"Like you said, Suzanne, I have no conscience. Oh, and spell 'conscience' as it means: f-o-o-l."

"No, I'll spell it like this: I'm- going- to- adopt- Laura."

No bomb could have been more anticipated, yet still so shocking on impact. I scrambled quickly for the perimeter.

"What? I never took you for a gold-digger, Suzanne. You want honest cash, why don't you just work the strip joints in Vegas?" It was a last-ditch effort, another Hail Mary in a game that really, really mattered.

"Fuck you! No, oh, Jesus, cancel that thought! You idiot! I wanted to take her anyway, but it was too difficult. I'm not married, already have a new-born and have a limited income. Now the problem's solved." That's right! She wasn't married! That was the one remaining hope.

"Well, you said it right there, Suzanne. You're not married and have a kid out of wedlock. Not that it's a big deal anymore, but the adoption hierarchy has its official blue-noses. You're not in a rich family like Lacey's, you know. You're just a broke grad student with questionable morals. Too them, that is. I'll bet the doctor could find a family that would really love her and need her." I put my sincerest spin on that, drenched with artificial syrup.

"Can it, Ben. I've got the university connection, the money and the doctor's approval. I have a good chance. Just calm down. No one is asking anything from you. No one's squeezed water from a stone since Moses. Go wake up and take a shower. I can smell your night-on-the-town from here. Get a coffee and relax. In the future, when you come around to my place to visit Abraham, you don't even have to notice her. You know, ..."

"Yeah, I don't have to do shit. Let me tell you, Suzanne, you're crazy. You could have saved a lot of time and effort and just gotten knocked up in high school. It would have led to the same thing."

"I don't know about that, Ben. I've got friends, I've got university daycare and I've got money. The last is the hardest thing, don't you think? Now there's enough to last through fieldwork and the Ph.D. Then the kids will be older and I'll have a job. That doesn't sound like a welfare mother to me."

"Wake up and look at yourself, Suzanne. Is it worth it? When, uh, Lori could get a family that really wants her?"

"I know myself, Ben. I've had my eyes open for a long time. It seems some of us need a boot in the ass to wake up, though, you know? Go shower and get your flight. Oh, and her name's 'Laura.' We'll see you when we see you."

"You'll be..." I found myself then in the humiliating position of talking to a dead phone. My stomach was churning and my hands were trembling, either from the tequila or the talk or both. It seemed that behind every hurdle stood another.

The shower was turned on full in hopes that the sound would cleanse a nagging thought from my mind: you started it all. You and the fucking back-room desk! The inner voice kept on talking, but as the shower brought my blood alive, it became muted and feeble. My confidence returned. No, it wasn't my fault. It was Lacey's for leaving her private papers in a public desk. She had run from Steven's ghost and had passed him off like a venereal disease. Bitch. Now the bastard had come to live under my skin.

By the end of the shower I had convinced myself that it was maliciousness on Steven's part that had caused of all my misfortunes. While the hardness of life mocked the existence of an omnipotent and loving God, the reality of nasty spirits seemed not only possible but inevitable, *a priori*. In light of my travails, it seemed uncomfortably logical that the ghost of that clumsy oaf had been pulling at my errant strings and was now casting his spawn before me, laughing at every discomfort. The glint of his hairy specter was almost discernable in the hot mist, and I was not at all certain that this was entirely the work of the hangover.

In fact, as the morning's business wore on, his sweaty presence became so real that I barely remembered leaving my parents at the airport for my flight to Detroit. It was force of habit alone that pulled me through the necessary procedures, as every proof of his existence was argued away for the sake of my sanity. Yet with each argument, the thought of his presence brought with it a sense of relief, providing an excuse for my own blunders that had led to so many disasters. The contradictions of thought brought a sense of relief and anxiety, at once and in tandem.

On the plane, I crunched into my window seat and instinctively hid from plebian conversation behind a book, where my thoughts were stood before the magistrate of reason. The verdict was that my suffering was due to alcohol poisoning, although six shots and three beers did not seem adequate. It was far beyond my normal consumption, but hardly heroic. But science was science. The only spirits that existed were volatile chemicals carried on the nervous system. There were no ghosts howling through the 'ether.'

In spite of this sensible reasoning, though, a portion of my mind persisted in its anthropomorphic indulgence, which began to edge towards panic. The claustrophobic conditions of the plane only added to my discomfort, and it became necessary to repeat over and over the certainty that all would be right once on land again and detoxified by time.

'It's just the alcohol. Just wait. It's just the alcohol. Just wait.' The need for this mantra then struck me as indicative of a pathological disorder, which only increased the need for it. Realizing this vicious feedback loop, it came to me that the loop itself was emanating from pure evil. The g-force of the jet accelerated the panic, causing me to mumble the mantra aloud, bringing further thoughts of horror. Good God, what if I lost it on the plane? How could I live that down?

Hours passed like days, but as we reached the eastern shore of Lake Michigan, my panic had been corralled into a hellish corner. It seemed certain that the worst was over. The Lake, however, followed its nature heedless of my suffering. Caught in the same air currents that made the famous lake-effect snow, the plane dropped dramatically in a fraction of a second. People screamed and old women crossed themselves before the pilot came on and calmly explained to us the nature of the disturbances. In his best Buzz Aldrin accent he assured us that everything was under control, but that we should fasten our seatbelts. No shit. In the next minute we were subjected to several more of these lurches, each like a plummet into death itself.

By the time we had cleared the front and were nearing Lansing, my soured stomach was lodged permanently in my throat. I felt that I would either die or puke on the surrounding passengers, one or the other inevitable and both inconceivable.

Although the 'seat belt' sign was still lit, nature could not be forestalled, and I was forced to lurch for the isle and an open lavatory, crushing several toes unapologetically along the way. Once there, the jointed doors were kicked open, then pushed closed with my buttocks as I knelt at the commode. The accidental touch of my hands on the cold stainless steel of the rim caused a shiver of disgust before rising vomit erupted from my mouth into the caustic blue antiseptic water. The smell of the disinfectant brought on another wave, and the revolting taste in my mouth, another. I paused and wiped the drool from my lips and waited for the next. After an anxious moment's pause, it seemed finished. My head ached upon standing, but a normal calm returned, and after the toilette was flushed along with the sour smell, I knew it was over. I swore then and there to never drink so much again and meant it. That bit of foolish youth would be left behind without regret.

It was an odd trip back to my seat. While the specter of Steven had been slain, my actual vision seemed to have clarified to an astounding degree, as if my glasses had been cleaned for the first time in months. Everything stood out in such stark relief that my initial astonishment began to collapse once again into panic. I tried to slide gently back into my seat, an impossible task which caused the two people on the outside seats to recoil at the memory of my last passage and pull in their crushed feet as far as possible. A brief look in their faces during my struggle revealed every line and every thought as well. This did not bode well for my mental stability, and I quickly turned my attention towards the window once in my seat. The vision that met me was appalling.

In a line that blotted out the horizon, a massive wall of clouds had piled up as if stopped by a dam, the work, no doubt, of the moist Lake Michigan air colliding with the dry, cold air inland. In spite of my conventional reasoning, however, the vast, tumbling wave of undulating gray struck me with terror, as if it had been a tsunami towering over my head. It was not only huge, but appeared alive as some areas rose like subterranean bubbles above the dark surface while others sank into pits, suppurating like molten lava. Above it all, stray rays of the setting sun cast a pinkish light on the writhing mass, toning it as if it were a vital organ secreting juices in an immense mass of offal. This mixture of images that came to mind, of crushing natural forces and seething, living organs, overcame all my defenses and left me gasping for sanity. I was being swept away by the awesome power and the terrible mortality of this living world.

It is impossible to say what would have happened if the scene hadn't changed so suddenly. Could sanity be so fragile that it could collapse in a moment? But things did change. As we left that horrible, undulating wall, the farms and homes and fields of central Michigan gleamed underneath with the scant and delicate light of winter sunset. Our altitude was such that the windows in the homes and the cars in the driveways appeared to be accessories to exquisitely made dollhouses.

In the rush of relief that their sight brought, it came to me how fragile and beautiful was our life on earth, so hopeful and proud before the great powers of nature and death. As the evening lights in the streets became visible, I felt that we were like phosphorescent algae floating in the summer sea, throwing snaps of light into the world like bubbles from soda pop, proclaiming our mysterious force with astounding brevity. It occurred to me that each of these flashes of light expressed a quality from the full spectrum of colors, from the vile to the sublime, which together cast a radiance as white as diamonds, every gleaming ray an exuberant shout of existence. My mind seemed to expand with these images as I understood them as proclamations of love, then as enormous forces of will that rose from pure desire to push back the void, each fraction of a living moment requiring total strength and concentration and commitment. From them rose their personifications in the guises of a struggling Atlas and the suffering Christ, in a frustrated Sisyphus and in God in His Risen Glory. We, too, were the light thrown from these forces, defiant and joyous, triumphant and perfect in each moment that we prevailed against the great nothing.

Tears came as I hid my face in the window. The passion and nobility of life and the conflict and the pleasure and the pain that existed to fashion it coursed through me in a shining stream. There could be no other way, and it was perfect in its balance and its courage, worthy of our tears in joy and laughter in tragedy. There could be no other way but to have terror so that we might have the wonder and beauty.

The contradictions of life struck me then not as a maddening enigma, but as the infinitely clever design of an omnipotent genius who deserved our complete love and devotion. It came to me that there was a natural law that denied life, insurmountable but for the workings of a divine logic that turned the law back on itself by a magical slight-of-hand. Another flash had me see that the necessary limitations of our mind could be transcended in moments of grace or transformation, and that one might understand that all, mortality, infinity, all of it could and did fit into everything else, impossible as it seemed to normal consciousness, to the world demanded by sanity. I felt in those moments like the first man of antiquity who learned of spheres and gravity and perspective and understood at last how he could stand whole and firm on a round and spinning world. It all made sense. Then it all disappeared, leaving only wonder and exhaustion.

It was not until after, in the terminal, that I began to analyze my experience and my predicament. Around me, the hard, bright halls teamed with an irritable parade of ill-smelling travelers, none of whom seemed holy or magical or wondrous. Suzanne's future, freely chosen, no less, seemed tedious and contentious and ultimately disappointing. How different was she, after all, from those people who lived in the houses I had seen from the plane, from these people who did not live lives of bright courage and reverence, but of vice and boredom and fear? What enormous joke had my detoxifying nervous system played on me? If one moderate hangover on a plane could cause that, what would a man who was raised on prophecy see after 40 days of starvation and solitude in a desert?

I had no bag to retrieve, and went straight to the limousine service just outside the shining automatic doors. I stepped into the cold and found my queue, and looked into the last light of the winter sky. Far to the western horizon still lingered the bank of clouds that had brought on my astounding mental aberration, and it held me, mesmerized, until a new sensation broke the spell. It, too, was a revelation, but it remained carefully enclosed within my rational and personal boundaries. Still, it pointed to where I had just been; it pointed out that we didn't know what this was, this existence, and that we couldn't understand creation and death and the infinite, let alone the reasons for it or even the mere physics of it all.

Yet we could get to know it better, couldn't we? Wasn't someone always there for us, an artist, a philosopher, a prophet, to hack out another path and point 'that way' to a greater vision we could choose or not? Weren't we all shown a way, at least once, and given to decide? Didn't we all know, all of us, that we would face that great wall of clouds sooner or later? Didn't we all know that, wherever we had been in life, we would someday stand before its looming finality?

Once there at the end of life, it came to me as a certainty that we would take one last look behind ourselves and see – choose to see - either love or spite before we were absorbed into the source.

It struck me then that it could not be known which path in life would bring us the greater joy or sorrow before the last moment. It did seem certain that living with that finality before us would bring a greater peace now. It also seemed certain that the choice to live with this mystery as a talisman lay before me at that moment to take or not.

Thoughts roiled. In choosing the infinite, what was there to lose? Did I really gain from the smallness of my room, the silence of my books, the creeping poison of professional envy, the crush of peer sniping and intrigue? Would that life prepare me for the rising wall of clouds that must be met by everyone? Could a chance to know another world more alien than any exotic tribe really be refused?

The questions led instantly to my relationship with Suzanne. That, somehow, was the key. Of course, in that lay money as well. I could make it through fieldwork with Suzanne, and the irony delighted me: Steven's illegitimate child would support me! Whose ghost would be laughing then? On the other hand, whose world had been turned upside down by an inscrutable power that had been so vigorously denied? For it seemed now that my destiny was as inexorable as the course of the Nile, whose muddy waters had once born Moses in a basket of reeds from the humble house of Israel to the exalted court of the Pharaoh.

After taking a seat in the rear of the limo, it occurred to me that

Suzanne had known what my decision would be all along. What could possibly have caused her to acquiesce to her burden and to our union? Was there something unknown in me for her, some hidden well that could be tapped for sweeter water? Or were her choices like mine, empty gestures that could no more direct her fate than a pawn could dominate a game of chess?

The clashing concepts of will and fate finally took their toll and drove me into a deep sleep in the darkening car. From this spilled a dream, a dream of me, or someone like me, talking to the baby Laura who was now a school-aged girl. This man was telling the story of her father, of how his broken hand had moved her from a land of persecution to this one, to her new mother and father, as gracefully as a river flows to the sea. With a gentle reverence that flowed through me from him as if we were two beings in one, he told her of this man who now looked out for her from a star beyond the moon, his other hand in God's, from a place we would both someday know.

www.ingramcontent.com/pod-product-compliance
Lightning Source LLC
Chambersburg PA
CBHW021454240626
47154CB00002B/371